Sick as our Secrets
Book Two of the Utopian Testament
Jim Christopher

HTTPS://WWW.JIM-CHRISTOPHER.COM

Published by Jim Christopher.

ISBN-13: 978-1-7355362-4-8 (ebook)

ISBN-13: 978-1-7355362-5-5 (paperback)

Cover design by Matthew Revert (https://www.matthewrevertdesign.com)

First edition

Published 18 January 2022

For Dad.
I guess you finally know something I don't.
For what it's worth, I agree with you,
and I hope we're both wrong.

Nothing makes us so lonely as our secrets.

——Paul Tournier

Prologue

Find him, Starlight.

Irene didn't hear the words. They arrived in her head, a thought or compulsion carried in the air she breathed, through her lungs and into her blood. The waxing moon watched her. A yellow pupil on the universe, focused on her alone. The light sliced through the row of trees, illuminating the uneven path.

Save him.

She stumbled forward, propelled by the words. Gravel should have shifted under her feet, and the night must have hummed with sounds of living things—insects and coyotes that lived in the darkness. But she sensed nothing. As her body cut a wake in that stillness, Irene experienced only the echo of the words.

Her father's words reaching through everything. The ground, the air, her skin and bones and guts, all quaking from the volume of his voice in her head.

Find him.

The moon's spotlight dragged across the scrabble and dirt ahead. She floated, following the shifting yellow beam as it passed over the flats between the dark hills. The light slowed, centering on two figures. A man and a child.

Her heart raced. The man was someone she sought. Needed to find. Her brother, Wes. A yearning knotted in her, a need to run to him. Grab hold of him before he could disappear again. But her body would not cooperate.

Save him, Starlight.

She followed them into a corridor of plants—a strait of aridity cutting through the sea of lush and spindly leaves tickling her skin. Wes and the child disappeared in the shadow of a stout tower squatted over the field. She waited in the thick miasma of flavors seeping out of the vast sprawl of vegetation—skunk and pine and rust that pinched her sinuses.

Through the thick shield of leaves, she could see the platform above. Her brother reappeared there. The boy followed moments later, his small face peering over the railing and down. Wes patted the child's back and stepped away.

An unfamiliar sensation took her. Not the words rattling her bones. Something more coherent and focused. A warmth that tickled her scalp. Cascaded down her nerves. Into her stomach. Pressing against her from the inside.

A bloom of joy warmed her cheeks, her arms light and hands tingling as bliss came. The field reacted with her—the tang on her tongue thickening, thin fronds creeping deeper into her personal space.

Something split in her face. Her fingers floated to her mouth as a crunch echoed through her skull and into her ears. A sharp welt swelled under her right ear as her jaw cracked in two.

The terror lasted a moment—a fraction of a breath of that tainted air in the field. Yet her heart slammed against her ribs. Irene's vision shook, watery with tears.

A new sound rose. A rumble in her chest that gurgled up her throat and erupted in a scream as her body tore itself apart.

And it felt wonderful.

Chapter One

F inch opened his eye as his adrenaline spiked. The yellow moonlight was bright enough that his sight didn't need to adjust, but the wash of red on his ceiling told him that the tires scraping across the loose dirt outside weren't part of a dream. He knew it was too early for anyone to be driving through his land. Hell, there was never a good time for someone to be on his land.

He heaved his body upright, watching his numb feet touch the floor before attempting to stand from the bed. The large picture window faced west, giving him a full eye of the untouched Texas hill country without hinting that the property bordered the highway just a few dozen yards from his home. Finch loved this view. It helped him isolate from the strangers that would gawk at him and pity him for his appearance and condition. Except now. A set of phosphor-red taillights played through the scrub brush dotting the flats in front of the hills. The vehicle was running without headlamps. It didn't want to be seen.

Finch moved to the window, confident that the darkness of his bedroom would conceal him from view. The truck skirted the edge of his dried-up pond and skidded to a stop. The adrenaline tingle in his chest faded, leaving a hollow anxiety. They would have only one reason to be there. The only thing on Finch's land besides his home.

The truck's headlights burst on. Light scattered off of the aluminum shell of the Airstream trailer by the pond, casting enough luminance for Finch to catch his reflection in the window—his scarred and swirling pink-and-brown skin evident even in the minimal light. Finch stepped deeper into his room on a reflex, wanting to hide his appearance from even himself, but movement outside focused his attention back to the truck.

Two men dragged a limp form from the cab; long, straight hair swept the ground as they teamed the rag doll like a stretcher. Worry flowed through his chest, then solidified to fear as the men passed the vehicle's headlights. The person in their arms lived in that trailer. Finch's only confidant and friend. Irene Allard.

He bolted to the closet and threw on the T-shirt and sweatpants laying on top of his hamper. He reached to the shelf above him, unlocked his gun safe, and wrapped his fingers around the grip of the Desert Eagle. He lifted the pistol in his hand, grabbing the thick preloaded magazine and driving it into the grip with the other. He chambered a round as he moved out of his bedroom and on to the second-floor landing.

His movements tensed, not from his anxiety over Irene, but from his broken body. Chemical burns covered almost all of his skin, and his taut scars limited his motion as if his skin were clothing a size too small. Descending the stairs, keeping his attention on his dull feet, plodding from step to step, Finch acknowledged he should be dead. Two years prior, as he had laid in a bed in Uvalde Hospital, smothered in gauze and ointment, he had prayed for it. An end to the constant suffering. But he hadn't died. Instead, on that day, a warmth had overtaken him. Filled him like inebriation, starting at his toes and working up into his legs and torso. His sloughing skin had tightened on his bones and muscles, and his nerves had tingled as a numb awareness had come to his damaged body.

The joy of two years ago had gone. Now numbness taunted him, prevented him from running through his home as quickly as he wanted. As if to mock his thoughts, his foot missed the last step on the staircase, and Finch fell into the banister. He didn't stop to check his body for injury. Irene was in danger. He moved through the kitchen and reached the sliding door that led into his backyard. The lock snapped as he flicked it free, and he eased the door open. Any sound from the door's metal track drowned under the rumble of the large-framed pickup speeding up.

The vehicle turned, approaching him now, and Finch ducked behind the table and chairs as the dusty light from the headlights splayed in his direction. He waited as the truck passed, hearing the change in the timbre as the vehicle's tires transitioned from gravel to asphalt. He rose and ran as best he could, feet clomping against the artificial decking until he reached the yard, then hoofed it towards Irene's mobile home.

The lights of the trailer were off, but the entrance stood ajar in the yellow moon's shine. Finch probed the gap with the deadly end of the pistol, easing into Irene's home. The Desert Eagle played across the cramped space, ready to destroy anyone who shouldn't be there. The air carried familiar odors: the billowing hint of the gin Irene loved—and something else. Familiar to Finch, but foreign in Irene's home. The earthy taint of marijuana.

"Irene?" His voice croaked through the tight space. "You okay?"

Nothing. Finch pivoted the gun down the length of the trailer. There were only two doors in the place: bedroom, bathroom. His feet padded through the kitchen, and Finch cursed as his toes knocked against an empty liquor bottle. Past the galley, his eye shot to the tiny lavatory. The clutter of makeup Irene never wore, an open tube of toothpaste resting on the lip of the sink, dribbles of white goo spattered across the lid of the chemical toilet.

The accordion bedroom door was closed but not latched. There was nowhere else she could be. Finch pushed the vinyl divider aside.

She lay in her bed. Clothed in her usual jeans and threadbare T-shirt. Prone, her limbs spread like batter spilled on a griddle.

"Hey, *coneja!*" Finch whispered. "What the fuck is going on? Who were those guys?"

Silence. Not dead—he could see her chest expanding. He took a hand from the gun and shook her shoulder.

"Wake up, Irene!"

Nothing. Placing the pistol on the bed, Finch rolled her over. A second shock of adrenaline racked him at the sight of her. Blood caked her face, and streaks and spots of dried red covered her front. Had those men stabbed her? Struck her? Finch ripped open the bloody shirt, expecting a gaping wound requiring medical attention he couldn't provide. Instead, he found Irene's porcelain skin intact. Pristine and glowing in the moonlight radiating through the windows.

His pulse skipped. The sight of the blood with no source told a story—one from his time in Uvalde Hospital. Where his mortal burns had healed into the scars and pocks that composed his skin now. A story he craved to hear again.

"Did you find him?" He hadn't intended to say the words out loud.

His hand reached for her head. He didn't want to force himself on Irene. And he wouldn't have, not in any other circumstance. She was the one person who knew him, who saw beyond the depth of his mottled scars. Finch would rather die than betray the one genuine friendship he'd had in his life.

But the possibility was here. Now. Finch needed to know more than he needed a friend.

His hand moved under her neck. To that small divot at the base of her skull. A jolt of current coursed from there, into his palm. A connection opened, Irene's psyche unfolding like a book in front of Finch. Shadows and feelings. Memories. Finch expected some order to them. Some story that would recount how Irene had ended up bloody and in her bed. Instead, he found a hot mess. Disjointed images, stretched and warped so he couldn't tell memory from fiction.

It took several moments to organize the pile of thoughts. Irene's normally sharp mind was dulled—they had drugged her with something. Why? He peeled away layers of her mental haze, trying to understand.

A long journey congealed in the disorder. Blisters on her feet from hours of plodding. Not by choice, but not forced either. Highways and farm roads. Where those streets ended, Finch found the bookend of a memory. A metal sign, mounted between two wooden posts, scripted lettering clear amidst the drug-induced stupor: UTOPIA FARMS.

The mental dam in Irene opened once Finch moved past the placard. A slew of impressions cropped up, their authenticity growing questionable as details in her mind struggled like desperate rats drowning in a pool. In the rabble, a face stood out. Leaner than he'd seen in Irene's photos. But still recognizable after all the stories. The nightly chats with her. He knew this person. It was her brother, Wes Allard. Wanted by the police for murder. And by Irene for answers about their father.

"You found Wes?" Finch huffed. After two years of searching, here he was alive, living on this place called Utopia Farms. "*Dios mío!* You fucking found him!"

And there was someone else with Wes. A young boy, orbiting the gravity of Irene's brother like a moon. A tickle crossed Finch's belly. Could it be? Had Irene completed both of their searches somehow?

He ripped apart the memory, ignoring Irene's whimpers. The boy's face came into focus, and Finch's heart leapt. Dark hair and amber complexion. The jawline familiar to him. The brow creased now, but recognizable. And the telltale nose of the family line.

She'd done it! She'd found Emerson!

Finch sobbed, his vocal blubbering lost on Irene's passive mind and listless body. His dead skin couldn't sense the tears, but he knew he was crying. From joy at finding his lost treasure.

And grief at what he would have to do to get Emerson back.

Chapter Two

"You can't just bury it like that, Terry!" Hawk had to scream into the radio to hear himself over the diesel engine of the backhoe as its bucket dribbled fill dirt over the hole in the ground.

"Terry! Stop!"

Hawk's speaker stayed silent. The excavator whined as the arm swiveled out, trailing a cloud of dust and bringing the cab into view. Crammed behind the spidery control levers, Terry's round face stared vapidly out of the window.

"Goddammit, Terry!"

The bucket stopped, clumps of dirt rattling against the metal freight container in the ground. Hawk sheathed the radio on his belt and ran to the treads of the machine, then hauled himself onto the short mesh girder that provided access to the cab. The hollow percussion of dry soil and stone smacking the metal roof told Hawk he had moments before Terry swung the boom back to the pile of fill, spinning the cab and tossing him to the ground.

Hawk reached for the handle as the cadence of falling earth slowed to a patter. The door slammed open with the boom rotation kicking in. He gripped the roll bar and punched into the cab, wrapped his fist around Terry's left hand, and forced the stick back to its neutral position.

The rotation stopped with a rattle like old bones.

Hawk took a breath, then raised his gaze to Terry. The man melted into the cab's corner, his pudgy face framed with expensive wireless earphones. His eyes were wide now, focused on Hawk.

Hawk's knuckles creaked as he tightened his grip around Terry's hand. The man was careless, and Hawk didn't trust him with his safety. Seizing Terry's frozen surprise, Hawk combed the headphones off the man's head. A whimper escaped Terry's throat, a noise Hawk found satisfying.

The earphones flew into the dirty air. Then Hawk's hand snapped back to Terry's jowls.

"What's the rule, Terry?"

The man's eyes widened. His lips quivered.

Hawk leaned in closer. His voice lowered to a whisper, his speech slowing to enunciate each word as he held Terry's attention. "What. Is. The. Rule?"

The layer of fat in Hawk's fist jiggled as the terrified man gulped. "No... no headphones in the cab."

"In the cab?" Hawk pressed.

Terry blinked hard. "No, no, I mean... no headphones on the site."

Hawk smiled, trying his best to hide his irritation and reinforce the positive response. "That's right. No headphones on the build site. Why do we have that rule, Terry?"

Terry gulped again, eyes shifting away from Hawk's stare. Hawk tracked the man's gaze to the pack of Camels and the radio seated in the cupholder near the boom lever. He nodded, waiting for Terry to piece it together.

"Say the words, Terry."

"Buh... because you can't hear the walkie," he stammered.

"Exactly." Hawk released the man's face. He killed the excavator engine before unwrapping his talons from around the fat man's fist. Terry's hand recoiled from the knob like it had bitten him.

Hawk reversed from the cab to stand straight. The merciless sun had already burned the back of his neck with the tingling warmth of sunburn. The ongoing drought had left everything desiccated—the ground, the plants, his lips and skin. Hell, Hawk could feel the brittle crumbling in his own soul. He scanned over the boom, around the hole in the dusty earth Terry was working to fill.

"And what happens if we can't hear the radio?"

"People could get killed."

Hawk nodded and looked at the site. "Yeah, yeah, that's right. We don't want people to die, do we?"

"Well, but Emerson can fix 'em up, so..."

Hawk's jaw clenched at the man's arrogance. He stared into the wide hole scratched into the earth. Terry's ignorance would fill it, overflow from it, and drown the entire build site. Hawk hissed through his teeth, "He can't bring anyone back to life, Terry. If you run over one of the day laborers? Smear their guts into the ground? There's nothing Emerson can do!"

When the man didn't respond, Hawk shot his gaze back into the cab. "Do you understand, Terry?"

"Yes... yes, sir. I do."

Hawk turned out the cab's plexiglass window and pointed to the open earth. "Speaking of safety, where's your spotter?"

The weak sigh that leaked from Terry's shaking lips told Hawk all he needed to know.

"You're using the excavator without a spotter?" Fresh anger warmed Hawk's chest. "That's reckless!"

Terry's melon head bobbed. "I just thought I could fill in this hole right quick and knock off early."

"Dammit, Terry! This unit isn't ready to be buttoned up yet! We still need to fix the drainage and support because this damned drought's making the ground open up. And we can't do that until the next load of gravel gets here later today."

Terry's mouth flopped in protest. He thumbed over his shoulder as he said, "Yeah, but I did the first two containers already!"

Hawk snorted. "And they're already caving in, you dumbass! We've gotta dig 'em up and set 'em right. Unless you think Jaime will be okay with all this work collapsing around him?"

Terry's face fell. Hawk pulled in a deep breath as he stood upright once more.

"In fact, call in a spotter and crew right now. Fix this shit"—Hawk motioned to the half-filled gash in the ground—"and start clearing the top layers off the other ones."

"Aw, c'mon, Hawk!"

"No, dickhead. You wanna use the excavator, you're using the excavator. And you're going to be damned careful, you get me? Those containers are about five grand apiece. Any damage to 'em and I'll make sure it comes out of your hide."

Terry wiped a thick hand down his greasy face, smearing his disappointment to his chin.

"Literally your hide, Terry!"

The fat man startled at that.

Hawk hopped to the ground, kicking up a cloud of dust. He turned to the cab, ensuring he had Terry's full attention. The radio snapped off his belt, and he jabbed the antenna towards the enormous machine.

"I'm going to radio at random times today. If you don't answer me within a few seconds, I swear to Christ, Terry, I will send you to the farm. I don't care who you're related to or whose patch of Texas we're standing on."

The panicked twitch in Terry's eye confirmed that he understood.

"Bossman for Hawk." The radio in Hawk's hand buzzed as it tried to carry Jaime's thick baritone.

Hawk turned from the excavator, hollering to Terry, "Well? Get on it!"

Outside of Terry's earshot, he raised the walkie to his face and said, "Go for Hawk."

Jaime's voice crackled back. "We got a customer heading in. I'm occupied and need you to take care of 'em."

Hawk sighed, then thumbed the radio's talk button. His tongue squirmed to tell Jaime to get off his ass or hire some real help. "Sure thing, Boss. While I have you, I need to talk to you about Terry. He's going to end up killing someone."

A pause. Jaime's breath came through the speaker. "I get it. But he's Blair's brother, okay? And Terry owns the land. So we gotta indulge him." The radio squealed as Jaime finished.

Hawk replied, "Maybe he can go back to doing a shitty job of running the kennels? The cops rarely care if a dog dies, do they?"

A longer pause. Hawk could imagine Jaime placating Blair as they lounged on the porch of the main house, downing mint juleps.

"I'll talk to Blair. Get on over to the dispensary."

Hawk grinned. Help might be coming after all. "Will do. Hawk out."

Chapter Three

The electric motor whimpered as the golf cart rolled to a stop. Hawk set the brake and lifted his sweating ass off the vinyl seat. The dispensary's storage unit looked like any barn on a working ranch: a corrugated metal box, almost three men tall. A thirteen-foot garage bay sat closed at the far end, and downspouts speared enormous and, thanks to the drought, useless rain barrels at the building's corners. Mud and shit-covered swallow nests encrusted the upper curve of each gutter.

Hawk entered the building. Inside, the calm air contained enough humidity to chill him despite the parched Texas afternoon. He cleaned his hands at the mudroom sink, then kicked off his dusty work boots and slid his feet into his waiting pair of camouflage Crocs.

The shoes quacked on the concrete of the massive storeroom as he walked between rows of wooden shelving units—many of which he had built himself. They were stuffed floor to ceiling, front to back, and edge to edge with Mason jars of various sizes. Jars glowed under the LED lighting with the telltale pastel purples and greens of dried product. Index cards taped to the shelves marked the dates the buds had arrived from drying and trimming.

The shelving opened onto the loading dock. A rolling bay door allowed access for anything up to the size of a semi. They hadn't gotten to use it yet, but Jaime had thought ahead when he'd laid out the storeroom design. Thanks to Emerson's gifts, the ranch produced a ton of amazing product, and once their distribution license came through, the plan was to explode onto the virgin Texas market of legalized marijuana. The garage sat closed, three steel reinforcement plates welded across the door to prevent surprise entry.

Hawk squeaked past the empty bay, towards the far door that opened near the dispensary. The guard by the door nodded and smiled, and Hawk worked to remember his name before reading "Phil" off of his nametag.

Instead of a greeting, Hawk grinned back, then exited the warehouse on a mission. A wall of yelps and barks hit him as he stepped into the blazing air. The dispensary was an old double-wide by Terry's kennels. Technically, Terry owned the entire ranch, while Jaime threw a ton of money at him for use of the land. Unfortunately, Terry had not been content to stay on his side of the business or compound.

The wooden steps to the dispensary creaked under Hawk's feet, and the door rattled as he yanked it free from the settling frame. Inside, the air was stale, as was the stare from the college kid standing on the other side of the makeshift plywood counter.

"Hey, apologies for keeping you waiting, friend," Hawk offered. "We mostly sell by appointment."

"Should I come back?" He paled. Nervous. A first-timer.

"No, no, it's fine," Hawk said, smiling to relax the kid. "Just letting you know for next time. How can I help?"

"I, um... I need to get some weed. They said to ask for the *yook*?"

Hawk approached the counter as his brows raised with curiosity. "'They'? Who are 'they'?"

"Oh, um..." He looked around, as if "they" were standing right behind him. "My frat. Said this was the place to get it?"

Hawk's smile broadened with genuine pride. "Utopia Farms is the only place you can get Utopia Kush. It's our own strain. Grown outdoors in the Texas sun and air." Hawk looked to the window beyond the kid, where the dust kicked up by his car was still settling over the dirt lot. "If you can believe anything grows in this drought."

The customer smiled as he gulped, the thick, moist sound picking at Hawk's patience and making him want to finish the transaction as fast as possible.

"How much are you looking to buy?" Hawk sighed.

He shrugged. "I'm not sure. They said to get a lot, but..." He worried his lip as he continued, "I've never done this before."

Hawk nodded. "No worries. What's your name?"

"Colby."

"I'm Hawk." He held out his hand, and the kid took it. "Don't worry, I'll walk you through this, okay?"

Colby relaxed, shoulders shrinking and his diminutive frame somehow becoming smaller beneath his sweat-soaked T-shirt. "Thanks. I don't want to look like an idiot in front of my brothers."

Hawk forced his smile and chuckled. "I get it. Nobody wants that, Colby. So, we sell by weight. By the ounce. Did they give you any idea how much you're supposed to pick up?"

Colby shook his head. "Not specifically, no. It's for a party."

The wood groaned as Hawk leaned into the counter. He pulled his memo pad from his back pocket and yanked the pencil nub he kept in the metal spiral. Flipping to a clean page, he asked, "How many folks you expecting?"

Colby's eyes drifted as he considered the question. "Around a hundred?"

Hawk did some quick math, guessing where needed and padding the hell out of the numbers. "Five ounces should cover it."

The kid nodded. "And how much is that?"

"Utopia Kush is three fifty an ounce, so you're looking at seventeen hundred and fifty bucks."

Colby blanched.

"Is that a problem?" Hawk asked. A spear of irritation creased his brow.

"No, it's good. I'll figure it out," Colby replied.

"But you can pay that, right?" No sense in doing the leg work when the customer couldn't pay.

The kid scrounged into the pocket of his athletic shorts like he was digging for gold, and rummaged out a wallet. "You take credit?"

Hawk nodded. "We do, in fact, take credit. I'll also need your driver's license."

Colby dropped a credit card and license on the counter. Hawk collected them.

"Give me a minute to get you into the system and run the balance, okay?"

Colby nodded and wandered over to one of the folding chairs near the window, and Hawk pulled his smartphone from his hip and opened the Texas dispensary client registration app. He scanned the barcode on the license, and after a moment, the app returned with verification that Colby Snell of Austin was in good standing with the Texas justice system. Hawk entered the strain and weight into the app, then swiped the credit card through his phone's built-in reader.

His radio squawked. "Bossman for Hawk."

Hawk lay down his phone and unsheathed the radio. "Go for Hawk."

"Go secure," Jaime demanded.

Movement caught Hawk's attention. He looked up at Colby and found the kid's eyes white in panic as his ass lifted from the metal chair.

He offered Colby a relaxed smile. "Don't worry; he's asking me to use a secured channel, is all. Don't go anyplace. I'll be right back with your *yook*, okay?" Hawk stepped through the rear door of the renovated double-wide, then flipped the secure switch on the radio to encrypt the connection. "Hawk secure. What's up, Boss?" He walked to the warehouse door.

"We've got a new customer. Alpha-negative. Do we have any right now?"

Hawk reached for his back pocket, where his notepad should have been. He cursed himself when he realized he'd left it on the dispensary counter. He thumbed the talk button. "I don't think so. I'll have to verify and get back to you."

The radio belched. "No, Hawk. Not later. I've got this ass-hole on the phone, and they're ready to pay. I need to know right now."

Hawk sighed. "I think we have some around. I'll find it."

The radio squelched. "Good man!" Jaime's voice lilted with encouragement. "Make it happen. Bossman out."

Shit. Hawk had just made a promise to Jaime, and he wasn't sure he could keep it. He flipped the radio back to non-secure operation before sheathing it and swallowing his regret. His fingers found the doorknob, and he reentered the dispensary warehouse. One thing at a time. He'd deal with this customer, then figure out how to make Jaime happy.

From a pile near the loading bay, Hawk pulled out an upcy-cled cardboard container—one emblazoned with the logo from some generic brand of picante he wouldn't eat if he had another choice—and moved to the whiteboard bolted on the wall near the shelving. He double-checked the list of dates for the shelves, finding which were cured and ready for sale. He pulled five single-ounce jars from the shelf, set them into the box, and folded the lid closed.

The return to the Texas heat tingled his lips, and Hawk made a mental note to have Blair pick up some lip balm next time she was off-ranch. He reentered the dispensary, where Colby paced the floor and chewed on his thumbnail.

Hawk smiled at him, giving the box a gentle shake to rattle the glass jars. "Five ounces of Texas's finest!" he announced. He set the box on the counter and took up his notes. He flipped to the dogeared page labeled, in his sloppy pencil print, *The Farm*.

His heart sank as he scanned the list. A nervous twitch fluttered under his left eye as he double-checked whether he could keep his promise to Jaime. No alpha-negs. There was an alpha-pos, and a beta-neg, but no alpha-neg. Shit! Jaime would be pissed.

"My license? My card?"

Hawk chewed his lip, remembering the task at hand. "Um yeah, sorry." Hawk pocketed his memo pad and plucked up his phone. He unlocked the device, and a red box appeared, stabbing his eyes with the message *Transaction Declined*.

He took a breath, swallowed his fear of Jaime and irritation with this green kid. His dry lips cracked from his friendly smirk as he turned his phone to Colby.

The student's face fell. "Ah, shit. My parents must have cut me off."

Hawk slid the credit card back across the counter. "Sorry, Colby. Any other way to pay?"

Colby shook his head. "My brothers will kill me. I promised I'd come through! Is there anything I can do?" His voice strained, desperation squeezing on his throat.

"I feel ya," Hawk offered. And he did. He'd made his own promise, and he knew that if he failed to deliver, he'd have to worry about more than a mild hazing. "But we don't offer credit services here."

Hawk needed to get rid of this kid, get on to the next task. Find that alpha-neg. He sheathed his phone in the holder on his belt and picked up the driver's license from the counter. Gripping it between two fingers, he pressed it into Colby's trembling hand. The kid ripped open his wallet, and Hawk's eyes landed on a key piece of information.

His hand snatched the kid's wrist, rotating it to get a clear look at the bright red card poking out of the wallet's sleeve.

A blood donor card. Deep crimson behind bold white letters that spelled out the start of a solution to both of their problems. His gaze lifted to Colby, and the young man's face soured with confusion.

"Your blood type is A-negative?" he asked the kid.

Colby's eyes squinted. "What?"

"Your blood type," Hawk enunciated.

The kid balked at the change in demeanor. "Yeah, I guess so. What does that matter?"

Hawk let go and shifted his weight as he considered his options.

He could make this work. The kid would get his weed, and Jaime's needs would be met.

The gun slid from his thigh holster and slammed on the counter. The thud of the Glock against the plywood silenced the college brat.

Colby's face widened with fear.

Hawk made sure the business end of the pistol was visible under his hand and cleared his throat, recapturing the kid's unraveling attention. "You really want that weed?"

Colby's lips quivered, and he managed to nod his head without taking his eyes off of the gun.

"Because there's something I want, too. Something you happen to have."

College boy's eyes broke away from the weapon and snapped up to Hawk. They glistened, brimming with panicked tears.

"Hey, Colby, don't be upset, okay? We're gonna help each other out here, is all."

Chapter Four

A pin hammer smacked her temple. The clack ricocheted behind her clenched eyes as sunlight bleached her eyelids. How many hours had she been asleep? The stitch in her back said too many, but the rest of her body screamed not enough.

"Irene..."

The voice pierced her skull. Her hand flopped off the bed and found the floor, fingers tingling against the cool linoleum. She wanted that against her face.

The hammer came again. Irene winced but stayed conscious. She nudged her body from the bed and let it slop to the floor. The soothing temperature change did nothing to tame her racing heart or exploding brain. Christ, had she drunk that much? She couldn't remember.

"Irene!" The voice again. Yelling. Angry. "Open the door, please!"

She moaned, her voice broken and dry.

More beating against the trailer. Incessant. *Bam, bam, bam, bam, BAM!*

It needed to stop. Irene heaved herself off the floor. Slapped her hands over her ears and clamped her eyes shut. Her will pushed a scream out of her gut, through her filmy mouth.

The hammering stopped. Blissful silence blanketed her, broken only by the rapid thudding of her pulse in her head, the rasping of her shallow breath, and the burn of her dehydrated throat.

Irene swam in that moment of relief, and then the trailer lilted under her as if the ground itself were opening up. Her hand shot out, catching her before her face smacked the floor.

She used the forward momentum to heave up on her knees, then get her feet under her. Her hands gripped the door frame, and she used it as a ladder to pull her wrecked body upright.

The narrow living space pulsed and spun in front of her. She shut her eyes against the carnival funhouse effect, pushing against both sides of the door frame to steel herself. The spin was all in her head. She wasn't moving. Not really.

With a wobbling step, she slid one hand to the wall of the bathroom. Her mouth salivated, fast and thick. A warning.

Without opening her eyes, she felt her way to the toilet. Hands groped for the lid. Spit dripped from her lips. Her gut tightened, and she slapped the plastic cover up as her gorge rose.

After a few heaves, the fist clenching her abdomen relaxed. She breathed easier, even as her pulse sliced through her head several times a second. Dehydration shrunk her skin, and her body ached with false fever. But at least the world wasn't spinning anymore.

She rinsed out her mouth at the sink, flushed the toilet, and hobbled her way through the kitchen to the trailer door. The small silhouette in the privacy glass was familiar—the lean frame and close-cropped hair of Sheriff Coleen Dietrick. Irene cursed in her head.

"Please, Irene," the sheriff hollered.

Irene's teeth gritted together as she shoved open the door.

"For fuck's sake, Coleen, stop yelling!" The vibration of her own voice was nauseating.

Dietrick's face soured with concern. She splayed her long fingers in surrender. "I'm not yelling, Irene."

And she wasn't. But the sound still hurt Irene's head. That, along with the laser intensity of the sun on her skin, pressured Irene back into the dark calm of her home. She covered her eyes from the brilliant light and waved the sheriff in.

"Jesus Christ." Coleen gaped at her living space, and Irene took in the boxes and bottles that littered the floor.

"Sorry. Here, give me a sec." Irene pushed the closest box out of the way with her foot, the jugs of liquor inside rattling in response. "What are you doing here?"

The sheriff leaned against the counter behind her. "I tried to call. You're not answering your phone, Irene."

Irene's gaze lilted around the trailer. Where the hell was her cell? She blinked to clear her head. "Christ, Coleen. I'm sorry but... this is awkward, you know? I don't know the etiquette here."

The sheriff sighed, her face tightening as her hand went to massage her forehead. "I know, Irene. That's on me. I crossed a line, but right now I need you to work past that."

Irene hugged herself. The search for her family had intersected the two women's paths a few years ago. Back then, Coleen had been Sheriff Dietrick. Professional and pragmatic. But in the time since, they had grown close. The sheriff had opened to reveal Coleen. Their time together had bled beyond work. They had learned from each other. Irene had shown her friend some simple tricks with data, and Coleen had introduced her to Texas culture. Helped her settle into the arduous cycle of searching for Wes. Following leads to nowhere. Ignoring the disappointment seeping through every nerve of her body, and compelling herself to keep going. Start over, search for Wes, and get some answers about what had happened to her dad.

And then Coleen had thrown a wrench into the machine. After a long and sweaty night of line dancing at the Leon Springs Dance Hall, followed by beer and brisket at their favorite barbeque joint, Coleen had kissed her. The affection was unexpected, and Irene hadn't been able to think of a sensible reaction. She'd ended up blurting out, "I'm not gay."

Coleen had replied that "Hey, spaghetti's straight until it gets hot and wet," and the evening had become more awkward from there. Ever since, their relationship had carried extra weight. A discomfort neither managed effectively.

"I mean that, Irene. Your friendship is important to me. I don't want to lose it over something stupid." Coleen sucked in her lower lip. "But that's not why I'm here."

Irene's head pounded as she knit her brow. "What do you mean?"

Coleen stood, squaring her frame and radiating authority as she turned back into the sheriff.

Irene's gut fell, her hands moving to catch it. "What the hell is it?"

Sheriff Dietrick swallowed, her throat pulsing with the effort. "Irene, we found your brother."

Irene's brow relaxed as a wave of relief and anticipation flooded her chest. A laugh rumbled out of her. She would achieve what she had been seeking for the last two years: answers, clarity around her father's final days. An explanation for the shitshow in the hospital. Her search was over!

The sheriff raised a hand, stiffened her lips. Her demeanor made Irene swallow her joy.

It was Coleen, not the sheriff, who met her nervous stare.

"Irene, I'm so sorry. Wes is dead."

Chapter Five

The excavator's diesel engine purred awake from behind the hills separating Hawk from the build site—a sign Terry had somehow lollygagged into work. He checked the time on his phone: nine o'clock. Almost ninety minutes of the day wasted by Terry's laziness.

The cart reached the tread path from the main house to the equipment shed, and Hawk stomped the accelerator until it hit the floor. He wasn't in any rush, but the breeze on his face was a minor comfort in the glowing heat. God willing, the day would close with the drainage under the shipping containers fixed. The work on this new farm was veering off track, thanks to Terry's ineptitude as a foreman.

Around the last hill, the site came into view. An excavator's boom reached out and down into the hole Hawk knew was there.

He squinted, trying to glimpse Terry in the cab, looking for the flash of the shiny red over-the-ear headphones he shouldn't be wearing. The sun's reflection off the plexiglass made it impossible to see. He sucked in a deep breath, centering himself as he blew out between pursed lips, directing the air down across his sweat-laden shirt. The skin under the clinging fabric tickled with the chill.

The fork in the path approached. Left to the new farm, to check on the foreman and the crew. Right to the equipment barn and the tractor he would use to move the tiny houses away from the collapsing trenches near the farm. Hawk debated until the last possible moment. He turned left after deciding he trusted the Earth not to open far more than he trusted Terry not to fuck things up.

The cart rolled to a stop in front of the office. Hawk slid across the bench and heaved himself to standing to face the construction activity. He pulled out his radio, verified it was still on the channel used at the build site, and hit the push-to-talk button. "Hawk for Terry."

A response snapped back: "Yeah, go for Terry."

Good. The asshole had ditched his headphones today.

"What's your plan to get the gravel beneath the containers?"

There was a long pause before Terry's reply squawked. "I'm gonna chain the container to the bucket and lift it a few feet. The crew can get under there and move the rock easy enough."

Hawk groaned. "Terry, that's dangerous and stupid. Just raise the entire thing out of the hole and give the crew room to work safely."

Another pause. Hawk looked up to the sun's blaze gleaming off the cab window. He could sense Terry glaring at him from behind it.

"Sure thing, Hawk."

"I'll be in the mobile if you need a hand. Let me know. Hawk out."

Hawk walked around the cart to the side of the prefab portable building. He started the generator that powered the office, the noise diminutive in the excavator's roar. He gave the site one last visual review before mounting the steps and opening the door.

The air inside was stifling and stale, the odor of papers and toner dusting Hawk's sinuses. He powered on the window unit mounted in the trailer's wall, the sound of the generator outside purring louder to keep up with the power needs of the air conditioner. The breeze from the AC was at least ten degrees cooler, and Hawk savored the chill before opening the mini blinds to give him a line of sight on the crew.

The top of the closest container peeked from the earth. Heavy chains webbed from the pothook of the bucket, stretching to each corner of the freight container, where the thick hooks of the red lever binders pierced the shackles welded to the frame. The roof of the blue-painted steel box gleamed in the sun as the heat rising off the metal made the chains and bucket dance in the air.

Something about the scene stuck in Hawk's craw. He waited for the boom to lift, to pull the box clear of the pit. Nothing moved except for the crew walking around the edge of the hole and peering in. Hawk put his hand on the radio, waiting to scream at Terry if those workers lowered into the hole with the immense steel box still floating there. But then the container rose. Slow, gentle, steady motion. The white lettering of the logistics company logo peeked out of the ground.

The knot in Hawk's head tightened. Terry was following directions. Yet something still irritated him. The scene was wrong, somehow. Hawk chided himself for thinking it. Everyone deserved the chance to make right. Hell, Hawk knew he was a living example of that. Even Terry deserved the benefit of a doubt.

Then the problem latched together. The rhyme snapped into his head as if he were hearing it: *Use the reds in a truck's beds; for heavy fellows, use the yellows.*

Adrenaline flooded his chest. The red binders only supported 1,500 pounds; they were only good for securing hauls to a trailer. The crew needed the yellow binders for loads this heavy.

Hawk pulled open the door. The container's bottom edge had already cleared the ground by a good six feet. Too high. A man stood between Hawk and the excavator, his hand pointing right as the boom rotated the freight container over the ground. The beaming red of the lever binders shook in the heat. Hawk yanked his radio to his mouth.

He saw it before he heard it. Flecks of red shooting away from the scene. Then the whine of steel shearing. He stopped on the steps as the near edge of the massive boxcar came down and flattened the spotter against the ground. The site faded behind a powdery dust cloud.

Everything froze under the burning sun. Then came the clatter of the chain rattling through the pothook. Hawk ran into the filthy mist, squinting against the dust stinging his eyes, trying to keep his direction straight as he spat out the tang of copper and clay on his tongue. Somewhere ahead, a groan floated through the grimy cloud. Hawk slowed. Strained to hear against the clang of the chains hitting the ground and the rising voices of the crew as they processed what the hell had just happened.

Then Hawk found him. The spotter lay on his back, eyes wide in the falling dust, hands pressed against the corner of the freight container sunk into his middle. Hawk leapt over him, dropping his radio, and slammed into the steel. He heaved with every fiber of muscle. Even as the stupidity of what he was doing hit him—the uselessness of his meager strength against the weight crushing the spotter—he felt the container shift and lift up off the injured man. It took Hawk a second to realize he wasn't doing this. It was the weight shifting as the heavy chain fell on the far side, tilting the container up and off the broken man's body.

The opposite corner landed, spewing up another cloud of earth. Hawk turned to the spotter. Blood sputtered from the man's mouth and nose and leaked from his flattened groin and twisted legs. His jeans already bloomed with crimson, and his hands clamored for Hawk, for someone to help. Hawk reached for his radio. Not on his belt. He had dropped it. He scoured the ground for the black walkie and found it next to the man's crushed thigh. Hawk snatched it. Brought it to his mouth. Slammed the talkback.

He had moments to save this man. He sucked in the dry air, the metallic sourness of blood suspended in the mist. The dirty breath burned his throat as he shouted, "*Go for the bell! Go for the bell! Go for the bell!*"

Chapter Six

"F ound you!"

Emerson's voice carried into the pecan trees. The umber trunks spread away from him in a man-made pattern, the pale green and yellow canopies mingling to provide enough shade that Emerson could play outside with his friends. The trees glowed with thin and steady tangerine halos, making it all too easy to locate the deep cornflower aura radiating at the end of the orchard. "Chris, you're up a tree! Second from the end!"

An irritated groan carried through the trees, and Chris's halo pulsed with bright white divots as it lowered from the tree. Emerson's smile fell as he realized he had annoyed Chris again.

"It's no fun when you're It," he whined. "There's no place to hide where you can't see us!"

Emerson walked towards the other end of the grove. Chris's posture matched his collapsing aura, shoulders slumped with surrender and lip bursting into a pout.

"I can't help it," Emerson said. "I can't turn it off."

"You could close your eyes, dummy!" Chris called.

Emerson shrugged. "It won't matter. Your light looks so much like a shit stain I could smell my way to it."

The white marks became lightning bolts. "Shut up. You said it was blue!" Chris's aura throbbed with waves the color of brick, a warning that he was losing his patience.

If he kept pressing his friend, Emerson knew his aura would erupt in lemon and silver. The play would end, which Emerson didn't want to happen. And also, Chris might punch him.

Emerson stopped and leaned against a pecan tree while Chris finished his descent. The irritated color pattern glowed around his friend, strong and even now that his feet were on the ground. Chris folded his arms and propped himself against his own tree, facing Emerson but looking at the dirt between them.

The impulse to manipulate his friend's halo came to Emerson. A reflexive desire to fix the negative feelings he'd caused. To put his fingers into the light and twist it to the steady calm blue of Chris-at-play. And Chris would react, his mind following his light to happiness and calm, and they would continue the game uninterrupted. Emerson could erase the bad feelings as easily as he could erase a stray pencil mark from paper. Behind the impulse, Emerson heard Hawk's guidance as if the man were whispering in his ear: *Use your words before your gift.*

Emerson pressed his hands into the pockets of his shorts. "It is super blue, Chris. You're right. And it's powerful. I guess that's why it's so easy to see through the trees."

His friend's face rose as the negative colors faded to a coppery sheen. "Really?"

"Oh yeah," Emerson said as he smiled. "I could see it from the other end of the ranch. Through the hills, even."

Chris's halo strengthened as his lopsided grin stretched to one side of his face. The metallic shine faded back to the rich color Emerson had seen in books with underwater photos of the ocean. His friend's posture straightened, arms flexed in front of his chest in some kind of power stance.

"What about now?" Chris's voice grunted through his clenched teeth as his cheeks flushed. "I'll bet it's even more bright!"

Emerson laughed as his friend's halo dimmed with the point-less exertion. "No, Chris, it doesn't work that way!"

Chris released the pose with a sigh of disappointment. "Whatever. Let's find Layla, I guess." He looked down the rows of trees, towards the ranch house. "You see her anyplace?"

Emerson scanned the orchard, then the stale grass yard beyond that buffered the new barn and old kennels. Layla's light wasn't dim as much as it was thin. "Demure" was the word Mom had used when Emerson had tried to describe it. Delicate, almost afraid to shine. Even standing next to him, the dim orange radiance of the pecan trees would have consumed her aura. "Nah, her light won't give her away. Do you know where she went?"

Chris raised a finger to Emerson's house. "When I started up the tree, I noticed her heading 'round back."

The two boys walked towards the house. The rippled bark of each trunk they passed left a pleasing tingle in Emerson's fingertips. Past the last tree, Emerson's yard opened around the large white house, and they stepped into the brutal glare of the sun. The ground was crunchy with straw grass drying from the heat. As they walked, Emerson avoided the gopher holes in the yard.

"Why don't y'all water the grass?" Chris asked.

Emerson shook his head. "Jaime says it doesn't matter. That we could water it all the time and it would still be dead." He looked up to the wraparound porch. The white siding gleamed in the heavy sunlight. In the shade under the awning, Barfly napped, the goofy golden Labradoodle blanketed in her ever-green halo. The pink blob of her tongue was visible under her shiny, black nose, and Emerson wondered if it was wiggling like it sometimes did when the dog was dreaming. "Should we get Barfly to help find Layla?"

Chris slapped Emerson's shoulder as he replied, "Good idea!"

Emerson whistled, the loud way with his fingers on his tongue, like Hawk had taught him. Barfly's ears rose and flopped as she stumbled into a semi-upright position. "C'mon, girl! Find Layla!"

The dog didn't need prodding. From her seated pose, Barfly leapt over the porch railing, sailing, graceful and pretty until she hit the ground in a tumble. Her aura wiggled with embar-rassment. Emerson patted her head to restore her confidence. "Good girl! Now, where's Layla?"

The dog stared at him, panting in the heat of the sunny yard.

"Barfly," Emerson repeated. "Where is Layla?"

The dog's eyes met his, but Emerson found no understand-ing in them.

"Lay-lah!" Emerson enunciated. "Where is Lay-lah?!"

The dog's tongue stilled, her pointed cheeks falling in thought as her rubber dog lips relaxed. Her halo wobbled with recognition and concern, the dog's thoughts almost visible in the shifting light: *Where the hell is Layla?*

With a snort, the dog's nose hit the dusty ground, and she started wandering, sniffing her way in a crooked path across the yard towards the playground.

The boys followed at a walk, unable to keep pace with the dog's wandering search. Emerson watched his dog crisscross the yard and smiled when he spotted the telltale tracks of Layla's crutches. He pointed at the pockmarks in the earth, the arrhythmic evidence of her feet scraping between them. "Looks like Barfly's on her trail."

The dog oriented, her path centering as she sped up to a trot. Chris followed, calling back, "C'mon, Em! I bet I can find her first!"

Chris and Barfly disappeared around the corner of the house. Emerson smiled, pleased with himself for having used his words before his gift back in the orchard. A bead of sweat tickled its way down his neck. He wiped it away, pushing his hand up and through his short hair.

"Got her!" Chris's voice echoed against the hills bordering the yard, followed by the sharp percussion of Barfly's yaps. As Emerson reached his backyard, he noticed the dog first, tail dancing with her front end low to the earth. Chris stood next to her, leaning against the toolshed.

As Emerson approached, Chris pulled Layla to her feet, securing her upper arms into her crutches as her halo beamed wisps of gold through her usual bland sage. The faces of his friends inched closer to one another, and Layla's aura brightened.

Emerson smiled at the change in their lights. The way Chris's aura surged against Layla's, the colors mingling, like how watercolors oozed together to create new colors. "Wow, you really like each other!"

Her smile faded as she looked to her feet. She shifted on her crutches, her slight frame stabilizing around her limp legs. "What do you mean?" she asked, a rim of orange embarrassment pulsing outward from her core.

Emerson gestured at her light, even as he knew she couldn't see it. "Your halos. Both of you. Your lights are full of... happy. You like one another a lot. That's all."

Layla's smile inverted, her eyes and her halo collapsing with shame. "Shut up, I do not!" The stippling of silver surrounding her told Emerson she was lying.

Chris stepped back, dark colors of confusion radiating out from his chest.

Emerson felt confused too. "Why would you lie about liking someone?" he asked.

"I'm not lying!" Her voice rose as her halo faded.

Chris's posture diminished. "It's okay. Let's just play a different game, okay?" His tone was flat, clipped. Like Jaime sounded when he pissed off Mom and just wanted the fight to be over.

The dog, having found Layla, wandered off into the shade. She fell over in a huff and began cleaning herself with her tongue. Envy pooled in Emerson's gut for the simplicity of her life and thoughts. Her steady light.

"But... it's a good thing, isn't it? You like each other?"

Layla's eyes were saucers as her gaze fell. The clack of her crutches marked her hasty departure, her voice warbling in her wake, "I hate you, Emerson! I can't believe you said that!"

Emerson sighed, and his own colors darkened as he tried to work out what he'd done wrong. If Layla and Chris could see his halo, see each other's light, this friendship would be so much easier.

He turned to Chris, who walked in the other direction, his light sputtering and unreadable.

The reflex to reach out returned. Instead, Emerson considered calling out to his friends. Before he could work out his words, the deep drone of the iron dinner bell filled the bleached air around them. Another resonant clang followed, the air humming with danger as the noise bounced between the house and the hills.

The bell!

Someone was hurt. Jaime tolled the bell only when it was an emergency. Emerson closed his eyes, reached out with his own light. He felt his halo entwine with Chris's. Then Layla's. Their auras throbbed with his. Then he stretched farther. Through the house, to Jaime standing on the front porch with his hand on the bell and his violet aura swirling around him. To his mother, napping upstairs in her bed under her scarlet blanket of light. He reached farther out, finding the rattlesnakes and jackrabbits and mesquite beetles and mice in the hills. The birds that had returned to the pecan trees now that the human games were over. Across the field and through the equipment barn, the entire ranch shrinking as his light expanded to fill it. The crew working the build. Uncle Terry, Hawk—and between them, Emerson found a shattered halo. A flicker of a failing light, close to being snuffed out altogether.

Emerson focused there, narrowing his aura through all the living things between himself and that broken person.

The connections formed. The injured man's light linked to Hawk's. Hawk's to the workers' on the site. From there, it stretched to the wildlife in the surrounding hills. Then through Layla. And back to Emerson. He imposed his healing will on the living currents that linked him to the dying man. Emerson straightened the radiating beams as he went. Forced the halos in the chain to grow, to become whole and pretty again. He pushed until he reached that broken light, that tear in the beauty that he needed to stitch back together.

The wounded light moved. Doubled in brightness. Closed into a full halo. Not perfect, not as lovely as it should be. But shining. And it would continue to shine.

When the aura would move no more, Emerson retracted his halo from the build site and pulled it back across the hills. As it shrank through Layla, he heard the muffled thud of her metal crutches hitting the grass. Contained in himself once more, Emerson opened his eyes and released his breath.

A path of lush emerald grass stretched away from his feet, carpeted the ground beneath Layla, and disappeared at the base of the hill where the sod became dust. Layla stood straight, her white T-shirt now glowing against the backdrop of the fresh flowering sagebrush that cut through the hill behind her. Her tanned arms hung free at her sides, the crutches lost in the overgrown grass hiding her feet.

She flexed her hands. Shook them out. Lifted her feet off the ground one at a time, pulling each free from the overgrowth of grass that clung to her shoes. Each ankle took a slow roll, as if Layla had to remind herself how to use them. Then she turned around, her face blank and eyes hazy.

She stared through Emerson, and her gaze hovered for a moment before it fell to her legs. She blinked a few times, and then a dreamy smile rounded her cheeks, as if she was recognizing the limbs as hers. After a breath, Layla stooped to gather her crutches.

She stood back up, taller than Emerson was used to seeing her. A swish of her dark hair stuck against the perspiration on her neck. Layla's eyes pinned Emerson now, the sage in her aura deep and powerful and flecked with a steely blue.

"This doesn't change anything," she said, turning on her working legs. "I'm still mad at you, Emerson Hunt!"

Chapter Seven

"How's Nacho?" Jaime's concern carried over the secured radio channel.

Hawk brought the walkie to his lips, keeping his voice low. "Doc's with him now. I'll let you know what she says."

"You think he'll live?"

Hawk knew that wasn't what his boss was asking. He needed to know if they had a body-sized problem to clean up today.

"Yeah, the kid saved his life. I mean, he was almost in two pieces, Boss. Just a question of whether anything happened when Em put him back together. And how much Nacho remembers."

"Good. I like the guy. And you're certain no one saw?"

Hawk shielded his eyes against the morning sun and looked through the wavering air towards the food tent. The crew sat idle and calm, relaxing in the warm shade of a canvas canopy. Most drank water; a few lay on the table benches, napping.

"If they did, they ain't acting like it," he replied.

"Good. That's good news, isn't it?"

Again, Hawk caught the meaning beneath Jaime's platitudes. If the crew had seen Emerson's handiwork, Hawk would have had to silence them to keep their secret safe. He counted the number of workers on the site today. An even dozen, including Nacho. More than they could manage.

A squelch from the radio derailed his sick math. "Unless I hear otherwise from you, I'm assuming things are managed over there." Jaime's tone tightened with impatience.

Hawk sighed. "Yeah, I'll let you know either way. But something's gotta be done about Terry, Boss. Get him off the work site. Right now. He's a fucking danger to everyone."

Jaime's exasperation rattled the speaker. "What the hell do you want me to do, Hawk? He's Blair's brother."

Hawk scraped his teeth over his tongue, gathering the sulfurous grit into a wad and spitting it out. Jaime was a beast until it came to the boy's mother. With her, Jaime froze, clutching his pearls like there was nothing he could do.

"If you don't act, someone will end up dead, Jaime!" Hawk had spoken faster than he could think, and he released the talkback to curse into the tepid air. Irritation and grime burned in his throat as he reengaged the radio. "I'm just saying he would do a lot less damage on the farm. He might even contribute to the ranch."

"Jesus Christ, Hawk!" Jaime's voice had tightened to a whisper. Blair must be within listening distance of him. "*You wanna put Terry in the farm?*"

Hawk chuckled. "*On* the farm, Boss," he clarified. "On the farm, not in it. He can..." Hawk almost suggested Terry harvest the product, but an image of the man yanking juvenile growths and hacking up healthy plants made him shake it off. "He could work security. Double shift, morning and afternoon. The heat would be a punishment for his incompetence on the build site."

Hawk rode the hiss of the static as Jaime considered the request. "I'll think on it."

An irritated smirk cracked Hawk's desiccated lips. "Tell you what, Boss. I'm sending him over to secure the farm. If you come to a different conclusion, let me know. Hawk out."

The click-clack of disabling the secure channel and sheathing the radio felt loud in the still air. The build site should be noisy. Machines moving the earth and men screaming about it. Instead, an uncomfortable silence smothered the area, as if the land and air were holding their breath to keep from blurting out the secret of what had just happened.

The shipping container rested on the ground now. While Hawk had been dealing with Nacho's injuries and post-Emerson disorientation, Terry had replaced the red lever binders with the stronger yellow ones, hoping no one would notice. Hawk stood at the scene of the incident, next to the crater of blood-stained mud already dry and cracking apart. He scanned between himself and the construction office, thinking back over what he'd seen. The taut chain releasing its energy, hurling the bright metal away at an angle. Hawk eyeballed that path until he found the unnatural, shiny red against the sickly Texas dirt.

He walked to the binder: a long lever of metal connecting two chains that ended with thick metal hooks. The device was whole except for the clean snap in one hook. As his hand wrapped the lever, Hawk confronted Terry in his mind, exploring possibilities that ended with burying the heavy binder into the incompetent man's head and then—maybe—calling for another bell.

The squeak of the mobile office door pulled him away from the daydream. Robin Travers stood on the top step, waving him over. Hawk felt tension leave his shoulders at the doctor's relaxed posture.

"You're gonna smash someone with that, aren't you?" she called as Hawk approached.

His lips twitched at the pleasure of the image. Yet the shame of having his emotions exposed compelled him to toss the snapped binder by the office steps. "Considering it, yeah. How is he?"

Robin's hand came up to shade her eyes, the direct sun leaving a glow in her tight auburn curls. "Physically, he's fine. A few lingering bruises, a really nasty one on his hip. Nothing that won't heal on its own."

"Anything... weird?" They needed to find a word for when Emerson's healing ability caused unintended side effects. Sometimes there would be a fresh scar, or one would go missing. Other times, it was unspeakably worse.

Robin shook her head. "Nothing. There's a tattoo close to the bruise, but it looks intact."

Hawk's chest relaxed as he sucked in the stale air. The anxiety returned as Hawk moved to the next problem.

"Did he say anything about workman's comp? Or calling an ambulance?"

Her face wagged from the steps above him. "No, says he doesn't need to. He asked if we'd give him some marijuana. I think it's a good idea. Cannabinoids are anti-inflammatory. It would ease the pain and help him heal."

Hawk snorted. "That won't be a problem. Christ, most of the labor already takes some payment in weed, anyway. What else? How's his head?"

Robin came down the steps, followed by the musky wake of her sweat. "Walk with me a bit," she said, leading Hawk away from the thin walls of the prefab construction office. After a dozen paces, she stopped and turned to face him, the Texas sun behind her turning her features to shadows. "He says the chain snapped, and the corner fell and knocked him over. He recalls being pinned under it, seeing his waist disappearing beneath it. But he doesn't remember being crushed. He thinks he got lucky, that it somehow landed just right to hold him down without tearing him apart."

Hawk blew out his relief. He had hoped Nacho would piece together some kind of explanation on his own. Things went easier that way.

He pointed with his chin to the office. "So you didn't need to use it?"

"The 'roofie pen?'" Robin's laugh was guttural and wet. She pulled the single-use syringe from her rear pocket, the needle still sealed under a protective plastic cap. "No, I didn't dose him. I didn't see the need."

Hawk closed his eyes, thankful that the mess wasn't sloppier. The hypodermic Rohypnol pens had their purpose. They were reliable at erasing about a day of memories, or at least making them so scrambled they wouldn't form a coherent story. Time was the only drawback—it took at least an hour to work, as many as twenty. While it was simpler for folks to explain away bouts of sleep than the miseries of the farm, Hawk hated having to use them at all.

"So we're okay?" he asked.

"As far as I can see, we're okay," she replied, her soft tone soothing his nerves.

Hawk rubbed a hand through his hair, and it came away slick with sweat. The heat was still rising, already bordering on unbearable. "You want some water? I'm heading over to the tent if you want to join me," he offered.

"Can you hang back a minute?" The doctor's voice had turned tentative. "I need to talk with you about Emerson."

Chapter Eight

H awk squared up with the doctor, giving her his full attention. "Sure, what is it?"

"Layla was playing with Emerson and Chris when the..." Robin pointed towards Nacho in the office. "When the bell rang."

A pang of anxiety tightened his ribs. "Oh, shit. Is she okay?" Hawk's concern was complicated. Robin's daughter was one of only three children regularly on the ranch. In that role, Layla played an essential part in Emerson's social development. It was important that she remain well, because Emerson needed her.

"Yes. I mean, she was in the fray when Emerson did what he does. She's been walking without crutches for two hours, which is great and all..."

"But you want to make it permanent," Hawk huffed. This was a conversation they had not revisited in months, and it irritated him she would bring it up now. He had bigger problems to contend with. They both did. "Look, Doctor, we've got a solid arrangement here, and I know you understand it. Four years of work, and Layla gets her legs back. Besides, you realize Emerson hasn't figured out how to keep the palsy away forever."

"No," Robin waved him off, her tone apologetic. "Hawk, I'm not trying to argue about our contract. It's only..." Her gaze wandered as her voice cracked.

Hawk's impatience opened into worry. He had grown to care for Robin and her kid. Not romantically; Hawk had no time for that. But in getting close to Robin, Hawk had found similarities in their stories. Her choices had ripped her from her comfortable life as a talented general surgeon in Austin and plopped her here, indentured to Jaime and Blair. Their reasons for staying were similar. For her, it was her kid's health; for Hawk, it was survival.

His hand went to her shoulder. "Robin, what is it? Whatever it is, we'll figure it out, okay?"

She nodded, wiping her eye. "Layla has a crush on Chris. I didn't realize. Layla hadn't even talked to me about it until today."

"Okay, yeah," Hawk offered, unsure why this was upsetting her. "They're growing up, and it's going to happen, right? It's just the three of them, so—"

"But Emerson could *see* it. He knew Layla was sweet on Chris by looking at her. And then he blurted it out to both of them." Her eyes narrowed with unease.

The picture clicked together in Hawk's mind as Robin continued. "Layla doesn't understand these feelings, Hawk. How to process them or express them. Learning that is part of growing up, right? But Emerson sees and announces her feelings to the world. He's taking that away from her."

Hawk's hand slipped down her arm, and he took her fingers in his. "I get it. There are no secrets around Emerson. He can read your damned soul, and it's amazing and terrifying all at once."

"Hawk," she pleaded, "if he wasn't a kid, this would be borderline emotional abuse, wouldn't it?"

He sighed, not from frustration, but resignation. Emerson was getting older. No one had his perspective on the world; no one else on the planet had experience to guide him to use his abilities. Hawk tried. Something had clicked early in their relationship, and for some dumb reason, the kid listened to him more than Jaime. But Hawk knew he was no role model.

"You're not wrong, Robin, okay?" He gave her fingers another reassuring squeeze. "Emerson's a good person, though. His thoughts are simple. Pure. This isn't intentional or mean. Hell, I'd bet money the poor little shit doesn't even recognize what he did."

She nodded, her lips quivering with sadness or relief; Hawk wasn't sure which. He let them stand in their silence, the heat of the sun prickling his skin. Hawk released her hand. He covered having to wipe off her sweat by hiking up his jeans.

"I promise to talk to Em about this, okay?" he offered. "Tonight, when he and I head up the tower to tend the field."

She smiled, mopping her eyes on the collar of her shirt. "Thanks, Hawk. I feel silly for making such a thing about it."

"Don't," he replied. "Inside this compound, we're all like Emerson, figuring this shit out every day without help. It's good that we can rely on each other."

"Thank you," she repeated.

Hawk turned south. The distant tower at the center of the marijuana field swayed in the heat.

"Anything going on in the farm tonight?" he asked.

"Yep," she replied. "At least two. Maybe three. Jaime will let me know."

Hawk sucked in a deep, dusty breath as his attention lagged back over the inactive build site. His gaze landed on the laborers not laboring under the food tent. It was approaching lunch, and the cook stoked the grill to cook for the idle crew. He swallowed the curse on his tongue at losing so much time.

"I know that look," Robin said. Hawk's eyes found her sky blues, now relaxed. "Stop worrying about what isn't getting done, okay?"

He scoffed. "Good intentions won't get me anywhere. Getting ranch shit done is the only reason I can stay. Same as you."

He stepped towards the tent and considered how to organize the day's work. Robin's tense grip on his bicep stopped him, and she moved into his way.

Her face soured with disappointment. "Listen, Hawk. Things could have been a lot worse here. Give yourself a break." The woman's gaze fell to the crater left by the shipping container. "Someone almost died today."

Hawk patted the hand on his arm. Terry's round form melted on a wooden bench as he waited for his free lunch. "But today ain't over yet, is it, Doc?"

Chapter Nine

Coleen's hand raised from the driver's side window and waved as she maneuvered the cruiser down the gravel road. The car faded in a dusty cloud, the timbre of the engine shifting as it made the turn onto Highway 46.

Irene turned around and walked towards her trailer door. The short time in the sun had left her parched. She needed water. She needed more sleep. She had experienced enough of everything else for one day.

The tingle of eyes on her gave her pause. She looked back down the gravel drive, then across the dead pond. Her gaze flitted over the barren yard to the immense wooden deck on Finch's home. There, she found the stare she could feel.

He stood in the shallow shade of the house as the sun cut its way through the morning sky. He held a coffee cup, and Irene assumed it was full of the blistering, bold roast he drank every day. How anyone could drink hot coffee in this heat, Irene could never fathom.

She raised a hand. Not a wave, more of a salute to her friend and landlord. Finch did the same, then set his mug on the banister of the porch and pulled out his phone. He was texting her, and Irene realized her cell was still in the mobile home.

The buzzing rattle came from the bedroom, where her phone lay on the floor next to the bed. After thumbing through the lock screen, she found the text from Finch waiting for her.

Everything ok over there?

She would say she was fine. The sheriff had dropped by for a social visit. That wouldn't sound odd. Her relationship with Coleen was personal and professional. But as her thumbs worked the virtual keyboard, she was honest.

No, not really.

Finch's reply was immediate: *OMW.*

A few minutes later, his thin shadow crossed the dirt in front of her Airstream. She opened the door before he could knock. The lanky man held steaming mugs in his hands. He passed one to her as he entered the trailer, and while she accepted it as a courtesy, she found the earthy odor of the dark roast enticing.

"Thanks, Finch," she said before sipping the black brew. The mixture of heat and caffeine massaged at her hangover from the inside, and the rich, woody flavor was refreshing despite the stale warmth filling her trailer.

"So, what happened?" he asked as he leaned against the kitchen counter. "I saw the sheriff's car, figured she was just checking in. You don't look too good."

Irene tried to sort out her thoughts as she took another swallow of coffee. She looked for a place to start.

Finch knew all about her search for her brother and the mystery surrounding him. In fact, Finch had lived part of it with her. The two had both been at Uvalde Memorial Hospital during the Exodus. Irene had been tending to Wes. Her brother's injuries had been severe, his blood loss critical. A single gunshot had destroyed his thigh and severed his index finger. Finch had been there too—a patient in the Burn Unit several floors below Wes's room. They hadn't met until months later, at an Exodus support group. Their shared experience of the chaos that day provided a bond, gave their relationship depth beyond that of tenant and landlord. Something like a casual friendship, but with shared secrets. Irene equated it to therapy: she could talk with Finch about things she wasn't comfortable discussing with anyone else, and vice versa.

"It's about Wes," she said.

Finch froze, his mug touching his scarred lips. "They found him." It was an indirect question, his flat intonation making it sound like a statement.

Irene shook her head and looked at the floor. "They found his body, Finch. Wes was murdered."

The shattering of Finch's coffee cup startled her. She glanced up at the tight swirls of his face.

"Shit, sorry," he slurred. The scarring on his lips limited their movement, giving Finch's face an unreadable quality and his speech a slight lisp. His gait stiffened as he looked over the mess of her kitchen.

Irene pulled a stale towel from the counter. "No, I'm sorry. I guess that was a bombshell." She set her mug on the table and stooped to clean the mess by Finch's work boots. "I should have softened the news."

Her friend stepped back as Irene wiped up the spill and collected the shards of ceramic. "Not for my sake," he said. "It's not like I knew him. I'm just... shocked. For you. Does that make any sense?"

"It does." She rose and dropped the soggy towel on top of the pile in the sink. The pieces of porcelain tinkled against the dirty dishes as they worked their way to the metal bottom.

"Did the sheriff say what happened?"

She shook her head as she grabbed her coffee off the table. "Just a few ugly details. No real context."

A silence pressed against the close space. Finch stooped in the kitchen, his posture rigid as his mismatched eyes moved over her face.

Another wave of regret washed through her. "Christ, Finch, I'm sorry," she offered. "Can you sit for a bit?"

"Of course," he replied, moving to the bench seat Coleen had occupied earlier. Irene slid across from him and placed her mug on the table.

"Dumb question, but are you ok?" His eyes moved in staccato bursts, the opaque bluish-white of his left in sharp contrast to the deep brown of his right.

"I'm not sure. Honestly, I'm pretty hung over, and I don't think the facts have landed yet."

Finch nodded, placing his hands flat on her tabletop. "Whatever I can do—"

"I know," Irene cut him off and took a swig of the coffee. "I won't be shy about asking, I promise." She knew his offer was genuine, and the small token of kindness from Finch pried something loose. Irene felt the swell of tears as her sinuses closed.

"I'm supposed to identify his body tomorrow." Her voice creaked as she spoke, the tears finding their way out. She locked her gaze on the bronze crescent the sun left on the surface of her coffee. "Coleen says..." Her words shook, shredded by grief.

"Jesus," Finch replied. "Is that necessary?"

"I'm the only living family." Irene wiped her hand down her face, smearing wetness from her eyes across her cheek. "Coleen says I'm not required to, but it would help speed things along." She blinked away another tear before she looked up at Finch and his emotionless expression.

His thick lips parted. The whiteness of his teeth was at odds with the patchwork flesh around his mouth as he stumbled to find his words. "Easier for her? Or for you?"

A bloom of gratitude warmed her chest. Her lips cracked into an involuntary smile as the sensation relaxed her into her seat. "I hadn't considered it that way. I assumed she meant in terms of closing my brother's case."

Finch bobbed his head, a stiff motion a stranger would have mistaken for discomfort. "I doubt that's what she meant, Irene. She cares about you. You should realize that by now, *coneja*."

She broke his gaze, looking at her cooling coffee. Her hands gripped the mug as she tried to control the flush rushing through her cheeks. Coleen had made it clear how much she cared about Irene. It was more than Irene could reciprocate.

"Looks like you do understand," Finch murmured. Irene found his face, his half smile bulging into his cheek under his working eye. The expression on anyone else would look cruel, a sneer at her discomfort. She knew it was the best grin Finch could muster.

Another silence elongated the moment, this time providing a buffer of comfort between them.

As Irene sipped her coffee, Finch cleared his throat. "You thought about what it means?" he asked. "For you?"

Irene understood what he was asking. He understood why she was here. He could reason that her goals were unattainable now. Was she going to leave?

Her mug tapped the tabletop, and she sighed. "I guess I'm heading back to Boston, Finch. There's no reason for me to stay."

A grunt huffed out of Finch. Irene watched him, waiting for some tell of the emotion behind the noise. His eye scanned her, revealing nothing.

"Do you think Coleen would agree with you?"

The question filled her with shame. Her desire to run back to a normal life was making her selfish. Leaving would hurt Coleen, especially if they failed to work through their current issues first. She swallowed a lump of regret at thinking only of herself.

"Don't forget about the people who care about you," he added. "That includes me, *tarada*."

The insult cracked her discomfort. Levity washed over her guilt.

Finch leaned back, rolled his shoulders. "Keep that in mind. Whatever smart stuff you'd do in Boston, you can do here. And the thing you need to consider?"

Irene smiled, knowing some snark was about to come her way. "What's that?"

"The food's better here, *amiga*. The company too."

She chuckled, as grateful for the endearment as she'd been for the gibe.

Finch stood, a process of deliberate movements and sighs that made Irene wonder just how uncomfortable it was to live in Finch's damaged skin.

"Let me prove it to you tonight," he said after he rose to his feet. "I've got brisket in the pit already. Come over before sunset; we'll eat. Get a little hair of the dog in you."

Irene smiled, although the thought of drinking anything with alcohol made her stomach roil. As Finch moved to the door, she shifted from the bench and stood.

"Sounds lovely, Finch. Thank you."

He nodded as he swung open the door, a stifling heat rushing into the space. He stopped, and Irene followed his gaze out past the edge of his dried-up pond.

"Something else?" she asked. "Need me to pick up food or something?"

After a pause bordering on uncomfortable, Finch shook his head and plodded out of her trailer into the relentless sun. The flimsy door slapped shut behind him, the snap tapering off in the tight space around her, leaving Irene with no distraction from her guilt at wanting to escape, even if it meant leaving the feeble man to fend for himself.

Chapter Ten

Late afternoon promised the best sex. The dissipating heat in the air. The way it let sweat linger on Blair's body, cooling it enough so that Jaime's hands were warm where they found her. The low sun stippling through the blinds, creating patterns of light that moved in tides on their bodies—across Jaime's rocking chest, highlighting the contrast in his deep hazel skin under the pressure of her pale fingers, or the divots where his brick muscles gripped his sternum. Blair knew Jaime disagreed, that he was more of a morning guy, but for her, this time of day created an ideal canvas for making love.

Her gaze drifted to the clock on the nightstand, where the steady LED light showed it was just after four in the afternoon. Of course, this luxury came from more than the time. Blair knew herself—she couldn't get into it if her mind was elsewhere, and right now offered a beautiful lull between responsibilities. Emerson, Chris, and Layla were playing or doing homework somewhere. The day's chores were close to done, except for supper and the cleanup after. This was when Blair could turn off all the noisy bits in her head. Focus on being thankful. This house, built for her and Emerson. This enormous ranch, as big as the town where Jaime had found her and her son. The privilege of not having to worry about money. Or their future. And the security of living with a powerful partner.

Blair was very grateful for Jaime and all he had done for her. And she had just finished showing him the depth of that gratitude. His tension melted beneath her, his grip on her hip and thigh loosening and then falling away. His amber eyes wandered and blinked in an unfocused haze as she eased down, her fingertips moving to his face so she could enjoy the light tremor on his lips before she kissed them.

Her head nestled into the nook between his neck and shoulder. Their mingling odors enveloped her as the ridge of her nose found the fleshy spot behind his jaw. She listened to his breath and his heartbeat, the rhythm of his body slowing over several minutes as she stroked the line of his collar. At some point, his palm found her again, coming to rest on the curve of her ass. His tell that the bliss of fucking had waned. His mind was ready for conversation again.

"What happened to the guy?" she asked.

Jaime grunted. A rising tone. A question.

"The construction guy. The reason Hawk told you to ring the bell. How'd he get hurt?"

He groaned again, the tone falling now. "Just an accident on the site. He'll be okay. Thanks to Em." His fingertips caressed her butt, and Blair wiggled to his side until she could see his expression.

"But what happened, Jaime? That he needed the bell?"

Jaime shook his head, a slight but deliberate movement. "It's nothing you need to worry about."

She lifted her head. The air was cool on her cheek as she perched on an elbow. Jaime's face remained stoic. They stared at one another for a stretch, then he raised an eyebrow.

"What?" he asked.

"Don't do that," Blair pressed. "Don't you go keeping things from me, Jaime."

He sighed, an irritated and impatient sound that she took as dismissive.

"Hey!" She clambered to straddle him again. "I'm serious!"

"What?" he repeated.

Blair pushed on his chest and pointed at his chin as she leaned into him. "Do not hide stuff from me, okay? Don't tell me that shit's fine while you wave off the stink!"

Jaime's hands locked behind his head. "I'm not keeping anything from you, Blair. I just don't think you really want to know."

She stared into him, letting her silence be her response.

"It's not something you can unhear," he offered. "It was a serious accident. If Hawk hadn't rung the bell, Nacho would be dead."

"Nacho?" she asked. "The guy's name is Nacho?"

Jaime nodded, lips pursing with regret at the apparent slip of his tongue.

"What happened to him? How did he get hurt?" She shifted her weight backwards onto his hips as she waited for the answer.

After a deep, contemplative breath, he unlocked his hands and brought them over his chest. Hovering one flat over his pecs, he explained, "Terry was in the CAT, lifting a container out of the ground, and Nacho"—he wiggled a fingertip on his other hand before placing it on his pectoral—"was spotting him, and..."

His palm slapped over his fingertip, startling Blair.

"A binder broke, and the container landed on Nacho."

"Jesus! It crushed him?"

Jaime nodded, returning one hand to support his neck while the other found Blair's thigh. "Part of him." His calloused fingers slid up to her hip, squeezing the blade of her pelvis as he added, "From about here down."

Blair tried to imagine it. Jaime's grip closing on her. His strength snapping her. Crushing the bone in less than a flash. Shoving her organs around. Bending legs in directions they shouldn't go. And then her having to live through it. Her body revolted with a shiver.

"But he's fine, Blair." His fingers released her hip and slid down to the gooseflesh on her thigh. "Emerson did what we taught him. He saved the man's life."

Blair rolled out the tension in her shoulders. She scanned Jaime's chest, avoiding his gaze as she asked, "Was it Terry's fault? I heard Hawk on the radio say something about it being Terry's fault."

Jaime's throat clicked as he swallowed. That noise—the sound of Jaime massaging words, curating his thoughts—was all the answer she needed.

"He's my brother, Jaime. He ain't smart, but—"

"It's not that he's dumb, Blair. He's careless."

"Okay, but he's family. And Em don't have more than me and his uncle anymore."

Jaime remained silent. Pensive.

"I worry about Em. Living with so few people around? He's only got two other kids to play with, for fuck's sake. We should surround him with folks, you know? Help him learn who he likes and doesn't like, that kind of thing."

The depth of Jaime's tiger eyes bore into hers. Silence stretched the time until Blair broke his gaze to follow the trim of the pillow supporting his head. Her attention wandered up into the woodgrain of the headboard, landing on the dark, eye-shaped knot permanently staring back at her.

"Me and Terry, we're the only constant thing for Em. Everyone else will come and go. Layla, Chris, they'll leave the ranch someday. He'll probably never see 'em after that. Christ, even Emerson's worthless father couldn't stick around."

Her brow furrowed as her confidence crested. Her hand fell to Jaime's thick fingers, and she lifted them off of her leg and into her fist.

"I don't want Terry leaving the ranch, Jaime."

Her lover groaned. "His mistakes cost money, though. And shit's tight enough here. You realize how expensive it is to provide a full life for a ten-year-old inside of a few dozen acres?"

Blair squeezed, her thin fingers cracking against Jaime's stone digits. "But Emerson's the one who makes this all possible, Jaime."

He groaned again, more adamant. Blair expected a fight about money. About running the operation with a skeleton crew and balancing the books. A conversation to make it seem like she wasn't pulling her weight with Emerson or the ranch.

Instead, his fingers opened, enveloping hers in reassuring warmth. "I won't throw him out, okay? I won't."

Blair met his stare once more. His face relaxed, eyes round and sincere.

"I won't do that because it would hurt Emerson," he added. "But honey, I can't trust your brother with a lot of responsibility. He can go work the kennels. That, or Hawk'll put him on a security detail."

Blair smiled at the thought of her brother patrolling the crop field. "He'd like that, I think. Make him important, carrying a gun, keeping everyone safe."

Jaime rubbed his hand down his face. "None of us need Terry with a pistol, Blair. He'll have a radio and something nonlethal. Pepper spray, maybe."

She sighed, resignation unwinding the knot in her chest. Jaime was right—Terry was careless. He had more desire to be seen doing something than doing it right. A memory surfaced of Terry's prize dog, Lucifer. The stocky Rottweiler mix had worked her way out of her kennel and attacked a customer as they'd walked into the dispensary. Jaime had demanded Terry put her down, and instead of calling in the vet to make it peaceful for the dog, Terry had grabbed a gun. Three fucking shots to get it done. The echo of Lucy's howl after the first shot goosed Blair's flesh once more, and she knew the reverberation of the dog's gurgling cough before the last crack of the gun was going to keep her awake tonight.

For now, Blair stuffed the memory under her concerns for her son. She released Jaime's hand and pulled the smooth, pearly satin bed sheet over her shoulders, creating a tent to block the moving air from the ceiling fan.

"You're right," she murmured.

Jaime pulled the sheet closed over her belly. "We'll find a place for Terry. There's plenty to do around here."

Blair nodded.

"And Emerson doesn't have it that bad, hon. The people here care about him."

She bit her lip. "He seems happy most days. He talks about Hawk a lot, you know? I think he's good for Em. Like a big brother."

Jaime smiled. "Yeah, they have a bond, don't they? Em listens to him, like... really hears Hawk when they talk. To be honest, I'm jealous."

Her lips pouted at that. "Ain't no reason for that. He loves you, Jaime, he does."

"Sure he does. I only meant I wish I could be..." His gaze wandered, as if the words he sought were floating beyond Blair's stark crimson hair. "Hawk can be vulnerable. Show the kid weakness. I never learned how to do that. Hell, my dad whipped me for crying."

Blair swallowed now, a lump of regret from memories of her own actions with Emerson. She wasn't always a decent mother, but she wanted to be.

Jaime's face mirrored her feelings. "I can't compete with him, can I?"

Blair smiled, her flesh warm under the bedsheet as a tickle of sweat caressed her belly. She relaxed into his frame, her groin pressing into his. His eyes widened the slightest bit, the signal that she was hitting the mark.

"There ain't no competition, *buey*."

She pushed against him, the pressure expanding through her groin as Jaime sucked in his lips with a long sigh.

"Now, love," she hummed. "Ain't that better?" She leaned down to his face, her lips brushing his as she continued, "Aren't you glad you told me what happened?"

His tongue extended to meet hers. She pulled away, teasing him. "Don't it feel good that we talked?"

He lifted his head, mouth groping for hers. She eased farther back.

"Say it," she whispered.

His breath creaked, the angle of his neck odd and unnatural as he strained to kiss her.

Blair closed the distance, tasting the salt of his cheek as she sang, "Say it, Jaime."

"It's good." The powerful man's voice wobbled like a purr from a lion.

Blair smiled and rotated against him again. "What's good?"

"Us talking." His hands moved under the bed linen, finding her body and pulling her torso down towards his.

"Damn straight," she whispered, her breath brushing his cheek. "You gonna keep shit from me anymore?" She retreated, pushing into his chest and increasing her leverage as she ground into him. "You gonna keep secrets from me?"

"Oh... no," he groaned through the pressure and pleasure she was putting on him. "No secrets. No—"

The squawk of the radio on the nightstand startled him, and in his flailing, his crown cracked against headboard. Blair struggled to stay on him as he rolled beneath her, the experience too similar to riding a mechanical bull for her not to laugh.

"Ah shit!" he grunted, a hand shooting from under the sheet and slapping for the radio.

"Hawk for Boss," the walkie hissed as Jaime knocked it to the wood floor with a clatter.

Blair leaned off him, letting him roll onto his stomach. He reached out from the bed, the satin top sheet scooting off of his back and exposing his naked ass. Blair couldn't help herself. She struck, seeking the tight flesh with her thumb and finger.

"Go for *BOSS!*" At Blair's solid tweak of his butt cheek, the last syllable shot up an octave and several decibels. He turned, scowling and slapping her hand away. "Sorry, go for Boss," he repeated as he rotated onto the bed. He shot her a hurt look, almost pouting as he mouthed the words, *Stop it!*

Blair waggled her eyebrows and pinched the air with her fingers. That got a smirk from Jaime as Hawk's voice rattled in the crappy speaker.

"Hey, I need some extra time with the kid tonight. Doc asked me to talk to him about what happened today."

Blair's brow fell. "What does he mean?" she whispered.

Jaime shrugged and thumbed the talkback. "Can you elaborate?"

The rasp of a sigh came through the transmission. "Yeah, nothing major. Layla was in the mix of it today, so there's that. But also, she's upset. They had a bit of a fight, her and Em. I told Robin I'd explain some stuff to him."

"What kind of stuff?" Jaime pressed. Blair nodded.

"Um..." The radio belched static for a moment, then Hawk's voice returned clear as day, "It sounds like he's revealing some hidden feelings between his friends. Stuff they're not ready to have in the open."

Jaime cocked an eyebrow, asking Blair without words if that made any sense to her. She shook her head *no*.

"What's that mean, Hawk? Dumb it down for us."

"Okay, let's see..." Another moment of static before Hawk's voice came across the air. "In a nutshell, Layla has a crush on Chris, and Emerson saw it. And then he told Chris about it. In front of Layla. You know, standard kid-with-mystic-abilities-coming-of-age stuff."

Her heart sank. Blair slid up on her haunches, wrapping the satin sheet around her again. Shit like this was getting more common as Emerson got older. He saw things other people couldn't. Their genuine feelings, even if they were unaware of them. Hawk had coined a phrase: *There are no secrets from Emerson Hunt.* And he was right. There was no point lying around her son. He would blurt out the truth. It was the reason Blair could trust Jaime and love him—she knew he was being straight with her, because Emerson had told her so. People couldn't pass a lie when Em was nearby. But the benefit of her son's gifts came at the horrific cost of Emerson being alone in so many ways.

"Shit," she murmured. Pulling the sheet close and tightening it around her shoulders, she said, "Tell Hawk I'll have Em ready in ten minutes."

Jaime thumbed the radio. "Yeah, all right. Em will be outside in ten."

"Outside? Outside where? The compound is huge, Boss."

"It's a ranch," Blair blurted as she slipped off the edge of the bed, the wooden floor cool against her bare feet.

"Outside," Jaime repeated. "Meet him at the wooden thing." He released the talk button, looked at her and asked, "What did you say?"

"It's a ranch." Blair grabbed her panties from the floor. "Not a compound."

Jaime blinked and, after a moment, offered a dismissive shrug.

"What wood thing? The pecan orchard?" Hawk asked.

Jaime huffed, irritated. "No, dammit, the wooden *thing*. With the bars and the tire swing? Right there, in the yard. The wood... the thing!" His hand pointed to the walls, to the space outside, as if Hawk could see it over the radio.

"The... playground? Do you mean the playground?"

"Yeah, that's what I said, dumbass. Ten minutes, at the playground. Em will be there. Boss out."

He flipped the radio on the nightstand and ran his hand through his crew cut, scratching the back of his skull where it had clobbered the headboard. "You know, sometimes I wonder why I bother speaking English to that asshole."

Chapter Eleven

"**G**od, I wish that asshole would speak English to me," Hawk murmured as he sheathed the radio.

The tiny house looked plumb. He'd need a bubble level to be sure, but it would have to wait until morning. The house now stood by the drying huts, close enough to the electrical and water hookups, but avoiding the crevasse opening around the marijuana field. Moving it had taken a lot longer than Hawk expected, with one set of wheels kissing the trench as he maneuvered the bulky trailer away from the gap. The image of his home's precarious rocking in his side-view mirror brought him close to shitting his pants for the second time today. But the truck was powerful, and the forward momentum righted his small home.

Hawk pushed the power cable into the receptacle on his house and tightened the twist lock, giving the whole thing a solid yank to test the connection. A narrow soffit covered the electrical panel to protect it from weather. Hawk opened the access door, held his breath, and threw the main breaker. The hint of light coming through the small window above his head showed that the electricity was flowing, that his bathroom light—and the rest of his home—was getting juice. He exhaled, shaking his head at how much he distrusted his own work. Every damned time he had to move this house, he expected it to fall to pieces. It never did, but he could not shake the thought.

The access panel latched closed with a satisfying clunk. Hawk moved to the tractor parked in front of the trailer. It started with a growl, and Hawk pointed the beast towards the equipment barn. As it crawled down the worn path, Hawk turned to double-check that his house was standing, that the lights were on, and the place hadn't caught on fire in the twenty seconds since he left it.

The house was fine. It was Hawk that needed work. Of all the improvements he had made to himself in the last couple of years—learning electrical, carpentry, and plumbing skills, managing the build site, keeping sober with a field of free weed growing outside of his door—there was still a level of self-confidence that eluded him. Hawk was an impostor wherever he was and whatever he was doing. He had no formal education except high school. Instead, he had spent his life figuring shit out.

The ranch gave him a home, a safe place to continue figuring shit out, albeit on a smaller scale. Jaime and Blair provided everything he needed. Security, a job, and, of course, free health care from Emerson. But that kid gave him more. A purpose. Hawk smiled as he brought the tractor into the barn, reminding himself of the life he was rebuilding. No one knew him outside of the ranch anymore. Hawk hadn't left the grounds in almost a year, instead focusing his energy and time on things within his reach. Things he could control. The dispensary operation. The build site. And being a friend to Emerson.

He traded the tractor for the golf cart. His ears relaxed when the grumble of the diesel engine was replaced by the quiet whirr of the electric motor. Now he could hear the click and buzz of insects in the tall grass. As he drove along the path, the colors cooled faster than the air, and the tension he had built up over the day fell off him like broken bits. Nacho was alive, the work was getting done, Jaime would be okay with it.

Hawk rounded the hill and turned the golf cart south towards the main house. An orange tint painted the dead yard as the sunset stretched over the pecan trees. He steered the cart between the house and the orchard, making a beeline for the "wood thing with the bars and swings in the yard," chuckling to himself over Jaime's inability to land on the word for it.

Emerson appeared around the corner of the ranch house, hauling ass towards the climbing wall on the playground. A moment later, Barfly tore past, eyes bright and tongue hanging out of her smiling maw, a bead of spit tracing her path as she raced to catch her boy. Emerson leapt to the lower grabs, sneakers scrambling for grip while the dog came at him. Squealing with delightful suspense, he reached for a higher hand hold as his foot landed, launching him up the wall with Barfly nipping his laces.

Hawk parked the cart next to the one Jaime kept at the house, relishing the kid's laughter after the stress of the day. The odor of Camel Lights hit him, and he glanced at the house's wrap-around porch to see Blair leaning into the railing, a nub of a cigarette in her hand, watching her son with a worry on her lip.

"Hey there, Blair," Hawk called.

She turned to him. A half-smile crept up her cheek as she took a drag. She blew out the smoke, blue and pink in the rays and shadows created by the sun setting behind the pecan trees. She motioned for him to join her on the porch as she tapped the cigarette out against the railing.

The steps creaked under his weight, and Hawk noted the deepening split in the bottom tread. Jaime would tell him to fix it only after it broke, maybe sliced into someone's foot. Hawk pulled the memo pad from his back pocket to add it to his list of eventual to-dos, right under lubricating the storm door hinges.

"How're you holding up?" Blair asked. Her voice was demure, and Hawk assumed she was trying to keep Emerson from hearing their conversation.

"Long-ass day," he replied in kind. "But, as Dr. Travers likes to remind me, it could have been worse. How about you?"

"Oh hell, I'm fine, just worried for him." Her gaze floated to Emerson, now perched on the highest platform of the playground, hiding from his dog. "Em can do such incredible things, but he's so..." Her words trailed off with the remnants of her last drag.

"Innocent?" Hawk offered. "I used the word 'pure' to describe him earlier today."

Blair shook her head. "I guess that sounds better than 'dumb.' How can he see people like he does, and not understand how to interact with 'em?"

"Ah, well..." Hawk stood for a breath, unsure of how to respond. He had learned to measure his words with Blair, especially concerning Emerson. They both watched the kid, listened to his giggles as the dog seemed to forget where he had gone and start sniffing the dried scrub grass in a near panic. "I prefer his innocence to the alternative."

"How do you mean?"

"Well, the kid sees your soul, you know? Like I say, there are no secrets from Emerson Hunt."

Blair flipped around and planted her backside against the railing. "Yeah?" she prompted.

Hawk swallowed the discomfort of Blair's steely stare. "Sure. I mean, think about what you could do with that. If you *weren't* innocent. Or dumb, or whatever."

Her eyes glazed, unfocused. Hawk imagined her playing scenarios in her head as she tucked a lock of her straight scarlet hair behind her ear.

"If you could see into folks, into their emotions? The way Em does? What damage would you do to get what you want?" he continued.

"Jesus," she hissed. "Sounds like his fucking father."

Hawk flushed. He didn't intend for the conversation to go this direction. Emerson's biological father was a big-ass no-no topic.

"I'm sorry, Blair, I didn't mean..."

"No," she cut him off, her lips ticking up in a brief smile. "No, I ain't mad, the thought of it is terrifying is all." Her eyes tilted to the playground as her voice lowered. "I can't help but wonder about what kind of person Em would become growing up around that man-whore. Because you're right. If Em wanted something from someone, he'd get it easy enough. That's how his snake-tongued father did. Took what he craved. From whoever had it."

Her body shivered from some internal thought or image as her eyes returned to Hawk's. "It's intimidating, you know? Raising a kid like Emerson? I don't know what I'm doing."

Hawk laughed. a smile stretching his cracked lips. "No one knows what they're doing, Blair. Hell," he nodded over her shoulder, towards the young man on the playground, "even he isn't aware of what he can do. Uvalde proved that, right?"

Blair swallowed, nodding.

"We're all figuring it out, right along with you. With your son. Doing the best we can to make him a good person. There is nothing more we can do."

She hugged herself, thin arms crossing her flat belly and crafter's fingers gripping into her sides. "Yeah," she sighed, lips tightening to a line as her diminutive frame leaned against the railing. "Yeah, I suppose."

They stood in the stillness, the sunset's light and shadow decorated with Emerson's laughter and the dog's harrowing whines.

Feeling a lull in their exchange, Hawk changed the subject. "Speaking of, I was hoping you could convince Jaime to step into the compound tomorrow. Help with some stuff."

"Ranch," Blair corrected.

Hawk blinked. "Yes, sorry, the ranch. Anyway, with your brother off the construction site, I need a person to run it, and I can't do that and manage the dispensary until I find a replacement for Terry."

"I'll make ' em get out of the *casa mañana*, okay?"

"Appreciate it, Blair. I could use his help at the farm. The ground is caving, not sure why. I need the excavator down there to see what's what."

Blair shrugged, disinterested in the details of running the compound. Hawk stepped towards the stairs. He cupped a hand by his mouth and hollered, "Last tour of Utopia Farms leaves in one minute!"

Emerson's giggling and the frantic searching by Barfly stopped, and Hawk found kid and canine stares on him. The boy slung himself onto the fireman's pole, and his hands squeaked against the metal as he slid back to the earth. The dog's face returned to its natural silly grin, and she lopped straight for the golf cart.

"Hey, Hawk?" Blair's voice had her usual volume again, the full edge of her drawl carrying through the air. He hesitated at the stairs, a tinge of nerves tightening through him.

Had he said or done something wrong?

He turned to face her, and his gut unclenched as he found her face kind, relaxed. Her thin lips parted, paused as if she were second guessing her thought. "I appreciate you wantin' to be part of all this," she said. "And all you do for my son. This place..." Her focus drifted to the orchard and the sunset. "This home for Emerson wouldn't be what it is without you."

Pins and needles raked his skin, a chill in the blaring heat. An endearment from Blair? It was only the second one Hawk had received from her in the three years he'd been working and living on their land. Now it was his tongue stumbling, words failing to form as Hawk studied this pretty and delicate thing Blair had set between them, trying not to crush it with his clumsy and calloused fingers. He wasn't used to praise, not from Blair or Jaime, but neither from his previous life, before the ranch. It was awkward. He didn't appreciate what to do with it. A piece of kitsch with no purpose except to remind you of who it came from, taking up space without providing function in his tiny footprint of a life.

Right as the pause turned uncomfortable, he blurted, "Um... thank you, Blair. I was about to say the same about you."

Chapter Twelve

Hawk landed on the driver's side of the bench, Emerson already planted beside him and Barfly wedged into the narrow rear-facing seat.

"Are you ready?" he asked the kid.

"You bet!" Emerson's eyes gleamed with a familiar anticipation of their nightly adventure. "What are we doing tonight?"

Hawk considered the question as he engaged the key and tapped the throttle. The cart eased forward, and he steered away from the house. Their ritual was routine, but Hawk made sure it was never boring. Every drive to the farm became a story—a riverboat journey down the Amazon, or a tense cat-and-mouse chase as they hid from aliens trying to eat them.

"I have something special in mind," he replied. Moving into the straightaway, he eased the cart up to top speed, making sure the dog didn't roll off the rear seat. "Just hang tight for a minute."

Hawk sped along the path, the last of the sunlight painting the scrub with shallow hues similar to the Utopia Kush that filled the dispensary warehouse. As they passed the edge of the hill, Hawk looked back at the house, watching it disappear from view. After another thirty seconds of driving, he slid the cart to a stop.

"What's here?" asked Emerson. Usually, the first stop of their adventure was some kind of landmark. An anchor for the story. The build site office as a submarine, or the kennels as a monster barn. There was nothing around them except the warm, empty expanse of Texas twilight.

Hawk pulled himself to standing and turned to Emerson. He found the boy's brown eyes wide, expectant, looking for a clue. Hawk held his gaze, a slow smirk growing on his face.

"You're driving," Hawk said.

The kid's eyes widened as his mouth fell open. "But... I can't. Mom says I'm not allowed, Hawk!"

Hawk pursed his lips, as if considering the logic. He made a show of standing tall, a hand shielding his eyes as he pretended to search the barren space. "Yeah, but I don't see your mom here. Do you see her anywhere?"

Emerson gulped as his gaze swiveled, his shoulders hunched with anxiety. He gave the area a solid once-over, then looked at Hawk. The kid shook his head, his drab hair sticking to his sweaty forehead as his rounded cheeks wiggled.

Hawk patted the driver's seat. "Then scoot over and take the wheel."

Emerson glared at the steering wheel. "But I've never—"

"I'm going to teach you," Hawk cut him off. "Besides, I've been driving all damned day, and I'm tired of it. I want to be driven for a little while." He walked around the cart, cajoling Emerson across the bench.

Emerson shuffled to the driver's side. He planted his feet on the plastic floorboard, spreading them beside the pedals. He sat on his hands as if afraid to touch the steering wheel, and his shoulders cinched up to his ears.

Hawk seated himself and put a reassuring hand on Emerson's back. "It isn't scary. It's actually a lot of fun. I think you're going to like it, Em."

"I just..." Emerson relaxed into the seat. "Mom will be angry. I don't want that."

"Yeah, neither do I. Believe me. So, we won't tell her, okay?"

"I can't lie to her!" Emerson whispered.

"Me neither," Hawk admitted. "And I don't want us to."

"But Hawk, sometimes she asks me about our adventures at bedtime, and I tell her the story you made up. If I lie, she'll know, and she'll be mad."

Hawk nodded as the kid spoke. "Emerson, we won't lie, okay? If your mom asks about tonight's adventure, you say I was too tired to make one up."

The kid's face relaxed, thoughtful.

"Not a lie, is it?"

After consideration, the boy shrugged. "No, it's true. You said you're tired."

Barfly huffed from the second seat, her head rising from her paws so she could investigate the delay in her routine. Her beady stare twitched to Emerson behind the wheel.

"Ready to do this?" Hawk asked.

Emerson slipped his hands from under his legs. He gave up a slight nod as his fingers eased around the plastic steering wheel.

Hawk glanced to Em's small feet hovering over the brake and accelerator. The kid was stiff as a mannequin.

"First off, just relax." Hawk pointed to the pedals. "Do you know what those do?"

Emerson nodded, a wry smile spreading on his face. "I've watched you a lot. The long one means 'go,' and the fat one means 'stop.'" The kid's voice dripped with anticipation.

"Awesome. Could not have put it better myself." Hawk laughed. "Are you planning to smash both pedals at once?"

The kid's brow fell. His gaze raised to Hawk.

Hawk smiled. "We might get tossed apex-over-appetite if you do that. So, do you need both feet in the air?"

Emerson followed his stare. Instead of answering, he lowered his left foot to the floorboard next to the brake.

"Good choice!" Hawk sat back in his seat, pressed his feet into the floor, and gripped the handhold in the roof, bracing himself for a bumpy ride. "Now, tap the gas. Let's see what you can do, kid."

Over the next ten minutes, Emerson piloted around the east side of the compound. The kicks and spurts smoothed, Emerson feeling how the vehicle started and stopped, steered, and moved. Hawk gave positive direction as necessary, but mostly let the kid delight in learning something he shouldn't know.

They ended up at the build site, where Hawk prompted him to park near the freight container. Barfly hopped off the back and trotted ahead. Emerson engaged the parking brake and killed the motor without being shown how, and Hawk realized just how much detail the kid was taking in.

Em's gaze lifted to the plexiglass windshield, to the accident site beyond. The boy's cheeks flattened as his smile faded. "This... this is where the guy got hurt," he stuttered. His voice sounded like it had when Hawk had asked him to drive the cart. As if he was worried about landing in trouble for participating in this.

"Yeah," Hawk replied. "I wanted you to see it. You saved someone's life today, Em."

Without prompting, Emerson walked to the shallow pocket of earth where Nacho should have died. The bold red stains from the accident had blended to a neutral brown, and Hawk was thankful that the blood was not visible in the waning embers of daylight.

"Here, he was here." Emerson pointed at the impact crater as his dog sniffed and licked the greasy dirt. "And you were right there," he said, indicating a spot nearby. He pivoted back to the hole, his brow falling. Hawk assumed he was reviewing the details he could remember from the morning.

"He'd been crushed," Hawk offered. Bending down, he picked up a small rock and tossed it at the steel shipping container a few dozen feet from them, and it clattered against the side. "By that."

"I know," Emerson said. "His guts were squished. His legs weren't there anymore. That big bone? In your waist?" The kid asked for the word by patting his hands against his hips.

"Your pelvis?"

Emerson nodded, "Yeah, that. His was in thirty-three pieces."

The detail stunned Hawk, even though he'd seen Nacho's destroyed body. But it was the kid's delivery that shook him: matter-of-fact, almost liturgical.

"He would have died," Hawk said. "You saved him, Em. You did that today."

Emerson swallowed, his throat bobbing as his lips tightened in a diminutive smile.

The dog dragged a paw across the dirt and gave it a few licks with her tongue. Hawk toed her away as he pulled out his phone to check the time. It was getting close to the magic hour. Robin was under the farm now, preparing. Emerson needed to get to the tower.

"Come on," he said. "We need to tend the field and get home. You going to drive us there?"

Emerson's face lit, cheeks bulging with a smile that exploded on him. He didn't answer but ran back to the cart, claiming the driver's seat before Hawk could.

He smiled and pulled the radio from his belt. "Hawk for Terry."

"Go for Terry."

"Status on the field?"

"All quiet here, Hawk."

"Okay, I'm bringing Em over. Radio if something changes. Hawk out."

He sheathed the walkie and took his spot next to Emerson. Noting their imminent departure, Barfly barked once and ran to the cart. The dog jumped on Hawk's lap and crushed his balls before crawling to the rear seat. Hawk's groan was drowned by Emerson's laugh as his small foot released the brake.

The ride to the farm was smooth, Emerson comfortable driving the cart. Hawk had him park next to the expansive field's only path. His boots hit the ground with a pale crunch that was echoed by Emerson jogging into the loose dirt of the aisle. A pang of anxiety pinched Hawk's chest as Emerson disappeared into the long shadows of the field.

"Hey, Em, wait up!" he hollered. "You're not supposed to be in the farm by yourself!"

Chapter Thirteen

The field swallowed them in a thick, musky vapor as they walked the aisle towards the center clearing. Jaime called the scent "skunk," but Hawk had smelled skunk weed. This was sweeter. Heavy, and still off-putting, but less offensive than other strains. During one of their nightly tends, Emerson had described the odor of their Utopia Kush with a concise precision: the farm stank like "rusted fruit."

The security lights on the central stand filtered through the plants, leaving patterns of sharp shadows on the ground. The path opened into a circular clearing. There, a metal tower grew thirty feet into the sky, with a broad crow's nest at the top that was invisible in the powerful field of the security lamps.

Emerson bounded up the tight spiral staircase with the speed and certainty that came with youth. Hawk followed at his own pace, each unforgiving steel step aching his feet, the sound of his boots on the steps occasionally accompanied by the pop in his left knee. Below them, Barfly chuffed and fell to the dirt in a lump, licking herself.

Emerson paused at the final landing. The stairs ended in a trapdoor to the crow's nest, and Emerson waited for Hawk to release the bolt and lift the heavy door. It heaved open, and they crawled onto the tower platform.

The crow's nest was a small space, round like the field, with thick rebar railings welded to posts to prevent anyone from falling to their death. Hawk soaked in the view. The sodium lights cast a dusky glow across the farm, revealing details and contrast that appeared artificial. Beyond the haze, the shadow of the hill consumed the land. Small spots of light from his tiny house, the equipment barn, and the drying huts cut through the darkness and blur of the security lights, but no solid detail came to his eyes. Above the hill, the sky exploded. Crimson led to purple, which swirled into the blues and blacks of oncoming night. The entire scene created a surreal sense of disconnection—the farm close, an illuminated island of white and green stranded in a black sea of nothing, bordered by the vivid flow of an ocean of color. It never failed to leave Hawk cowering in awe.

Emerson joined Hawk, leaning into him as he also took in the view. After a few moments, the kid asked, "So, how many times tonight?"

Hawk blinked away his reverie and pulled out his phone. Robin had texted him a few minutes before: *3 cycles. Ready when u r.*

"Three," Hawk replied.

"Three?" Emerson turned to face him, lips pursed with curiosity. "We never do that many!"

"Can you... is it a problem?"

"No," Emerson said. "Just sounds like a lot. The field looks plenty bright to me."

Hawk rechecked the message from Robin. "Well, three is what we need. That cool?"

Emerson shrugged.

Hawk texted back: *starting now.*

"Then let's go." Hawk stepped back as Emerson bowed towards the plants. The kid's breathing slowed; his body stilled in concentration. What few sounds creaked from the field below them settled to silence.

After a few seconds, he lifted his gaze to Hawk. "Done!" he sang.

Hawk never questioned the kid's ability—he had seen it so many times he knew it was real. But watching him work this way felt disappointing. There was no revelation, no *ta-da* moment that told Hawk something miraculous had happened like there had been this morning with Nacho. The only signal that anything had happened was a waft of fresh resinous odors rising from the field.

Of course, Hawk knew that wasn't true. Below them, under the farm, the actual miracle had taken place.

His phone vibrated. A new text from Robin: *Good heal. One down. Give me five minutes. I'll check in when ready.*

Hawk replied with a simple *k* and noticed the boy watching him.

"Let's take a break," Hawk suggested. "I want to talk to you about today."

Emerson's brow scrunched. "What? The crushed guy? Did I do something wrong?"

Hawk smiled. "Of course not, Emerson. Not at all. Let's sit."

The kid slid to his bottom and scooted to the edge of the platform, his legs under the railing and his feet dangling in the air. Hawk mirrored him, finding relief in taking the pressure off his feet.

They sat side by side, watching the day fade as Hawk decided where to start the conversation.

"Tell me what happened with Layla this morning."

Emerson shrugged, his arms folding across the railing. "We were playing, like always. Then she got mad at me."

Hawk nodded, side-eyeing the kid. Emerson's gaze drifted away, a tell that he was holding back.

"Why do you think she got upset?"

"Because I fixed her legs?" His intonation rose, as if he was asking instead of telling. "I had to move through her to get to the crushed guy, and she's pissed that I didn't fix her legs forever."

Hawk paused, giving the kid space to hear himself. As intuitive as Emerson was when it came to recognizing the emotions of others, he sucked at turning that perception on himself.

Probing questions flipped through Hawk's brain as he searched for a way to get the kid talking. Most of them were accusatory. Yes and no responses that forced the kid to admit fault.

"Can you think of any other reason?" Hawk asked.

Emerson dropped his forehead onto his arms. His reply came in a whisper. "No?"

Hawk gave him another moment before asking, "She wasn't mad at you before you got her legs working?"

Emerson's stare remained lowered. "Yes, she was," he admitted.

"So then what happened, just before her colors got mad?"

Emerson shifted to look at Hawk. The light shining beneath them stretched strange shadows on the kid's cheeks, elongating his confused expression into something morbid and accenting the tremble in his lip.

"I don't know," he cried. "I saw her and Chris and how they glowed together. They enjoy each other, Hawk. The way Mom and Jaime do."

Hawk rubbed Emerson's back while the kid wiped his hand across his nose.

"Does it make you feel yuck? That they feel something for each other?"

"No!" Emerson spat. "It makes me happy!"

"You don't sound happy about it."

Emerson's hands gripped the rebar railing as he shrugged off Hawk.

"You seem bitter, Em. I know I can't see things the way you do, but I recognize anger."

"I'm not!" Tears worked out of Emerson's eyes, glinting in the underlighting.

Hawk leaned into the space separating them, keeping the kid's gaze and softening his own voice. "Then tell me. You look at yourself, your colors, and tell me what you see."

"I don't need to, Hawk!"

"Please, Emerson. Be honest with me. Use your words."

The kid's face collapsed. He wiped a forearm across his wet eyes. "I'm not angry at Layla or Chris. Or anyone. I'm happy they like each other. It gives them a reason to stay!"

A sudden tug yanked against Hawk's mind. "To stay? You mean here, at the compound?"

Emerson nodded, tears bubbling out now.

"I'm sorry, Emerson, I still don't understand. Why—"

"I know they don't want to be here," Emerson interrupted, his voice thinning with stress. "Not the way you do. I know Layla is only here until Mom lets me fix her forever. Then Dr. Travers will take her away. She'll be gone."

Hawk put his arm back around the kid, letting the boy's head nestle to his chest.

"And Chris too. He only comes over because of Layla."

The knot unraveled in Hawk's head. "And you think if they're fond of each other, they might stay?"

"Yeah," Emerson whimpered. "I can see it in their halos. They don't *like* me, Hawk. They just *need* me. When that's over, they won't want to stay with me."

The knot snapped. There were no secrets from Emerson Hunt.

"You're scared," Hawk whispered.

"I'm scared," Emerson admitted with a shudder. "I'm scared I'll end up the only kid here again."

Chapter Fourteen

The clatter of Hawk's phone vibrating against the metal platform ripped through the moment. Hawk grabbed the phone, frustrated at the interruption but grateful at the same time. He hadn't expected the discussion to wander where it had, and he needed a chance to think.

From Robin: *Ready for round 2.*

Hawk blew out a breath.

"Yeah, I know," Emerson sighed. He pulled himself standing. He stilled a second time, along with the world around them. In that peace, the weight of the hanging conversation pressed on them like the growing darkness past the lights.

Fresh, piney odors again enveloped the stand, rising on a tide of warmth from the field. As Emerson worked, Hawk's thoughts raced, scouring for some way to guide the kid through his minefield of emotions and circumstance.

Emerson eased to the floor, sitting cross-legged and facing Hawk. His eyes pleaded.

Hawk didn't have a plan. He just started talking.

"Nothing about your life is regular, Emerson. You are one of a kind. There isn't anyone on this planet that can understand what it means to be you."

The boy's face remained still.

"But your ability lets you see the experience of anybody you want."

"Almost anyone," Emerson corrected.

"Right, almost anyone." Hawk struggled to forget about the "lightless man"—the one individual Emerson had ever encountered who had no halo. The person who had set so much in motion for so many people.

Hawk heaved his legs onto the platform so he could sit square with the boy. "You feel alone... because you *are* alone, in a lot of ways. And being alone is scary."

Emerson nodded.

"Yet everyone is an open book to you. You know everything you want about every stranger you meet, right? Just by staring at their light?"

Emerson concurred again.

"Okay, now consider how those strangers experience each other. They can't see anything deeper than clothing or skin or hair. Where you see health, desires, motives, everyone else has to stop at blue jeans and blonde hair."

Hawk paused, considering how to make this a dialogue instead of a lecture. "So how do they learn about each other?"

Emerson rolled his eyes. "They use their words. I get it, Hawk. And I've been doing that—"

"Yes, you're right, but it's more than just using words, Em. People *choose* their words. They pick which colors to reveal, which ones to keep hidden away."

The kid's brow furrowed. Hawk had gotten him thinking.

"The lightless man," Hawk declared. "What did you learn about him?"

Emerson's lips parted in shock. Like the boy's father, the lightless man was a taboo topic. Hawk was treading a precarious path, but opportunities to help Emerson learn from his mistakes were rare. He couldn't let this one slip away.

"Nothing. He was just... a hole."

"Nothing? Look around the lack of light. What could you sense about him?"

Emerson's gaze wandered, his cheeks swelling in a grimace of memory. "He was... dirty. And he smelled like onions. He was scary."

Hawk swallowed the growing lump in his throat. "Was he? Or were you frightened at not knowing everything about him?"

Emerson paused, peering through Hawk. "Mom says he had a gun, that he was hurting people."

Hawk waited for a breath to steady himself. "Yes, okay, but what did the man say? What did he do?"

Emerson remained quiet.

"Did he hurt you? Or your mom?"

"No," Emerson admitted.

"Did he scream? Was he mean with his words?"

"No, he was nice to me. He even gave me a present."

Hawk waited now, letting the boy churn on their exchange. He studied the dark unknown past the lights, trusting that his home was there, that the work site lay beyond, and that the world was still turning.

"See, that's how the rest of us do it, Em. We spend time and effort learning about one other. We have to choose our actions, decide which bits of ourselves to share with another person and which bits to tuck away."

"Tuck away? You mean like keeping them secret?" Emerson asked.

"I suppose so."

"Mom says secrets are bad, though."

Hawk sighed. "Not always. I mean, she is right, keeping secrets can hurt people, but what I'm talking about isn't the same thing."

Emerson's face contorted with confusion, but his stare stuck to Hawk. It was time to bring the lesson home.

"Emerson, what will your mom do if she finds out I let you drive the golf cart?"

His eyes widened. "She'd be mad, Hawk! At both of us! Please don't!"

Hawk placed a reassuring hand on the kid's bent knee. "I won't, don't worry. I won't tell her unless she asks, okay? But look, now you and I share something that neither of us shares with your mom."

The kid's round cheeks softened.

"It's a secret, right?"

Emerson shrugged.

"But it's *our* secret. Not yours, and not mine, but ours. We're making a choice to keep it between us."

The boy's stare lightened.

Hawk continued, "That gives us something unique, something special that only we share. It helps us..." Hawk searched for the right words. "It lets us trust one another, Emerson."

Emerson frowned, unconvinced.

"What if Chris found out about the golf cart?" Hawk asked. "What if he told your mom?"

"That would suck," Emerson said. "We'd be in trouble."

"Sure we would! A heap of it! How would you feel about Chris after that?"

Emerson's expression melted into a somber mask as Hawk's phone vibrated. Another text from Robin. She was ready for Emerson to do his thing.

Hawk replied to her: *Give us a few minutes.* He placed the phone in his lap.

"I'd be really, really mad at him," the kid admitted.

Hawk nodded. "For sharing your secret? The way Layla is mad at you for sharing hers?"

"Yeah," Emerson whispered, his face heavy with understanding.

"Would you trust Chris after that?"

"No." More whispering.

The phone vibrated again. Another note from Robin: *Blood is flowing but sure take your time up there whatevs.*

Hawk sighed, irritated. He looked at Emerson, ready to ask him to tend the field, but Emerson was up. He stood by the railing, studying the farm with a familiar focus. An enveloping calm rose from below, traveling up Hawk's spine, releasing the knots in his back and shoulders.

Emerson turned to him. "Done," he murmured.

Hawk rose, stretching his healed body into the thickening evening air and sniffing the tingle out of his sinuses. "You might be done, but we aren't. Not yet."

Emerson sighed, radiating defeat. "What do I do, Hawk?"

"You need to tell me that, Emerson. What needs to happen with your friends?"

Emerson shrugged, and his gaze fell to the metal floor.

"What's missing between you and them? What do you and I have that you don't have with your friends?"

Emerson's eyes rose to his, pensive. After a moment of chewing on his lip, he replied, "The secret? About driving the cart?"

Hawk teetered a hand between them. "Sort of. What does the secret give us, Emerson?"

The young boy's lips relaxed as the pieces came together. "Trust. We trust each other."

Hawk nodded, a smile reopening the crack in his dry lips. The kid's last jolt on the field seemed to have petered out at Hawk's neck. "Exactly. And that's what you need to rebuild with Layla and Chris."

Hawk pulled him into a hug, and Emerson reciprocated. "But how?" Emerson asked, his voice muffled by Hawk's shirt. As they separated, the kid repeated, "How do I do that?"

"Well," Hawk said as he guided Emerson towards the staircase, "you told their secrets, right? That cost their trust. So maybe share some secrets back with them."

"But I don't have any. They've seen what I can do." The kid descended the metal steps ahead of Hawk.

"Well, then the three of you should make some."

"Make some what?"

"Some of your own secrets."

"Like you and I did tonight?"

"Yep, just like we did."

The ping of Emerson's sneakers on the steel stopped as he paused and looked over the lighted field. The kid worried his lip, sucking it between his teeth as he scanned the darkness. Hawk recognized the young boy's expression: the wandering gaze, shoulders set with determination. He was thinking through the problem, working things out in his own mystical way, and the sight brought a smile to Hawk's tired face.

"I think I know what to do."

Chapter Fifteen

G rey clouds diffused the morning sun. The hazy glow made it hurt to watch the world moving past the passenger window. So Irene clamped her eyes shut while Finch drove. She must have fallen asleep, because she jumped when he killed the engine.

Uvalde Memorial Hospital. The modern building dominated the other end of the parking area, its manicured grounds rising into rows of windows stacked eight floors high, each floor broken by a thin line of light-brown stucco. This place—this was where she had last seen her brother. Where she had begun her quest for answers.

Now she found herself back here, to see Wes one final time. Her pattern-centered brain could not ignore the symmetry. She would remember this place as the bookends to the most insane two years of her life.

"It's gonna rain," Finch mumbled. His bent fingers waved over the building ahead. Irene's stare tracked to the darkening sky.

"Bullshit." She yawned, flexing her jaw joint. "I would feel it coming."

Years ago, Wes had broken her jaw. During an intervention, he had lashed out at her, ended up cracking the bone in two. A metal plate now supported the bone, with screws securing the surgical steel to the outside of her mandible. As the barometer rose, so did the dull ache in her face.

Finch sniffed. "The sky don't lie, but your bones might."

Irene's head fell to the seat, then pivoted towards Finch. The man's gaze remained forward but darted around the building and parking lot with a nervous energy. Like her, Finch had his own experience with the hospital—months of treatment for chemical burns. A pang of guilt and shame shook her. He never left home unless he had to, but today, he was playing her caretaker. She could have driven herself, but Finch's concern for her well-being had outweighed his social anxiety.

"Thank you for bringing me here. I know this brings up shitty memories for you. It must be weird to be back here."

Eyes forward, Finch shrugged his shoulders.

Irene's phone chirped. She pulled it out of her backpack and found a text message from Coleen: *Let me know when you're here. I'm in the lobby.*

Irene sent a quick reply that she was heading in. She turned to her friend.

"You can come, but I don't expect you to."

His gaze tilted to her, his one tawny eye wider than normal.

"I... I'm gonna wait here. But please, take the time you need."

Irene hopped out of the truck and heaved her backpack over her shoulder. Finch had parked in the farthest corner, where spaces were plentiful and foot traffic minimal. As she closed the door, she noticed the floppy Aussie fedora in Finch's hand. He shoved it on, brim pulled down to hide his face from passers-by.

She crossed the parking lot, feeling the lift of a small breeze under her hair. Finch might be right: it could rain. What with the drought that had shadowed the search for her brother, it would be fitting for a monsoon to hit today.

The automatic doors slid open with a whisper that drowned in cacophony. Visitors corralled in the area, waiting to pass through a security screen.

She found Coleen waving her over to the security counter. The sheriff was in her khakis today. On the job, she was casual, but never sloppy. Irene had only seen her in the uniform once before.

Coleen rounded the desk, took Irene's arm, and led her through the checkpoint. They cleared the rabble and rounded a corner to a bank of elevators.

In the sudden quiet, Irene found herself in a firm embrace. Coleen had removed her Stetson and wrapped Irene in a tight hug, and Irene realized she was clutching the woman back. As they released one another, Coleen replaced her hat, and her face grew somber.

"How are you holding together?"

Irene shrugged. "I don't know, to be honest."

"Appreciate you doing this. It's never easy."

Irene wiped a hand on her nose, trying to brush away the chemical vapors of cleaners and medicine. "It is strange to be here again." Her eyes floated past Coleen to the window behind her. Outside was an open-air atrium. Centered in the window's frame was the bench where Irene had cried when hell had broken loose around her.

The sheriff reached across her and tapped the button for the elevator. "Well, we only need you to identify the body, but..." She turned to catch Irene's gaze. "Take as much time as you want with him, okay?"

The ping of the elevator's arrival saved Irene from having to respond. She followed her friend into the oversized lift, where the sheriff poked the button for the lowest floor.

The doors opened to silence and stillness. A bland, painted cinder block hallway stretched ahead. Irene walked a few paces behind Coleen, and the sound of the sheriff's boots tapping on the linoleum tile echoed in the empty space. As they passed a few open doors, Irene caught glimpses of what appeared to be workshops—tools hanging on pegboards, a rack of artificial limbs. One tiny room was someone's office, crammed full of books and papers. Irene imagined having to crawl over the desk to sit behind it.

She turned to find the sheriff's face solemn.

"You've never done something like this before, have you?"

Irene shook her head.

A gentle smile appeared on Coleen's face. "In a nutshell, the mortician will pull Wes's body from the freezer and uncover his face. All you have to do is give us a sign if it's him."

Irene nodded, as if practicing for what she had to do next.

"I'll answer your questions as I can, but, this being an active investigation, there's not a lot we can discuss."

Irene kept her focus ahead. The itch to avoid the entire situation reached her feet, and she fought the urge to bolt to the elevator.

Coleen must have sensed her discomfort. "All right, then, let's go."

The sheriff eased open the oversized swinging door and stepped through. She gestured for Irene to follow.

The morgue was at least ten degrees colder than the hallway. Irene's flesh retreated against her bones. Coleen placed a hand on her back and led her to the far side of the room, where square freezer metal doors lined the wall. Irene homed in on the one open door with its tray still inside the freezer. A slash of light struck across the opening, showing her only a flat sheet laid over the rack, with curving shadows suggesting an organic shape deeper in the cavity.

Motion caught her attention. The mortician stood, letting his pen fall on top of whatever paperwork he had been completing. The man was young and pale, with thin glasses and thinner hair, and his face carried a gentle, neutral expression that Irene assumed was part of his training.

Without speaking or acknowledging them, he grabbed the handle to the body tray. He eased it smoothly and slowly from the hole in the wall. The rack was empty at first. Nothing but a pale-green sheet wrapped tightly across the flat steel. Then a shape emerged. Irene recognized the form of a hand, the cotton cover wilting over the knobs of the knuckles, the fingers looking thick and stubby beneath the sheet. Then sharp angles appeared, an abrupt rise in the blanket, followed by an organic slope to the unmistakable contours of a human face.

A wave of anxiety crashed against Irene, rocking her back until she leaned into Coleen. She steadied herself, counting her breaths as Coleen's hands supported her.

"Ready?" The mortician's voice squeaked over her rushing pulse.

Chapter Sixteen

The dog followed Emerson, Layla, and Chris out the front door, bounding in anticipation of afternoon play.

"If it rains, y'all run inside, you hear?" Mom's voice carried over the clank of dishes landing in the kitchen sink.

"Okay, Mom!" Emerson hollered back, letting the screen slam shut.

Layla and Chris stood a dozen feet apart on the porch, neither of them looking near the other, their lights reserved and dim. They were uncomfortable with one another. And with Emerson too. He knew it was his fault. And Hawk always said, *You have to own your mistakes.* It was up to him to fix it.

"I'm sorry about yesterday," Emerson began. They faced the yard, but their auras perked up. They were listening. "I forget I can see stuff other people can't, and I didn't mean to make things all weird."

Chris's head pivoted in Layla's direction, while her gaze remained on the yard.

"But I'm gonna make it up to you today, if you'll let me. I have an idea. I think you'll both enjoy it."

The thump of a crutch marked Layla's pivot. She met Chris's gaze, and they both shrugged. Emerson smiled as their auras brightened with curiosity.

"First thing: I gotta tell Barfly to stay here. Otherwise she'll give us away."

Now Layla's and Chris's curious glances turned to Emerson as he plunged his hand into the dog's aura. He pulled on the bright blues and greens until Barfly's happy pants slowed to a yawn.

"You stay here, girl," he said, rubbing her face as her eyes slid closed. "You stay here and nap while we play."

The dog plopped to the wood floor of the porch, rolled onto her side, and released a long sigh.

"Okay," Emerson whispered, standing back up and turning to his friends. "She'll sleep now. We can go."

Emerson headed to the porch steps, hearing Chris's murmuring sneakers and the clank of Layla's crutches following him.

"Where are we going?" Layla asked.

"Well, first, the backyard. I'll explain there."

As Emerson walked across the yard, Chris tore past him in a blaze. "Race you there, slowpokes!"

Emerson watched him disappear around the corner of the house. He glanced back at Layla. Her face wore a smile that didn't carry into her dull halo, where rust and grey showed her icky feelings. He waited for her to catch up.

"You want to run like Chris?" he asked.

Her face grew dour. Emerson sucked in a breath and gulped it, scared he was upsetting her again. He walked towards the corner, and her clunky gait followed.

"Layla, I understand what I did and want to make it right."

"It's okay." Her voice was soft, her light dimming and disappointed.

"It will be, I promise," Emerson said. He stepped out of view of the front porch and the kitchen windows. As Layla worked her way there, Emerson chewed his lip. "Just now, when I asked if you want to run…"

"I said it's okay," Layla repeated, her voice strained and tired, brick-red spirals of frustration spinning from her core.

"No, I was asking. Can we make that part of today? Is that something you want?"

Her eyes lit up. "But won't you get in trouble?"

"Only if Mom or Jaime find out. You can't tell them or I'll get a whoopin'." Mom hadn't switched him in months, but this might make her mad enough to pick it up again.

"I don't know, Emerson. I mean, I would love to run, but—"

His fingers touched her belly, and the hole in her gentle radiance closed.

Her stare unfocused, Emerson laid a supporting hand on her shoulder while she caught her balance. A smile bloomed on her cheeks as the haze lifted off of her, her aura strong and full now. She giggled, a tender sound that warmed the inside of Emerson's chest.

He helped her take a few orienting steps forward, her crutches up as she tested her legs. Once she was steady on her feet, Emerson let go.

"Thank you!" Her voice came in a sweeping breath, her excitement showing real and genuine in the gold rays of her light.

"Let's catch up to Chris," Emerson replied.

Chris leaned against the shed, his face brightening as Emerson and Layla arrived.

"Now we'll see who's the real slowpoke!" Layla laughed.

"Come on." Emerson guided his friends behind the shed. "Leave your crutches here; we're going on a hike."

Layla leaned the aluminum walkers against the clapboard wall. "So where are we going?" she asked. Emerson looked back over the yard, to the spot Layla stood yesterday. The healed grass had faded from the lush emerald to a sickly yellow in the crushing heat. He traced it into the hills, where the scrub and mesquite flowers withered.

He pointed up the dying path. "Over there."

"Then let's go!" Chris hollered. He raced off, shoes crunching on the paling runway.

"Not so fast, buttface!" Layla screamed. She wobbled on her fresh legs for a few steps, then found her balance and ran after Chris.

Emerson beamed, pleased to see the lights of his companions glowing and strong. He set off, trailing them up the hill.

Chris stopped at the crest, waiting for them. Layla sidled up next to him, panting at the unfamiliar exertion. As Emerson closed the gap, he pointed at the slope winding to his right.

"Let's go farther up," he said.

"Are we hunting rattlesnakes?" Chris asked. It was a common suggestion—he wanted to catch rattlers in his hands and let Emerson heal any bites.

"No, dumbass." Emerson climbed ahead of his friends. The rocky soil scrunched under his sneakers, and the ground radiated heat under his chin. The air was heavy, leaving him sluggish and wet. "We're going to play a game together."

Emerson led them up the slope until they were level with the roof of his house. Then he cut left, working a switchback that led down to the flat ground by the farm. Stopping before they wandered behind the next hill, Emerson pointed towards the expanse ahead. "I want us to play in there."

Layla and Chris remained silent, their faces and halos confused.

"What do you mean?" Layla asked.

"I mean, we're going to play hide and seek," Emerson said. He turned his head, nodding towards the wide circular field of pale-green growth below the hill. "In the farm."

The eyes of his friends widened. Chris's lips trembled, but Layla found her words and said, "Emerson, we're not allowed in there. My mom said never to go in there, that it's dangerous."

"I know," he replied. "But I do it every night, and it's fine. They're just plants."

"Oh, I don't know," Layla gasped.

"It ain't dangerous. They just want you to think that so you'll stay out of it. They don't want us breaking the plants, because they sell 'em." Emerson turned to Chris, saying, "You're always saying hide and seek isn't fair because I can see your light, right?"

His friend nodded, lips still moving in uncertain shock.

"In there, the light from the plants is so bright, I can't see anything else."

Chris's narrowed stare moved to the farm. "Really?"

"Yep," Emerson confirmed. The plants radiated a thick purple glow, and from the tower, it was difficult to make out any individual plants or animals over the halo noise. "So what do you two say? Hmm?"

His friends locked eyes, their auras popping with shades of anticipation, each waiting for the other to make the first move.

Emerson started down the slope, loose clods of dirt tumbling ahead of him. "Who's going to the farm with me?"

Chapter Seventeen

The mortician billowed the top of the sheet. He eased it down, Irene seeing in her periphery as pale tones of flesh were exposed. Her eyes refused to move from the man's solemn expression.

He stepped away, hands clasped in front of him. Coleen gave her a reassuring squeeze, and Irene forced her gaze to the uncovered head on the rack.

The body was Wes's. The sandy blond hair was longer, shaggy. His face was thin and drawn, from rigor mortis or his drug use, she wasn't sure. His lips parted to show his upper gums, a distinctive shape she called "fish mouth." She'd assumed this expressed indignation. An aura of superiority.

She was wrong. His motionless body, empty of any psyche, showed her the expression was only his stupid face. Nothing more.

"Irene?" Coleen whispered.

"It's Wes," she croaked.

The sheriff moved a hand across her back. "I'm so sorry, Irene."

"Can I..." Irene spoke before she could stop herself. "Can I have a minute with him?"

Without a word, the mortician headed for the doors across the room. Coleen's hands left Irene to allow her to stand on her own.

"Take as long as you need. I'll be right outside."

The room fell silent once the door closed behind the sheriff, and Irene found herself alone with her brother. The thing she'd chased for the last two years.

Her chest was a roiling kettle of emotion. Wes—part of him—lay still before her. She wanted an explanation of their father's last days. Something that might make her experiences since his death sensible. Her default stony belligerence around Wes bubbled up, and, to her surprise, dissipated. Envy percolated at his lackadaisical approach to everything, the way he'd shirked responsibility and stranded her with questions. The ebb and flow of emotions and memories came fast. A shiver ran over her ribs, and she wrapped her arms around her gut to hold herself in place. Words raced through her mind, overloading the path to her tongue.

"I'm sorry."

Her voice was foreign in the sterile room. And her words stunned her. In the silent wake they cut through the chemical-scented air, her body found a calm.

"I'm sorry, Wes," she whispered. "I'm sorry I hated you for things you can't help." She took a shuddering breath. "I still hate you, in so many ways. And I am so, so sorry."

Irene wanted to cry, but nothing came. She watched the un-moving skin of his pale lips.

"You know, Dad talks to me," she continued, checking over her shoulder to make sure Coleen was still out of the room. "I don't understand how, or why. But... his voice comes to me. Maybe not his voice, but his words? I'm not sure how to describe it."

Wes remained quiet.

"It's been happening since he died, and it's always the same. It's always 'Save Wes' or 'Save your brother' or some shit like that."

Her stare fell to the sheet collapsed into the space where his chest should be. She lifted a tentative finger, sneaking the cotton a few inches lower, exposing her brother's collarbone. Her breath caught at the line of ragged and ruddy flesh. She threw the sheet over him, covering the gore.

"But I failed, didn't I?" she asked no one. "I wasn't able to keep you safe. From whoever did this to you. From yourself. And the world."

Tears came as the next words formed.

"From me."

Irene let herself cry through her ambivalent emotions. Around her, the universe vibrated with the voices of the scream-ing dead.

"I don't know what Dad expects me to do, Wes. Now that you're gone, what the hell does he expect me to do about it?" Her tone soured. Anger again. Injustice. A mixture of sorrow and frustration threatening to wrench her composure apart.

With shaking fists and weeping eyes, she focused on Wes's dead face.

He gazed in wonder at the ceiling tiles.

She steadied her breath. "I'm sorry that I couldn't give you the benefit of the doubt. Not that you earned it, but that's not the point, is it?" She gulped the lump in her throat. "If I got the chance to do it again... I dunno, Wes. I think I would choose trust next time? Wouldn't I?"

Wes held his tongue in his fish mouth that was just a part of his dumb, tear-blurred face.

"If we could rewind, I hope I'd choose family instead of... instead of..." She tried to swallow the realization. "Instead of my ego."

Wes stayed silent. The way the dead should be.

"I want to believe I would. And that'll have to do now. Won't it?"

Irene seated her backpack on her shoulder and wiped her eyes one last time over her brother.

"Goodbye, Wes."

Chapter Eighteen

Uncle Terry walked the edges of the field, wearing a massive belt that carried a radio and dangerous-looking equipment. Hawk had started the security patrol to keep people out of the farm and stop them from stealing the plants. If the kids were going to get busted, it would be by Uncle Terry.

Emerson peered around the rock that hid him and his friends from the man's view. "Get ready," he murmured, moving past the boulder, giving Layla and Chris room to move. Emerson watched his uncle's light throb to the steady beat of music in his headphones. "He's close enough to hear us, but he's got headphones on. So don't worry about noise. Just try and stay hidden."

The other children nodded, eyes tense with anticipation and excitement.

His uncle rounded the curved edge of the farm and disappeared from view. "Now!" Emerson hissed, bolting from behind the rock. He kept low, even though his ninja crouch wouldn't hide his bright white t-shirt blaring against the ugly brown dirt if Uncle Terry turned back. His eyes locked on the field ahead, and his legs warmed as they pumped. A line of metal stakes bounded the edge, with strings weaving away to support the top-heavy plants. Emerson breached the field, the temperature and humidity rising along with the familiar sweet-metal odor of the plants. A few steps in, he spun to check on his friends.

They ran together, hands interlocked and held up next to their faces, which stretched with delight while their halos ringed with the fear of getting spotted.

They caught up to Emerson, and after a moment of silent celebration, Emerson ushered them deeper into the thicket.

"It smells awful!" Chris complained.

"I know," Emerson said, "but you get used to it quick." The plants towered over them, arranged in something Hawk called a "daisy pattern" that packed the most plants into the space. It also limited visibility to a few feet in any direction. The shade was plentiful, the air between the growths thick and wet. It carried a heft Emerson wasn't used to breathing, and his shirt was soaked with sweat.

"Where are we going?" asked Layla.

Emerson looked up through the pointed leaves crawling off of dense, bushy stalks, finding hints of the gray skies above them. His eyes teetered through the gaps until he spied the brown rust of the metal tower.

"There," he said. He put his face next to hers, tasting her apple shampoo in the air. He let her site along his arm and finger as he pointed at the tower. "That's at the center of the field. We can play there."

"This place is huge," Chris chimed. "You sure you can't see our light in here?"

Emerson smirked. "I can right now, dummy. You're standing here beside me."

Chris's expression lit up. He bolted ahead, a few plants in, and called back, "How about now?"

Emerson stopped and looked into the surrounding miasma of purples. The plants radiated their steady lilac colors, the collective aura creating a mask that hid Chris's cornflower blue. The only other colors Emerson could see were his own shades of gold.

"I don't see any of it," Emerson whispered back, moving farther into the plants until he saw Chris. "You listening? I can't see it around the light of the plants!"

Chris's face beamed. "Finally! A fair game!"

Emerson chuckled as he maneuvered through the stinky jungle. He rounded the base of a plant and found himself in the clearing. One of the four supports holding up the tower was in front of them, and the others splayed in a square on the open ground with the spindly plants walling them in. At the very center was the metal spiral staircase.

Chris and Layla emitted small noises of wonder and pleasure at the sight, and then Layla fixated on the stairs. She jogged ahead, put her hand on the railing, and tested her legs on the first step.

"I could do this; I'm able to climb these!" she declared. Her beam was genuine, her halo pushing out with a yellow Emerson had never seen from her.

"No, we can't," Emerson murmured. "After a few steps, you'll poke over the plants. Remember Uncle Terry? He might be looking."

The smile didn't waver. "Still," she sighed, her eyes and mouth relaxing with wonder. She planted her foot on the next step, then followed with the other, her grin quivering into a giggle at the novel experience Emerson realized he took for granted.

"Okay, let's do this," Chris said. "Emerson, you're It by default. Layla and I will go hide."

"Fine, but stay in the field. Try to keep away from the outer edge. Also, don't shake the plants too much or they'll notice. "

The other kids exchanged knowing glances, their faces tensing with anticipation of forbidden dangers.

"Oh, and try not to cross the main aisle." Emerson raised a hand towards the open corridor through the plants. "If Terry's walking by when you do, he'll see. You can see all the way down that aisle."

They both nodded.

"Fine! Get on with it, butthead," Chris said.

"I'll count to ten. You two better move!" Emerson said, covering his eyes with the crook of his elbow as he leaned against the metal stairs. Even without his sight, the pair of lights from his friends was visible with the pale glow of the purple field behind them. As Emerson counted, their shines scuttled to the lavender haze, then split in separate directions before dissolving into the deeper purple.

A tight discomfort grew in his chest. He opened his eyes and studied the wall of plants and their merging violet glow. A flickering sound grew, a rustling as the wind rallied. There was no sign of Layla or Chris. For all he knew, he was alone in this field. His friends might have left him here, run home to tattle on him and get him a switching as payback for his behavior yesterday.

He sucked in a deep breath, letting the humid air tamp down his fear, and squared his shoulders. As unpleasant as this experience was for him, it was necessary. Trust would build into relationships. That's what Hawk had told him last night, thirty feet above where he was standing now.

He stepped out from the cover of the tower, heading towards the spot where he had lost track of his friends. As he considered where to head into the greenery, something smacked him on the face, just above his right eye. From the impact, it might have been a June bug, but then the thing on his forehead moved. It didn't tickle as much as trickle onto his eyelid, which fluttered closed on reflex.

Emerson wiped his hand across his eye and found liquid on his fingertips. Another pelt landed on the top of his head. He turned his gaze skyward, where the bottoms of the clouds had darkened and their surface roiled with slow-motion energy.

A third droplet materialized, falling from the sky and splashing on his lips, leaving a sweet flavor there.

Rain! It was raining! Mom had said something about it as they left the house, but he'd never thought it would happen.

He smiled, excitement boiling in him. Rain hadn't fallen in years, and now it was wetting his skin. Dull thuds of water hit the dried ground around him, their cadence quickening.

And a peculiar odor joined the sweet rust in the air. An earthy scent that somehow left him cool and secure. He laughed, giddy, holding out his hands, hoping that the sky might bless his fingers with its tears.

His reverie crumbled when Layla started screaming from the field.

Chapter Nineteen

Irene watched the town of Hondo pass by her window. The pattern of low-profile buildings relaxed her. A cycle of wide metal barn structures converted to feed stores, the stucco gas stations, and wooden clapboard-sided restaurants offering the "best whatever-kind-of-food-we-serve in Texas" entered and left her periphery as she focused on thinking about nothing in particular.

The rain ebbed and flowed, each cascade of sighing water lasting longer than the previous one. In the parking lot across the intersection, a woman stood in the falling rain. A young girl clung to her leg, eyes to the sky and squinted against the thick droplets. The child smiled, relishing the novelty as if her soaked clothes were a gift on Christmas morning.

A rumble shook Irene in her seat as the pickup rolled over a set of double train tracks. The sensation felt odd. Out of place.

"Are we taking a different way home?" She turned to Finch. He'd tucked his Aussie fedora low on his head, the brim pulled over his eyes. "I don't remember crossing a railroad."

He nodded. One of his gnarled fingers gestured to the road ahead as he replied, "Yeah, I have a quick errand. Not out of the way or anything. In fact"—he turned to her, lifting the hat higher on his forehead—"I'd appreciate your help with it. If it ain't no trouble."

"Of course not, Finch." Irene looked up the curving road. A small country lane, just big enough for two cars to pass one another. "Where are we going?"

"Well," Finch sighed, his voice straining with reluctance, "the short version is, I'm out of weed. So we're picking up more."

Irene chuckled, and it grew into unanticipated laughter. "At least it's something important!"

Finch huffed, playing hurt. "Aw, come on now, it helps with my appetite!"

"I know," Irene replied. "I'm just busting your balls, Finch." The levity was a welcome break from the sadness and rain of the last half hour.

Finch set his fedora again, his lips tightening before he spoke. "Now, the longer version is that I'm out of weed, and I'm buying a metric shit ton more of it."

Irene felt the tug of intrigue. "Like, how much?"

"Seven ounces." His voice carried a gravity that contradicted the diminutive measurement.

"Is... is that a lot? It doesn't sound like a lot, Finch."

Now Finch chuckled. "I guess it depends. Seven ounces of water isn't much. For pot, it's a lot." The splotched skin on his forehead rose with thought, unable to wrinkle. "Should last me a solid three months, I figure."

Irene's brow rose. "How much do you usually buy?"

"About an ounce or two. Every couple of weeks."

"Okay. Why are you stocking up, then?"

"Because I can." Finch turned to her, his eye gleaming. "Even with it legal, you can't get more than a couple of ounces. The great state of Texas doesn't want its citizens succumbing to *reefer madness.*"

"So, you're breaking the law?"

"No, that's the thing." Finch's hand ruffled in his shirt pocket. He pulled out his phone and set it under his leg, then worked back in for something else. He handed Irene a slip of paper, and as she unfolded it, she noted the telltale signature scrawl of a doctor's prescription. "Because of my..." He trailed off. Irene turned to find him working through his words, as if they were difficult to force out of his scarred mouth. "... my body. My physical condition. I can buy more than a recreational amount."

Irene handed the script back to him, and Finch worked it into the pocket along with his phone. Her friend didn't usually discuss his scars or how he'd gotten them. The topic wasn't taboo, but Irene was never comfortable asking for more information than Finch might offer on his own. That it had come up in casual conversation surprised her, and she was sure it mortified the hell out of poor Finch.

"So, where do I come in then?" she asked. "I can't imagine you need to team-lift seven ounces of anything."

Finch smiled, his discomfort appearing to ease. "Simple." He looked at her again, his blank face stoic as the downpour hit the window behind him. Yet his working eye conveyed enough emotion for Irene to realize what he needed.

She returned his grin. "You want me to talk to the actual, real-life people, don't you?"

Relief eased over Finch, his gaze turning to the road and rain.

"Yeah," he said, his voice thin with chagrin. "With an order this large, they won't just leave it outside for you to pick up, you know? Someone's gotta go in, hand them the cash. I don't want..." His words trailed off, and they didn't need to be spoken.

For the last eighteen months, she had run most of Finch's errands for him. Anything that required interactions with people was something he tried to avoid. Getting Finch in a room with other people was rare—outside of the Uvalde support group, Irene had never seen him in public. She often wondered how different the man had been before the marring of his features, before the accident had taken his confidence and pride from him. Finch was capable—his large house and his stretch of land near Boerne showed he had made plenty of money in his "before" times. But whatever had happened had replaced the man's capability with those horrific scars.

Irene caught herself staring at his skin. Not in disgust, the way others stared at him. Not in wonder, either. But in grief. She saw Finch, past the ugly surface and into his person. Who he had been, before the mutilation of his flesh, would have been quite something to experience. Irene missed a man she'd never known.

Anxiety raced through her like mercury. The shadow of her brother's crimes and disappearance, her search for him, his death—Irene considered the scars these would leave on her. What pieces would she leave behind here in Texas? Were they the best part of her? Would these people—Finch, or Coleen—would they look at her someday, perhaps stand over her dead body, memorialize her as they wondered what the hell had happened to the pragmatic and intelligent fighter beneath her scars?

The thought occurred to Irene: it could be a mistake to return to her previous life. She might let these people down the same way she'd let her brother and her father down.

She wiped her eyes, willed the crying to cease as her gaze drifted to the windshield. A steady rain fell and would soon create rivulets of runoff along the sides of the winding road. The few cars on the streets had slowed, the drivers moving with pedantic care through the storm.

"Almost there." Finch hollered to make his voice heard over the weather beating on the vehicle. The wipers spun side to side, hurling puddles of water off the windshield only to have them replaced with more by the groaning sky.

Irene saw the haze of commercial lighting out her window, but the rain made it impossible to identify any businesses. The only legible sign was for a township, and it passed through the foggy headlamps, close and slow on her side of the truck.

Tarpley, Texas. Population, a few hundred people.

Moments later, Finch eased the Chevy onto a gravel drive. The scenery opened outside the vehicle windows, a short expanse of flat ground disappearing into a glistening film as rain collected on its surface. Farther away, the large puddles and pools faded into the gray film. The driveway appeared out of that nothing, passed them, and disappeared back into nothing. The image left Irene feeling isolated and vulnerable.

As if to punctuate her emotions, a brilliant slash of lightning ignited the surrounding haze, refracting through the weather into some end-of-the-world inferno. Irene waited for the thunder, but there was none.

"Jesus Christ, are we safe, Finch?"

He laughed, keeping his eyes on the drive ahead and both hands locked on the steering wheel. "This is pretty normal. It's just been a minute. You've never seen a Texas storm, have you?"

Irene remained quiet, white-knuckling the dashboard and door grip to steady herself.

"It'll run off quick," Finch continued. "Or it won't."

Irene took some solace in Finch's lackluster reaction to the exploding sky. A dark wall appeared in the thick mire ahead. A line of trees: a boundary marker. Another sign blipped through the headlights: UTOPIA FARMS.

As if triggered by the truck passing the trees, the rain decreased to a mild drizzle, opening the curtain to reveal an open space, maybe sixty feet wide and not as long, circled by an array of animal enclosures. Across the area, she found a dilapidated double-wide propped on blocks. A hand-painted plywood sign staked in the ground read dispensary. Behind the home loomed a bulky and industrial-looking barn, with everything beyond shrouded in the strange weather.

Finch parked in front of the mobile home and killed the engine. The sound of the raindrops crept louder around the still cab. Irene waited, assuming Finch would offer some kind of instruction on what she needed to do. Buying pot was something she'd never done before, legally or otherwise, and she had no insight into the etiquette of it. She turned in her seat, the ripples of water leaving crawling shadows across the dash and her friend's swirled skin.

Finch's hands still clenched the wheel, and his gaze stayed forward, looking at the dispensary. His throat expanded in fits as he swallowed something thick.

"Hey, you okay?" she asked. Another shadow moved over his face as a rivulet of rain slithered down the windshield.

"Yeah," Finch croaked after a moment. "Yeah, I just..." He turned his head towards her, his eye hidden beneath his hat. "I just wanted to say thank you."

"Of course," she replied, frowning at the big stink he was making. This was just another errand, even if it was new to her. "It's no problem, Finch. I'll need to know what to do, though."

Finch's stoic face bowed. One of his hands peeled away from the vinyl steering wheel and stretched across the cab. One of his ruddy fingers slipped under the latch of the glove box and popped it open. Irene's heart skipped as he revealed one of the largest pistols she had seen in her life.

Finch reached in, fumbling for the large envelope under the gun, and she relaxed again. He held the thick packet out to her, and her fingers found the paper stuffed to capacity with the thick, pliable feeling of linen and an unmistakable heft that told her she was holding a massive wad of cash.

"Tell 'em you're here for my pickup. Hand 'em that. Bring me the box."

"They won't need your ID or anything?"

Finch shook his head. "I'm a regular. They've got my info already."

Irene shrugged. "Easy-peasy, I suppose."

She peered out over the dashboard, plotting her path from the truck to the steps, hoping to avoid as many mud puddles as she could. Figuring the break in the weather wouldn't hold for long, she cracked open the passenger door.

"Be right back!" she sang, and Irene slid out of the truck.

Across the cab, Irene tucked the envelope into her shirt and hugged it against her chest before jumping out into the rain. She gave a nondescript holler at the weather and slammed the passenger door. Finch tracked Irene through the windshield as she hopped from spot to spot, her small body hunched over the pile of cash next to her breast, trying to keep it dry.

His hand returned to the glove box and wrapped around the handle of the Desert Eagle. He pulled the heavy weapon out, checked the safety and the chamber, and set the gun in his lap.

The rain hissed at him, growing loud and angry as it came in sheets and then buckets. Irene made it to the steps, her hair a mottled mess against her back and face. She wiped a hand over her brow as she looked back at the truck. Finch had the high beams on, and her expression of wonder at her situation pulled on an emotional thread. If Finch didn't know better, Irene might have been digging through his own personal shadows.

He was going to miss her. He longed for the chance to say a proper goodbye. Irene was the closest thing Finch had made to a genuine friend since his skin melted off. If today worked out, it would be because of her presence here.

Finch swallowed his guilt. She would be okay. She was strong. Fierce. Tenacious. Not the coy cliché of a dog with a bone, lazy and greedy, wanting to be left alone. More like a rabbit on the run. Improvising, forced to make smart choices. She'd need those skills today to outsmart the dogs she was about to tussle with.

Irene yanked open the door and disappeared inside.

"*Corre, coneja,*" Finch whispered. "It's time for those dogs to give chase."

Chapter Twenty

T he long leaves and stems whipped Emerson's cheeks as he tore into the line of plants that circled the clearing. Emerson recognized the sound of a damaged halo: Layla's scream had been from surprise and pain. His eyes darted, searching the glow and shade for his friend. He couldn't see more than a few feet in any direction. The explosion of life around him sucked away any hope of catching Layla's demure aura.

Emerson stopped a dozen plants in, turning his head, listening. The only sound was the increasing frequency of thuds as thick drops of rain bombed the spindly leaves.

Another scream. To his left. This one was visceral, his friend's voice cracking and raw. No surprise this time, just pain.

Emerson bolted, gaze bouncing across the farthest plants he could see, looking for any sign of her. The rain's patter on the plants grew to a steady hiss, the water finding its way through the canopy and wetting Emerson's hair and shoulders.

Over the whispers of the drizzle, he heard the staccato of sobbing nearby. Dodging the wide base of a mature plant, he saw her. He hopped over the prone body, trying to figure out what had happened.

She was on her back, face wet, hands hovering over her left leg. Layla's knee made a hard turn and disappeared into the loose soil. Her light was erratic, difficult to see against the overwhelming purple luster. But Emerson knew she had broken her knee.

"It hurts, Emerson!" she cried, voice raspy and raw.

"What happened?"

"I was running, and I sank in the ground. I heard a snap, and now it just hurts really, really bad!"

"Can you move?"

"I don't think so!"

Emerson looked closer at her knee. Her calf disappeared under the dirt, with the joint of the knee bent the wrong way. Her foot had landed in a deep, narrow trench that slithered a path between the plants.

"I think you've broken your leg," he said.

"Fix it!" she screamed. "Make it stop hurting!"

Emerson reached for her belly, for the spot where her halo became putty to him. He stopped, thinking through what would happen.

"Please!"

"I can't," he replied.

"Emerson!" Her hands balled into fists as her body shook, making ripples in the mud.

"No, Layla, I can't fix it until your leg is free."

The desperation in her cries grated at his heart. He wanted nothing more than to heal her. Right now. Take away the pain. But he knew what would happen if the leg remained planted in the earth.

"Layla, if I fix you like this, your leg will stay bent. I need to get it out of this hole first, okay?" He tried to make his voice even, the way Hawk did when things got crazy. That always made Emerson calm under whatever pressure was building around him.

"No!" she shouted. "No, don't!"

Chris's wide and shocked face rounded the plant ahead of them. His eyes asked, and Emerson answered. "Her leg broke, but it's stuck. We have to lift her out, you and me, so I can fix her."

"What?" Chris's voice ramped up several octaves. "Emerson, maybe we need a grown-up!"

"No!" Layla grunted. "No, don't tell my mom!" Her breathing steadied, forming a seesaw rhythm of violent inhales and exhales. Emerson tracked her light as best as he could, noting the inward turn of the halo. She was building her strength.

"We can do this," Emerson said, holding Chris's gaze. "You and me, we free her; then I heal her."

Chris's face was wet. Emerson wasn't sure if it was with tears or rain.

"I need your help, Chris! I can't do this by myself!"

His friend's lips trembled with his halo, his eyes wide with fear, but a single nod signaled his commitment to the plan.

Emerson turned to Layla and stooped to her. Her eyelids fluttered, but she breathed deeply. Emerson saw how the beat of her own heart was causing her pain, as her aura shook in time with her pulse.

"Layla, I'm going to stick my hand in there." He pointed at the crevice that swallowed her leg. "I have to make sure you're not stuck on a root or something."

She nodded, her breath hitching.

Emerson's hand eased into the space. His fingers found the trembling flesh of Layla's calf and shifted loose wads of fibrous and intricate white roots off of her skin. Her leg was hidden below the ankle, surrounded by crumbles of clay and dirt. The field was slurping her in like a noodle of spaghetti.

"I'm going to touch your foot, okay?"

Emerson didn't wait for her response. He laid on the ground, his face near the trench, and began moving dirt away from her shoe with delicate fingers. As he brushed the skin on her shin, Layla yelped.

"Sorry," Emerson said. "Sorry, but your foot has to get free from the dirt."

Layla's strength cracked, and she started sobbing again.

Emerson looked up at Chris. His light carried a steady deep blue now. He wanted to help. "Kneel there." Emerson nodded to the other side of Layla, across the narrow gap. "I think we'll need four hands for this."

Chris's gulp was audible as Emerson tucked his face next to the trench. He scooped away the dirt, his fingers found wetness. The weather was increasing. His friend landed on his knees.

"What do you need me to do?" Chris cried.

"I need you to... easy, now... move the roots, dirt, and mud away from Layla's foot. Try not to touch her leg if you can help it."

Chris's hand slid into the trench alongside Emerson's. The white of Layla's Keds was soon visible, and Emerson felt a flitter of hope. It was coming free.

"Almost there, Layla," he hollered. "Just one more second."

When the lighter brown of her shoe's sole became visible against the red clay, Emerson worked his fingers beneath it. He cradled her foot in his right hand and reached his other one to her belly, to the center of her light.

"Chris, get your hands under her calf. Don't lift until I say so, okay?"

Chris whimpered and complied.

"Layla," Emerson shouted, his head close to the ground and pointing away from hers, "in a second, we're going to yank your leg up, and I'm going to heal you."

"Okay." Her voice steeled, but her breath hitched with anticipation. Emerson's hand tightened around her shoe. His other fingers clenched around her halo.

"Ready..." Emerson opened his hand over her stomach.

"Set..." Chris's arms tensed, his thin bicep muscles visible under his soaked shirt.

"LIFT!"

There was a sickening crackle as they pulled on her leg. Emerson poured his light into hers, pushing away the injury and pain, reshaping her halo into something solid. Layla released a gasp, then sucked in a gaping breath and held it as her aura grew. The sage deepened and gave way to a pinkish hue Emerson had never seen from her. Her knee rotated back, the wet snap and gurgle of her tissues tamping until the leg was straight.

The halo throbbed, radiated outward again. The pain and the injury were gone. Emerson let go of her, and Chris followed. Their gazes moved to Layla's face, and the two boys watched her blink away the dreamy haze Emerson had left in his wake.

"You okay now?" Chris begged, his voice still trilling higher than normal.

Layla grunted. A peaceful sound. She pushed herself up to sitting, one hand in the mud, propping her up, while the other gingerly probed her fixed knee. She bent the leg, hesitant at first, then with more energy as her confidence grew.

"Like it didn't happen," she murmured, her face relaxed and gaze unfocused. She looked from Chris to Emerson, then back. "Thank you, thank you both."

The ebb of adrenaline chipped away at Emerson's spirit. Chris was in the same boat, and they fell back on the soggy ground. Emerson stared through the finger-like leaves into the darkening sky. Bolts of water were falling now, the rain growing into a storm. He hadn't noticed the weather pick up while they were helping Layla, but he felt the soak in his hair, the extra weight in his shirt and shorts. He wiggled his toes, feeling the squish of water sopping his socks.

The three of them lay silent for several minutes, letting the crescendo of rain soak them and the ground. Above the hiss and bluster of the weather, the surrounding plants rattled in the wind.

"Emerson?" Layla finally spoke. "I don't want to play on the farm anymore."

That got a chuckle from both boys. Emerson pulled himself to sitting, wiping the mud from his hands onto his now-brown shirt. "Neither do I," he replied. "This was a dumb idea, I guess."

"No!" Layla and Chris shouted over one another.

Chris continued, "No, this was *kickass*! Layla just isn't used to having legs is all."

"Shut up!" Layla tapped Chris on the shoulder, a playful punch. "I'm surprised you didn't get swallowed up whole!"

Chris laughed, and Emerson couldn't help but follow suit. "Still, I think that's enough for one day," Emerson offered.

His two friends nodded their agreement. The boys stood on their own, each offering a hand to Layla. They took a moment to make sure her legs were usable. Then Emerson looked through the jungle for the tower to orient his way out of the farm.

A splash of orange against the pale mud caught his eye. An aura. Not a whole one. As if he'd glimpsed the top of it, while the rest was buried in the earth below them.

He shielded his eyes from the rain as he struggled to make sense of the sight. The tangerine circle rippled like a bubble flexing in the breeze. Rays of life seeped outward, their barest edges visible on top of the earth.

He gasped as the orange blob of light moved. Something living and large was under the field, and it was coming towards Emerson and his friends.

Chapter Twenty-One

T he flimsy door snapped shut on its spring. The rain sloughed off of her and onto the bare plywood floor around Irene's shoes. She acclimated to the still air while catching her breath after bolting from the truck. Irene swung the water off her arms and onto the floor, then eased the envelope out of her bra, careful to keep the wetness of her T-shirt away from the money.

She took in the dispensary. At first, she figured she was in the wrong place. This wasn't a business; it was a demolition site. The remnants of a double-wide were obvious if you knew what to look for—the cabinets against the wall that had once been part of a kitchen, the countertops replaced with cheap, rough-hewn plywood. At her feet, the floor was raw sheathing, carpet tack clinging in random places near the walls. It was dusty, and a moldy smell suggested the owners might just hose it off whenever they felt the need.

She had missed the guy standing behind the counter. A compact man dressed for outside work—a long-sleeved, heavy cotton button-down hanging over a pair of faded jeans. He watched her with a smirk of amusement on his tan face as she absorbed the building and slung the rain off her body.

"Ain't much to see," he said, calm and welcoming. "We haven't invested in the storefront yet. Just the product."

Irene smiled at him. "Whatever works," she replied.

She laid the money on the plywood counter between them. As her gaze followed the envelope, she caught sight of the gun holstered to the guy's thigh. The second one she'd seen in less than two minutes. What was it with Texans and their fucking guns? Every male in the state was a closet ammosexual.

"How can I help you?" he asked. "I mean, I assume you're here to buy weed; otherwise, you're very lost."

Irene chuckled. At least the guy had a sense of humor. She found a name tag clipped to his shirt pocket. Phil.

"I'm here to pick up an order for Finch."

"Holy shit, yeah," he huffed, his ruddy cheeks bursting with a smile. "It was a slow day until he called us. Now we're going to close early!"

Irene glanced at the door and the rain beyond. "Solid plan. I doubt you'll be getting many drop-ins with the crazy storm."

The screech of a radio pulled her attention. Phil was murmuring into a walkie-talkie, and Irene heard Finch's name.

She slid the envelope of cash towards him. He swiped it up with calloused fingers and thumbed through the bills, lips wiggling as he counted in his head.

"Perfect," he said. He bent under the counter, and a metal clang Irene assumed was a lockbox echoed from there. The man rose with a groan, the sound of a laborer who felt the time of day in his back muscles.

"I'll just need your ID and prescription," he said. His eyes found hers, wide and expectant.

A jarring unease filled her chest. "Um, I'm... I'm not Finch, I'm his friend. He's in the pickup outside." She thumbed over her shoulder, pointing through the thin walls of the gutted mobile home to the parking area.

His kind eyes hardened. "Well then, your friend needs to run in here and show us his ID and prescription."

"I'm sorry," Irene said through a sudden tightness in her throat. "He's got a medical condition and is a little shy about it."

His face soured as his head cocked from side to side. "Listen, I can't sell this much weed without validating he's got a script. He'll have to come in here himself."

There was a pregnant moment where they locked stares—Irene at a loss for protocol, and Phil at a loss of patience. As it became uncomfortable, the man broke the silence. "I can give you the money back and cancel the order."

Her unease sharpened in her gut. She wanted to do this for Finch, without him having to confront anyone. "Let me have a word with him," she said. "I'll be back in a minute, okay?"

"No worries at all," he replied, his tone pleasant if not patient.

Irene headed outside. Finch's truck still sat in the mud twenty paces from the steps, idling in the rain with his high-beams reflecting against the whitewashed siding of the dispensary and making most of the scene unseeable.

Irene waved into the light. She neither saw nor heard any response.

Sighing, she dredged through the muddy yard to the truck's driver-side door. As she pulled it open, she said, "Finch, I am so, so sorry, but they need you to come—"

The vehicle was empty, and the words died in her throat. Irene backed away, looking about for her friend. The parking area contained nothing but the whispers of the falling sky.

"What the hell, Finch?" she murmured. Maybe he'd wandered off to take a piss? Except that wasn't something Finch would do. He'd worry about encountering someone. Afraid of their reaction to his face. No, Finch wouldn't leave the truck without a safe place to go.

She eased the door closed and hoofed it up the steps to the dispensary. She spun inside and shook the water off herself again. Low voices sounded clearly beyond the wet hair over her eyes.

"Something's wrong," she said. "I'm not sure why, but he's not in his truck anymore." She slicked her sopping hair back against her scalp, which revealed two people behind the counter. The man from before, and another carrying a cardboard box.

This second man stared, eyes agape and boring into her. In them was a blue and gray she associated with lies. His jaw worked up and down as if he were chewing on his words. Irene glared back, unable to reconcile what her senses were showing her.

The box slipped from his hands and hit the floor. The rattle of glass marked the impact.

His blond hair and light complexion, darker now as if from working under the sun. A bulky frame, lean and solid. The face of a person she knew, thinner and hardened with work.

His lip trembled, then his voice broke. "Fuck! What the fuck! Why are you here?"

After years of living with it, years of replaying memories over and over in her head, she recognized that thin, warbling tenor in a heartbeat.

Her legs melted, and she collapsed against the stripped plywood wall as her arms steadied her against the frame of a window. The edges of her vision blurred as impossibility knotted up her mind.

Despite the thick moisture in the air, the water on her cheeks and lips, her throat had dried up. It took Irene three tries to get the single word off her tongue.

"*Wes?*"

Chapter Twenty-Two

"I just... I identified you." Irene's chest locked open, her heart drumming in a frantic beat. She could not inhale. "Your corpse! In the morgue!" Her head was yelling, but her body worked in whispers. "You... you're dead."

Wes's hands, balled into fists, went to his sand-colored hair. His eyes fixed on her, their shape changing from surprise to the same panic Irene was feeling herself.

She couldn't believe her senses. Her years-long search for Wes had ended twice in the same day.

"How are you here?" he yelled. "You've gotta go, Irene! You can't—"

"No." Her breathing caught up with her. "No, Wes. That isn't the big mystery here, okay?"

Her brother's gaze fell with resignation.

"Wes? They found you... your body. I saw it!"

Wes's shoulders slumped forward, his hands landing on the counter between them. "Fuck," he sobbed. "Fuck, Irene. That should have been the end. Why the hell are you here?"

Her brow knitted, her brain unable to follow the meandering conversation, unwilling to reconcile the fact that she was speaking to a dead man.

"She said she's with someone else," Phil offered. "That huge order we got? She's here to pick it up."

Wes's stare rose to the ceiling. "I don't believe it."

"Neither do I," added Phil.

The snap and click of the handgun in the man's hand stole her breath. Irene saw the pistol as it bumped the countertop, the barrel pointed in her direction. Phil's grip relaxed over the weapon, ready to lift it on a whim.

"Who's with you?" Wes asked. His voice carried an ache, and his eyes conveyed exhausted desperation.

Her confusion congealed to fear, a weight she felt in her gut. Her head shook, overloaded with fact and emotion. "Finch," she creaked. "My friend."

"Bullshit," the other man spat. After a still moment, Phil nodded to Wes. "Go check it out; she said he left his truck a minute ago."

Wes heaved himself over the counter, pivoting on his ass and plopping his feet on the floor. Irene couldn't look away from him—the surreality of her brother, alive. His movements familiar but new. That corpse in the morgue—she must have missed something. Or maybe her mind had tricked her, letting her see Wes, so she'd move on with her life. As he passed, the miasma of odors unlocked the lingering doubts and confusion. The sweet odor of his sweat, the stale funk of weed, and the lime-scented deodorant he always wore.

This was Wes. He was alive.

The door slapped shut, and Irene's gaze unfocused as she watched him. For a moment, fear tickled her. An indescribable feeling that her brother might disappear into the storm, that she would lose him one more time.

She peered through the plexiglass window into the torrent of weather. She caught Wes's shadow in the truck's cab as Phil's voice rose behind her.

"You stay put!"

She spun around to face his hard stare, his demeanor moving from service to malice. The gun's barrel gaped at her from the man's extended arm. His eyes laser-focused on her, his free hand pulled a walkie-talkie from his belt and moved it to his mouth.

"Boss? Dispensary. We might have a security issue," he spoke into the unit.

In the space of a blink, a response came back.

"Go secure." A heavy voice. Gruff. Large.

The man's thumb flicked a switch on the walkie.

"We're secure."

"What the hell is going on?"

Phil's eyes narrowed, his gaze shifting across her dripping body and face. "A woman showed up to pick up that large-ass order. She's freaking out, something about being at the morgue earlier today."

The door to the dispensary opened, and Wes returned sopping wet. He held her backpack in one hand; the other wiped slicks of rain from his face. He moved towards the counter, tossing her knapsack over the plywood before hopping over himself.

"The truck's empty. This is hers; it was on the passenger—"

The squawk of the radio cut him off.

"Who is she? What's her name?" the speaker hissed.

"Shit," Wes whispered. "You called Boss?" His gaze flickered from Phil to Irene and landed on the raised pistol.

Silence spun as Irene took in the depth of the barrel.

"Well?" Phil demanded, holding up the walkie. It coughed as he released the talk button.

Irene swallowed, a hopelessness swallowing her right back. She'd walked into this room to help a friend and now had a gun in her face. Fucking typical: she locates Wes, and as a result finds herself in dire straits. Her heartbeat rushed in her ears, ebbing and flowing, angry and scared.

"Irene," she squeaked. "Irene Allard. Wes"—she nodded his direction—"is my brother. And he was dead this morning."

Phil turned the radio around. "You catch that, Boss? Irene Allard."

The white-noise whispers from the radio gossiped in the surrounding space, marking every increment of distance between the gun and Irene with a hum and energy.

The static broke, suspending the three of them in silence again.

The voice hissed on the speaker. "I'm on my way. Shoot her before I get there, or I'll shoot you."

Chapter Twenty-Three

F inch lumbered past the shorter wall of the trailer. The ground gave under his numb feet, making the walk cumbersome and slow. He shambled through the thick air towards the wide metal storehouse.

No one was there. Finch wasn't sure if he'd got lucky with the shit weather or if guards always stayed inside the warehouse. He wished he'd planned better. Learned the operations and personnel here. But he'd had no time. The slipshod idea of distracting the boy's family with Irene, paired with the stopping power of his .50-caliber handgun, would have to work.

He rounded the near corner just as the door clicked open. Finch froze, willing himself to be invisible to whomever was walking out of the building. He lifted his gun, bringing it level, in case the interloper spotted him.

A muffled "thank you" echoed around the corner. Footsteps sloshed towards the dispensary. Finch chanced a glimpse around the warehouse's rusted facade. Through the pelt of rainfall, Finch saw him.

Irene's brother, Wes. Alive, and about to come face to face with his sister.

An itch crawled to his cheeks as Finch smiled, his fragile lips splitting and cracking even in the damp air.

He had to move. Get to the house and find the boy. The diversion wouldn't last, and, seeing Wes walking into the dispensary, Finch knew the clock was ticking.

He slogged through the thinning mud, the muck sucking on his boots with each stride. When he reached the corner, he peeked around it.

No windows in the building's length. A closed rolling garage door. Another security door, at the far end. Two dim floodlights, flickering on and off in the murky air. A field lay beyond, flat and open until it melted into the falling rain. A grove of mature trees existed in that gray mist, according to the satellite imagery he'd found on Google Maps. Next to the grove, a house. Emerson should be there.

The dirt solidified as he walked, the dead grass giving the earth hold against the falling torrent. He couldn't run. The coordination and sensory feedback he needed had burned away. So he moved with purpose, watching each step and making his movements deliberate. After a minute, he looked up. The silhouettes of swaying trees cut through a light, the rustling of their panicked leaves audible over the steady hiss of rain.

He glanced back. Behind him, the puttering warehouse floodlights diminished to a mottled gray void. He wondered if Irene and Wes had seen one another yet, and what would happen after they did. He shuddered. Was it never knowing what would happen to his friend? Or just the chill of the weather soaking through his leathery hide?

Under the canopy, the shower felt less severe. From the home, a brilliant light radiated between the rows of trees, casting long and twisting shadows as branches flailed in the growing wind. Finch lurked towards the house, using the shade of the thick trunks to hide.

The last set of trees stood between him and Emerson's home. Whatever tingle of anticipation had seized him on the field was growing. He had searched for so long, and now the prize was right in front of him.

An organic movement caught his eye. Something crossing the porch's floodlight. The shadows of the trees slithered with the wind, but this one remained fixed and strong. A person. Crossing the porch. He looked at his senseless hand, making sure he still had a grip on the Desert Eagle.

"Emerson!" Her voice carried through the storm, a mild drawl pushing through the dribbles and splashes. It echoed between the branches, then against his skull.

The insipid voice of Emerson's bitch mother.

His grip tightened on the gun. He raised it level, bracing his arm against the tree trunk, aiming for the heart of the shadow. He would kill her. Leave a gaping hole in her chest. Breach the house. Find Emerson. Take him. Disappear.

"Emerson!" she hollered again, louder. "Time to come inside!"

His finger came off the trigger. Where the hell was he?

Finch's arm shook as he lowered the gun. He was so close. Emerson was here, goddammit. Somewhere. Finch needed to find him.

The silhouette moved, projecting darkness across Finch's eye. He slid behind the trunk, unsure if she was able to see him. Her form spun, and her voice came again, muttering something about following simple instructions before a slamming door cut her off.

He reviewed the aerial map of the compound in his head. Where else would Emerson be? The house, the grove of trees. He traced the map with a mental finger. Utopia Farms was massive, with lots of small structures perfect for a young man to hole up in during a storm.

Finch didn't have the time to waste searching.

A noise broke his self-pity. A huff, coming from the other side of the tree. His fist tightened on the pistol, ready to destroy whoever was approaching.

Another pattern cut into the light, moving in a different way from the mother. More of a wobble than a walk. It took a moment for Finch to recognize the strange gait, the rotating shadow of a wagging tail. The opaque form belonged to a canine, not a human.

He peeked past the trunk. The curious stare of a Labradoodle waited for him in the pouring rain.

The dog's body tensed. She stood a dozen feet from him, but outrunning her was impossible. Damp curls mottled flat to her muzzle, giving her a wise frown as she studied Finch. Her nose jutted towards him, nostrils wiggling as she sampled his scent.

Finch eased to a knee, bringing himself level with the dog's snout. He held out his hand, letting her take in his smell.

She skulked into the distance between them, tasting the air as she approached.

"Hey there," he croaked.

Her head cocked to one side.

"Hey, little puppy girl, how are you?" He tried to put a lilt in his voice. It came out as a creak, yet the relatively carefree sound belied the frustration he was feeling.

The dog's tail rotated in a happy circle as her face relaxed into a curious stare. She took a few steps closer to Finch. She panted, steady and content as her nose rubbed against Finch's outstretched fingers.

"You remember, don't you?"

Her tail spun faster, the wiggle running along her body as recognition came. Her sniffs and huffs grew into whines, her lips peeling away from her teeth into a smile.

How was this dog alive, still keeping to the boy and his mother? As her excitement at their reunion wore off, the dog leaned into him, licking any exposed skin she found. Finch wished he could feel it.

His fingers rubbed into the soaked fur of her crown, and for a moment, Finch relaxed in the joy of being seen without pity or judgment.

"I missed you too, girl," he muttered between face lickings.

She nuzzled into him. Finch stood and gazed at the animal, moving his hand to the dog's neck.

The jolt of energy hit his fingers as the dog's uncomplicated psyche unfolded around him. The garden of shadows the dog had cultivated. Simple and few compared to those of humans.

Food. Play. And, as Finch expected, Emerson was the focus of it all.

He zeroed in on that core hole that defined this animal's drive. He pulled at it, stretched the shade and hollow of her boy as large as possible. The dog let out a pathetic falling whine. Her body strained as her paws danced on the ground. She panted now, the huffing irregular and stressed as her eyes searched the surrounding space for what she wanted most.

"You wanna find where Emerson is too, don't ya, girl?"

A crack echoed from the gray haze surrounding the dispensary and warehouse. Not the roll and rumble of thunder—a gunshot. Far enough that the echo arrived with the report, yet Finch flinched with pain. He closed his eyes, acknowledged that the sound likely marked Irene being murdered.

His regrets would have to wait. Today would cost him everything.

Her sacrifice would not go to waste.

Chapter Twenty-Four

T he orange wisps licked at the toe of Emerson's shoe.

"We gotta go, now!" Emerson huffed.

"What's wrong?" Layla asked. Her voice sounded as tired as Emerson's legs, and he didn't need to see her aura to know that the day's wear and tear had pushed her to her limits.

"There's... *something*," he replied, his tone more clipped than he intended. "Something big! Under the ground!"

"*What?*" Chris shouted, his voice echoing into the field.

Emerson turned and grabbed his hand. "Just get moving!" he hissed.

They formed a train through the thicket. Emerson leading Chris, Chris guiding Layla. Emerson wormed his way through the daisy spiral of plants, doing his best to keep them moving in a straight path away from the thing.

They rounded a cluster of plants. Emerson glanced left to find they were circling around towards the back of the tower. He was leading them farther into the field, away from the house. In another minute, the tower would be between them and the main aisle out of the field.

He chanced a look back, maneuvering his head around Layla and Chris's exhausted forms to peer into the purple splotchwork for the distinctive orange glow. He found nothing but oozing tones of violet. Then he pushed his focus beneath the edge of the field's intense aura.

He slid them to a stop, and his friends huddled into him as the rain continued to pelt their faces.

"I don't see it," Emerson offered, a glint of hope in his voice. "Maybe it isn't following us."

As he spoke, the sharp tangerine glimmer eased into view. The outer ring of the halo oozed through in the mud, the stipples of falling rain mixing with the aura's prickly shape.

"Shit," Emerson groaned.

Chris's hand tightened on his. A whine bubbled through his lips.

"About five plants that way." Emerson pointed with his free hand back the way they had come. The light coasted through the earth in a straight line, unimpeded by the dirt or plants, and it eased towards them at a steady pace.

Emerson rounded the plants to keep them moving away from the underground entity. He glanced back, finding the glow of orange had brightened and drawn closer than before. To avoid the plants, he and his friends had to adjust their serpentine path, which slowed their progress. This thing, whatever it was, didn't seem to have that limitation. It crawled as though the earth were air.

The inner layers of the halo were sharp now. Whatever it was, the thing was big. Lurching several feet beneath them. And it was at least the size of a person.

"It's coming right at us! We need to run!" He let go of Chris's hand, pivoting around to take Layla's. "C'mon," he pushed, "help Layla move faster!"

The two boys held Layla steady as they raced ahead. The mud sucked on their shoes as they moved, the rain not heavy enough to thin the viscous muck and ease their travel. Layla squeaked, an uneasy sound that betrayed the twist of pain in her pale-green aura.

Chris's arm went around her waist as he spoke. "I got you; keep going!" Her weight shifted away from Emerson, and he let go of her hand. He turned, the orange spines of the thing's halo just one plant behind them now.

"Faster!" he shouted. He spun to follow and found the earth heading up to him instead.

Emerson landed with a wet slap, having fallen face first into the mud. He flipped over, wiping the filth off his eyes with the back of a hand. Layla and Chris were on the ground too. Layla's legs were folded beneath her, the wetness of her face now a mixture of rain and tears. Chris knelt beside her, his eyes stretched with unbridled panic. Behind them, the deep-orange glow expanded, the inner lights showing amber and apricot as it closed in on them.

Emerson lunged at his friends. Wrapped his arms around them in a bear hug as the edge of the halo breached them.

"It's here," he hissed.

The collective group held their breath as Emerson's vision filled with the lightening tones of the thing's core. It was easing just feet beneath the surface. Emerson squeezed his crew tighter and clenched his eyes shut, knowing this would do nothing to stem his awareness of its presence and motion.

The aura tensed. Impatient. Hungry. Emerson's mind conjured countless horrors of what the thing might be. Giant worms from movies Mom said he shouldn't watch, that tracked prey on the surface by sound. Burrowing monsters born out of the darkest corners of imagination. The amber grew around them, Emerson tightening his bear hug on Layla and Chris.

It was right under their shivering and soaked bodies. Emerson sensed it, mere feet away. Hovering beneath their huddled and muddy pile. The aura reached out of the ground, rotating through the sage and blues of his friends, overwhelming the powerful purples of the field. The desire to understand it wrestled against Emerson's innate fear.

His light pierced the ground and lunged for the core of the monster chasing them. He strained through his nerves to scramble a hold on it. He connected with it, and details emerged from the light. The thing took a shape. An identity.

Emerson relaxed, confused by what he could see in his third eye and unable to reconcile it with his knowledge. The aura was a person, in the ground. Someone familiar.

Chris whimpered as Emerson let go of his friends and stood. The aura beneath them eased away from them, heading off in the same direction they had been running.

"I can do it. I can run," Layla offered.

Emerson's gaze moved from the underground halo to her eyes. They piqued, and her thin lips carried a tremble on them that betrayed her fear.

Emerson shook his head, wiping a hand across his face to clear the water and confusion. "It... the thing under the ground..."

"What?" Chris whined.

Emerson looked at Layla. "The thing in the ground... I think it's your mom." His voice came out raspy, punctuated by his confusion and racing pulse.

Layla's face scrunched. "What do you mean?"

"I mean"—Emerson turned back, pointing at the orange glow moving at a walking pace away from them now—"your mom is the light under the field."

"Is that a joke? Because it isn't funny!"

Emerson watched as the light of Dr. Travers slowed. It pivoted in the ground. Emerson struggled, a throbbing coming to his head as he focused on that underground aura. He could nearly make out her physical form.

"She's stopping," he continued, his finger pointing at a spot just beyond the plant wall ahead. "Right over there."

Emerson spun to his friends. Chris helped Layla up to her feet while she stared in the direction that Emerson pointed. Her brow screwed tight, her face tired with worry and weather.

"How is my mom in the ground?" she asked, her gaze disoriented and wandering across the puddles and mud. A tomato layer of confusion rimmed her light.

"I don't know." Emerson slapped his hands to his sides. "But there she is." He peeked at the doctor's halo, her identity obvious to him now that his panic had subsided.

The round circle of orange and ambers slowed to a stop a dozen feet away. A row of plants separated the kids from the glow, giving Emerson a partial view of the aura as it played amid the bruise-colored shine from the plants. Between the stalks, the embers rose, with more of the halo's crest breaching the ground. Emerson's confusion grew again as the center of the aura rose level with the surface of the farm.

"She's... I think she's coming up," he said.

The three of them froze, confusion and exhaustion locking them with indecision.

"Should we run?" Chris asked.

"But if it's just my mom—" Layla started.

"Yeah, but we'll still be in big trouble," Chris replied.

Emerson held up a hand, a signal for them to hold. For a long moment, his friends waited as Emerson studied the light hovering just under the surface a few plants away.

"What's she doing?" Layla whispered.

Emerson shrugged, keeping his eyes on the underground aura.

A sharp bang reverberated from behind the plants ahead, causing the children to flinch. Emerson tensed and stared into the brush between them and the sound. A hand grabbed him—one of his friends pulling him away from the light.

The aura of Layla's mom climbed out of the ground with a metallic scream.

Chapter Twenty-Five

The barrel of the pistol reached for Irene, threatening to swallow her life in one loud gulp.

"Wait a second!" Wes cried.

"Boss said to shoot her," Phil stated, as if her death was a tick on his to-do list for the day. His arm straightened, the firearm tracking towards her forehead.

Every muscle tensed, full of the pressure to run but frozen with fear. Her amygdala was taking over, that primitive layer of the brain that only knows fighting, feeding, fleeing, and fucking. She had studied it in her biology classes—the expanding perception that comes with terror, the elaboration of stressful moments caused by the saturation of neurotransmitters and hormones. It was useless information right now, and she wondered if this was going to be her last stupid thought.

Wes's hands clamped on the gun. The line of the barrel pivoted from Irene as Wes slammed into Phil. Her fright became flight, and those hormones and neurotransmitters moved her ass to the exit.

As the flimsy door opened, a spray of water slapped her face. She turned away, a reflex, and caught a glimpse of Wes struggling to keep the weapon in Phil's grip from moving in her direction. She bolted into the rain, leaping over the steps and losing her footing as soon as she reached the mud. The pickup was only ten feet ahead. She scrambled her feet back under her and ran.

She rounded the truck, the headlights blinding her more than the rainfall. Her hands tracked the front panel to the driver's-side door. Irene flung it open and heaved herself behind the steering wheel.

A commotion moved in the intense brilliance of the truck's headlamps. Irene looked through the windshield. Wes and Phil wrestled on the landing outside the door. Wes had him in a bear grip. The slick of the shower and amplified light from the high beams revealed Wes's lean and tense muscles pinning Phil's arms to his sides. The flat black of the handgun still twitched in his hand.

She went for the ignition. Her fingers gripped the flange of the switch, and she slammed it forward.

The truck wouldn't start.

She looked down. The keys. Where were the keys to the pickup? Against any logic, she gave the starter a second shove, hoping it would turn, spark the engine to life. It remained locked in place.

A ruckus pulled her gaze up again. She caught the sight of the men toppling down the steps and landing in the mud, their different shapes and forms now merged into a single ugly gray amoeba writhing on the ground.

Her flight instinct tickled her legs once more, and she launched out of the cab and into the storm. She ran from the trailer. From the gun. The haze of the wet air covered the yard, the faint outline of kennels marking a gap. The entrance that led to the road.

If she got enough of a lead, she could disappear into that fog. Hide. Sneak off under the storm's bustle.

Her soaked sneakers made sloppy sounds as they drummed against the earth. Her breath heaved, and her heart exploded and contracted to keep her moving.

Shouts rose behind her. Angry ones, scared ones. She didn't turn to see.

The kennels solidified into view as she pushed forward. The bend of the gravel drive was visible not a dozen feet ahead.

She should be faster. She used to run sprints. Her soaked clothes made her heavy, but her lack of self-care over the last few years weighed her down more. The tang of rising bile hit the back of her throat.

Another desperate shriek rose above the hissing rain. Her legs pumped with fear.

The driveway straightened out as she rounded the edge of the kennel, the straight gravel drive disappearing into the mist. *Follow it. Find the road.*

A jolt ran through her leg, and the horizon twisted ahead. The loose rock expanded around her as her feet left the ground. She fell into the gravel with a heavy crack that was far too loud.

Her hands fumbled beneath her, and she heaved herself up and launched herself forward.

She landed again, hard. Her senses shook. The shushing of the shower thinned to a murmur as her body reacted to an injury. Something was very wrong with her right thigh. Static screamed from there—not pain but its disorganized prelude.

She rolled to her side, lifting her head enough to watch the crimson bloom expanding on the knee of her jeans. The noise in her leg sharpened, and the hum in her ears burst to a wail.

Movement drew her eye past her sneakers. Out of the glowing mist came a person, a shadow backlit by light refracting through the saturated air. The figure congealed into a man, arm stretched out, holding a gun. The raindrops scattered off him and created a strange, radiant halo.

Searing agony crashed inside of her skull. The figure faded as the edges of her vision trembled. A second ghost flew out of the mist, running to her and landing on his knees in the gravel.

Hands took her face. As her consciousness succumbed to the shock, Wes's eyes glared into hers. Ribbons of water hung from his cheeks and nose, dripping onto her. She couldn't hear him. But she could sense the vibrations. Wes was screaming. His lips moved. Between that and the rattle of his voice through her bones, she registered his words as she retreated into the black.

Why didn't you stay away?

Chapter Twenty-Six

"Head that way!" Emerson pointed past the tower to the aisle leading out of the farm.

Chris held Layla's arm, supporting her as they dashed from the groan spiraling up behind them. His eyes shot back, then away in the direction Emerson pointed.

"But that'll take us in the open!" he cried.

Emerson huffed, speaking between the slaps of his shoes on the ground. "I know, Chris, but the ground is solid. It'll be easier for Layla to run."

Without replying, Chris led them, panting, into the clearing. Emerson took Layla's free arm to offer more help as their feet thumped them under the tower. The air was heavy from rain, but cooler out of the plants. Despite being exposed, Emerson found the widening space comforting. Whatever the hell was breaking out of the ground didn't sound like Dr. Travers. It didn't even sound human.

Past the tower, Layla slipped in the mud. The boys caught her before she fell.

"I can't make it!" she cried. "My palsy is back! My legs aren't working anymore!"

Emerson glanced back—nothing was crashing through the plants, coming to eat them. He motioned for Chris to ease Layla down and then stooped to her. He didn't ask permission, but wrapped his hand around her chakra, the core of Layla's person radiating between his fingers as he rotated it, shaped it, moving wisps and glow into her thighs and calves, through her feet, and into her toes.

"There," he huffed, "you should be able to run!"

They lifted her up by her arms, and her tentative legs unfolded. After a few steps, Layla shrugged them off and jogged towards the main corridor.

"Not too fast," Chris cried. "You'll get hurt again!"

"I'm fine, Chris!" she panted, her legs stretching out behind her, cycling her forward. Emerson struggled to keep pace.

They left the tower behind. Emerson peeked over his shoulder, ensuring that no tangerine halo was emerging from the thicket, fangs bared, enraged eyes piercing through a swirl of mist and froth. The space remained empty. He ran to catch up to his friends.

The field's purple radiance closed around them, funneling them into the path out of the clearing. The shortening of his perception made his gut roil. His attention darted from plant to plant, looking for movement, a glint of color, anything to suggest another living thing in the thicket. As his gaze crossed the path, he saw Chris and Layla leave the clearing and enter the aisle, their struggling auras dampened by the tight wall of plants.

The end of the field came into view, fog beyond hiding the switchback over the hills. The surrounding stalks swayed as

Emerson's lungs burned with the stinky air. His shoes pounded the mud, faster, faster, towards that empty void.

Layla's rhythm broke. Chris slowed to help, but she recovered before hitting the ground.

"Just a few more steps," Emerson huffed. Spit flew from his mouth, a wet streak running from the corner of his lips across his cheek. The air became crushing, the dense plants holding the heat as it tried to escape in a ghostly haze.

The edge approached, the view beyond expanding to show the faint suggestion of the boulder by the hill. Emerson smiled. He could see it. They were close. They would be home in minutes.

His friends broke out of the farm. Chris let out a barbaric yawp into the open space, a holler of victory and relief that echoed off the hill ahead. The sound carried a joy that mirrored Chris's exploding yellow light.

They were going to make it!

As he breached from the field, a force slammed him to his side. He was off his feet, his mind heading in one direction while his body jerked in another. Emerson's face splashed into the muddy grass.

"Emerson!"

Layla's voice. His friends stood close to the boulder. Chris's lips tremored, his light broken with black rips of fear. Layla's hands were over her mouth; her eyes were wide and panicked, looking at whatever had knocked Emerson down. Their lights spewed out, patternless and terrified.

Something heavy landed on him. Talons sunk into his torso, pushing him into the sloppy ground and gripping wads of his shirt and skin. A terrifying growl shook the air. Warmth bloomed in Emerson's shorts as he pissed himself, expecting the monster's teeth to tear him to pieces.

The claw lifted him. Tossed him on his back with a moist smack.

Above him, obscured by the damp air, loomed the staggering shadow of an enormous man. His aura was deep and red. The color of blood.

"Emerson?" The voice was tinny, tentative. Nothing like the rumbling and violent growl from the field.

The figure stooped. Emerson's body sank into the puddle as the man came close, the shadows on his skin and the mist in the air giving him a distorted, hateful appearance.

"Shit, Em. Is that you under that muck?"

Emerson's body relaxed as he realized who the face belonged to.

He sucked in a breath and exhaled it with relief.

"Yeah, Uncle Terry, it's me."

Chapter
Twenty-Seven

"Dammit," Hawk snapped, watching the blood leave the woman's leg and pool on the floor of the warehouse. "Radio Blair to ring the bell, Jaime!"

Jaime closed the distance between them and jabbed a finger into Hawk's sternum. "No way." His voice had lowered to a rumble, as if frustration and rage rattled inside his chest.

"She'll bleed out!" he cried.

Jaime threw up his hand, jetting even closer to Hawk so their noses almost touched. Close enough to Hawk that the man's musky sweat overpowered the funk of the product that filled the warehouse.

"Then let her," he hissed, his tone tight over the sizzle of rain on the metal roof.

Hawk took a breath. Jaime was prepared to let Irene die and then force him to clean up the aftermath. Jaime stepped away from him, and Hawk exhaled into the space left behind. His stance relaxed, the physical distance from Jaime giving him a modicum of comfort.

"Why is she here, Jaime?" Hawk's hands went to his hips, and he slumped his shoulders to appear as non-threatening as possible. "We need to keep her alive to find out, don't you think?"

Jaime grabbed an empty Mason jar, thumbing the ridge of the opening as he considered the question. His expression darkened in the silence.

"No," he grunted. "No, not this time, Hawk. Wes had his chance to take care of his sister."

"Jaime—"

"Hawk, no." The boss's voice was firm, his demeanor steady and rooted. Resolute.

The change left Hawk with a lump in his throat.

Jaime studied the jar as he continued. "We owe him, Hawk. I haven't forgotten. Wes brought Emerson back to us after that shitshow at the hospital. Got him home safe to Utopia."

Hawk jumped at the pause. "He did, Jaime."

Jaime's gaze shot up, and his perturbed expression silenced Hawk. The silence grew as his thumb rang the rim of the jar.

"He's got a bond with Emerson. The kid likes him. That's half the reason I let him stick around."

Hawk kept his mouth shut. Jaime had something to say, and he needed the space to say it. The dark of his eyes stayed locked on Hawk.

"And it ain't like there's a place for him to go. Wes Allard is a cop killer. In the great state of Texas."

Hawk nodded. "He is."

A smirk landed on Jaime's face. "They'll roast 'im, Hawk. Yeah?"

Hawk swallowed his discomfort. "They will. If they don't shoot him on sight."

Jaime's lips expanded to a grin. "Good point. So he's stuck with us. At least, as long as we'll have him."

Jaime's stare fell to the glass in his gorilla hand. Tendons and veins rippled under the flesh as they tightened. "But I gotta be honest, it's getting to where he's not worth the trouble that surrounds him."

Silence. Bossman's eyes peered out under the hood of his lowered forehead.

"What about you, Hawk? Do you think he's worth it?"

Hawk considered his response. Jaime's words had nothing to do with what he was asking.

"I do," he creaked.

"You don't sound convinced."

"Of course I am, Jaime. Wes has done a lot for the ranch. For the business." Hawk's gaze drifted across the rows of glass jars stacked on the shelves, then unfocused through the wall to the farm. "He volunteered to help figure out what Emerson can do, don't forget. That wasn't pleasant for him."

Jaime lifted his head, eyes glinting under the fluorescent lights. "Yeah."

Hawk worried his lip, the tender skin still raw from the earlier sun.

"But that sister of his. We can't let her keep operating, Hawk. She can't go."

"Go?" Hawk asked, shrugging.

"I won't let her walk out of here. I gave Wes a chance to lead her away. Hell, I thought the idea was fucking genius. What could be more definitive for her than finding her brother's god-damned corpse?"

Hawk's lip split under his teeth.

"But it didn't work. She's here, and she'll keep chasing Wes unless we stop her."

"Yes, but... don't you want to know *how* she found us? Him?"

Jaime's stare narrowed. Hawk could see he was considering the notion. "We don't know if she came with anyone. Or she may have told someone she was coming here."

Bossman blew out a sigh.

"She's friends with that sheriff, right?" Hawk offered. "We know that—"

"Fine," Jaime murmured, his posture relaxing.

Hawk sucked in a breath and held it.

"Fine," he repeated. Louder. Definitive once more. "Take her under the farm, get Robin to patch her leg. Then get Wes to talk with her. Find out the how and the why of her being here."

An involuntary smile spread Hawk's lips, and he flinched at the cracking flesh.

"Something funny?" Jaime asked.

"It's just weird, talking about him—about Wes—like he ain't even here."

Jaime hurled the jar. It speared past Hawk's head, leaving a breathy *whoosh* in its wake. A thunderclap rattled the room as glass shattered against the steel garage door.

Jaime's massive, calloused fist wadded into Hawk's shirt, and Hawk's feet floated off the ground as the man lifted him until their faces were level. Once more, Hawk smelled the strange cloud of Jaime's person.

"Because he ain't here, Hawk! He ain't anywhere, get it?"

Hawk swallowed, unable to answer.

"Wes Allard died," he spit. "They found his corpse in a dried-up creek in Utopia. The man is no more. He's gone, and fuck-all if we keep talking about him otherwise."

Lost for words, Hawk bobbed his head. Jaime dropped him on his feet with a jarring shove.

"At least he *was* dead, until his fucking sister somehow walked into the same room with him," Jaime continued, composure easing back into his tone.

Hawk smoothed his shirt with his hands. His voice shuddered, "We'll figure it out, Boss."

Jaime nodded. His eyes teetered off Hawk, passing over the unconscious woman to the garage door. He wagged a hand at the pulverized glass that covered the loading bay floor.

"Get someone to clean up that shit. It's dangerous to leave it like that."

Chapter Twenty-Eight

"What the hell you doin' here?" Terry asked, his halo fading from an angry maroon into a disappointed brick red. He pulled Emerson up by his shirt as he spoke, then wiped his muddy hands on his jeans. "You and your friends here"—he motioned to Chris and Layla—"y'all ain't allowed at the farm, and you know it."

Emerson took a moment, breathed, and then rubbed the grime from his face. He felt the stings on his cheeks and shins now, slivers of exposed skin whipped raw from running through the plants.

"We were only playing, Uncle Terry. Layla got hurt, and then something started chasing us," Emerson offered.

Terry's hands planted on his hips just above his packed utility belt. It held several small round canisters with danger-red caps that Emerson recognized as pepper spray. Plus, Uncle Terry had crammed a plastic yellow pistol into a holster on his thigh. It was a TASER gun, and while it looked like a toy, Hawk had taught him that it was a dangerous weapon.

The squat man turned at his waist, studied Chris and Layla. "Get the hell over here!" he demanded, jerking his head.

Emerson's friends held a strange mix of emotions. Their auras jittered with fear and radiated with cool colors of relief that Emerson felt as well. Chris led the way, taking Layla's hand as they approached.

Terry's stare fell on Layla, gliding across her lean frame to her long legs.

"You're the doctor's kid. Where're your crutches? Ain't you a cripple?" he asked. His gaze shot to Emerson, and his mouth slanted in a smirk. "Nephew, wasn't she a cripple this mornin'? Am I recallin' that correctly?"

Emerson nodded. The punishment and shame he would experience for using his gift without permission were nothing compared to the imagined horrors breaking out of the ground behind them.

"I have CP," Layla said, her voice tentative.

"Well, looks like you're feeling better, sugar." His gaze bored into Emerson as he side-spoke to Layla. "I'm sure you got special attention from little Em here."

"We just wanted to play together." Chris stepped forward, placing himself between Terry and Layla.

Terry wiped a hand over his mouth as his halo darkened. Purples. Not like the aura from the field. His was deep and carried a crimson hue. The shade of it left a tingle of anxiety in Emerson's chest. This was a cruel color.

"That's mighty tender, boy. A great tale of your friendship. But y'all have broken several basic rules of the ranch here. Playin' on the farm, healin' folk without your mom's say-so. No mention of the goddamned heart attack you screamin' your way outta that field nearly gave me!"

With the stress of getting caught, Emerson had missed the obvious slur in Terry's words. The continuous sway in his body. Those small floating bubbles of nothing that came to his shimmer after he drank lots of beer.

Terry spat onto the soaked ground. "I think we need to discuss an arrangement?"

"What do you mean?" Emerson asked. "Aren't you going to tell Mom?"

Terry swiped the radio off his belt and held it up in his hand. "I can. Simple enough. She'll whip the lot of you, though."

In the corner of Emerson's vision, Chris and Layla shrank into each other. A new panic welled up at the thought of his mother's wrath. Making a mistake was one thing. But Emerson had defied her explicit rules. Twice. There was no doubt she would leave marks on him.

"Yeah, I can see your gears turnin', Nephew." Terry replaced the radio and leaned over, hands on his knees, until their faces were level. His words carried an odor like sour bread. "But what you ain't thinkin' yet, Em?" Terry's voice had softened, lowered to a near whisper, as if he were sharing a secret. "The thing you gotta consider here is what your mama will do to your friends."

Emerson's brow knotted. "She wouldn't whip 'em. They're not her kids."

Terry's eyes widened. "Oh, of course not! That ain't what I'm sayin', Emerson. What I'm sayin' is... how long you think she'll let 'em stick around the ranch? Given their less-than-positive influence on her boy?"

Emerson's thoughts poured into the opening pit in his chest. Uncle Terry was right. His gaze shifted to his two friends—his only friends. Chris stood tall, but his aura surrounded him in a painted portrait of fear. Beyond, Layla hugged herself, a tremble visible in her arms and aura. He tried not to imagine his days without them on the ranch, worked to keep the memories of boredom and the expanse of loneliness out of his mind.

"Not if you don't tell her." The words left Emerson's tongue before the idea had formed.

Terry sneered. He wobbled on his feet the way the thicket of plants behind them swayed in the wind. His crude purples bloomed stronger.

"I suppose you're right, Nephew." Terry sighed, shifting his bobbing head towards Layla, Chris, and then to Emerson once more. "But what reason do I have to keep this from your mama?"

Emerson's confusion must have shown on his face, because Uncle Terry continued.

"I'm askin' what you're offerin'," he clarified.

"What... what is it you want?"

Terry's round face relaxed. He leaned into Emerson, close enough to whisper. "For starters, you can use your power on me. We won't tell your mama; it'll stay between us, okay?"

Emerson looked past the violets and voids reaching out of the man's core and searched for a physical problem reflected in his light.

He shook his head. "I can't see nothing wrong with you, Uncle Terry."

Terry's acid breath fell into Emerson's ear and down his neck. "Remember when I went to Del Rio a few weeks back? See, I spent some time and money there and—" His uncle chuckled. "Well shit, Em, I think I got the clap."

Emerson pulled away, searching for his uncle's eyes and trying to understand the words and hues of pink shame tinting his aura. Before he could ask questions, a scrabble from the hills caught everyone's attention. Uncle Terry bolted upright at the sound of Barfly bolting out of the misty switchback and barreling towards them.

The dog broadsided Emerson and knocked him back to the soggy ground. Barfly pinned him under her wiggling front paws and whined like she hadn't seen him for years. Her warm and rough tongue flopped against his face, over and over, the scratchy surface tickling his whipped-raw cheeks.

Behind the dog, Terry's purples rotated towards blues. His color of curiosity.

"Who the fuck are you?" His uncle's tone was rigid, his voice projecting into the hills at something Emerson couldn't see. Then his light exploded in yellow fear.

Thunder. The shock of warm spray stole Emerson's breath, blurred the world. Emerson rubbed the muck off his eyes so he could see.

His uncle's light was a flicker and disappeared. Emerson worked to understand what he was seeing; the space where Terry's face had been was now filled with gleaming brown particulates that sank through the moist air.

He pitched forward, landing across Emerson's legs. Emerson should have heard something—a wet splat as Terry's body hit the earth. Instead, his ears surged with a mellow ring. Chris and Layla clutched one another. Their gazes gaped away from Emerson towards the boulder at the base of the hill.

A shadow hovered there, tall and straight in the swirling gray. A man. His halo twisted, black, evaporating into the surrounding mist. His arm stretched towards them, and his fingers gripped a massive, smoking pistol.

Chapter Twenty-Nine

As much as he hated Blair's brother, as many times as he'd daydreamed of doing it, Finch regretted the mess and the noise. But Terry had seen him approaching, was reaching for his own gun. One of them was going to shoot first, and Finch figured it may as well be him.

The fat man's head disappeared.

At the gun's report, the children cowered as if the crack was weight carried on their shoulders. Emerson's dog struggled free of his grip, still whining and crying. The longing for her boy had dried up when the gun had fired. The hound ran off, tail stuck to her asshole, a bundle of terrified curls and limbs.

Finch lowered the pistol. Pointed it at the earth. He wasn't a threat. Not to these kids. Their stares were on him. Three sets of eyes, bleach white, surrounded by brown grime and smears. A girl. Two boys. One of them was Emerson; he couldn't tell which. He should know. He should remember enough to see him under the layers of filth.

The echo of the .50-caliber fluttered through the humid air, carrying into the surrounding haze that hid other people, people with their own weapons. The clock was ticking.

"Emerson?" he croaked. Finch lurched towards the children; their eyes were fixed on him as he scoured them for any sign of recognition. At each step he took, his gaze flipped from one boy to the other, details failing to emerge from under the caked mud on their faces.

"Emerson!" His throat stung, and the force of the words jarred the children as much as the gun's report had.

The standing kids turned their heads and stared at the boy on the ground.

Finch stepped closer to them. The girl shrieked, a sound of terror and disgust. Finch's eye snapped to her, her expression familiar even beneath the banal mask of dirt. The girl had seen his face for what it was.

He continued forward, watching her eyes and mouth melt through the phases of disbelief, morbid curiosity, revulsion, and wonder. Finch recognized them all, had seen them so many times since his skin had become scars.

He smiled at her as best he could manage. It helped knowing that this would be the last time anyone would look at him that way.

The children froze, petrified in place as he passed them. Emerson struggled on the wet ground, trying to crab-walk away from Finch and towards the field.

Finch tucked the gun in his waistband, seating it under the small of his back. Then he lifted his hands up, palms open, doing his best to appear harmless.

"I ain't gonna hurt you, Emerson. That's not why I'm here."

The boy's crawl became a mad scramble, but the slippery mud fought against him. Finch lumbered to him. "I've been searching for you. For years now," he said. The gap between them shrank with each deliberate stride. "Tryin' to figure a way to get us together—"

The mud slid under his step. Finch glanced down to find his boot planted to his calf in the bubbling muck. He pulled, muscles straining against the suction and the unstable ground to lift the buried foot out of the sinkhole.

His gaze shot up to see the three children sprinting to the tall plants that faded into the mist.

"Wait!" he shouted, the desperation in his voice obvious and thick. "Just wait!"

His hands reached under his knee as his ass smacked the ground. His arms pulled up on this thigh, and his free leg pushed against the earth until it gave up his foot with a meaty slurp.

"Emerson!" he hollered.

The boy, who had been within arm's reach, disappeared into the dense growth.

The golf cart slowed, approaching the bend at the base of the hill.

Hawk peered over his shoulder from his stooped position on the rear seat, where he was applying pressure to Irene's wound.

The bullet had shredded the thigh right above her knee, and she had lost a ton of blood.

"Why are you slowing down?" he asked.

Jaime held up a finger. "Did you hear that? Was that a fucking gunshot?"

"Yeah, it was," Hawk replied, turning to Irene. "Looks like Irene brought friends. All the more reason to keep her alive; so can you get a move on, Boss? She's fading here."

Jaime engaged the accelerator, and the golf cart lurched ahead. Irene's face bobbed with the change in force, her flaccid lips and cheeks rippling with each bump in the path.

The rain had started once more. The cart's all-terrain tires did little more than slide them forward in the mud. Hawk watched as the edge of the hill passed him, then the equipment barn with the smaller golf cart and tractor parked in their spaces. The air was heavy with moist heat rising from the earth. Irene's blood congealed between his fingers, warm even against the air, and sticky. The tackiness of the blood and the visual of the ruined thigh nauseated him enough that he had to look away.

Hawk huffed as their speed decreased again. Before he could demand an explanation, Jaime spoke. "What the fuck is this shit?"

Hawk strained, his cramped posture preventing him from turning around without releasing his hold on the tourniquet. He could see a person prone in the muck. Jaime was out of the cart, jogging the last dozen feet.

"Who is it?" Hawk cried.

Jaime's fingers rubbed his bristly hair. Then they slapped to his sides. "I think it's Terry."

"You think?" Hawk asked, confused.

"He's got no face anymore."

Hawk removed a hand from the makeshift tourniquet and pivoted to see. The body lay face down, its head pointing into the aisle. Mud covered most of it, and Hawk noted the rusty tinge of the sludge. The cone of space revealed by the cart's headlamps was full of telltale angles and whiteness of bone shards peppering the brown muck.

"Jesus Christ," Hawk whispered. "Did he shoot himself?"

Jaime tilted his head, toed the side of Terry's head with his boot. He stared at it for a long moment. "I don't think so, Hawk. Someone shot him in the head. Large bore." He yanked the radio from his belt. "Something we don't carry on the ranch."

Jaime thumbed the talkback and lifted it to his face. "All hands, this is Boss. We have a security breach. Unknown number of armed intruders. Implement lockdown protocol. Arm yourselves and seek shelter until you hear otherwise." His voice never cracked, never rose above a conversational tone.

"Boss?" Hawk called, pointing to his patient with his chin. "Let's get her into the farm so we can figure this shit out?"

Jaime nodded and moved to the vehicle. The radio squelched as he replaced it on his belt.

"Jaime? Jaime, it's Blair!" Her frantic voice betrayed a deteriorating state of mind.

At last, the man's face showed concern. A crack in his stern brow line as the walkie flew back to his mouth.

"Blair, get Emerson and the kids and lock yourselves in the safe room!"

"I can't! Emerson ain't here!"

Jaime's gaze rose to meet Hawk's, his dull expression sharpening to razor panic.

He was rushing now, yelling into the radio. "What the hell do you mean? Where is he?"

"He went outside... play with... friends!" The radio signal faded in and out of static. "I called for him when it started raining, but... didn't come! You got to find him, Jaime!"

The cart was moving again, Jaime making a beeline for the center aisle. Hawk turned around, keeping firm pressure on Irene's leg. As the vehicle bumped and skidded over the broken ground, Hawk's body wedged hers into the seat and kept her from flopping out.

The funk of the farm came to his nose before the outer edge of plants passed. As the tall stalks and reaching branches whipped by, Hawk's eyes scanned for movement or muzzle flash. And for Emerson. At once, he felt exposed, helpless in the blind of the narrow aisle, a ready target for whatever gang or cartel was prowling the grounds.

Amid the rain and the danger, two thoughts repeated in Hawk's head: *Find Emerson. Save Irene.*

Chapter Thirty

The field swallowed Emerson and his friends. He looked over his shoulder for the man—his scarred face and cat-o'-nine-tails halo. There was only the green barrier of plants and the purple of their auras.

They had bolted back into the confined space and limited sight lines. The field that had terrified them with sounds and ideas only minutes ago now offered safety against a known threat. Emerson could still taste it, that tang of pennies that flows from a split lip. Except what he was tasting wasn't him. It was Uncle Terry.

Layla and Chris flew steps ahead of him, their feet slapping the muddy ground. Emerson moved faster than earlier, propelled by the idea of getting away from that burned man.

The killer's face had been nothing but swirls and scratches of flesh. Emerson had seen far worse when healing people, though. The physical deformity didn't scare him. It was the aura brimming from him.

Black. Luminescent. Reminiscent of a shiny stag-beetle carapace. As strong as the field's violets, but spiraling into a coil, wrapping the stranger the way barbed wire twists into a fence-post. Emerson had encountered nothing like it. Where everyone else's auras radiated out, pushed against the surrounding light, this man's did the opposite. It pulled into him. Fear surged at the visual memory, urging Emerson deeper into the field and filling him with terror that the coiled halo might reach out and entangle him too. Suck him in. Devour his aura. Make him a part of the monster that had killed his uncle.

Chris and Layla hauled ass around the next plant. Emerson rounded the other side, trying to close the distance to his friends. He glimpsed one of their sneakers disappearing past another leafy growth and adjusted his course.

He passed the plant and found only the periwinkle glow. No sign of Chris's earthy blue or Layla's pastel greens. He stared across the flat surface of puddles reflecting the haze of the sky above him, small peaks and ridges of soaked earth dividing them.

He pivoted, scouring the ground. Searching the growth. Nothing.

He had lost his friends. A new panic welled under his sternum as Emerson questioned where he was. What direction he faced. Was he running into the field? Out of it? The mist obscured his anchor landmark—the tower at the center of the clearing—and with the security lights off, Emerson couldn't figure out where it was.

He spun on his heels. The plants looked the same. The fence of purple and green was unvaried. There was no gap. No glint of the outside world.

The man was in here too. Tracking him. Emerson felt the pull of the monster's vile halo in the field. The ropes of black twisting between the stems, poised to stab out at Emerson and tear his own light to shreds. From where had he run? That was where the scarred man was. Emerson had no clue, and his fear turned to tears.

A rustle. Behind him. He whirled to see. Plants swayed in the wet wind. Warm water sprayed across his face. He turned into it, gasping. The lilac haze closed on him, swallowing him. He drowned in the skunk odor.

Something heavy landed on his shoulder. Emerson screamed as fingers tightened into his flesh.

"What the hell are you kids doing here?" Robin demanded. "You know you're not allowed on the farm!"

Confusion railed through her. The kids—her kid—should not be here. The farm was the only part of the ranch forbidden to the children, and the part that held the darkest secrets.

Layla shrieked, a pitch of terror that unraveled to sobbing as she embraced her mother's middle with a death grip.

"Where are your crutches?" The question sounded moronic as she asked it, given that her daughter had run into her full force on her own two legs.

"We need help!" Chris huffed. "Someone's shooting people."

Robin's confusion dissipated as the bigger issue boomed to the top of her mind. She had left the bunker to run to her tiny house and grab something to eat when the warning of armed intruders had come over the radio.

"I know. Let's—"

"Mom, he's right behind us!" Layla cried.

"What do you mean?" Robin asked, then cringed at the irrelevance of her own words.

Layla released her, pointing the direction they had come. "We ran out of the farm, and Emerson's uncle caught us. But then he got shot. By another man. He's coming this way, Mom!"

She saw her daughter then. Past the broken rules and the abuse of Emerson's ability. She was muddy. Scratched bloody and scared. Smeared with greasy tears.

"Oh, God!" Robin moved the children in front of her, ushering them towards the storm cellar doors a few rows ahead. "There's a place we'll be safe, don't worry."

"But Mom—"

"No talking. We need to move," Robin huffed. She pushed and pulled the kids through the plants, finding the painted concrete slab and metal doors of the shelter.

"Just wait—"

"Shh!" she hissed. "Be quiet; we'll be through this in a second."

Robin fumbled with the keys in her jeans pocket, grabbing the padlock and chain on the door with her other hand. She opened the lock with smooth, practiced moves, and the chain clattered to her feet.

She yanked on the heavy steel, the metal hinges grinding, releasing a horrid growl into the thick air.

"Get down there, now! This door is louder than Gabriel's fucking horn, and whoever is chasing you just heard it!"

She moved Layla in front of her, directing her to the concrete steps and into the pale, yellow LEDs of the bunker's entrance. Her daughter protested, but Robin insisted with a rare use of physical force.

Chris wiggled out of her fingers as she reached for him next.

"But Dr. Travers," he pleaded, "what about Emerson? He's still out there!"

Chapter Thirty-One

A hand clamped over Emerson's mouth as another thumped into his chest. He left the ground, held aloft by a strength matching Jaime's. But this wasn't Jaime. The small crescent of finger flesh he could see was pink and ruddy, not the calloused tan of his mom's boyfriend. And this man had an odor, like the stale fruit of the field, but stronger. Something vaporous and medicinal that burned his sinuses.

The plants whipped by him. Emerson was carried, disoriented, the directions shifting around him as he was whisked through the field. His arms dug into his sides from the man's bear hug. Something bit into his wrist as the man shifted direction.

The barrel in Emerson's front pocket—the pepper spray he'd taken from Uncle Terry's belt. His fingers found the shape, but with his arms pinned, Emerson couldn't get into his pocket to retrieve it.

The burned man stopped, holding Emerson off the ground. The man's chest pressed into his back, expanding and contracting with the sound of his labored panting. The purple miasma of the field's halo pulsed as Emerson's blood rushed to his ears.

In his periphery, the gleaming ebony whips of the stranger's aura writhed into the glow of the plants. The way his light shaped and slithered—more tentacles than aura—it wasn't something Emerson had thought was possible.

After a minute, the man's breathing slowed, but his grip around Emerson didn't loosen. Emerson's skin tightened as the intruder's lips eased to his ear.

"Not a sound," the man murmured. "I won't hurt you, but I swear I'll shoot whoever comes near us, and I don't want to kill anyone else."

Emerson kept still except for curling his fingers. A snag on his fingernail told him he'd found the pocket's seam.

"Nod if you understand."

Emerson nodded, his eyes watering from the sting of the man's medicinal scent. The tapered ends of the dark coils turned to him. Snakes eyeing their next meal. *How is he controlling his light that way?*

"I just want to talk to you, okay? Nothin' bad is gonna happen to you." The man's breath emitted more foul odors, spicy and sharp. Emerson tasted it between the gaps of the stranger's loosening grip on his mouth.

Emerson's wrist flexed forward, achieving an unnatural angle to get the tips of his fingers under the seam of the pocket opening. A pang of pressure shot through his forearm and up to his shoulder. His fingertips breached the pocket, but the pivot of his wrist and the hold of the man against him prevented him from reaching the cylinder.

Then his mouth was freed as the man's hand came away. Emerson's feet touched the ground.

The cloth opened around his fingers, and smooth metal rolled into his grip. Emerson knew how to use the pepper spray. His mom had showed him once when he'd asked her what the bright-red rod on her keys was.

His thumb landed on the notch on the lever. He rotated it counterclockwise to enable the spray. Emerson heard a grunt, a heave of air leaving his lungs, and the faceless man squeezed.

"Don't move," the man said. "This won't hurt. You won't enjoy it, but it won't hurt."

Emerson's fingers had the cylinder. He tried to lift his arm. To pull the weapon free. The intruder locked on his bicep—it was pointless.

A warmth on Emerson's neck tensed his flesh once more. Not the man's breath this time. The sensation was even, steady. It was the man's skin, his hand curling around Emerson's collar.

"What are you doing?" Emerson blurted. The tightening on his neck sent an immense pressure along his spine, as if the man was going to fold Emerson's torso in half.

"Shush now," he whispered. "No talking. No moving. Don't fight me; just let it happen."

A panic grew, raw and unconstrained, as the shining black tethers of the man's venomous aura sank into Emerson's chest and slithered up his throat.

Stories careened through his head. Things Mom had told him. Ugly details of what happened to children whose parents didn't love them as much as she loved him. He struggled against the fabric of his pocket, his arm heaving against the immense power of the man pinning him. His shoulder rolled up, his arm sliding against his ribs as the pocket seam scraped against his fist.

A sharp zing radiated from the man's fingers, a shock that tensed the muscles in Emerson's neck. His body convulsed, yanking his hand from his pocket.

Emerson bent his elbow over the man's thick grip, rotating the spray towards his own face. He would hold his breath, clamp his eyes shut. Shoot the pepper spray over his own shoulder and into the man's face. When the man let go, he would run, eyes shut, not breathing, until the man's screams and coughs faded into the rustle of the field.

With luck, Emerson wouldn't trip. He would get free. Scream for help, and maybe Hawk or Jaime would hear him and come running. They might reach him before the stranger could gather himself again.

Thoughts of escape were pushed out by the tendrils worming through his torso. The black rays crept up into his mind, and then down into his light.

Emerson pulled his halo inward. Surrounded his core with it. A protective barrier against the attack. The strange aura was already there, strands of shiny emptiness whipping through him. Barbs biting into him, tearing off bits of his own amber light.

"Let me in, Emerson." The stranger's voice was distant, even as Emerson felt the hot breath on his ear. Emerson's body went limp, his will to fight consumed by growing dread. A malaise welled through him, surrender wringing the strength from his muscles, and his arm fell back to his side.

Emerson was aware of his fingers relaxing, of the metal cylinder rolling past his fingertips to the ground. But he didn't care anymore. The fear that had eaten at him moments ago was washed off by incessant waves of misery. He realized how isolated he was. How few characters played a part in his story. How careless he was with their feelings. The danger he had put Layla and Chris in today, no thoughts in his head but the terror of losing their friendship.

"That's it..." the man's voice echoed.

Loneliness bloomed in him. A dark and delicate flower supported by the barbed aura of the burned man. The petals opened, spreading a shadow across his mind. Emerson saw his individuality, his uniqueness in a world of mundane people. His ability to help others, which only isolated him from everyone. People using him for their own gain. Jaime. His own mother. The shadow deepened, tamping any glimmer of light or hope, until it blocked his very thoughts and feelings.

A tear welled in his eye, breached the lid, and slid over his mud-crusted cheek.

"... just let me in."

Chapter Thirty-Two

"*E merson!*" Blair's voice cracked, her throat raw from screaming for her son over and over. The name left her lips. It carried into the orchard, the field. Bounced from the hills behind the house then again from the warehouse hidden in the mist of weather.

The echo remained the only response.

Her boots sloshed in the muck as she retreated through the pecan grove. The pillars of the porch cut deep grooves in the floodlight, made sharp by the humidity. The saturated air did nothing to pull the sweat off her skin. Instead, it collected on her, squished in every nook of her body as she moved in the muggy air, searching for her boy.

Simple fucking directions. She had given her son simple directions to come inside if the weather changed. All the children had heard her. She crossed her arms, stomping through the trees as rage nipped at the heels of her panic. Thoughts of finding Emerson offered relief—an image of her holding him, his cherub face buried in her chest the way he used to. Then the scene turned sour as she saw herself cutting a switch from the surrounding trees and using it to remind him of the importance of following her instructions.

She neared the edge of the grove, the house ahead of her lost in the blinding white sun of the porch lights. Again, she called her son's name, and again it radiated into the hidden void around her without a response.

Emerson should have a radio with him. Or maybe a tracking device. He was too important to let run amok. She'd make Jaime research it, find a solution. So they'd always know where Emerson was.

Jaime would argue, claim that the dog was enough. Barfly kept him safe, warned them about vagrants on the ranch. Stepped between Emerson and intruders who got too curious, keeping them at bay until Jaime showed up and took control. But Barfly couldn't tell them where Emerson was now.

Frustration mounted as she reached the midpoint between the orchard and the house. The playground sat to her right, the metal gleaming in the porch's light and the wet air. Haze consumed the land to her left, the silhouette of the hills visible against the gray.

She spun on her heels, taking in the ranch's breadth. She couldn't decide where to search. The ranch was expansive, and outside of the yard and orchard, there weren't many places Emerson could go play. Where they allowed him to play. His normally compliant demeanor made it difficult for her to fathom where the hell he might be.

As she debated, a squelch broke the silence, startling her. She reached for the noise on her hip: the walkie screeching an incoming transmission.

"Robin for Boss."

Blair fumbled with the device, trying to unlatch the thing from the waist of her jeans.

"Not now, Robin." Her boyfriend's tone carried an impatience Blair recognized. The radio snapped loose from her waistband, and she lifted it to her ear.

"Listen," the doctor continued, her voice fighting against the static, "I found Layla and Chris. I've moved them under the farm. They're safe here, but Emerson is still in the field someplace!"

That decided it. Blair ran to the extra golf cart parked by the porch. She threw herself behind the wheel and engaged the electric engine with a set of practiced moves. She would reach the farm in five minutes.

"I'm there now," Jaime replied. "We're heading your way with an injured woman. Gunshot wound to the leg. Prep a table for her."

Blair slammed the throttle to the floor, and the vehicle eased forward with frustrating lethargy.

"Jesus... okay, I have questions, but they can wait," Robin said. "The kids say that there's a man chasing them. They saw him shoot one of the security detail, so they ran into the field. He's still out there, Boss."

Blair maneuvered past the house and pointed the cart towards the tip of the foothill that divided the ranch. The small wheels slid in the mud. The entire cart threatened to heave over until the tread caught on the gravel of the trodden path.

The speaker blared in her hand. "Noted," Jaime said. "I'm dropping Hawk and the woman at the bunker, then I'll go find the kid."

Blair lifted the radio to her mouth, her thumb slipping off the talk button once before catching it. "Jaime, Blair. I'm heading to the farm to help search."

The static shattered. "Blair, no! Get to the house! Lock yourself in the safe room!"

"Go fuck yourself," she replied into the walkie.

"Goddammit, Blair," Jaime growled, the twist in his voice tightening. "People are dying out here!"

"Jaime, I'm comin' to find my boy, and that's all there is to it." She set the radio in the cart's cupholder, where it rattled as she bounced along the sloppy wet path.

She knew where her boy was. The rough area, at least. And that he was in danger. When Blair located the person threatening Emerson, she would tear off his balls. Then she'd calm down and confront Emerson's open defiance.

The hills scrolled by through the sinking mist. As she navigated the dark path, the lights of the cart bouncing across the vertical lines of rain, a steady hiss whispered through the air. The sound left her suspended. Waiting for a signal to disrupt the noise. Like the buzz from the walkie waiting for a reply.

The path split, and she turned south. The radio thumped against the side of the plastic cupholder. Something she'd heard wasn't sitting right. A mundane detail under the immediate terror of a gunman. Her brow furrowed as she tried to replay the conversation she'd just had.

As the cart sputtered past the utility barn, the tower of the farm faded into view, the pointed roof of the upper platform a geometric grey anomaly against the organic contours of the slopes. The field was a dull, pale splotch of gray in the rain.

Blair steered the cart between the hills and the field, making a beeline for the center aisle.

The hiss of rain swelled into a roar as the details of the radio chatter came back to her. She shook her head, sure of what she'd heard but unable to fathom its meaning.

Blair snatched the radio from the cupholder. She thumbed the talkback.

"Jaime? It's Blair."

A moment of static, then his reply: "Go for Jaime."

"What do y'all mean by 'under' the farm?"

Chapter Thirty-Three

"What do y'all mean by under the farm?"

Hawk recognized the edge in her voice. The tenacity of a dog with its bone.

Jaime must have recognized it too. He sighed. "Fuck me standing, I don't need this shit." The radio flew to his mouth as he stammered, "There's, uh... an emergency shelter. Built right under the farm."

Jaime killed the volume on the walkie, cutting off Blair's next question. Then he motioned at the double steel doors with his free hand, ordering Hawk to open the bunker. Hawk tightened the tourniquet, checking Irene's lips for color, before launching out of the cart and jogging to the storm-rated doors. The green metal shutters sat atop a concrete frame, hiding steps that led into the subterranean shelter. Hawk grabbed the handle near the center seam and gave it a pull.

The doors refused to budge. The security bolts were latched.

He pulled his radio. "Hawk for Doc, open up. It's us."

Jaime whistled. Hawk looked up to find his arms hooked into Irene's armpits, heaving her rag-doll frame off the rear seat.

"Little help?"

A series of metallic clacks rang from beneath the storm doors—the sound of Robin releasing the interior locks. Hawk moved next to Jaime and took Irene's back and knees, and they eased her out of the back seat.

Hawk slid his arm up her back and took her weight. Her body melted, her neck and head lax over his bicep as her legs dangled limp. His left hand sucked against her blood-saturated jeans. The tourniquet had loosened, and her wound was leaking again.

Jaime went to the doors, grabbed the handle, and pulled. This time, it pivoted on its hinge, metal scraping and releasing a tinny screech that shook the air. Hawk approached the opening, turned around, and shifted backwards down the concrete steps as Irene flopped in his arms.

At the base of the steps, Robin was waiting for him.

"What the hell is going on, Hawk?"

"All I know is she needs help, Doc."

She looked at Irene's face. "Jesus Christ, isn't that—"

"Yes," he interrupted. "It's her. She's lost a shit ton of blood."

Robin's eyes found Irene's exploded knee and widened. She spun towards the dark tunnel leading into the ground. "Let me get a gurney, one sec."

"Hawk!" Jaime's voice echoed in the tight concrete room, punching heavily against Hawk's ears.

Hawk turned back. "What, Jaime?!"

Jaime spoke as he lowered the cellar door. "Lock this behind me. Don't open it unless you hear from me."

"Yeah, okay. What about you?"

"I'm gonna find Emerson, and then I'm gonna kill the fucker who's invaded my compound."

The hinges squealed, and the steel door clattered against the concrete baffle. The sound faded as a new one took its place: wheels rolling on the plywood flooring. Hawk turned to see Robin pushing a hospital bed through the narrow tunnel.

"Set her down. Help me get her to the operating room," she said.

Hawk eased Irene onto the stretcher. Her blood made rust-colored stains, stark on the white linens even in the subdued yellow light of the entrance.

He rounded to the head of the bed, letting Robin lead them into the main bunker. As Hawk pushed Irene forward, the bed's wheels rattled across the line of French drains that separated the entrance steps from the buried shipping containers that made up the underground shelter. The gurney consumed the corridor width, the corrugated steel walls passing a foot on either side. Dim lights provided just enough illumination for Hawk to see the grain of the floor passing under his feet.

The bed reached the end of the darkness, a heavy curtain backlit by white pouring around its edge. Robin pulled the drape away, letting Hawk push the stretcher across the welded threshold between shipping containers.

Ahead, three more containers lay end to end, a protracted hallway that ended with another weighty curtain. Intense LED lighting bounced off the whitewashed walls and exposed detail that had not been apparent in the weather outside: the filth and dried blood on Hawk's hands, Irene's weeping wounds, the clots forming on the frayed fabric where the bullet had shredded the leg. Her skin had paled since the dispensary, and her lips remained flaccid as Hawk jogged the bed through the long hallway.

Robin passed her office door and pulled back the curtain with a sharp scraping sound. She held it open, and Hawk steered the bed into the larger operating area.

The room comprised two shipping containers welded together on their long sides. The plywood floor carried into the space from the hallway. Hawk eased the gurney under the large, round, medical-grade light that was suspended from the ceiling by a sturdy arm, while Robin ran to a metal cabinet.

She pulled instruments from the cabinet and piled them on a surgical tray. She rummaged through them, found a set of blunt-tipped scissors, and worked at cutting and unwrapping the denim on Irene's wounded leg, edging up to the shredded knee. The fabric clung to the injury and the dried blood around it, and as Robin exposed the wound, she turned her head to look at him.

"I can't fix this, Hawk. Her leg is fucking hamburger. We need Emerson to do it," she said. "If we were in a hospital, they'd amputate to save her life."

Hawk ran a hand through his hair. "Just keep her alive, Doc. Keep her alive so we can talk to her." He turned to the bunker doors to engage the security bolts like Jaime had instructed, then called over his shoulder, "Keep her alive until we get the kid here! Oh, and Doc?"

Robin didn't look up from her patient. "What is it?"

"Restrain her. When she wakes up, she'll start swinging."

The steel rattled against the concrete, alerting everyone in earshot. Jaime scoped the surrounding field as he moved to the golf cart. He scoured for something fixed in the liquid motions of the leaves in the wind. Nothing.

His hand left the gun on his thigh. He slid into the driver's seat and engaged the engine, then circled back to the clearing at the center of the field.

The rain had picked up, pattering on the plastic roof and splatting the ground in sporadic, heavy drops. The vegetation opened around him, a foundation pylon for one of the tower legs a dozen feet ahead. Jaime eased the cart around it, accelerating towards the tower's far limb.

He hopped out of the vehicle before it was still, his hand rummaging into his jeans pocket for his keys. As he jogged to the large electrical box mounted on the leg of the tower, he flipped through his keys to find the one that unlocked the padlock securing the wide metal switch that controlled the tower security lights.

The lock opened and fell to the ground. The heavy lever resisted him as he heaved it up to engage the power.

Then it clacked home.

The dismal gray of the weather disappeared in a blinding wash of yellow and white sodium lights. The wall of the field surrounding the tower appeared out of the gloom, a phalanx of stalks and branches popping into existence. Even the air glowed now, the thick strands of falling rain refracting the light above him.

Jaime listened. Tried to hear something past the hiss of the weather on the plants. Over the dull thuds of the water rolling off the metal roof several stories above him. Seeking any disturbance over the mellow hum of the electrical circuit.

He debated how to start. Emerson was, as far as he knew, still in the field. Perhaps with the gunman. Or maybe hiding from him. Either way, Jaime didn't want to announce his approach.

In his mind, he drew a line from Terry's body, just outside of the main aisle of the farm, to the bunker door. The kids had run along that line. Emerson had too.

He slid the Glock out of its holster and jogged forward. His ears and eyes tensed as the thicket closed on him.

Chapter Thirty-Four

T he boy went limp against him as Finch exposed his psyche. The core of his drive, the central fear that bore the load of how Emerson defined himself. It lay bare before them both.

Finch smiled his crooked grin. He'd expected something deeper. More complex. Emerson was a child still, but he had experiences unique across the universe, and a continuous insight into those around him. Yet his thinking remained simple. His fears were common.

"You do not know what you are," Finch whispered in the child's ear. "No one here has any notion of it either."

The boy remained putty in his grasp, his head resting on Finch's bicep.

"You compare yourself to others and view yourself as the outsider. You want their acceptance. That makes you vulnerable to their whims."

Finch listened as the patter of rain picked up. He pulled away another layer of Emerson's psyche, finding familiar faces and feelings.

"Your mother... her lover... your friends... None of these people have any idea what it's like being you, Emerson. The things you can do. Yet here I am, hitting the taproot of what makes you—the single drive in you that is fed by all the others. The one that stitches you together."

The child shuddered in his grip.

"Look at it! Look right into it! What do you see?" Finch asked, knowing the boy wouldn't speak. "You see your mother, the woman who birthed you? Raised you? One of a few people close to you, someone who loves you because she has to?"

Another rattle ran through the child's limp frame. Emerson's languid sobs rocked through Finch's hand and arm.

"Where would her love go if you were like everyone else? If you weren't useful to her? Would she keep you on this ranch? Would she have kept you at all, boy?"

Emerson's slight body shook. Finch had to be delicate, but time was short, and this might be his one chance.

"She whips you, doesn't she?" he whispered next to Emerson's ear. "I see it in there, Emerson. The extension cord in her hand. Doubled over and landing across your back."

The boy jerked, as if the switch had struck him.

"How many times? And for what end?" Finch asked. He didn't need an answer, just needed to ask the question. The kid would understand. See the shameless disregard his mother had for his sensitivities and safety.

Finch closed that loop, moving on to the next.

"And her man. He's supposed to keep you safe. Protect you."

The body relaxed again as Finch moved his focus off Blair.

"What would he do to you if you stopped using your gifts for his gains?"

Another level of psychological defense peeled back.

"What purpose would he have for you then? What value would your mother have?"

Emerson's breathing hastened as Finch found memories the boy had tucked away. Customers wanting to hurt others without consequence. Others who desired only to live, to love their folk longer, and Blair or Jaime denying him the chance to help.

"What does he do to people he doesn't need anymore? He hurts them, Emerson. He hurts them through action and inaction. Looks like you know some of it. You'll learn all of it, eventually. He hurts people, and he uses your divine nature to do it. And your bitch mother wants him to. And for what? For money?"

One final shudder racked the boy's bones. Then he was still. Empty of defenses, his mind locked with fear. Broken, ready to be rebuilt.

"You come with me, Emerson. Come with me, and I promise you will never be alone the way you are here. No one will use you like they do here. You are not a tool to be held in an infantile grip, boy! You are a force of nature, your ability woven into the very fabric of the universe that surrounds us. And these people cannot help you understand."

Finch waited, felt the boy's chest expand against his arm once. Twice.

"But I can. Come with me, and no one will ever wield you like this again—"

The air exploded around him, light from bright flood lamps swallowing him and drowning his vision. An artificial sun burned over the field, the flash blurred and amplified by the falling rain.

In the sudden brightness, Finch pulled his hand up to shield his eye. His bond with Emerson had broken, and Finch struggled to regain awareness of his surroundings.

In the confusion, Emerson slipped from his grasp. Finch stumbled on his numb feet, trying to find his balance.

"Emerson!" he cried. "Wait! Stay with me now!"

A gritty scraping came to Finch's ears. Off to his right. He found the boy on the ground, crawling but not running away.

"That's good," Finch said, spying the boy's shifting form a few feet away. "You believe me, don't you? I can teach you who you are. Show you who you can be."

The child rolled over. Finch could make out facial contours now in the harsh light and shadow.

"You never need to be alone. Or appease anyone, ever again."

For a long moment, they stared at one another. Finch had seen the boy's fear, and Emerson would realize he was telling the truth.

The child's arm floated. Tentative. Then with purpose.

Finch smiled. He had found Emerson. The boy belonged to him now, safe from Blair. Finch reached out a hand to help Emerson off the ground.

Emerson didn't reach back for it. Confused, Finch blinked to clean the haze from his eye.

The boy gripped something red and metal. As Finch tried to discern its identity, the tiny fist clenched.

A liquid flew to Finch's face. A strange sensation at first—a rare tingle and warmth on his calloused cheeks.

Then the pepper spray struck his working eye, and the world faded into a searing blur.

Chapter Thirty-Five

A strobing flash of heat lightning rippled through the air behind Blair, revealing every visual detail of the field. Her foot stamped something soft but unyielding, and the world rotated around her. She landed on her front, hitting the mud and sending a thick sludge up her face.

Another burst, but this one didn't fade.

Blair twisted and found her leg draped across a body. In her rising panic, she kicked, crab-walking away from the gore. The toes of her leather boot hooked against the body's arm, and her frantic energy rolled the corpse onto its back.

Blair froze. The head was there. Most of it. His face was missing. But she recognized her brother.

Terry was dead.

She forced in a breath through her closed throat. The white static of shock threatened her, grief trying to swallow her focus. She couldn't deal with them right now. The reality of her predicament shone clear in the artificial light. Someone was here, killing people. Her son was here somewhere too, running through the sea of plants as waves of wind rocked them on their roots.

Her desire to scream faded, and a familiar feeling replaced the dread in her chest. A righteous anger warmed her muscles as she climbed to her feet.

Nobody would hurt her boy. She wouldn't allow that to happen. She was his mother, and she would protect him as long as she lived.

Her eyes fell to her brother's corpse and stopped at his waist. Blair knelt over the body and, holding her gorge, worked the TASER gun out of the holster on his thigh. She checked the weapon. It appeared undamaged.

Blair flipped the safety lever. The gun was live, ready to use. Her finger felt the trigger guard and rested there, like Jaime had taught her. It had a single shot. If she needed it, she would make it count.

Her breath even and steady, Blair aimed the TASER ahead of her and stepped into the column of light shining down the farm's aisle.

"Hawk, she's lucid. If you want to talk to her, now is the time."

Irene turned her head, struggling to catch a sliver of the room. The doctor—or at least the person dressed as one—remained out of sight.

Echoes of boots slapping a wood floor crescendoed as someone approached. Irene counted twelve steps before they stopped.

"Did she say anything to you?" The lower tone of a man, reverberations in the room making the words difficult to hear. Yet she recognized the voice. Irene strained her neck to see, but the rails of the gurney blocked her view.

"Nothing of consequence. I figured you'd have more luck."

Another murmur, too low for Irene to make out.

More shoes on wood. A softer sound, drifting away.

As seconds passed, she could sense someone there, watching her. A predator salivating over her vulnerability.

One heavy thud marked movement. The watcher, closing on her. Irene saw shadows flopping against the corrugated walls as he stepped into Irene's field of view.

Wes.

"Hey, sis." Wes's tone was quiet and tempered. He dragged a stool up to the bed, adjusting the height before easing himself onto it. His fingers made for hers, and she fisted her hand.

An avalanche of questions tumbled down her mind, the haze of whatever medicine was veiling her injury making it impossible to focus on one.

"Why is she calling you 'Hawk?'" she asked.

Wes chuckled, revealing his gums. A sight that pulled Irene back to the morning, to the morgue and Wes's fish mouth.

"That's my name now," he replied. His stare narrowed and turned to her leg. "How are you feeling, Irene? Are you in pain?"

She did a mental inventory and shook her head before refocusing the conversation. "I don't feel it," she said. "It's bad, though. I can tell I need a hospital."

"No, we'll take care of you," he promised, again trying to hold her hand as she yanked it from him. The restraint prevented her from moving past a few inches, but Wes took the hint.

"The fuck you will," she hissed. "Where the hell am I?"

Wes snorted. "You really don't know?"

"Of course not!" A heat rose in her. Frustration. The tumbling questions cracking against each other before they could reach her mouth. "Wes, how are you alive? I saw your corpse in the morgue!"

"We'll get to that," Wes said, his countenance calm. "But first, I need to know how you found me. And how many people are running around the compound." His gaze flitted to the ceiling. "And what the hell they want."

She chewed her lip. "I wasn't looking for you."

"Bullshit." Wes's expression darkened. "Irene, I don't believe that. My boss won't believe it, either."

"I went to the fucking morgue today, Wes! Where I identified your body! I thought I left you there, goddammit!"

Her brother watched her, mulling over her words. "Then how did you end up here, Irene?"

Her mind scoured for details from that morning, the building storm, and Finch's errand. "Finch brought me."

"Who is that?"

"Finch? He said... he had a pickup at the dispensary. He's one of your regular customers."

Wes shook his head. "Today was his first order."

Her brow tensed and her brain heated as it fought the drugs to put the pieces together. "He said that—"

"Who is he?" Wes interrupted. "How do you know him, Irene?"

She shrugged, the linens crinkling under her shoulders. "He's my landlord, I guess. I live on his land, and I run errands for him because of his..."

"His what? Is he disabled? Injured?" Her brother's voice had turned tense, and his lips formed a stern line.

"He's covered in burn scars," she blurted.

Wes looked away, his brow tightening with anger as he stared out of the room.

"What?" she asked. "What about it?"

His gaze returned. "He's here for the boy."

Irene's thoughts faltered. "What... what boy?"

Wes stayed silent, studying her with an unrelenting stare that knotted her stomach.

Her discomfort bloomed, the heat of her own frustrations percolating in her skull as she shoved her voice through her tight throat. "Wes, what boy? What the hell is going on here? What is this place?"

After a few seconds, Wes sighed. "You sure you don't remember?"

"Remember what?" She teetered on a scream as her body and mind struggled against their restraints.

Wes reached for her once more. She pulled away, but this time Wes forced his hand onto hers. His grip tightened to a firm pressure, a gesture of reassurance that she didn't want. He held steady as she yanked against the cuff, cussing at him while he remained silent. After a moment, Irene realized there was no point. She stilled, pressing herself into the bed, away from her brother.

His eyes lingered on hers, displaying a patience she wasn't expecting. He'd always been reactive. The two of them quarreled, their history more like that of boxers than siblings. This stillness was new, and Irene wasn't sure whether his calm made him safe or more dangerous.

Wes cleared his throat. "Irene, this isn't the first time you've found me. This isn't your first visit to Utopia Farms. Hell." He lifted his gaze from her, carrying it over the pleated metal ceiling. "This isn't even your first visit to this godforsaken room."

Chapter Thirty-Six

The mud drew the heat out of his cheeks. Finch applied more of it over his clamped eye, then let it sit and dry while he caught his breath.

He was more than blind. The boy had targeted his only working sense. Now, any awareness of his surroundings came only through the otoplasty openings in the melted skin over his ear canals.

Sounds had no direction, no location. Without his vision, Finch was unable to orient himself. The hiss of drizzle and the whoosh of wind left him immersed in a vast space full of static and danger. And somewhere in that noise was Emerson.

His fingers touched the clay covering his eye. It had thickened but remained damp. The chemical heat of the pepper spray still radiated there. It needed a few more minutes to have any effect.

He'd lost his orientation when the kid had attacked him. The surprise and the sudden burning had sent Finch reeling, spinning away. He reached out with a hand, hoping against hope that it would find flesh. The child, acknowledging that a life with Finch would be better than staying here.

His fingers found the narrow trunk of a plant. He anchored himself to it, honing his focus until the plant was the center of the universe. His back leaned against it, and the rain pattering on the leaves drowned out other sounds.

Finch sat in the little bubble the plant created, shielding himself from the shower. Emerson may be two feet away. Or Blair's brutish lover could be staring him down. A gun in his thick mitt, aimed at Finch's skull, bracing to end his life.

The longing to call to the child was overwhelming. Finch had seen his fear and measured it. Emerson was alone here, surrounded by family who were unable to help him and had no hope of teaching him to handle his gifts. Hell, the boy *knew* it too. Finch had seen it in him. Under the layers of basic survival and security, Emerson was aware of what his caretakers were using him to do. And yet he had run to them, even after Finch had torn open his psychological defenses and given him full awareness of how fucked up his life was here.

Finch swallowed and coughed from the latent burning in his throat. The sensation was sickening and familiar to him. As if every nerve had been plunged into a deep fryer. His skin tightened in response, despite the humid air.

A thought occurred to him. A possibility. Emerson may not have run from him. Finch had sensed a change in him, perhaps enough to allow Emerson to see past Finch's monstrous visage.

Another swallow, this one burning his esophagus and making his stomach lurch.

"Emerson?" he croaked, his voice hampered by the clench in his chest.

He pivoted his head left, then right. A tic he'd adopted to help compensate for his missing earlobes and localize sound. No response came except the rustle of the plants in the wind. He hoped the boy was in that static, close enough to listen.

Finch cleared his throat and spoke again, louder. "Emerson?" His voice carried now, and a fresh fire filled his sinuses as he exhaled. "Emerson, if you are there... if you can hear me... just listen."

The whip and tatter of leaves and branches was the only reply.

"I know I look a fright. But I ain't no monster. I ain't here to hurt you."

Finch paused for several breaths, listening.

"You're wondering why I killed that man out there? Because he was gonna keep me from you. You're the reason I'm here, boy. I'm here to save you, to get you away from here."

Finch listened to the patter and thuds of water splashing the ground.

"You don't recognize me, not like I am now. But I promise you—"

The snap of a stem, maybe a dozen feet ahead. Not the fluid rhythm of moving plants, but the keen crack of sudden force. Finch rotated his head, straining to hear more. He licked his lips—the greasy minerals of the earth smeared there, along with the sharp sting of the pepper spray. He leaned on the trunk, getting his boots under him, and stood.

"I promise that if you mend me, you won't see a monster."

Finch listened again. He wasn't sure, but he thought he perceived a hole in the soundscape that enveloped him. A place where sounds dampened, where the field held its breath.

"Heal me, Emerson. Know me. For who I am, not what I look like. And I promise you'll want to come with me."

Finch stood in the open, the thump of the rain against the brim of his hat drowning out the other sounds of the field.

"I haven't lied to you, Emerson. You needed to see what was what. I won't never lie to you the way your mother does. The way she lets others lie to you. I won't use you, or let others use you."

Finch brushed his eye again. The mud crumbled against his touch, leaving a gritty dust. He plucked off his fedora and lifted his face to the precipitation. He wiped the muck off with his fingers. The yellow light filling the field seeped through his eyelid, and a blood-red glow formed as the mud disappeared. He finished scraping off the dirt using one of his shirttails, then blinked once. His eye screamed, tears cascading over his cheek, but he worked through the pain, blinking more, letting the brilliance of the sodium lights sting as shadows turned into light.

He was seeing movement. Whip-like dancing of the marijuana fronds flopping in the sporadic gusts. He replaced his hat, focused on his breathing as the pain in his eye diminished.

The boy had stayed close. He felt it. The child had heard Finch. And just like Finch was listening now, Emerson was waiting for more.

Finch pulled in a sigh, ready to explain everything. Convince Emerson to approach, lay hands on him. Then they would leave this place forever.

"*Emerson?*" A female voice sailed through the wind and rain.

Finch held his breath as he swiveled his head, trying to locate the direction from which the cry had come.

"Emerson? Come to me, honey!"

A pattern developed in the rustling of the plants. A consistency that no weather could create.

The pad of footfalls. Running away from him.

His tingling cheeks stretched tight as Finch smiled and rubbed off more of the dried mud, knowing he had reached the child.

Chapter Thirty-Seven

I rene huffed at her brother. "What are you talking about? If I had discovered you, you'd be in jail now, Wes! You're a murderer—"

"I can prove it," he interrupted. "If you'll listen to me this time."

A low hum filled the space. A steady sound that leaked down from above. Deeper than the whine of the constant electrical noise.

Irene nodded for him to go on.

"Blair and Jaime, they run this ranch. We built it around Blair's son, Emerson." Wes's face fell, and he looked at his fingers still draped over hers. "Emerson is why Dad needed to come to Texas. He's the reason I brought Dad here."

Irene waited for him to continue, uncertain where the story was heading.

"Emerson has a gift. An ability. He can see into people, see how their bodies have broken. And he heals them, Irene."

Her mouth twitched with incredulity. "Sounds to me like you let Dad fall for a con artist—"

Her voice caught as Wes raised his left hand. She wasn't sure what he was trying to show her, yet the display struck her as wrong.

"How many fingers did I have the last time you remember seeing me?"

It clicked as her eyes focused on his index digit. The one that shouldn't be there.

Wes continued, "When Dad shot me, I had my fist around the revolver. The flash severed my finger."

Irene countered, but Wes spoke over her.

"And yes, you're going to tell me you only saw the bandage, not the wound; and for all you know, the digit was never missing; and that your memories of it are flawed," he said. "Am I right?"

Irene swallowed. Those were the exact points she had wanted to make.

"Your memory isn't wrong, Irene. I left my finger on the bloody dashboard of a truck, but now I have it again. Emerson did that." He lowered his hand to the rail of the stretcher. "I was fading in that hospital. Not from the gunshot or the morphine. After what I did to get Dad to Texas, I wanted to die."

"You killed someone, Wes." Irene's voice was a near whisper.

"I did. I remember every fucking detail of it. And back at Uvalde Memorial, I was ready to give myself up to the police. I tried to help Dad, and in the process, I hurt countless others."

Wes raised a palm as Irene went to speak, silencing her before he continued.

"But then Emerson was in my room. I didn't know who he was. He... he put a hand over me. Moved things where they needed to be. The broken bone in my leg grew back. My finger regenerated."

Wes's gaze faded, as if he was watching the memory in his mind.

"He reached through me, even though he never touched me. And once he fixed the physical damage, Emerson did something else. I don't know how; I don't know what he changed, Irene. But he removed my addictions too. I could..." His gaze shifted, returning to the room. "They were just... missing."

Irene shook her head. "I've heard you say that enough times not to believe it. And you live on a fucking pot farm, Wes. I can't even begin—"

"I don't care if you believe it," Wes retorted, his tone matter-of-fact and lacking the emotional turbulence Irene was expecting. "What you believe has nothing to do with the truth."

Irene held the rest of her words.

Wes sighed, then continued. "After that, he stretched beyond me. Into the hospital. He stood there shaking on a stool next to my bed. His reach shot through me, and I was a part of it. With each soul he connected with, I could feel him fixing their bodies too. He went searching, and I realized what he wanted. Who he was looking for. His mother."

"Blair?" Irene confirmed.

Wes nodded, his focus returning to her.

"She was forty-three rooms away, Irene. Emerson healed every single person between him and his mother until he reached her. And then he restored her too."

Irene thought back to that day—what local news had called the Uvalde Exodus. She'd found herself in the thick of it. Patients exiting their rooms. Some were coherent, others mystified and lost. They had all displayed the same sudden and miraculous improvement in their health, but the outcomes were not all positive.

"I remember," she croaked. "A bunch of people hurt themselves."

Wes nodded. "The kid didn't realize what he was doing. He didn't even know he was able to do what he did. Until he did it." Her brother stood, rubbing his scalp as if the recollection was rain clinging to his hair. "It terrified him, what happened. Hell, it scared the shit out of me too!"

Irene studied him in his silence, looking for his tells that he was making this up: the tic in the corner of his mouth, or his stare popping up to hers to check if his story was holding together. She noticed none of them.

"How did you get here?" she asked.

Wes's sad eyes found hers. "I ran, Irene. I took Emerson, and I ran out of that room. We stole a car from the parking lot, drove to Utopia, and waited for Emerson's parents to come home."

"You ran from the cops," Irene said.

"I got the kid out of that shitshow," he corrected. "And before you dig in your heels, I wanted to turn myself in once Emerson was safe."

"Why didn't you?"

"Jaime talked me out of it. Offered me a life. Protection. Emerson seems to admire me, and I think that had something to do with it."

Irene sighed. "So you skirted the consequences?"

Now Wes smirked, and his gaze floated up, through the wall, to something distant. "I changed them, sis. I needed to stay near Emerson. Help him however I could. That boy will change the world. And after all the energy I spent destroying it, I figured helping him is a way to..."

"Atone?" she asked.

Wes thought for a moment, then nodded. "Jaime moved us here, to the ranch. But it wasn't a ranch then; it was nothing but kennels and unused land. When the state legalized pot, we started the farm. We built up a closed life to protect Emerson."

"And you," Irene added. "This ranch protects you too."

Wes sighed. His expression was glazed, his face drawn and tired. "In a way," he whispered, "but it doesn't come free."

She wasn't certain how to take his words. There was no deference of responsibility in his demeanor like she'd expected. Just a look of sadness. A wide emotional space opened between them, and Irene realized that the last two years had been much longer than they'd seemed. She shook off the empathy.

"You said I was here before?" she asked.

Her brother's eyes rose with his breath. He turned and walked across the room, approaching a large metal cabinet. Drawers clanged open and closed as he searched.

"If that's true, why don't I remember it?" she pressed.

Another clattering drawer, and Wes went to grab something as he started speaking.

"Just above us is a tower at the center of the marijuana field. Every night, Emerson and I climb up that tower, and he uses his power to heal the crops." He slammed the drawer and turned around, an object buried in his grip. Wes approached the bed once more. "Emerson makes them grow. Between the drought and the cheap dirt, it's the only way we can farm anything here."

Her gaze flicked from his hand to his face. Sadness pulled his lips in a worry.

"When he heals that way, at a distance, it's... indiscriminate. Things don't always come together as you'd expect. You saw it in Uvalde, right?"

Irene didn't want to recall—patients wandering off, their bodies rejecting their medical adornments like oil in water. Breathing tubes, IVs, catheters scattered in pools of effluvium and blood throughout the hallways of the hospital. She closed her eyes, letting the haze of the painkiller blur the thought.

She nodded once.

"Four days ago, me and him climbed the steps up the tower. We stood on the platform and Emerson did his thing. He restored the farm."

His attention went to the object in his palm. He considered it, rolled it in his fingers before continuing.

"Then there was screaming. In the field below us. Security rushed in, and... It was you, Irene. You were hiding among the crops. Security found you because you wouldn't stop shrieking.

I flew down the steps, ready to shoot, and once I saw it was you, I realized what was happening."

Wes's eyes popped to hers. He held up the item so she could see it: a small piece of bent gray metal with several holes in it. Irene studied the object, trying to make sense of its shape—organic and curved, but precise.

"What the hell is that?" she asked.

Wes smirked. "I guess you've never seen this before." He tilted his head and brought the metal to his cheek, placing it beneath the joint of his jaw. Her pulse jolted, an anxiety the drugs couldn't tamp down.

"This is your steel plate, Irene. The one you got after I broke your jaw. You were there, hidden in the plants, watching us. And so Emerson mended you when he restored the field."

On reflex, Irene reached for her mouth, seeking to feel her jaw joint, but the restraints kept her hands in place.

"Your body did what bodies do when they're in Emerson's field of influence. It healed. And by doing so, it rejected this steel plate. Forced the screws right out of your bones."

"Bullshit," she said. Another reflex, as her fingers reached once more for her jaw.

Wes shook his head and dropped the plate on the surgical tray. He leaned over her and worked off one restraint, holding her arm as he said, "We ran you here, to this room. Robin had to cut this out of you. Excise the screws from your flesh."

Her hand came free, and she shot it to her mandible, fingers pressing and searching for the rigid bumps she expected there. Waiting for the pinch of her flesh against the flange of the plate.

Tactile sensations her body and mind had grown to accept as normal.

Her pulse raced when she discovered them missing.

"What the hell?" she gasped. Her gaze switched from nothing in front of her to her brother's face and found it drawn with regret. "I'd fucking remember that, Wes!"

Her brother eased her arm back into the restraint, and then he went to the metal cabinet once more. He opened the top drawer, grabbed something, and returned to her.

"This," he said as he lifted the object. "This is the reason you have no memory of being here."

Wes pulled a plastic cap off the cylinder in his grip, revealing a long, thin needle. The thing looked similar to an EpiPen, a single dose of epinephrine someone might use if they were allergic to a bee sting. Before she asked, Wes continued. "It's a hypodermic form of Rohypnol. Has a sedating effect, but we use it because it scrambles recent memories."

The meaning clicked together despite her mental fog. "You... dosed me? With a date-rape drug?"

Wes shrugged. "I mean... that's not what we use it for, but... yeah, I did. I had to."

Her stomach fell, the nausea caused by her injury augmented with revulsion at what Wes had done to her. Wes placed the hypodermic on the tray and sat on the stool near her gurney. He came for her hand and, unable to pull it out of the restraints, Irene balled her fingers into a fist. She wanted to punch him, hurt him even in some small way. The beginning of her retribution for his assault.

But Wes's hand clamped hers, and his other hand joined the pile of fingers. "Irene, listen," he said, his voice straining but not bitter. Concerned.

"Fuck you!" she spat.

"I get that you're angry, but you need to understand..." Wes's voice tensed. His expression hardened.

"Go to hell!"

"Irene!" he snapped. The authority in his tone was unnerving. She found herself expecting admonition, as if Wes had become the grown-up and she had just broken the cookie jar.

Her brother's stare penetrated into hers. His lips tightened again, even as they trembled.

"Irene, I had to dose you." His voice warbled as he spoke, the sound familiar to Irene. Indicative of the emotions rushing through her brother. Regret. Surrender. "There was no choice! I had to use this on you. I had to, because the alternative..." Tears fell over his cheeks.

Irene swallowed the lump in her throat. Around the shock, through the nausea and anger, the resignation in Wes's demeanor left a tingle of fear in her.

"What was the alternative, Wes?"

Wes gulped, then wiped his eyes.

"Killing you. And I wouldn't do that, Irene. Not when there was another option."

Chapter Thirty-Eight

B lair reseated her grip on the TASER and double-checked the safety was disabled.

"Emerson!" Blair cried. "Come to me, honey!"

The world scuttled in the breeze and rain. Quick bursts of wind rolled over the farm like waves on water, giving her momentary glimpses deeper into the sea of plants. The closed space amplified the noise of the storm. She wondered if there was any hope of being heard over the racket. Whipping leaves mimicked speech sounds, spinning her around as her mind kept finding voices where there were none.

Mom... The air howled behind her, mocking her search for her child.

She scanned the aisle, the tower lights forcing her to shield her eyes so she could see. The corridor was fluid in the storm.

"Mom!" The sound came from the other direction now. Blair followed as the wind cascaded over the field, and she glimpsed motion a dozen feet from her. The harsh sodium lights highlighted details—mud-soaked clothing and wide eyes that locked onto hers.

"Emerson?" she hollered. "Emerson, is that you?"

The roiling thicket swallowed the figure, but Blair knew what she'd seen. Her son, running to her. She moved in that direction, taking only a few strides before Emerson barreled around the bushy base of a plant and rammed into her.

His arms closed tight around her middle, and his head buried into her stomach. Blair hugged his head into her belly with her free arm, the other keeping the weapon pointed to the ground.

Emerson mumbled into her. Blair released her hold on him, and his gaze rose to hers. His eyes drooped with exhaustion, and his filthy cheeks were streaked from the lines of tears or rain, Blair wasn't sure which.

"We gotta go," he said.

"We are!" she replied, clamping her hand around his. "C'mon, let's get to the house. We'll be safe there." Her heart raced, knowing an invisible threat loomed close. She stomped down the path, heading the way she had come, the electric pistol pointed in front of her.

Emerson tugged against her. Without turning around, Blair yanked back, her son's weight shifting towards her.

"Mom," he cried. "Mom, wait!"

"No talking, Em. We gotta be quick, now!" She took another handful of steps, scanning the rumbling field for danger. The light was behind her, revealing a torrent of movement ahead. Whipping leaves reached for her. For her son. Green fingers that craved to snag them and pull them into the thicket. Flickers of light through the thick drops of falling rain looked like muzzle flashes—countless guns aimed at their heads.

Emerson's hand pulled out of hers. Blair spun, clenching a wad of his T-shirt.

"Keep moving," she hissed. Her son's emotional needs had to wait until they were safe. "We're in danger—"

"Not that way!" Emerson cried. Loud enough to expose them to the hidden evils out there.

Her grip left his shirt. It rose, and before Blair could fight the impulse, she watched her palm fly across Emerson's face.

In her adrenaline rush, she had hit Emerson harder than usual. He rocked on his heels, stumbling over himself, before splatting to the muddy ground.

"Goddammit, Emerson!" she hissed. "Keep your voice down and let's go! Our lives are in jeopardy here!"

Emerson tested his cheek with his fingertips, and Blair's heart crumbled. His gaze bored into her. He was stunned. Shocked. Not at their predicament, but at her. Her gut tumbled with a mix of fear and regret.

"I'm sorry," she said, speaking low. She stooped to him, cupping a hand to his shoulder.

Emerson scrambled out of her reach.

"Emerson, someone's killing people on the ranch," she explained. "Your Uncle Terry... he's dead. We need to—"

"I know!" Her child's voice came out hard. His expression sharpened to an edge. "I know Uncle Terry's dead!"

She spotted it then. Around the edge of his face, where the security lights erased the shadows. A rusty color in the streaks her fingers had left through the muck on his cheeks. Not the beige of the Texas clay, not the dark umber of the topsoil. Red, a vile shade of it.

"Oh, God," she whispered as she leaned closer to him. "God, Emerson, are you bleeding? Emerson I am so—"

"No!" Her son stretched away from her again. "This is Uncle Terry's blood, not mine!"

A stillness formed between them, even as the field rustled and the shower persisted. The facts clicked together. "You saw Uncle Terry get shot?"

Emerson nodded. His fingers stayed on his jaw, and his stare narrowed as he studied her. Blair swallowed her guilt at striking him, yet her cheeks flared hot, a stain of shame that the rain couldn't wash away.

"You shouldn't hit me," Emerson scolded. His tone was firm, carrying a confidence Blair had never heard from him. He rose to his feet, his palm still rubbing his bruised cheek. "If you loved me, you wouldn't hurt me!" His voice boomed out and faded into the turbulent haze.

Blair pulled herself up too. Her hands smoothed her denim shirt, the fabric heavy with moisture and clinging against her. The terrified and angry look on Emerson's face tore apart the story she had in her head—that she was his beacon of safety, his protector. She had never seen this side of her son.

She drew in a breath through the rain, a second apology forming on her tongue as water dripped from her lips.

"You know what?"

This voice wasn't the wind. Too close. The words enunciated in a familiar tone that sparked fear.

Blair spun on her feet, wobbling from the ebb of the earlier adrenaline. A man stood a few steps away, blocking their way out of the farm. In the brutal glow of the security lamps, Blair saw the swirls and bubbles of flesh that made up his face. His mismatched eyes, one sharp and hazel, the other a clouded, useless, milky blue.

Blair's gaze fell to the gaping barrel of the pistol in his hand, then back up to his burned face. She backed a step from the man and towards her son.

His patchwork flesh stretched into a sneer, and the expression pulled on something deep in Blair's emotional memory.

"The kid makes a brilliant point, Blair."

Chapter Thirty-Nine

At the burned man's growl, Mom's halo burst with white shock. She spun to face the man, and her light dissolved into sickly greens and tans. The edges of it trembled like when she argued with Jaime over money.

Emerson had a full view of the man now. Even from Emerson's prone position, with the stranger looming above him, a piece of what made the man a threat disappeared. The lanky arms showed through the sopping wet flannel, turning the oversized gun in his hand cartoonish. His frame was mousy, his posture stooped.

A strange sensation bubbled through Emerson—similar to the anxious static of seeing Layla and her crutches. It was guilt over this man. A sorrow at his condition. Emerson wanted to put hands on him, make his physical body right again. To reshape the monster's light until he was a monster no longer.

But the stranger's aura—against the glow of the tower lights, Emerson saw it well now. Not a halo, but a barbed, tar-colored rope, twisting around itself into powerful coils. It flailed out from him in violent whips as his body stood still. The glassy black wisps reached towards his mother, probing the edges of her shaking halo for a way inside. Each tentacle circled her as if to isolate her from the world.

Once again, Emerson didn't understand how the stranger was able to do such a thing. His own light focused in a single direction when he healed people like Nacho. A flashlight piercing the dark. But this man, his aura became another arm with countless fingers. An extension of the man's scarred body and mind. He controlled it in ways Emerson hadn't known were possible.

"You should be ashamed to call yourself his mother!" The monster's voice crackled over the wind's bustle.

The tentacles of ebony light tightened around Mom. Flecks of her terrified green crawled back along those obsidian fingers.

Her body shuddered. What the hell was he doing to her?

The man's gaze left Mom's face, and it fell onto Emerson's.

"Come with me," he said through tight lips. "I can give you a life these people can't. I can help you—"

A blue spark appeared over the man's mysterious aura, over the flood of the tower security lights. At first, Emerson wasn't sure if it was part of the strange halo, but the man's physical reaction made it obvious that it wasn't.

Emerson followed the glint of the thin metal wire to the TASER in Mom's hand. The weapon emitted a harsh sound—*clack, clack, clack, clack!*—and the scarred man collapsed in a heap.

Mom grabbed Emerson's hand and yanked him to his feet. Her fingers had a lock on him as she started running towards the tower. Emerson's feet flopped under him, uncoordinated, frantic to keep his mother's pace.

A howl ripped through the air. A scream that Emerson knew wasn't from bodily pain. This was emotion. If the sound was a color, it was the blaze at the core of a forest fire.

Emerson chanced a look back. The monster rolled on the ground, his hands flapping against the wires. He tugged them out of his body. The man's black light expanded, throbbing into frantic whips that battered the living auras around him.

"Jaime!" Mom's holler drew Emerson's attention forward to where another dark figure emerged from the field ahead.

The shadow's thick arms and violet light were around them before the details of Jaime's face formed out of the shadows.

"C'mon!" he huffed. "Let's get you safe!"

Jaime took Mom's hand, and the three of them chained into the field. Jaime led them with purpose, but not to the tower. Instead, he moved away from the aisle. Emerson's fingers clamped around his mother's palm, her desperate panic obvious in her death grip: *Don't let go or we'll lose you.*

Soon the tower was behind them, along with most of the ranch. Ahead, Emerson made out the crescent of steep hills that marked the southern boundary of Utopia Farms. They were running out of field.

"Where are we going?" The words flopped out of his mouth, clumsy as his feet as he tried to keep pace with the adults.

"Here," Jaime said. The tug of Jaime's strength carried through his mother's arm as they rounded a wide wedge of concrete planted in the ground. Jaime drove them around the far side, shoving Blair behind the short wall. Emerson saw something like the cellar door on their house—wide metal double doors with thick handles and hinges the size of his fingers. But the doors didn't connect to a structure. They lay between two bunches of crop, surrounded by a frame of concrete.

Before Emerson was able to ask what it was, Jaime was hissing into his radio. "Hawk? We're at the door! Open the damned thing!"

"On it, Boss! One second!" Not Hawk. Layla's mother. Dr. Travers.

Jaime stooped behind the concrete baffle with them, his eyes moving across the surrounding field. His gun drawn, pointed back the way they had come. Emerson scanned the space too, watching for the black light. Waiting for it to slither from the swaying stalks of the field.

A tinge of color pulled his gaze to the right. It was the orange of Layla's mother again. And like before, with Layla and Chris, it radiated from the earth below them. The aura glided through the earth, effortlessly, until it slid beneath them.

The light paused at the cellar doors as Jaime's radio crackled.

A series of metal coughs chuffed behind the doors. Jaime was shifting, gun still pointed into the field. His thick fingers wrapped the handle on the door, and he heaved. As the door moved, the rumble of the hinges rattled in Emerson's bones, and a horrific squeal shattered the air as metal and rust ground together.

Emerson recognized the sound—it was the metallic scream of the monster in the dirt, from when Layla's mom had started to crawl out of the ground. A part of his panic crumbled. There was no creature under the farm. The scream he heard had a source, the underground aura an explanation.

Jaime ushered them to the open door, where Emerson found concrete steps leading into a dark space. There, Dr. Travers waited, hands beckoning for him to climb down as a waft of cool air tickled his face. Emerson launched to the steps, his hand still locked in his mother's as she followed him into the dim passage.

His eyes adjusted as Layla's mom pulled back a heavy curtain, revealing a lighted hallway made of metal. Two figures solidified in the changing light.

A shudder of relief rattled his chest. Layla and Chris both ran to him, their feet clomping against the plywood floor, and Emerson hugged his two friends again.

Everyone was safe, and they were together once more.

Thunder boomed behind him. Emerson startled. As he spun to the bunker door, another recognition formed in his head. It wasn't thunder, but a sound he had heard earlier. It was the sound of Uncle Terry dying.

The explosive eruption had come from the burned man's massive gun.

Chapter Forty

H awk swallowed, hoping that his blunt honesty had clarified her drug-blurred thoughts.

"What?" A tremble ran through Irene's voice. An audible chink in her armor. "You'd kill me to protect yourself?"

"No. Like I said, I wouldn't do that. I never wanted to kill anyone, Irene. But I'm not in charge here. And Jaime and Blair let me live on this compound, as long as I meet their terms. But the compound doesn't exist to hide me. It's for Emerson."

Irene's eyes defocused as she considered that.

"They're trying to keep him a secret," she said. Her tone was mild now, thoughtful. She wasn't asking a question; she was stating the answer.

He smiled at her intelligence, her ability to see the next piece before it was on the board. It was something he had missed about her. A skill he wished he possessed.

"Yeah, that's the meat of it. Blair and Jaime, they don't want to draw attention to the kid. Hard to do when folks witness miracles whenever he's around."

Her gaze rose to the corrugated metal ceiling. A look Hawk recognized as her thinking face. Staring at nothing to see everything. Her lips worked as she rolled an idea around in her mouth.

"So you drug people so they forget?"

Hawk nodded. "Yeah."

"Does it always work?"

Hawk swallowed and shook his head. He hoped the implication was obvious to her.

Her gaze crawled to his. Sadness fell over her features.

"So if the drug hadn't worked on me..."

He let the question hang in silence for a moment. "But it did work. At least, we thought so. Then you showed up today."

His sister clenched her eyes shut, her head shaking the dust from her mind.

"Jesus, Wes. I don't remember any of it. The only reason I'm here today is because Finch brought me, I swear."

"I trust you, Irene. But my boss won't. We've run out of leash with him."

Her expression soured with confusion. "We?"

Hawk sighed, a flush of shame warming his cheeks. "I bartered, Irene. Two years ago. Wes Allard was a fugitive. There was no place for him outside of Utopia Farms. And he knew the kid's power, so... there weren't many options. But I saw an opportunity. I offered to work the compound, help protect Emerson from the world."

Irene considered his words, her gaze shifting with her thoughts.

"The attention around Emerson at Uvalde. Around the cop that..." Hawk stopped to reconsider his words. The highway patrolman hadn't just died. "The cop I murdered. It tapered off. I mean, except for—"

"Except for me," she finished the thought.

Hawk smiled. "I didn't realize you were in Texas until we discovered you in the field, Irene. I assumed you had returned to Boston after Pop's death. But you hadn't," he added, motioning to her in the gurney.

"After Robin excised your jaw plate and Emerson healed you, we tried to figure out how you'd found me. How you'd ended up on the compound. Who knew you were here. We questioned you for hours but got nothing out of you. You kept telling us you didn't know. That you simply woke up in the field, screaming."

His sister's gaze fell to the bed. To her wounded leg. Her skin reddened. Hawk recognized that shade, and that it meant frustration was building inside Irene.

He sighed and continued, "I believe you. Jaime doesn't. You saw the boy's talent; you learned I'm on the ranch—two problems that go away as long as the roofie pen was effective. But it was clear to Jaime, and to me, that even if you couldn't remember finding me—"

"That I'd keep searching. That I'd find you again," she offered, her tone quieting with introspection.

"Exactly."

Several breaths passed, Irene's rapid thoughts plain on her mumbling lips.

"Jaime wanted to kill you, right then." Hawk studied the rusting operating room. "Right here, in fact. But we talked him out of it."

"Again with the 'we.' What does that mean, Wes?"

"It means literally that. We—you and I—created an alternative. Something to keep you alive and let Jaime keep his indentured servant."

She fidgeted in her restraints, her arms pulling against the belts. "How, Wes? I'm never going to stop searching for you until—"

"But you found me," he interrupted. "Didn't you?"

Irene stilled in the bed. Hawk could see the logic train clicking together for her. Her eyes widened.

"The morgue," she started. "The body in the morgue, it's..." She shook her head, sense competing with her own perceptions.

"That was me in the morgue. And it's me here, right now, talking to you."

"The kid... Emerson..."

Hawk placed a steadying hand on her shoulder. Her frame trembled under his palm.

"Wes Allard had to die, Irene. He had to die, and you had to find him. It was the only way you'd run back to your life. The police get their killer, and Jaime and Blair keep their confidant."

The stunned expression stayed on her face.

"Jaime took Em up in the tower three nights ago. I was here with Robin—the doctor. While the kid was healing the field, she was taking a chainsaw to me." Hawk put a finger on his left shoulder, and drew a line above his heart, then down his chest to the base of his rib cage.

Irene's eyes and mouth expanded with horror. "Jesus fucking Christ, Wes!"

"They sedated me," he offered, trying to soothe her disgust. "Didn't feel a thing."

"But how could you be sure that... how did you know whe ther..." Her hands flexed in the cuffs, her fingers drawing in the air.

A sheepish smile stretched his face, and for the first time in days, it didn't bust a split in his chapped lips.

"We—Robin and I—we've done experiments on it. Well, I guess she does the experimenting. I'm one of the guinea pigs. We have a decent handle on what happens when Emerson heals severed limbs." Hawk looked over his shoulder, towards the hallway. "Robin's got a catalog in her office, documenting what we can and can't do."

"They just... grow back?" she asked, incredulous. "Even your head?"

With a shrug, Hawk replied, "Depends. On lots of things. The doc had to keep my body alive as she cut it apart, all while Emerson was doing his magic. But the short version is yes. In fact," he had to chuckle to hide his discomfort at the memory, "my new head was there before the old one hit the floor. I was able to watch it happen."

Irene swallowed her gorge. Her eyes shut, as if holding in her thoughts until they made sense. "So the Wes in the morgue was..."

"Think of that corpse as 'leftover Wes.' The half of me that didn't get healed."

Her head cratered into the pillow, like the story was sitting heavy in her mind. A jarring squeal echoed from the hall. The outer door opening. Hawk patted his sister's shoulder, turning to look her in the eyes.

"Irene, I will not let them do anything to you. Do you understand? We'll figure something out."

Her expression froze with shock. "Yeah, okay."

He grinned, trying to send a bit of calm to his sister. "Sounds like Boss is here with Emerson. We'll have your leg better than new, sis."

Hawk rose, giving her hand one last squeeze before he turned to the hallway.

"Wes?" his sister called.

He smiled back at her as he walked away. "Call me Hawk."

In the thrum of rain on the ground above, a tremendous crackle split the air. The sound slapped against the metal walls, reverberating in his bones.

A gunshot. Not inside the bunker, but still fucking loud. His ease evaporated. Hawk drew his Glock and pressed himself against the wall of the operating room. Holding a breath, he bounced his head around the corner, taking in the shelter in a blink.

Blair, Robin, and the kids. Not just Chris and Layla, but Emerson too. Crouched in the hallway. Beyond them, Jaime slumped over at the base's threshold, a heavy trail of blood leading up the steps, streaks of rain visible through the open bunker door.

Chapter Forty-One

F inch squeezed the trigger. The Desert Eagle shattered the air and kicked in his grip.

A dozen feet away, red spatter painted the open door, the bullet passing through Jaime's gut and ricocheting against the metal with a clang.

Jaime flailed, and his handgun flew from his fingers and landed somewhere in the muck behind the shelter door. Gravity carried him forward, and his body disappeared into the earth.

Finch ran, willing his stiff legs to bend farther than they should, for his feet to find stable land beneath him. Light poured out of the portal in the ground, casting disorienting upward shadows in the field.

He had to get to that door. Emerson was there, just beyond that steel barrier. Finch had reached him, and it was only a matter of time before Emerson came to his side. And Finch realized what Jaime or Blair would do to keep Emerson here.

Only a few feet stood between him and the bunker door, but his rigid and stumbling gait made it longer. The interior wall came into view, a smear of Jaime's blood tracing the steps that descended into that unknown space.

A hand reached from the dugout, and a head of curly blonde hair broke over the concrete baffle. Thick fingers gripped the interior handle of the open door.

"No," Finch grunted. Just three strides away. "Don't!"

The face turned. A woman, her terrified expression melting to horror as their eyes met.

"Close that fucking door!" A scream from the shelter. A man. Not Jaime's bellowing voice. Someone else.

Finch raised the gun. Clutched the weapon before he aimed. Another bullet rang off the metal as it fell. The boom of the shot dissipated, replaced by the clatter of the steel hitting concrete.

Finch dropped the pistol. His fingers moved under the handle, his arm and back heaving against the door. Against the person on the other side hauling it shut.

The door lifted an inch. Two inches. A tingle of hope fed his tired muscles, and Finch moved his fingers towards the gap. As they found a hold, the weight of the door multiplied. His grasp slipped off the handle. The door rammed closed against the concrete threshold with a final dull *thud*.

The tingle developed to a static in his chest. He clutched the handle with both hands. He heaved up, a strain racking his torso to its broken limit, and Finch heard the grinding of his own teeth through his bones as he struggled.

The muscles in his back screamed, and something tore in his belly as he struggled. The metal resisted. On the *clang* of a lock bolt hitting home, Finch realized he'd lost. He let go, stumbling away on numb feet until his legs gave up too. He panted on the wet ground, staring up into the rain cascading from the tepid gray sky, listening to the sequence of locks being engaged from inside the shelter.

A tremble ran up his thighs, then engaged his torso. Fatigue. Or maybe an echo of the TASER. Blair had landed one barb in his sternum, but the other had nicked the fabric of his shirt sleeve. It was an unlucky shot for Blair, but his soaked clothing had helped the weapon arc through him once before his flailing knocked the dart loose. The pain of the shock remained, an itch in his bones and tissues surging at random times. He closed his eyes against the rain, the sear of the pepper spray blooming under his eyelid.

He had come so close. Sacrificed Irene, then put his own life on the line. All to reach Emerson. The sounds of those locks slamming were hammers driving nails into the coffin of his plan.

No! His powerful mind revolted against his feeble body. The boy couldn't stay here. Finch wouldn't give up, not now. Not until Emerson was safe. The mud gurgled as he rose to his feet. He studied the door. The hinges were solid, the bolts hidden from him beneath the bulk of metal. The concrete appeared sturdy, a single piece instead of mortared cinder block that would easily break apart.

His fingers wrapped around the warm metal handle. His arm tensed, Finch careful not to cause further damage to himself. The door didn't give, not one millimeter. They'd secured it from the inside, and without applying massive force Finch didn't have, it would stay locked.

An exhausted rage boiled in his gut. Finch forced it to linger there. Useless thoughts paced in his head: beat the door; shoot it. None of that would do any good. His body left him the un-derdog in any physical confrontation. At least he had a chance with people—if his hands touched them, he was able to tear their psyches apart with his power. But this door was nothing but matter. There was no mind to manipulate. No desires to bore out. No thirst to stoke.

This was no longer a battle of physical or psychic will. Finch had to out-think Blair and Jaime to save Emerson.

His gaze moved to his feet. The Desert Eagle lay in the mud, next to a thick chain and heavy padlock. His back muscles screaming, he stooped to the ground, lifted the gun, and wiped it clean with his grungy shirt tail. He pulled the action and checked the barrel for debris. It was clear.

His gun held seven of the large-caliber rounds. He had used two so far. One for Terry, one for Jaime. No, three—he had forgotten the potshot he'd taken at whoever had closed the bunker. Almost half of his ammunition was gone, but it didn't matter. Even with infinite bullets, the steel would never yield to the pistol. He seated the weapon in the waist of his jeans, over his tailbone.

Finch felt a tickle in his mind. The shadow of an aggressive idea shaping as facts connected to each other. He lifted the chain and lock, a silver metal snake with a thick round head rattling in his hand.

He knew it was impossible to force his way into the shelter. At least for now. But he'd damned well make sure Emerson and the others didn't leave it.

Chapter Forty-Two

J aime should have made noise as he toppled down the concrete steps, but Emerson's ears were packed with the same
sonorous ringing that had marked the death of his uncle. Indigo
light scattered with Jaime's blood, wisps of his aura sticking to
the walls and floor, then fading into nothing. Around his prone
body, the halo stretched, thinning out. There was a flicker in it,
like Uncle Terry's right before he died. Emerson held his breath,
expecting the glint to disappear too.

Someone shoved past him. Layla's mother, checking Jaime.
Murmurs pressed into the air, words he could not recognize
over the buzz in his head. She reared at Emerson, eyes wide. She
waved him closer with a bloodstained hand.

"Heal him!" Her face screamed, but her voice was a hum in
his stuffy ears.

Emerson moved to Jaime. The man lay on his stomach, his
aura splitting with widening gaps of emptiness. Death was almost on him.

Emerson's hand hovered over Jaime's lower back, the spot
where the light was most accessible and tender. He slid his fingers in, and Jaime's halo righted to its crisp violet as the damage

to his gut repaired at Emerson's will. A cough and groan escaped the man's mouth, and then he was getting on his feet.

The ringing cleared, replaced by the sound of Robin's terrified yells.

"Someone help me! He's going to get it open!"

Jaime lunged, his massive fist wrapping the door's handle, and the door fell flush against the concrete.

"Close the locks!" Jaime hissed. Layla's mom worked around him, slapping bolts closed along the seam of the door, each emitting a thick metal grunt.

Emerson left bloody handprints as he crawled away from the steps. The reassuring arms of his mother enveloped him, and he leaned into her.

Jaime clung to the handle, using his weight to keep it secure. Dr. Travers flattened herself against the far wall, making space for Hawk to come to the doors. Everyone in the strange underground hallway waited, watched, listened.

A hush pressed the silence, the way air conditioning filled the room with sound at home. A low static that soaked them from above.

Rain. It was the hum of the rain on the ground.

Jaime eased his fingers off the handle and retreated down the steps. Hawk's hand went to his shoulder; his other pointed a gun at the metal door. The pressure on Emerson's chest grew as Mom squeezed him tighter.

Everyone's gazes fixed on the door, and their ears struggled to hear over the sizzle of rain.

"What is this place?"

Mom's voice made Emerson jump, a rush of panic welling in him even as his mother's tone remained calm.

Jaime turned to Mom, his core violet and blue, tainted with a curious brassy overtone. Emerson's fear relaxed to confusion at the change in color. He knew Jaime's aura well, could read the man like a comic book. He knew what was about to happen.

Jaime was going to lie to his mother.

"It's a storm shelter and a first-aid station," Jaime wheezed. He cleared his throat, the stress of lying showing up as copper pins and needles in his light.

"In the middle of the damned farm?" Blair asked.

Jaime stepped past them, motioning for Hawk to follow. Then he looked at Mom. His smile gleamed between his cheeks. His eyebrows rose, eyes earnest and forthright. But his halo told the truth.

"Where else would the workers go if a twister hit?" he asked.

Another lustrous deception.

Hawk and Jaime continued into the bunker, towards Dr. Travers's office door. Emerson turned away, tucking his face into Mom's shoulder as she adjusted her clutch on him. Emerson listened as Jaime argued with Hawk. Their conversation became muffled in whispers.

Emerson raised his head until his lips rested against his mother's ear.

He summoned an image of a butterfly coasting on the air. He would speak softer than that butterfly's wings, so there would be no chance of Jaime detecting his words.

"Mom?" he whispered.

She nodded. *Go ahead. I heard you.* A clomp behind him. Someone approaching. It was Hawk or Jaime.

"Jaime's lying to you."

A hand worked under his arm, and Emerson looked up into Hawk's blue eyes. His mouth pitched in worry, and as he spoke, Emerson could see the tremor on his lips.

"Emerson, we need you right now," Hawk said. "Please, come with us."

A grunt squeaked from Emerson's throat as his mom squeezed him tighter to her chest.

"Not today, Hawk," she sighed. "I'm not letting this kid out of my sight."

"Please," Hawk whispered. "My sister is here; she needs his help."

Mom's eyes widened. The tension in her arms slacked. At a nudge from Hawk, Emerson stuck a hand up the wall and stood.

Her mouth seemed to work faster than her brain. "How... how did she—"

"We don't know." The boom of Jaime's voice rattled the metal wall under Emerson's palm. It made his words bigger. Gave them a physical presence. "We need Emerson to help us find out."

Emerson unclenched his eyes. Jaime was over him, replacing Hawk's gentle hand with his own monstrous grip. He spun Emerson and hauled him through the hallway. As when Jaime had been dragging them through the field, Emerson's feet stumbled to keep pace with the gigantic man's stride.

Mom snapped behind them, "Where are you taking him?"

"Stay here, Blair," Jaime called back. "It'll be a few minutes."

"Wait!" Mom ordered. She pounded a fist against the wall, rattling the air the length of the hallway.

Jaime stopped, whipping Emerson around so they both faced Mom. Expressions of anger and meekness flopped across her face.

"What the hell is this place, Jaime?"

Silence. Pressure grew from Jaime's grip. Then, over the purr of rain, a sigh crept between Jaime's lips.

"I need to know who the fuck is running around our land. Who's shooting the shit out of our family. At the end of this hall, Hawk's sister is bleeding out. She knows who this asshole is. I'm taking Emerson back there to heal her. So she'll stay alive and tell us what the hell is going on."

Through the deep throbs of Jaime's purple indignation, Emerson watched his mom's halo rotate, spirals of piercing red struggling with a tame pink. Anger, mixed with confusion and fear.

Jaime continued, his tone stern and condescending, "Or we can wait here. Let her die. And take our chances with however many gunmen are waiting out there."

"I just want to understand—"

"So do I, Blair!" Jaime yelled. The surrounding aura pulsed with orange. Impatience. The color of having something better to do. "I want to understand how today turned into this shit-show! I want to know who smacked my guts against the bunker door!"

Mom shrank as he hollered, her reds turning to yellows.

"So unless you have some clue as to who Mr. Man-with-out-a-face-shooting-a-fucking-hand-cannon is up there?" He pointed up, gesturing to the ground above them.

Mom shook her head. Her face tight, like she'd swallowed something bitter. Diminutive silvers sliced through her halo. "Of course I don't."

Jaime turned away, pulling Emerson with him once more. "Then give us fifteen minutes."

Emerson's head whirled back, and he fixated on his mother's aura as Jaime pulled him away.

The bland words. Her hurt face. A voice from a dry throat. Her posture bent and submissive. Emerson tried to read it. Tried to reconcile what her body and words were telling him against the silver flecks of deception in her light. But he couldn't.

Mom had just lied too.

Chapter Forty-Three

The restraint slipped another half inch. Irene narrowed her hand, trying to compress her fingers and thumb to slip through the cuff. Since her brother had removed and reapplied the leather restraint, some give had appeared. Her wrist twisted inside the belt, and she could slip it up and down her forearm. A few inches, but it was something.

Voices continued to echo from outside the room. The stress level had dropped out there, but in Irene, tension wound into a tight coil. Over her injury and the drugs holding off her misery, fear hummed through her. She needed to get out of here, busted leg be damned.

Honesty wasn't a characteristic she associated with Wes. His assessment had taken time to settle in, but the implication was clear: whatever this place was, it was much worse than Wes was letting on. Because things were always worse than Wes let on.

She rotated her hand, struggling to catch the bulk of her thumb joint in the small gap where the cuff overlapped itself. Her bones didn't want to rotate that far, but Irene kept pushing through the building pressure on her shoulder and elbow. The painkillers were ebbing, bringing the edge back to her thoughts but also letting through signals of her trauma. Her torso shifted as she worked the arm around another few degrees, and her destroyed leg blazed with agony.

She froze, waiting for the wave to dissipate, struggling to control her shaking breath, trying not to scream. Her eyes closed, a haze of red pulsing with each crest of pain.

She opened them to find an enormous man filling her view. Something in his size, his dark features, pulled a thread in her memory. It wasn't until Irene saw the child with him that the pieces clicked together.

She'd seen them before. The day Dad died.

"You..." she huffed, more breath than sound.

The wall of a man smiled over her. He dragged the child closer to the gurney. "I was going to say the same thing." His voice was as big as his frame, and its reverberation against the metal box gave it an omnipresence.

Her body tensed, arms and legs taking the slack from the restraints. A primal reaction to the man's dangerous energy.

"What the fuck are you going to do?" Her voice warbled, her welling fear obvious.

His tired gaze shifted off of her. Down to the youth between them.

"Emerson?" the man murmured.

Emerson. The healer child. Irene took him in. He was filthy, his clothing ragged. Deep brown eyes, exhausted, confused. A scared little boy under a layer of mud and grime. Those eyes didn't look at her—they floated over her, taking in the space she occupied instead of her body. As if he wouldn't acknowledge she was here with him.

Then his stare locked onto hers.

The boy's voice was demure, silent as a breath even in the reverberating room. "Don't move, okay?"

Irene wanted to know why. What was going to happen to her. Before the question left her mouth, Emerson's dirty fingers flowed over her belly.

For a moment, the room shifted. Blurred out of focus, only to emerge with more clarity. Colors and details amplified—disparity in the bland paint on the metal walls; the advancement of rust in the corner, told in a story of reds and browns. Even the coats of dirt on the child's face sharpened into coherence: lines of tears through a dusting of filth over the smears on his cheeks, all laying plain the story of his day. Fun, fear, and now exhaustion.

Her eyelids fluttered, her sinuses opening rapidly and leaving a tingle under her nose. The stale, moldy air now carried a fresh floral scent. Her gaze traveled down her body.

Her leg was whole. Straight and true. The skin on her knee pristine. The only sign of her injury was the mess of blood on the linens and sliced denim beneath her.

"Holy shit." Despite her lucidity, her sudden sharpness, the statement came out slurred.

Irene looked up. Emerson was moving away. Past Jaime, to her brother's outstretched hand. Irene couldn't help herself—she smiled at Wes. Nodded. Longing to convey some understanding and empathy to him. Regardless of everything she knew to be true, Irene wouldn't deny her own senses and experience.

The child was real. Dad's quest to be healed was valid. Wes had known, somehow. Tried to rescue their father from his disease while she had worked to ease him into death. In the blissful wake of Emerson's magic, a truth resonated through her. One that offered certainty and terror.

Whatever Wes did to get their father to Emerson, Irene would have done too.

Words flopped against her skull, roiling over waves of confusion and joy. She wanted so much at that moment. Forgiveness. A do-over of the last two years. No, longer than that. She wished she'd had the truth sooner. In time to save their dad. To shift their fate off the crumbling path they walked, to live a different life where she and Wes and their father had trust and each other. Where they had family. It felt so possible to her now. Such an obvious choice.

"I... I didn't know..." she stammered.

Wes looked at her, lips tight in a line, as Emerson took his hand.

Her brother swallowed. "What next, Boss?"

The tentative sound of his voice reseated Irene into reality. Regardless of what she wanted, she was here. And she was in danger.

Jaime rotated, placing his bulk between Irene and Wes. His chest heaved in a breath, and he blew out a long sigh as he studied her face.

"Take him into the hallway, Hawk." His hand drifted to the standing tray next to the bed, his fingers pinching at something out of her view. "Stay in earshot. I'll call for him in a few minutes."

Jaime lifted something from the tray. In his meaty fingers, Irene caught a glint of silver. The roofie pen? Why use that now? Before asking her any questions?

The answer was obvious: he wouldn't. Her heart raced, and her arms tensed against their restraints, pulling them away from the stretcher rails as much as she could. Her gaze fell on the grey metal as it moved towards her flailing arm.

Long. Thin. Delicate in his sausage fingers. And deadly. Not a roofie pen.

Jaime was holding a scalpel.

Chapter Forty-Four

The field was a mire now. Water over sludge over mud. Finch's boots seeped deep into it, and the quenched ground sucked at his feet like he was food for the earth.

The dead grass of the clearing offered some respite from the sludge, and Finch's pace quickened. His soul ached. His scars were tight and irritated under the perpetual wetness.

Being in the open, unhidden and bold, was dangerous. Or it should have felt, in a manic way, liberating. Yet he experienced nothing over the ache and exhaustion soaking his bones.

The tower loomed overhead, providing a break from the constant wet pummeling of the storm. Finch fought the urge to slow down. In the moment of relative peace, a pulsing irritation cascaded along the spirals and patches of his skin. Even the numb parts of him were overwhelmed with the sensation. An ache from inside, radiating against his scars. He didn't dare stop. He feared he wouldn't start moving again.

The far edge of the clearing solidified in the rain, the center path marked by a curtain of gray. Finch headed to it, eyes focused ahead as the fetid-smelling crop closed in.

The aisle seemed to stretch, never ending, always more field hidden in the mist. A ripple passed through his head—acknowledgment of the self-sufficient little world Blair and Jaime had built for themselves.

All of it—the farm, the construction, the dispensary, the money driving it all—was all hitched to a yoke they forced Emerson to bear.

The thought enraged him. Blair didn't deserve the child. She was cruel. A selfish user of people, with no space in her life for someone once they stopped benefiting her. Finch knew this because he had lived it.

The wall of swaying green ended ahead of him. As the edge neared, the dark lumps of Terry's corpse resolved from the grey haze. Finch exited the field, the air growing cool in his lungs now, and approached the remains of Blair's brother.

If Terry'd had a face, he would have been drowning in the muck. Finch's gaze ran across the man's back to the belt around his thick middle. A shadow of the shocks and burns from earlier rattled under his skin as he noted the can of pepper spray seated in its holder there, the space next to it empty along with the holster that had been on Terry's leg.

Finch acknowledged his carelessness. He had focused on reaching Emerson rather than on his own safety. A sigh puffed his tight lips, and his mind raced with admonishment. He was no good to the kid dead.

His eye studied the surrounding gray expanse. Hills ahead, hidden by the haze. Finch turned around. The view was the same—mist and rain hiding the rest of the universe.

He willed his feet to move him into that unknown. What he needed was in there, waiting for him. His last hope of ripping the boy from his mother's covetous clutch.

It had taken him years to see it. Years of working to grow himself, of trying to build a normal life while using his dark talents to keep Blair and Emerson secure and cared for. And all Blair had wanted was more. The next level of living. Whatever step was above the one they were on. All of Finch's concern and effort had been forgotten as soon as Blair's interest grew beyond his ability to provide it.

Out of the mist emerged the long, bent snout of a monster. A pale orange; thick tendons attached to a single joint; an arm that ended in a massive maw of broad steel teeth.

Finch studied the frame of the excavator. Calculated how to get his broken body up the treads, into the cab. To reach that next level. To get the life he wanted. The one he deserved.

The one Emerson deserved.

Thick fingers clamped Irene's shoulder, and Jaime leaned his weight into her. She pressed into the bed, her arm locking between his rough grip and the hold of the restraint.

"You know," he said, his tone low and light in the narrow gap between them, "Robin's taught me a few things about human anatomy. Mostly stuff concerning Emerson's ability and how it works. Your brother's been a huge part of that. Sacrificed himself. Over and over. All in the spirit of helping us understand what Emerson is capable of."

A burn surged through her chest as she tried to squirm out from under his grip. The man's thumb crooked under her armpit, and he squeezed. Irene grunted through the focused tension that pierced the joint. If he wanted, Jaime could detach the ball from the socket.

"But some of the stuff she taught me, it's just common medical shit." His palm pushed down. Pressure built on her ribs.

"What are you doing?" she groaned through the discomfort.

Jaime's other hand—the one that held the scalpel—flicked in a tight arc of his wrist. Her breath caught, expecting a rush of agony. Her gaze lifted over his grip, her neck straining to give her eyes a view of what was happening to her.

No pain. Nothing except the pressure of Jaime's monster grip.

"Like the brachial artery. It runs through the underside of your arm. Branches into the radial and ulnar arteries in the forearm."

Irene stretched against the pressure, trying to discover what he had done.

"Look at me, Irene." The man's voice was still soft.

Her eyes locked on his. A smile stretched across his face.

"I just severed your radial artery. After I release your shoulder, you're going to bleed. In thirty seconds, you'll lose consciousness. Ninety seconds after that, you'll die."

His expression remained calm. Almost reassuring. At complete odds with the terror in his words.

"D... don't!" Irene stuttered. "Don't let go!"

But he did. Irene froze, her chest locked with the expectation of suffering. He sat back on the stool next to the bed. Silent. Watching. She pried her eyes off of him and looked to her arm.

She'd expected a horror show. Instead, a single thin and tidy puncture in her forearm trickled an insignificant stream of blood. She floated between confusion and terror—how could such a tiny wound be fatal? Panic won with the next beat of her heart, which sent arterial spray shooting from the diminutive slice in her arm.

"W... why?" Her throat tight, her voice pitching.

"I need to know who's on my compound, Irene. Tell me that and I'll bring Emerson back in here."

Another pulse. The blood poured across her forearm, splashing against the leather cuff restraining her wrist.

"I... it's Finch! My landlord! I don't understand why he's doing all of this—"

"I don't believe you. Why are you here again, Irene? What is this guy—Finch? What is he doing here?"

"I don't know," she cried. The scarlet pool bloomed faster than the slight cut should have allowed. The warmth of it reached through her shirt, tickling the side of her belly. "I really don't! He told me he was a customer, that he had an order to pick up—"

Jaime's hand wrapped under her chin, and he forced her gaze to his. "Bullshit!" he spat, the words flowing on the stale odor of cigarettes. "One time is a coincidence. I might buy that you found you way into my fucking compound a few days ago, somehow. I can understand that your hunger to punish Hawk—Wes—brought you here once."

Her view rocked as Jaime shoved her head against the bedding. He shot up, the stool clattering across the floor and clanging into the metal cabinet with a strange, unnatural echo.

A tunnel formed at the edge of her sight. A tingle faded into the corners of her body.

The scalpel jabbed towards her eye. "But there's no way you'd show up after we planted Wes's corpse for the authorities to find! You knew he was here! You remember the plan you came up with to deceive yourself!"

She shook her head. "I don't remember!" The tunnel closed in on her. Blackness spiraled around his meaty fingers, and a sting crawled up her limbs. The room was turning cold.

"Last chance, Irene. You've got maybe ten seconds of consciousness left. *Who the fuck is running around my goddamned compound?*" His voice boomed once again, pushing the darkness over her. Squeezing the blood out of her with sound.

"Please," she said, her speech cracking with a sudden parch. Her eyelids wanted to close, and Irene struggled to focus. She had to convince him she was telling the truth. What could she say to stop this? A mire surrounded her thoughts, making them awkward and slow.

Emptiness folded over her, a heavy, wet blanket of dark and cold. She wondered if Dad had gone through this in his last moments—this strange floating and sinking, the tightening of her chest and slackening of her mind.

Behind the veil of darkness, over the thrum in her ears, pierced a voice. Not words, just the lilting pitch of a woman's easy drawl.

Irene's head snapped clear; the seething cold tingle was replaced with a warm lift. She flushed with strength and vitality—colors grew vivid once more, and the tang of blood and mold soaked her tongue as the blackness lifted from her. And that cloying aroma of flowers—Emerson had saved her.

The woman's twang came then, her words now ringing clear: "It's a ranch, goddamn it. Not a compound."

Chapter Forty-Five

T he young woman on the bed snapped awake. The tight cut on her forearm disappeared. Whatever blood she'd lost had been replenished by Emerson's grace. Blair patted her son's arm, nudging him out from between her and Jaime.

The anxiety in her belly lurched as Hawk took the boy's hand. The metallic scent of gore sat in the motionless air as Irene's blood dribbled into the round drain set in the center of the floor. Blair's eyes followed the shining red stream—fresh blood, still liquid, seeping over the stale darker stains deep into the plywood.

The room wound tightly around the silence between them, and small sounds popped over the sigh of the rain hitting the ground: Hawk swallowing; Jaime's boots creaking on the fetid floor; Emerson sniffing back his tears.

Blair forced her gaze to Jaime. She found narrowed eyes, the deep ochre piercing in the crisp LED lighting.

"What the hell is this place?"

Jaime sighed, a disdainful smirk spreading on his face. "I told you, Blair—"

"No, Jaime. Don't tell me it's some safety bunker or first-aid station!" Her sharp voice twanged against the metal walls. It gave her words girth, a size and heft that gave her strength. "Jaime, why does this shitty hospital room exist under the farm?"

Her partner's face fell with resignation.

"Explain it to me, please." The edge sharpened on her tongue. "We've always said we don't keep secrets from each other. But this looks like a big goddamned secret you've been keeping!"

The man rolled his eyes. Not resignation, she realized. Impatience.

Blair cracked, the roiling unease in her lighting to a fire. "Listen, you son of a—"

"I'm not hiding anything from you, Blair." The resonance of his deep baritone shook the room, and the strength she'd felt before rattled off like costume armor. "You want to know what this place is? Fine, I'll explain all over again."

Blair's brow furrowed. Before she could ask, Jaime closed the distance between them.

"This room keeps you in your lifestyle, honey."

His breath was soft, carrying the smell of cigarettes and sweat that had the power to overwhelm her common sense, triggering primal and sexual urges. But here, in this small and disgusting space, the odors repulsed her. She backed away from him, feeling the crisp corrugated metal of the wall on her back.

"What does that mean?"

He smiled. Not the playful bedroom smile. The arrogant, scheming one. "I mean, what happens in this room gives us the money to support this ranch."

Blair shook her head. "No, but the weed—"

"The weed." Jaime's stare turned up to the ceiling, through it, to the plants. "We have a bumper crop, always producing at premium quality, thanks to your son." His gaze returned to her, his expression mocking and pitying. "We pull in more cash on our weed than any other grower in Texas, Blair. And after the state takes its hero's cut, after the labor gets paid, after the licensing and operations costs, there's barely enough money left to keep the ranch functioning."

The words hung in her head, jumbled with the dripping of blood in the drain. "But our cash flow; you said—"

"There *is* plenty of cash flowing. It flows through this room."

Blair studied Hawk's sister as she worked her blood-caked arm against the restraint chaining her to the bed. The answer was here, in this room. Yet Blair couldn't see it.

Something touched her belly. She peered down, finding a dirty scalpel resting against her bottom ribs. Jaime patted the flat of the blade against her, grazing her shirt enough so it moved against her skin. The glint of light on the red metal sent a shiver through her, and Blair tried to sink farther into the wall.

"We get five thousand dollars for a kidney," Jaime crooned as he slipped the knife across her abdomen. "Eight to ten for a liver."

Blair swallowed. His words tumbled through her mind and found no purchase. She understood what he was saying. That didn't mean she wanted to believe it.

"And then, the real moneymakers," he hummed. The blade followed the buttons of her shirt, between her breasts, where Jaime let it rest on her shaking sternum. "A lung? Easy forty thousand dollars. A heart, we make up to seventy."

Blair held her breath, tried to calm her rattling bones as the knife tickled the skin of her neck. She lifted her face, trying to peel away from the scalpel, but Jaime kept his girth on her, pinning her against the wall. His breath was on her cheek. Warm and stale in her nostrils. And then the coolness of the wet blade was under her eye. It slipped on her cheek, leaving a greasy smear of Irene's blood.

"Hell, even an eye gets us ten grand, Blair."

She swallowed the hard lump in her throat, trying like hell to keep her face from twitching with the scalpel next to her eye. Jaime retreated, easing the knife away and letting air between them. Trembling fingers found her cheek, and Blair wiped away the slick of copper-smelling gore left there.

"That's where our wealth comes from, sweetheart." Jaime's tone remained gentle, caring. Patronizing. "This room is under the tower. While Emerson's up there tending the crop, Robin's here, making the money."

The clues snapped together, leaving her chilled. "You're selling organs?"

Jaime nodded. He gestured with the blade to Emerson, still nestled into Hawk a few feet away. "And it keeps us in the life you love so much. Also courtesy of Emerson, even if he didn't know he was helping."

Her boy had heard all of it. His teary eyes told Blair he understood every word and nuance.

"You're using my son to hurt people!" she cried.

"Not at all," Jaime said, his voice playful and relaxed. "Just the opposite! You have any idea how many people we've helped? How many families are still whole thanks to him? To us?"

"This isn't right!" she hollered.

"Oh, come on, now! It's not like we're forcing anyone here, Blair. They're not awake for it. And they get paid. Most of the time."

Blair moved. It was her turn to take the space between them. "I won't let you use my son like this."

Jaime puffed a sigh and turned from her, gaze bobbing around the room. Distracted, looking for something.

"Do you hear me?!"

The man didn't respond. Instead, he took two leisurely steps to a large metal cabinet against the far wall. The contents of a drawer rattled as he flung it open.

"I heard you fine, Blair." His hand disappeared into the drawer, fingers rummaging for a moment before lifting something.

"This ends today."

Jaime shook his head. "No, it doesn't." He held up an object, showing it to her. As if she should recognize it. A bland-looking tube with an orange tip. He said nothing, but watched her. Studied her.

"What the hell is that?" she asked.

Jaime smiled. His thumb flicked the orange cap, popping it off and letting it bounce on the plywood floor a few times, revealing a thin needle projecting from the end of the tube. His expression froze her nerves, and her throat dried up.

"What are you doing with that?" she whispered.

Jaime spun the tube in his hand. The needle pointed down, Jaime's meaty fingers gripping the cylinder like a dagger. "I'm going to stick you with this, Blair. Like the last time you found out about this room. You'll pass out. Then you'll have a night of shitty fever dreams, and when you wake up, you won't remember this room or this conversation."

Her lover's thick lips pressed in a line, the skin around them paling with the effort. Then he turned away. Blair's shoulders hitched to her ears at the clatter of the syringe on the metal tray.

"Or maybe I won't," Jaime continued. "Maybe it's time you own your shit. Come to terms with the cost of sheltering your son." His other hand rose, the scalpel in his fingers, held as if he was looking to carve his signature into someone.

"Either way, I'll do whatever the fuck I need to, honey."

Chapter Forty-Six

J aime took two laggard steps to the stretcher. Irene's body surged, her wrist stressing against the leather restraint as the edge of his knife teased the flesh of her upper arm. The tip slipped into her skin, the barest of pinches. Then the tickle of blood. Warm, slick, and flowing a few inches beneath her armpit.

The mother's face broke, her earlier strength paling at the sight of the gore. Her gaze fluttered over Irene but stuck to nothing, then shot to Jaime as he spoke.

"You know me. You realize that everything I do is to keep Emerson safe. To keep *you* safe, Blair."

The fingers on the surgical blade twitched—the crossing of a T, no more. More blood flowed from the opening, and a groan peeled from Irene's throat as the tip slid its way into her muscle.

Wes's voice hissed through gritted teeth. "Jaime! Don't!"

Irene's gaze darted to him. A gun filled his hand now, pointed at Jaime's head. The two men stared each other down, not a twitch or breath between them.

Jaime kept the knife in her arm. Irene struggled to stay still, but a quiver rattled through her, a reaction to the pain that forced her flesh to scrape the blade even more.

"What the fuck are you going to do, Hawk? Shoot me? Save your sister? And then what?"

The scalpel carved another few millimeters. The wound widened, deepened. Cramps racked Irene's neck and chest; her body tensed, her sobs became guttural.

"Jaime!" Wes again, yelling now. Pressing the gun closer.

"Where would you go, huh?" Jaime chided. A sneer curled into his lips. "Without me? Without this haven we've built? You've got nothing beyond this, you understand? What will you do if you lose the ranch, you dumbass?"

A sear crawled into the muscle of her shoulder. The tension binding her body together dissolved into a bubbling panic. The pain of the wound flashed, and Irene convulsed.

Wes spoke in terror, his voice warbling near tears. "Please, Jaime, she doesn't know! This is pointless torture!"

She stared at her wounded arm, life once again rushing out of her. Serpentining the curve of her elbow and collecting around the restraint.

Jaime's words boomed in the tight space. They washed over the rush of her own pulse like a tidal wave. "I don't believe her, Hawk!"

Wes lunged at Jaime, rocking the large brute into the gurney. Irene's arm seared with white pain as Jaime yanked the scalpel forward. Each man locked on the other. Wes shoved Jaime into the bedrail, and something clattered to the floor. Voices rang through the tight metal box now—grunts from the fighting, hollers from Blair, and someone else. Someone screaming. Irene realized it was her.

The men tumbled off the end of the stretcher. Her attention shot to her arm. The incision stretched two inches, the flow of blood steady but non-arterial. Yet her suffering was exquisite and sharp. The depth of this cut a canyon to the earlier ditch.

Irene tugged, but the restraint refused to let go. She had to get free. Grab something she could use as a weapon. Was there another scalpel on the tray?

A woman's scream. Blair this time, her words unintelligible over the agony in Irene's shoulder.

Irene wrenched her arm, her wrist rotating in the cuff, but her hand still refused to fit. Blood smeared under the restraint, lubricating her skin and giving her a few extra degrees of twist.

Fingers landed on the cuff, prying the tongue of the restraint through the metal buckle.

"Hang on, I'll get you out of here," Blair stammered.

The belt loosened, and blood oozed between her flesh and the leather.

"Hurry," Irene begged.

The tongue flopped out of the buckle, but the prong still pierced the hole. The cuff gave a modicum of slack. Irene strained against it, earning another inch of freedom.

The wheeze of her heaving breath came to her, and it took her a moment to register the sudden stillness in the room. The grunts and tumbles of the wrestling had silenced.

Blair's fingers no longer worked the buckle. Irene glanced up to find them covering the woman's thin mouth, and then she traced her gaze across the bed to where her brother had been struggling with Jaime. She strained to see over the bedrail.

Wes crumpled against the cabinet, his hands at his throat. Palms flapped over the geyser of blood flowing out of his neck as the color faded from his skin.

Over the pain in her shoulder, she felt a tickle of hope. It brushed the tips of her fingers as they stretched to cling to the one piece of family she had left, the thing she had sought for over two years. Lost, then found.

Her heart broke. For the second time today, Irene would see her brother dead.

The light was chaos. Jaime's angry burgundy and lilac washed over Hawk's righteous pale blue as they slammed into the floor. The scarlet of Mom's aura burned as she moved to the bed. And the lady there—Hawk's sister—her emerald glow was intense and terrified.

Emerson absorbed it all. He couldn't help but see the halos. But from his vantage, balled against the wall next to the hallway, he could see Hawk straining, both of his hands pinning Jaime's arm to the plywood floor and throwing his entire body weight against it. His muscles shook against Jaime's strength, and bubbles of spittle formed on his tensed lips. Yet Jaime's fist inched up.

Mom was yelling. The woman in the bed was screaming. Behind him, Emerson heard Layla and Chris crying over comforting tones from Layla's mom. Hawk groaned through clenched teeth. In the riptide of noise, only Jaime was silent. His mouth stayed tight, and his eyes narrowed on Hawk as his hand rose farther.

A gleam came through Jaime's purples, a single flash that reflected his hand as it lashed out to Hawk's neck. Hawk's blue aura sputtered, and his eyes gaped with shock. Jaime's hand retreated, and a squirt of red followed from a wound in Hawk's neck.

Hawk's hands went up to cover the puncture, and Jaime shoved his sternum. Hawk's ring of blues curdled to yellows as he smashed into the cabinet, clattering the contents.

That paling buttercup hue—Emerson remembered it from the first time he met Hawk. At the hospital in Uvalde. Not the man's natural aura. It was the shade of death taking him. The pulse of Hawk's light shook with his body, alternating with spurts of blood from his neck. In the space of a blink, the ochre was fading.

Emerson thrust his halo through the space and the noise and the blood and the putrid odors that were more rusty and sweet than the plants above them. His light scrambled to connect with Hawk before his yellow disappeared forever. Like Uncle Terry and so many others Emerson wished he had saved.

His halo found his mother. The heat of her determined fire prickled across his skin, a bitter shame and guilt souring in his mouth and stomach. These were not his feelings—these were his mother's, as if he had swallowed her halo and become her. Her thoughts stayed hidden in a ruddy haze, but her emotions lay bare as their lights entwined.

The experience was familiar, but the intensity was beyond anything he'd felt.

Hawk heaved, blood trickling from his mouth now as his body tremored. There was no time to revel in the complex sensation. Emerson shoved his light farther.

Hawk's sister—the deep-green patterns and intricate details in her aura unfolded around him. Her confusion at not having the mental pieces lined up in a tidy row, the panic over her dying brother, the lingering terror of seeing a dead man walking. And exhaustion, not from today, but a lingering fatigue.

A pulse rippled through Hawk's crumbling halo as another spurt left his neck. Emerson stretched his aura forward, the ache like the one in his calves after a day of hiking and searching for rattlers in the hills behind the house.

He found Jaime, the violent ruckus of indigos and violets slippery, difficult to clutch. Emerson's light fumbled against the man's boiling rage.

Another fading wave from Hawk's light. Tufts of his halo tore away, matching the stemmed geyser from his neck. The color was leaving him, physically and otherwise.

Emerson pushed through the strain. His light balked as he tried to reach past Jaime's foul glow. The colors of Mom's boyfriend swirled in powerful eddies and spirals as Jaime rose to his feet.

Hawk's eyelids fluttered. They moved from his sister to Emerson. Emerson sought the connection, the blissful release of righting the tear of a broken halo. Hawk's hand fell from his throat, landing palm up on the dirty and bloody floor. As if he was reaching for Emerson. *Help me. Save me. I'm dying.*

Something rumbled under Emerson's light. A miserable, unfamiliar color. Red and heavy like Mom's fire, green and confused like Hawk's sister, and purple like Jaime's swirling anger, but as hollow as the spaces carved open by the burned man's black wisps.

The burned man—Emerson had watched him shape his aura. That stranger would stretch around Jaime's raging glow to reach Hawk if he had to. If that man could do it, then Emerson could too!

Hawk's eyes eased shut. The last curl of amber flitted from the man's center. Spiraled out from his core, leaving nothing in its wake. An intensity pulled down the corners of Emerson's mouth, and he fisted his hands and feet as his halo bent. Not a coil. Not tight and controlled. A fledgling finger of light. But maybe enough to reach Hawk. To save him.

Fueled by this strange feeling, Emerson lurched for that last fading ember of his friend.

Chapter Forty-Seven

"**E**merson, save him!" Blair screamed.

Hawk continued to bleed and pale. His body quieting and melting into the cabinet and wall.

"Emerson?!"

Silence. But Blair could sense his power moving through her.

Her gaze left Hawk as Jaime rose to his feet. He used the gurney for support, his weight clanging it into the steel wall. The knife remained in his grip. Blood soaked his work shirt. Not his blood, but Hawk's. Irene's. His stare locked on her, probing.

His eyes full of questions. Would she be any trouble over this? Did she plan to oppose him? Or would she get the fuck out of his way? Let him handle shit the only way he could?

Her eyes must have answered him, as he moved between Blair and the bed.

"This is your fucking fault, you know that, Blair?"

Hawk's gurgling faded as the drizzle of more blood finding its way into the drainpipe grew.

"You and your fucking wants. Always more! Never worrying where it's gonna come from!" He angled his back to her, facing poor Irene as she gawked at her bleeding brother.

"I never wanted this!" she cried, motioning to the disgusting room and its awful purpose. "I wanted security! For Emerson to be safe from people using him for shit like this, Jaime!"

Jaime huffed, putting his hand on Irene's shoulder and laying pressure into it. The woman shrieked, her attention torn away from her dying brother. "You have no idea—"

Blair slapped the side of his head hard enough to stop his words. He paused, dazed, his body immovable even after her best effort. Jaime shook it off as if clearing dust from his hair. He turned to look at her.

His expression wasn't angry or hurt. It was sad. A piteous rise to his thick eyebrows that mirrored the tone of his voice. "How could I have kept this place secret from you, Blair?"

He'd said as much already, but the words didn't make sense. "I've never been here, Jaime!"

A sigh eased through the growing smirk between his cheeks. He stood up, releasing the pressure on Irene's arm as she let out a strained sob. Standing over Blair, Jaime pointed at her with the scalpel dripping with other people's blood. "You always bitch that you need to understand. You want details of how the compound works, where the cash comes from."

She backed up a step, the teetering blade too near her skin.

"I took you through the pot farm, the operations and financials, showed you the costs to keep it running, the pile of money we have to defer to the state, the county, the city. It's not sustainable, not on our own."

She swallowed, confused. Not wanting to believe him. A metallic *ting* rang from the walls of the enclosure, disrupting her thoughts. Her attention fixated on Jaime, even as her brain screamed at her to get a glimpse of Hawk. Was Emerson restoring him?

Jaime continued, "Not without heavy investment for machinery, personnel, utilities. We'd have business partners here all the time. Nosing around. You expect them to keep Emerson a secret?"

Behind him, Irene twisted herself on the stretcher, rotating her bleeding arm against the restraint.

"Weed, we can grow. Money, we have to earn. And you sure as hell demanded more of it. The house and land weren't enough. You wanted to build Emerson's entire future life, right here on this spot."

Jaime motioned to the metal boxcar walls. "This *was* an old storm bunker, Blair. But then Robin and I adapted it to produce an added source of revenue. One with no regulation or fees. And no victims, every participant a willing volunteer."

"Except Emerson," she spat.

Jaime's brow rose. "Is that what's bothering you? That we didn't let him in on this?"

"Or me!" she cried. "You didn't tell me we were mutilating people for their organs!"

"You stood there!" Jaime bellowed, the metal walls ringing with the resonance of his baritone. "Right where your son is now!" His fist moved to her face. Blair expected a wallop across her cheek. Instead, the breeze of Jaime's movement carried his saccharine body odor. She followed his finger to her son cowering on the floor, his gaze latched on Hawk, his tiny body shaking with fear.

"You stood there while Robin and I laid out everything that happens here, Blair!"

"Bullshit—"

"You did. Hand to God, you did. And you said the same damned things. Lost your shit, ordered us to stop. Just like you're doing today. But you remember what happened next?"

She turned to Jaime. His face was in hers, his breath sour on her tongue.

"I showed you the books, Blair. You saw the bounty this room produces, how cheap it is to run. You found the next level of the life you craved, in the palm of your grubby hand. And you caved."

"I wouldn't—"

"But you did, Blair. You told us to keep the bunker going, with two stipulations. First, that Emerson never find out."

Jaime paused, leering at her, waiting. Something crumbled inside of her, some crack in the bedrock of her person.

"The second?" she squeaked.

Jaime's leer blew out into a full smile. The chaotic one that Jaime displayed when he landed a kill on a hunt or when he won an argument with Hawk. "That we dose you so you forget what you learned. And hide this room from you too. So you wouldn't wrinkle your pretty little brow over it ever again."

The man's face blurred, and Blair blinked the standing tears out of her eyes.

"Fuck you. That's a lie." The words floated out of her mouth, almost inaudible. Blair didn't even believe them. But they were all she could say, a whisper of a shield to defend herself.

Jaime shrugged, and his palm shot to Blair's chin. His fingers squeezed the flesh of her cheeks, cracking her lips apart as he forced her head to turn. She saw the hallway stretch away to the bunker doors, where the children cowered in the narrow embrace of Robin's arms. The two women locked eyes, sharing their terror. Guilt. Shame. All the feelings roiling in Blair's own belly. She could see them bubbling in Robin too. Jaime forced her face farther, tugged her gaze to the floor.

Emerson wilted there, his eyes drilling into Hawk. What was he thinking? What was he feeling? Blair craved to read her son the way he read her. Was his shaking the same as hers, stemming from the same terror? Or was Emerson steeling some new resolve?

"Ain't no secrets from Emerson, am I right?" Jaime's voice hissed through clenched teeth, the warmth and wetness of his spit spraying on her neck and cheek. "So go on, Blair. Ask him if I'm lying to you."

Chapter Forty-Eight

It was like trying to grab smoke with astronaut gloves. The last tender feather of light, the final delicate breath of Hawk. Yet the strength Emerson needed to shape his own aura to cradle it shook him. His body was close to caving.

A rumble grew out of him. Enveloped the space. Pressed out through the walls. Emerson's perceptions expanded: the life in the field; the bountiful creatures there; the endless sea of purple fuzz swelling in the wind.

The drab wisp that was Hawk tugged. It wanted to leave. Sought to spin off to wherever the lights go next, his mortal tapestry designed for no purpose but to unravel. Emerson gathered it. Corralled it closer to Hawk's empty body.

Screams. His mother. Hawk's sister. Layla and Chris crying. They mixed into the haze of the field, noise and distraction from this last fraying thread of Hawk's soul.

Emerson inhaled. Sucked in the colors with the air. The purple glow seething into the ground, roots seeping with power in the dirt outside the metal walls as his own aura struggled.

The amber fiber untangled. Emerson's grip was failing. He was losing the light! He was losing his friend!

Another scream. From inside of him. The noise of his halo lashing out, piercing any living thing it could find.

No one dies here. Nothing ends. Not today.

The lush violet radiated through the walls and ceiling now—the field responding to Emerson's emotion, its roots pressing against this awful metal room as it groaned in protest.

One last filament tied Hawk to this world. Emerson focused on it. Spiraled his halo around it. Willed the thread to grow. To weave itself back into the surrounding tapestry of light.

The coil of Emerson's light snapped, whipping out and away from Hawk and across the ground and field over their heads.

And the amber whisper of light ignited and exploded in a rage of tawny and blues. Hawk's aura stretched out, the same way as Emerson's did. A flame seeking a wick. A soul craving a vessel.

Emerson nudged the blue inferno towards Hawk's corpse. Despite his scalding anger at Jaime, the hollow of fear that he might lose Hawk, Emerson cracked a smile as Hawk's eyes peered open.

The smile broke as the wall behind Hawk buckled with a percussive snap.

"Please, stop!"

A warm tingle floated in Jaime's gut as he tightened his grip on her throat. A moment of pleasure at her pain.

Blair's wheeze shrunk to a squeak. "You don't have to do this!" If her face wasn't so near, Jaime wouldn't have realized she'd spoken at all.

The gall of this woman, speaking out of both sides of her mouth! Wanting the ends; not wanting to be troubled by the means. Jaime would pretend no more. He had enough trouble protecting the kid without the extra work of securing her fucking sensibilities too.

"Yes, Blair, I do," he spat, nudging the blade against her abdomen. "Sometimes carving up little bitches like Hawk's sister is necessary to keep Emerson safe. And I don't mind doing it, you know that. I work in the dirt and blood every day. But I'll be damned if I'm doing it so you can stay clean!"

Tears leaked from her eyes as her head nudged from side to side. "No," she croaked, her hands pulling on his wrist, her nails trying to pry his fingers off her throat. It was adorable, the desperation and pointlessness of her effort. A kitten clawing against a bear's paw.

Blair choked, "She doesn't know who's chasing Emerson, but I do!"

He opened his hand. Blair fell back against the wall, stumbling over her son. Her face was red, matching her vibrant hair, the hues amplified by the intense strip lighting and white walls of the operating room.

"What the fuck did you say?" Jaime had heard her, but the words—they didn't fit together.

She doubled over, hands on her knees, coughing, and spat a gob of phlegm at his feet.

"I asked you what you said!" he yelled.

Blair's face rose. Her eyes placative. Sad. And afraid.

"Who is it, Blair?"

Two breaths, he waited for the answer. Her gaze squared to his, and her thin lips closing in a tight line. The sadness in her face melted to terror.

Her stare floated to the floor, pointing with intention at her son. They stayed there for another breath, then moved back to Jaime again.

It took him a moment to understand. To snap it together. The intensity and rage in her stare. It *was* the answer to his question. The man shooting up the farm was the person Blair feared and hated most in this world. The cause of her destitution and her struggles.

The interloper was Emerson's father.

He nodded, a wad of guilt sinking in his throat that he swallowed before it could spew out in an apology. There was nothing he needed to apologize for. He wouldn't have hurt Irene if Blair had told him. She'd had her chance—when they'd entered the bunker, she could have reported her suspicions then.

"Why didn't you tell me?"

Her lips quivered as she rose, leaning into the wall for support. A clang of metal rang in his ears.

"I'm not totally sure it's him. He wasn't burned before," she stammered. Her voice trembled with uncertainty.

New rage balled his fists, his fingers squeezing the blade and shaking. He wanted to sink that edge into Blair's gut and twist.

"I know you fear him, Blair. From what you told me, you have good reasons. But goddammit, I can't protect—"

Before the words could leave his mouth, another metal *thump* hammered the room. Jaime's eyes darted and landed on the new crease in the steel wall over Hawk's body.

From behind Jaime came Emerson's petulant cry: "I don't think I can stop this!"

A second pucker snapped in the girding at the room's edge. Jaime's anger, his rage—they vaporized in the heat of fear.

"Emerson?" Jaime hollered, the bitter tang of raw nerves on his tongue. He spun to the child on the floor. "Whatcha doing, little buddy?"

Chapter Forty-Nine

J ust... another... inch...

Irene's arm twisted in the restraint. If she got her thumb into that small gap, where the tongue and cuff overlapped...

A wave of bliss enveloped her. The ache in the muscles of her shoulder dissolved, and a soothing, bubbling tickle took its place.

She knew this experience—it was Emerson, healing her and everyone else, yet the feeling was different. This wasn't a blink-and-you're-fine. Whatever the child was doing cradled her. Wrapped her in an Emerson blanket. Safe from any harm.

She tested that theory. Gave her shoulder a jerk, trying to wiggle her arm out of the cuff. Instead of a pang or ache or tear, her limb tingled, falling asleep in warmth rather than a chill.

The conclusion came to her along with a simple, determined thought: *Fuck it!* Teeth gritted in the expectation of anguish, Irene shoved her shoulder down. Her elbow locked, twisting too far and releasing with a wet crack that made Irene's stomach roil.

At once, the restraint let go. Her hand was free. Afraid she had mangled the limb, Irene forced her gaze to her arm.

Her fingers wiggled; her elbow bent where it should; her shoulder was seated and ready to go. No sign of injury.

Blair's cries pulled her back to the surrounding danger. Her fingers shot to the other arm restraint and rammed the tongue through the buckle until the prong popped from the leather. Two arms free.

As she rose to release her legs, an impatient, dangerous sound shook the room. The moaning of metal under stress. A thought percolated out of her pattern-seeking brain—the torrent outside, draining, eating away under this metal container, opening the ground beneath them, more and more, until there was nothing keeping this room from dropping into the dark aquifer abyss hundreds of feet below.

That isn't possible, right?

"I don't think I can stop this!" Emerson, calling out to... to anyone listening. His voice carried a tremor she recognized from chasing Dad and Wes: an agitation at having to watch events unfold out of your control.

Whatever Emerson was doing, it scared him. And that scared Irene.

She pried the cuffs off her ankles. Another groan rang out. More insistent. The metal walls rattled and vibrated the bed.

Blair screamed, and Jaime snubbed the sound with a hand around her throat. The scalpel hovered in his other fingers, near her stomach. He hissed at her. Too quietly to make out over the din, but the ruddy color of his neck marked his anger.

Irene was free. She could leave. But the ogre Jaime was between her and the exit. She needed a weapon. Anything to defend herself against this beast.

The surgical tray! Maybe there was a second scalpel there.

Irene's hands clamored for the stand.

Steel sheared behind her, its squeal burying the clang of the tray bouncing into the stretcher rail. She turned. The top seam of the wall ripped open, muck and spray plopping to the floor, the loamy odor covering the taint of mold and blood. Something spindly wormed through the opening. Explored the walls, as if seeking their weak spots.

Roots. From the plants above them. They squeezed the freight container, tearing it apart with her in it.

The tray bounced off the bedrail, scattering the contents.

Fuck. Fuck! Her eyes scanned the floor: gauze, blunted scissors, clamps.

Another sharp bang punched the room. In reflex, Irene's gaze shot to the wall over her brother's head. A new cleft bent the metal towards her, knocking the medical cabinet several inches forward.

It took a breath to see it. A visual detail failing to meet her expectation.

Wes.

His eyes peered open, set in a pale and sickly face, but focused and purposeful.

Wes was alive!

His hand shook, and a finger stretched out. Pointing at the floor.

Irene traced the line from his fingertip with her stare. Across the plywood bloated with blood stains. A PVC drain. Gauze and pads. A thick metal tube. No scalpel.

Another holler from Blair, and then Emerson. Followed by the walls themselves. Her stomach lurched as the room tilted, the shudder of metal mixing with the moist sounds of growth as the roots began to consume the bed, wiggling against her hand and leg.

She flopped over the bedrail, her sneakers smacking the wood, and spun to Wes. What was he trying to show her?

His attention and finger gestured to her feet.

There, between her blood-soaked and mud-caked sneakers was the cylinder.

Clear block letters on the label: ROHYPNOL.

Wes wanted the roofie pen.

The seam between the ceiling and the wall snapped apart. For a moment, Jaime saw the red clay that passed for soil in Texas, a deep brick color swirled with sienna. The dirt receded as a bland haze emerged from the mud. Fingers. Or worms. Whatever the hell they were, they tore open a cavity and imposed their way inside. The pale tendrils squirmed over the wailing metal as if scavenging for food.

"Get out of here!" he shouted. His gaze snapped to Blair. To Emerson. She dragged the balled-up boy towards the door.

The ground shifted under him. Jaime stumbled a few steps, palms landing on the cabinet and wall to catch his fall.

The clamor rose. Shrieks of bending metal became screams of shearing steel as the room begged for calm. And unfamiliar noises joined the fray—wet, sloppy sounds of life and water flowing into the buried shipping containers.

He spun, glimpsing Blair and Emerson running through the hall. Safe for the moment. And Hawk's sister moved as well. Somehow out of the gurney, crouched on her new, healthy legs. Her arm shot in an arc, and something skittered towards him. Then past him.

And into Hawk's waiting hand. He was alive! Slumped against the wall. All that bleeding wasn't enough to kill him. Jaime had to smile. He liked Hawk, enjoyed having him around. He was useful, and Jaime hoped the man escaped this collapsing grave with them.

The thought faded to dread as their eyes met. Hawk's gaze stabbing, chin sharpened by a clenched jaw. Skin ruddy with anger. His hand rose, holding the thing his sister had tossed his way.

The tube long in his grip. The needle thin and stabby. A Rohypnol pen!

Jaime spun, lurching towards the slanting doorway. Blair and Emerson disappeared deeper into the hallway as the threshold jerked several feet higher, revealing layers of earth that oozed into the space. The drop in Jaime's stomach made it clear: they were sinking.

His boots skidded on the greasy floor, banged against the metal cabinet as he clamored towards the doorway above him. Fresh clay squished under his hands as he clawed over it, its pliability preventing a solid hold.

His leg refused to climb. Jaime glanced back. Or down. He wasn't sure anymore.

Hawk's fist was clamped onto the cuff of his jeans. Jaime shook his limb. Kicked. Connected with Hawk's chest, but the man refused to let go. Instead, his other hand shot out, gripping the tube like a dagger.

Behind Hawk, the wall squirmed with blurry motion. The bleached tendrils slithered over his skin and clothes, as if to feed on him.

Jaime shoved again. Hawk's grip tore free, and Jaime struggled against the loose dirt on the floor. Scrambling for the hallway. Just feet away.

A pinch in his calf. Then a burn.

The edges of his vision blurred as nausea percolated in his gut. Directions wandered, but his gaze found the source of the pain.

The tube stood out of his calf muscle. The needle was embedded in his leg. White tentacles, the haze, whatever it was invading the room. It crawled up his ankle. Beyond, Hawk lay prone on the wall—or was it the floor now?—engulfed by a pile of the pale, naked branches.

Unconsciousness approached as the drug accelerated through him. Colors faded. Darkness crept over the white fuzz, and a hum drowned the screams of metal and people. His view zoomed on Hawk. Jaime's hands stopped listening to him, and they released the grimy floor. His muscles relaxed, his body melting into the deteriorating room.

He had to focus. Stay awake. Leave this bunker. Which way was out? His attention centered on Hawk. Hawk could help.

The man smiled at him, screened by blooming muted growth, and lifted a hand to Jaime's face.

Jaime's consciousness shriveled around Hawk's raised middle finger.

Chapter Fifty

I rene skidded down the sloping floor to her brother, passing Jaime's limp bulk.

"Get up, Wes! We gotta move!"

She grabbed her brother's hand and tugged. Wes groaned as the roots tore free around him and then reasserted themselves, snagging his shirt and jeans again before she pulled him free.

The room continued its slow tilt. Jaime's body slumped into the cabinet. Irene's foot slipped against the flesh of the man's shoulder, and she levered Wes onto his unsteady feet.

A crash washed out the groaning and whining of metal. Behind her, Irene saw the stretcher bounce against the wall, along with the surgical tray and an array of smaller items. The floor kept dropping. *Physics always wins.*

She crab-walked backwards over Jaime's body, hands wrapped in Wes's as he stumbled after her. The roots were covering everything. Walls, floor, ceiling, the gurney. They encased Jaime's legs with sticky white wrappings that slithered closer to her brother's lagging steps.

"Hurry, dammit!" she screeched.

She peered over her shoulder. The hallway inched higher, mud oozing in from the opening cavity. She turned, releasing one of his hands and reaching for the floor of the bunker, now hanging above a growing gap of dirt and emptiness.

Her fingertip nipped the edge just as the floor fell another inch. Her grip slipped, the verge to the hallway out of reach.

"Shit!"

The entire room moaned again, loudly enough that the rumble flowed through her chest, and the floor tilted another dozen degrees. The soles of Irene's sneakers lost their grip, and she scrambled to keep from falling, losing her hold on Wes's other hand.

Her foot landed on something solid. A hold. She looked to find Wes, one boot planted on Jaime's head and the other buried in the slithering roots. Her heel was on his palm.

He shoved. As he did, Irene leapt, reaching for the threshold.

The rough ripples of plywood scraped beneath her fingertips. Her grip tightened, the floor giving another inch and a metal crack exploding in her ears.

She glanced back as Wes tumbled, landing flat against the root-laden wall that was plunging into the earth. The wispy, bleached tentacles nipped at him. Raced over his legs and arms. Whipped across his face.

"Wes!" She wouldn't lose him again. Not after the last two years. Not after the last twenty-four hours.

He ripped away the pulsing wad of roots, fighting to reach the far side of the room.

"What the hell are you doing?" she called over the rumble.

"Get out of here, sis!" Wes struggled against the roots as they whipped at him with serpentine fingers.

"Fuck you, dickhead, I'm not leaving you!" she screamed. Her pinky finger slipped from the edge, and her ring finger threatened to follow it as the tilt of the room dragged on her body.

She reached up with her other hand, slapping at the stable hallway floor above her head. The ledge rose as she sank. The cool and slick clay filled her hand when she missed.

Another struggling finger snapped off the edge. The shelter continued to twist and rattle as she threw her arm up once more. She could feel it: the room was dying. If she missed this time, this disgusting hole would be their tomb.

A boom ripped through the room, tearing away her tentative grip on the ledge. Her body slid from the safety of the hallway, deeper into the dying room.

She had lost. Lost her life, and her brother.

As she slid across the muddy, blood-greased floor, a pleasant thought surprised her: at least she was with family once again.

It was worse than moving through the mud up top. The mud resisted you but didn't attack you the way these roots did.

Hawk's boot sank into the writhing mass, which latched around his ankle and crawled up his calf. As it did, he tore his other leg free and heaved it another step closer to the gurney set against the wall. Or the floor. Directions were mercurial.

His fingers folded over the metal railing of the hospital stretcher as the room shuddered with warning. The white fibers wrapped the other bedrail and sneaked across the mattress. The slithering plants under his feet shifted again, and Hawk's gut dropped.

"Ah, shit!" Irene's holler drew his attention, and he saw her slipping along the steepening floor, her hands flapping up for the rising door to the hallway.

Hawk turned to the gurney. This was it. Wherever this room was heading, it was going there now.

He yanked on the monstrous bed, his feeble body shaking with the effort. But the roots gave way, and the stretcher teetered towards him as the room sank beneath his feet. The eight-foot ceiling was shifting to the twenty-foot length of the shipping container as it dipped into the earth. He heaved on the bed, hauling it out of the roots and angling it to fall over the pile of plants covering Jaime's body. Metal clanged on metal as the bed cantered against the container wall, and Hawk wedged it into place with as much force as his tired body could find.

Irene's momentum slung her along, and her feet bounced against the bed's solid frame and stopped her descent.

Her head pivoted, a look of bewilderment on her face.

"Time to climb, sis!" Hawk was clambering up the bed frame, using it as a makeshift ladder to help him reach the disappearing hallway. Irene turned, found support in the railing for her feet, and climbed.

Hawk scampered behind her. She stood on the gurney's highest corner and stretched to the doorway once more. He scooted next to her, his head at her thigh as she strained to grasp the ledge.

"Here, let's try that again," he offered. He planted his feet into the bedrail, one hand steadying himself against the floor-wall as the other slid beneath Irene's raised foot.

She gave him her weight, tentative until Hawk egged her on with a yell. Then she shifted, the weight on his arm growing as she leapt up, and he shoved her away with every straining fiber of muscle that still worked.

The meaty slap of her hands hitting plywood was the sound of angels singing, and Hawk scrambled to the top of the bed frame. Irene pulled herself up, one leg over the lip of the edge, the other dangling in his face.

A sickening crunch echoed below him. Hawk glanced down. The room was shrinking. The ceiling closing in on the floor, the walls buckling shut. The container was a soda can getting squashed by Mother Nature and Emerson's untethered power.

"Come on!" Irene's voice. He looked up. Her arms reached to him, her face and hair shining with sweat and grime. Hawk stooped on the gurney's rail, rallying his body for one last burst of energy.

His legs engaged. Eyes locked on his sister. Arms up. Fingers splayed. Body loose in the air.

His hands wrapped around her forearms, and she clamped a death grip on him. She heaved, groaning against the strain as Hawk's feet scrabbled against the slick, sloping floor. Behind him, the cracking and squeezing of the container became incessant and deafening. The destruction closed in, intent on swallowing him.

Hawk was flying. Boots dangling, arms still secured in his sister's claws. He glanced down, the room now a gaping mouth full of loose detritus getting chomped by steel teeth just feet below him.

Then they were falling again. Back in the room. Into those gnashing metal jaws. Hawk let go. One last try to keep his sister safe from his choices. But she only clutched him tighter.

Irene, always taking the higher road. How could he protect her if she wouldn't cooperate? She needed to let him go, for her own sake.

As the thought cleared, he found himself collapsing onto the level floor of the hallway. He found Robin hauling Irene up by her waistband, his sister's underwear impossibly deep into her ass crack. A scene he could not help but find miraculous and hilarious.

"Move! Get away from the edge!" Robin's tone slapped Hawk back to the danger they were in. As if he needed extra reminding, the floor shifted under him.

Robin's thick legs churned, running from the destruction. Irene followed, working her panties back where they should be. Hawk stumbled to stand and found Blair, Layla, Chris, and Emerson huddled against the metal bunker doors.

His feet thumped the plywood, the monster's mouth falling behind them while its shearing cries grew to echoes as he reached the bunker entrance.

The group huddled together, crammed against the cellar doors. Hawk shielding his sister. Emerson clinging to his mother. Chris and Layla burying their faces into Robin's shoulders. A rumble came through the walls and floor as nature and gravity fought over the operating room. The far end of the shelter boiled in a mess of metal and mud, churning and spitting dirt into the hallway.

After a few tense breaths, everything stopped, the wall of noise dissipating into individual clanks and clinks, then a final groan of stress as the steel beast came to rest. The container's roof was visible through the doorway, with the bulk of it sunk deep into the ground. Most of the doorway was piled with earth—mud, clay, and the tangle of roots spinning out from the brown mess. A trickle of water spilled out of the mud and pattered onto the hallway floor before running into the new cavity of their would-be grave.

Irene was shaking in his arms. Except maybe she wasn't—Hawk was fighting the adrenaline too. The group detached themselves from one another but stayed huddled together, eyes fixed on the mess at the end of the hall.

Hawk didn't want to relax, sure that the bunker wasn't done sinking or getting crushed or whatever the hell was happening to it. But his body was telling him to sit. To give it a break. His ass landed on the bottom concrete step. It remained wet from the last time the doors had been opened. He didn't mind; every muscle sighed with the relief of sitting.

No one spoke. For several minutes, the only human sounds were coughs and sniffles. Hawk sucked in deep, long breaths, each loaded with the lush smell of the clay soil spilling into the shelter.

He broke the silence. "So, Emerson, that was new."

Chapter Fifty-One

"Jaime?" Blair's eyes grew wide. From fear or anticipation, Hawk couldn't tell.

The image of Jaime disappearing into those twining roots flashed through his mind, but he pushed it away. There was no time to dwell. Not for Blair. Not for any of them. He shook his head.

Her expression melted, eyes staring at something far away.

"We need to leave," Irene insisted. "Get back outside."

As if agreeing with her, the shelter sighed, metal moving against metal. A spark flashed at the trashed end of the bunker—electrical wires snapping loose from the collapsed room. The tight underground hallway was plunged in darkness, the walls disappearing into a boundless void. The kids cried out in fear; the emptiness filled with echoes of their bodies scrambling into the adults near them. Hawk felt Emerson's familiar fingers wrapping into his.

The darkness lasted a moment too long. Then the battery-fed emergency LEDs kicked in.

"It isn't safe here," Hawk admitted, "but we've got... that guy..."

He drew a blank on the name and looked to his sister for help. "Finch," she offered.

"We've got Finch running around out there, killing people. What are we going to do?" Hawk looked at the bunker door, checking the locks. "Christ, he's probably sitting there waiting for us to come out."

"I'll talk to him," Blair said.

Hawk turned to find Blair's pale stare piercing him. "Blair, not to offend, but what use is talking to this asshat? He murdered Terry, and he tried to kill Jaime. He's not looking for a conversation."

She swallowed, worrying her upper lip. "Because I know what he wants, Hawk."

Blair put her hands on her son's head. Emerson released Hawk's hand, then turned and hugged his mother's waist, his face lost in her midriff.

"He needs Emerson to fix him, heal his skin," Hawk replied.

Blair ran her fingers through Emerson's hair. "It's not that. Or at least, not just that. He wants Emerson." Blair's face soured, her twitching lips a prelude to tears. "He's Emerson's father," she whispered.

Chills shuddered through Hawk's chest, down his arms, tightening his skin on his bones. His tired gaze shot to Emerson. The young boy's eyes widened. His mouth slacked open, a tremor in his cheeks as he stared up at his mother.

"Mama?" he squeaked. "That... that burned man?"

Blair tightened her arms, pulling her son farther into her belly and wrapping his head in a powerful hug.

"Are you sure?" Hawk asked, regretting the fear in his tone.

"Not entirely. The burns are new. I ain't ever seen 'em like that before. And his name ain't 'Finch' either." Blair's attention drifted from Hawk to the ruined operating room. She swallowed hard. "But his body, his voice. The way he talks and what he says. It's more feeling than fact, but I'd bet money it's him, Hawk."

A thin wail seeped from Emerson's hidden face.

"Wait a minute," Irene interjected. "My landlord happens to be your kid's baby daddy?"

Blair's head pivoted, taking in Irene with a thin-lipped and narrow-eyed smirk.

"You sleepin' with him, honey?"

Irene blinked. "What was that?"

Blair's hands moved to cover Emerson's ears. "I asked if you're fucking the man."

Irene's face burst with disgust. "Of course not! I'm just his tenant—"

"No, you're not. To that man, everyone's somethin' different from what they think they are." Her hands lifted off her son's ears and returned to an embrace. "You're living there, sure. But if you ain't... well, if you ain't doing *that*, then he's using you for something else. That's how he works."

Irene's face relaxed, her eyes focusing on something she couldn't see.

Blair continued, "I was his wife. And the mother of his child. That done, he had no use for me. And he left."

"Why is he back, then?" Irene asked.

Blair looked at her son. She ran a hand over his filthy hair as he sobbed. "Because he found out about Emerson's power? Maybe the same way y'all did? I'm guessin', but that's what I think. Now he wants Emerson for himself."

"How did you meet him, Irene?" Hawk asked. There had to be a connection. Something that had drawn Finch and Irene to the ranch. Finch to his son. Irene to her brother.

She shrugged. Shook her head. "I met him at a support group after moving to San Antonio." Her speech was flat. Unimpressed. "He was at Uvalde Hospital during the... the incident. Being treated for a chemical or acid burn, I think." Her gaze bounced to Emerson and back. She shrugged a shoulder. "He didn't seem to want any friends, and I wasn't interested in making any. It felt like two introverts finding each other in a space full of people."

"He rents to you, though?"

"Yeah." Irene nodded. "A few weeks after we met, I mentioned my rental fell through. That I'd miss the next meeting because I needed to find somewhere to live. He offered to put me up in a trailer on his land."

Blair snorted. Irene's brow crinkled in confusion.

"Did you ever mention Emerson?" Hawk asked.

Irene shrugged both shoulders now. "I'd never met him. How could I?"

"You knew Dad and I came to Texas to find him, right? I told you in the hospital. We came to find the boy that could heal with his hands, get him to heal Dad?"

She looked past him, through the shelter doors. For a moment, her lips twitched and her gaze rose to the ceiling. Her thinking face.

"Yeah... yeah, I was open with him about it. Told him stuff I didn't tell the rest of the group. And he knew I was looking for you," Irene offered.

"Does solving this little mystery help us?" Robin begged. She sat on the plywood with her back against the metal wall of the shipping container. Her arms rested around Layla and Chris as they cuddled into her shoulders. "He's here, now, and shooting people. What the hell do we do?"

She was right, of course. Figuring out how Finch had found Emerson, how Irene had discovered the farm—none of it could save them from a bullet.

"We need a plan," she added. "A place to go that's safe from—" She ended the sentence with a wide sweep of her hand, gesturing at everything around them.

As if offended by her insinuation, the steel walls groaned.

"Could we... stay here?" Irene asked. "I mean, I know I don't understand the ins and outs of your ability, Emerson, but could you keep us alive down here indefinitely?"

Emerson's face turned out from Blair's gut. Streaks of tears on his cheeks glinted under the LED lights as he met Irene's curiosity. "I guess so?" he squeaked.

"So we wait here until, what?" Robin asked. She shifted as Chris nuzzled against her, Robin's face scrunching up as the kid pinched a rib or something. "He gets bored and leaves?"

"Until someone comes," Blair offered.

Robin snorted. "If Terry's dead, then everyone who knows about this bunker is in it right now, except Finch."

Hawk watched the two women stare at one another, as if an answer might appear between them. He silently cursed Jaime and the paranoid security theater he'd built on this ranch. If he'd wanted Emerson safe, he should have surrounded him with people. Built trust instead of distance.

"No one's coming," Hawk concluded aloud. The words felt heavy, like they might collapse the bunker further.

"And we can't wait forever," Robin added, pointing along the corridor to the pile of roots and mud pressing on the crumpled room. "This whole thing's gonna sink."

Layla murmured low, capturing her mother's attention. Robin kissed her head, offering a demure whisper in response.

Hawk took stock. He had the Glock. He slipped it from this thigh holster and checked the magazine. Ten rounds. "Anyone else have a weapon?" he asked. He slapped the mag home, checked the chamber, and holstered the gun.

Silence.

"Any weapons? Anything at all?" Hawk begged.

"What about those roofie pens?" Irene suggested.

Hawk glanced at Robin. She nodded, eyes pointed towards the closed door halfway between them and the destroyed operating room. "Top shelf of the cabinet in my office. I should have a few in there."

Irene was already picking her way to the door, hugging the wall.

"Blades?" Hawk asked.

Robin's face fell. "They were all in the operating room."

Irene returned with two of the Rohypnol pens and handed them to Blair and Robin.

"If we get to the house, we'll be okay," Blair said. "Once we're in the safe room, we can call for help."

"We're going home?" Emerson's voice squeaked as he stared up at his mother.

"Yes, we are, sweetness," his mother whispered.

Hawk put a hand on his sister's shoulder, bringing her face to face with him. "Is there *anything* you can think of that might help us against him? Any... weakness?"

Her face scrunched with thought. "He smokes lots of dope. He's... he's kind of feeble, honestly." Her tone and eyes turned pitying. "He can't even walk very well because of his injuries. Not terribly strong. Without that gun, he'd be defenseless. We could just knock him over and run."

"Do not underestimate him," Blair countered. "He's not a brute, not like Jaime. Not physically. But he's clever and cruel."

"The hills."

All eyes fell on Emerson, his muffled, soft voice capturing the group.

Hawk nodded. "What do you mean, Em?"

The kid wiped a dirty palm across his dripping nose, his eyes blinking around the space until they landed on Irene.

"You said he can't run good." Emerson pivoted his gaze to Robin, to the children against her bosom. "The way Layla can't walk good. I had to heal her legs so she could come through the switchbacks with us today. If we run into the hills, he won't be able to keep up."

Hawk offered Emerson a reassuring smile and nodded. The kid was thinking through his terror, solving the problem. "It makes sense. We're near the far side of the field. The hills wrap the southern edge and lead to the house. We open the door, break up the stairs, then cut a straight line south through the field. That's the fastest way to the hills."

"That's not much of a plan," Irene pleaded, Robin grunting in agreement.

Another rumble tickled up Hawk's boots, tingling the soles of his feet and stirring the anxiety in his gut. He crossed to the wall, putting a hand on the corrugated steel. The slight vibration was constant in his fingers. It swelled through the metal, a tactile purr growing to a growl.

"We don't have time to debate," he sighed. The rattle expanded, everyone tensing as it rose into the quiet like water filling a sinking ship. "Get ready to run, everyone. The bunker's not done collapsing."

Without hesitating for the group's protests, he stepped to the doors and began unbolting the interior locks.

Chapter Fifty-Two

The uncertainty in Hawk's voice tightened Emerson's chest. He never sounded this way unless things were going to be bad. Like when Lucifer had attacked that customer.

Hands slid between him and his mother. Her hands. She stooped to him, moving him so his face and her face were touching noses.

"Emerson, you don't stop, you hear me? You run. You hear gunshots, you keep running."

"But—"

"No, sweetness, no 'buts.' Not today. Today is running. When Hawk opens that door, we're hauling ass to the hills like you said we should. Don't worry about anyone but yourself. You. Just. Run."

Emerson shot his stare to Layla, just now gathering to her unsteady feet. Dr. Travers watched him with eyes that begged for the opposite of what Mom was telling him to do. Chris wiped his face, his cornflower halo still beaming, his soul bracing to go.

An image of Uncle Terry came to Emerson. His head disappearing. His light blinking out. There had been no time to save him after the stranger shot him.

Not a stranger. The monster was his father.

He looked at Mom, her face wrinkled and dirty, random red strands of hair falling loose from her ponytail and reaching away from her, mixing into the uncertain pinks of her halo. She had lied to Jaime about not knowing the man's identity. Emerson had seen it, and it had turned his colors muddy. He didn't understand why she had fibbed. Mom had always talked about his father truthfully, at least as far as her aura had told him. And those stories were awful. His father was not a nice man. Especially to Mom.

And then there was the truth Jaime had revealed. That the field was a colossal deception, stitched so Jaime could use Emerson without him realizing.

But not just Jaime. Dr. Travers too. And even Mom had known, and she had forgotten. No, not even that—she had made a choice to forget. To hide herself from the secret with another lie. To use Emerson for her own gain.

The corrugated panels appeared fuzzy as they rattled back and forth with the rumble. The intensity of it, the shaking of his insides—it reminded him of the burned man's light tearing through him, revealing his loneliness to himself.

That burned man—his father—he had known they were using him. That Emerson was their tool. A flush of shame rushed through his cheeks, followed by a rising anger in his belly at his family. But beneath those sharp emotions lingered a tingle of curiosity. His father had lived with his power. Learned how to hone it. Emerson wondered what he might have learned from him if he had stayed in his life. How to shape his halo without setting life ablaze.

Hawk and his sister hunched under the bunker doors. They each gripped a handle, ready to unfold the shelter doors like a book and let them pour out like the words. To Emerson's side, Layla stood, her mother and Chris holding hands in a chain.

Mom didn't hold his hand, though. Her palm was on his chest, hugging him to her.

Hawk eased back the last deadbolt.

The bunker was unlocked.

Mom crouched down, her body behind him, her hug against him tightening. "Remember what I told you," she whispered. "Those doors open, and you run like hell."

He would—Emerson would run like hell. Maybe he wouldn't stop at the house. Maybe he would run past it. To the orchard. Then the property line, the one Mom forbade him to cross. And then past that. To whatever was beyond. Someplace where Mom wasn't. Where his father wouldn't find him.

He would run from this place. From the secrets and lies they grew on the farm. Under the farm. Run, run, run, until his legs were nubs like too-sharpened pencils.

And he would take his dog with him.

Hawk raised his fingers. A countdown.

Three. Emerson felt heat in his legs, along with the growling of the shelter and ground around them.

Two. Mom's fingers clawed at his rib cage, her other hand moving to his shoulder as she crouched. Layla whispered to her mother, "I love you," and her mother said it back to her with a kiss to her head.

One.

Hawk and his sister heaved their shoulders into the doors.

A seam opened, and a line of grey sky filled the gap. Emerson's feet pulsed, itching to launch. Rain spattered the concrete steps.

The doors stopped with a rattle after a few inches. Hawk stumbled into them as they refused to open farther.

"What the..." Hawk pressed again, peering into the small opening.

Confused whispers came from Mom and Dr. Travers.

"That fucker chained the doors. He locked us in!" Hawk's colors shifted to a sky blue. Bewilderment. "Why would he do that?"

Hawk turned to his sister, then to the group. His expression melted, the way it did when he focused on something.

"Wait, listen," he said, tilting an ear to the gap.

Emerson held his breath, and the air was quiet because everyone else was doing it too. They were listening and sensing the rumble through the walls.

Hawk smiled, pivoting his gaze to them. "That clatter isn't the bunker. It's too regular. I think it's an engine—"

The shelter doors caved in with a demonic scream of metal and people. Teeth slammed through the seam of light, metal fangs on a wide head grinding into them, cracking them, scraping against them. Shoving the doors inward.

There were flashes of aura, then their bodies twisted in ways they shouldn't as the green metal smashed over them. The monster's rusting mouth sandwiched Hawk and his sister between the stairs and the crumpled steel doors.

Chapter Fifty-Three

The excavator's arm lifted out of the concrete shell. Finch gasped as the bucket's teeth cleared the doorway, dripping with blood.

Shit, shit, shit! Had Emerson been under the doors? Had he killed his son?

Finch snagged the Desert Eagle off the console and threw open the cab door. He fell more than climbed to the wet ground, catching himself at the last moment to stay on his numb feet.

He rounded the side of the backhoe and stared into the shelter entrance. Gun raised, he sighted straight into the hole in the earth. The chug of the idling excavator mimicked his racing heartbeat.

Both doors were caved, crumpled and pressed into the stairs and walls. Blood covered the concrete, rivulets pouring over the steps into the bunker as rain continued. On the bottom tread, cantilevered over the French drain, was a severed leg. Long, with the snapped end of a thick femur sticking out of it. An adult limb. Not Emerson's. It was too big. Finch felt the effervescent tingle of relief in his chest. A giddiness at the thought that maybe he had crushed Jaime, saving himself a bullet.

Finch counted the treads in the concrete. Ten. Ten steps and he would be with Emerson. He'd convince Emerson to come with him, or he would die trying.

Before descending, he listened. Strained his broken ears to detect any sound. Over the purr of the diesel engine, the hum of the steady rain, he heard nothing.

His boots helped him find traction on the small path of wet cement that wasn't covered with the crumpled doors. One hand on the pockmarked concrete for balance, he climbed into the shelter.

Piece by piece, step by slick concrete step, the space came into his view. Plywood floors, stained with dirt and mud, warped from prolonged exposure to moisture. Metal walls, vertical corrugations. And a dozen feet away, five people. Finch recognized most of them—Emerson and Blair, the kids who had been there when he'd killed Terry. Petrified, whiter than the walls of the room, the tall ceiling—ten feet or more—making them appear so very insignificant. They trembled, the shock of his violent breach still bouncing through their bodies. All of them, except Emerson.

His son stared at him. Through him. Mouth slack and eyes tired, unfocused. Not afraid. Not anymore. Resigned, perhaps.

That might be enough. Finch would take it.

He trained his gun on Blair. "I got no clue what y'all been up to. Must have been big, based on what I saw up top."

Finch lowered a step, peeking down long enough to toe the orphan leg out of his way.

"For a minute, I thought the plants were attacking me. The whole thing, all around that tower? Exploded like some god-damned green inferno. Caused one hell of a racket. Made driving that Caterpillar a real bottom-clencher. The growth nearly knocked it over."

Finch's feet were off the steps. On the level surface of the bunker. He faced the two women, the three children. Emerson's friends hid in the arms of the second woman. Blair cowered with their son as Emerson stayed planted just off-center in the hallway, holding that empty stare. A fitting image, a summary of their relationship.

Finch pivoted the gun to the unknown woman. Her flinching reaction told him what he needed to know. She was no threat.

A wet cough pulled his attention backwards. Keeping his aim on the group, Finch peered at the stairs behind him.

A torso protruded from beneath the door, the body crushed against the steps. Finch watched as the head creaked on its neck, the arm locked at an unnatural angle. The shaking face was thin. Lean. A man, but not Jaime.

"Goddammit," Finch hissed. He lowered to his knee, peeking at Blair and the group, keeping his gun trained on them. The blood obscured the injured man's features, but Finch could see strands of blond. His mitt landed on the man's forehead, and his thumb jerked open the flaccid eyelid.

Blue eyes.

Irene's brother, Wes. Pinned under the door by the excavator. He had hoped today would end well for them, for Irene and Wes to reunite. Work out their shit or not. To restart their lives together or apart. Either way, their search was done.

A strange reluctance pierced him. A regret so strong it should have had flavor, not that he could taste anything.

He whispered, soft so the others didn't hear, "I'm sorry, Wes."

The blue eye watered, either tears of sadness or a mere effect of his mortal injuries.

"I didn't want this for you, please believe that. Your sister was a good person. A rare friend. Someone who saw past the ugliness in people. Found their value. Made them feel it. But I suppose you already knew that."

As if in response, Wes's hand twitched. Fingers reached away from Finch. Past him. Across the steps.

Finch swallowed. Released Wes's eyelid, which stuck open as the eye studied something behind Finch. A sickening fear bloated his stomach. An emotional gorge he wasn't ready to confront.

He turned. The group remained frozen in the moment by the barrel of his gun. He shifted the weapon to his other hand and looked to the far wall.

Needing to see. Not wanting to.

The second door bit into the steps, a longwise fold pressing part of it into the concrete. Another body poked out from beneath the corner of the metal sheet. A sloppy mess of dirty brown hair sticking to a blood- and mud-caked face facing the ceiling. Two slender arms splayed over her head, like she had tried to dive out of the way of the Caterpillar's punch. He didn't need to shift her hair. To see her eyes. Finch understood what he had done.

He scuttled over to her, his free hand tugging on the metal. It didn't budge, lodged tight by the excavator's force. The pointlessness of trying to move it, to save Irene, became obvious—Finch had crushed her against the steps, and the door pinned her into the concrete at her waist.

Irene hadn't died at the hands of Blair or her lover. Finch had killed his only real friend.

A shocking wave of regret pulled on his gut, rocking him to a knee. But he breathed through it. His goal repeated in his head. A mantra that reminded him what was left to lose.

Save him. Save Emerson.

He rose, saying nothing to the corpse of Irene because she wouldn't hear it anyway, and turned to the others. Emerson remained a statue of exhaustion. Blair struggled to urge him deeper into the hallway, but their son stood fixed.

"Leave 'im, Blair. You had a good run. Made your money. But that's over now. Emerson's coming with me."

"Go to hell!" Blair cried. "I'll die before you take my boy!"

"You deserve nothing less," Finch growled.

He trained the pistol on her. Straightened his arm and sighted her head as her eyes widened; followed her as she dropped into a cower. Finch found Emerson's face between his aim and Blair, and he yanked the gun towards the ceiling.

"You piece of shit," Finch spat. "You'd shield yourself with our son?"

Emerson's stare remained sallow and his body immobile, even as Blair clamored to hide behind him.

"Can you see, Emerson?" Finch cried. "Do you realize she's using you, yet?" He took a step forward, causing the other woman to pull Emerson's friends down the hallway several feet. Emerson stayed fixed.

"She's using you now! Protecting her own life with yours! You have the gift, son. Not her. You get to choose how to use it."

Finch took another step forward, and an odd tickle reached into his gut. A glow that fed his body.

"Come with me, Emerson. Come with me, and no one can use you again. You'll be a god among the rabble. We'll shape this world into what *you* want it to be."

The warmth in Finch's belly spread. A tightening flutter moved over his skin, blissful and intense. He closed his eyes, afraid the sensation might leak out of them.

His son was reaching into him. Healing him.

Blair's twanging voice poked through his joy. "He'll never go with you, you bastard!"

Finch chuckled, his breath heaving as his body came to life. "Oh, I think you're in for a surprise, *pendeja*."

Chapter Fifty-Four

Her legs were wet. Maybe that's what had woken her? Jesus, had she pissed the bed?

But then, Irene didn't feel damp. She didn't feel at all. Her eyes groaned open.

Everyone was upside down, walking on the ceiling.

The bunker. Was it falling again? Wouldn't she sense it in her gut? But she was still. The room wasn't sinking.

The data congealed a moment later. She was on her back, staring into the hallway.

The realization grounded her. This was real, this confusion of knowing there should be more of her. She should have legs. They should exist.

Her head tilted forward so she could see if her limbs were there. If they had ever been there.

Her stomach disappeared under a sheet of green- and red-flecked metal.

She put hands on the steel, trying to shove it off. But it gripped her, wedged her against the sharp points of the steps that dug into her spine. The steel refused to move. The bunker held her in an alligator bite—the door crumpled over her, the steps biting from beneath.

Maybe she was stuck here forever. Maybe this was where she lived now. On the steps. In the shelter. A steel slab for a blanket.

Warm clarity dribbled through her mind. A comforting buzz that, as pleasant as it was, carried dire implications.

Emerson's power.

Reality lost its blur. Her body was crushed. In mortal tatters, and Emerson was the only stitch holding it together.

This wasn't like before, though. The bliss was missing, nothing close to the thrill she'd experienced in the operating room. As if Emerson was restraining himself. Because Irene wasn't whole. The part of her that remained was merely... alive. Sort of here, but not all present.

She lowered her head to the steps. A few paces from her, Finch stood on the ceiling—or the floor. His arm extended, pointing that huge pistol into the hallway.

Aiming at Emerson. Or his mother.

Odors became clear. The tang of minerals. Machine oil? Or was that mold? Some copperish edge she didn't enjoy. Her gaze drifted to the steps holding her together. She found the resin waffle of the sole of someone's work boot. Her arm moved to it. Pushed it aside. The boot connected to a leg, but the leg didn't connect to anyone.

This wasn't her limb. She couldn't feel any legs right now, but this one definitely didn't belong to her. It had a holster around the thigh. Under the gross part.

It didn't matter. Once Emerson let go, there would be nothing left of her.

Another wave of healing crashed through her, the force of it smearing her thoughts like the tide spreads sand on the beach.

She focused past the tip of the boot. The other door lay wrecked against the steps. Her brother's face peeked out from the close edge.

Wes was pulverized too. One eye hung open, the shallow blue stark against the clay crust and blood over his face. It looked past her. At the tiled ceiling of the morgue at Uvalde Hospital. Wes was dead, again. *I guess third time's a charm.*

The buzz under her skin became an itching swarm. She heaved her lungs against the binding steel. She clenched her eyes. The healing energy wanted her to move. Breathe. But she had no room for it.

Her eyes popped opened on Wes. He focused on her now. Watched her with that pale-blue iris. She wanted to see life in it. Wanted it so badly that she pretended it was there. If she pretended hard enough, she would believe it. And she could spend her last breath the way her father had. Say words that would haunt Wes until his final moments too.

Wes blinked. Not pretend. If she'd imagined it, it wouldn't have been so slow. A creak, at most. And real. The movement was too mundane to be her imagination.

That meant Wes was alive. Like her, living but not whole. The rest of him creamed under that door.

Emerson was keeping both of them alive. She thanked him. Not out loud.

Emerson.

Irene let her head tilt backwards. Finch was there, gun in hand. Emerson standing in front of him. Blair shrinking down the hallway with everyone else.

Would Finch kill Emerson? Or steal him away? Either way, her brother was dead. She was dead.

What could she do? Her world had become so limited. This metal tent was her home. Her universe. She had no way of fighting him. She had no legs to chase him. Except the spare leg on the stairs.

The image popped to her like the snapping of a button. That leg. The one with the holster banded to the thigh.

The holster that contained a gun.

His skin was moving. Scars unfolded along his arm, the patchwork flesh unwinding into something natural.

Emerson belonged to him. This was his son's way of welcoming his father back into his life.

Finch opened his eyes.

The pistol wavered off his target as his body swam in the flowing bliss. Finch watched a flash of red hair move on Emerson. Hands yanking on his ratty shirt. Blair, trying to haul him away.

She was shouting. The words were indistinct over the bubbling in his head. But her voice—the timbre expanding with every syllable, the increasing clarity and depth as his ears re-formed. Her screams fascinated him. They had dimensions to them—location, direction. And there were layers now. The patter of the rain, echoing between the metal walls, waiting to be heard over the crying children. It was a symphony.

"Leave 'im, Blair," he croaked. His voice was shaking. He heard himself yelling, but he didn't know what he sounded like anymore. "You've lost him."

Emerson took a step forward. Towards Finch; away from Blair.

Finch smiled. His eyes... they were watering! Tears. He could cry tears!

He blinked until they tickled his plump cheeks. His son remained blurred and distorted. And the light echoed too. Like the sound, the walls amplified it.

Blair came at Finch with a fury belying her tiny frame. Her hands rammed at his face, her screams at his ears. She scratched at him, fingers peeling into his new flesh.

The wondrous tingle filled his arms as they lifted. Bones free in their skin, muscles unbounded by scar tissue. He shoved Blair against the wall by the other cowering woman. His hand came up, wavering with the unique sensations and the weight of his gun, and he squeezed the heavy trigger.

Blair's shoulder disappeared. She spun on her feet, the bullet twisting her like a broken marionette. She collapsed to the floor.

A shudder racked him, obscuring the joy of shooting Blair. A realization that his cooked eye was functioning again. There were two Emersons now. Two of everyone and everything. One real and one ghost. Nausea followed, and Finch had to close his new eye to keep from falling over.

"Yes!" he cried, the glee overtaking him. His voice pitching in his reverie. "I knew you would see I'm here to help you!"

Emerson closed another stride.

Finch cackled. From the tickle in his groin. From the relaxing of his muscles and skin. Novel dimensions formed around him. A slick bitterness in the air. A coppery flavor. Did air always have that taste? Had he forgotten?

"You don't have to be afraid, son. Mom can't hurt you. Not no more. Now that I'm here, I'll keep you safe." The roiling changes throughout his body made it difficult to think, much less speak. But he had to. He had to share his love and admiration for what the boy was doing for him.

It was over. The stares. Children screaming when he approached. The fucking sanctimonious pity from nobodies. People with nothing to show for their lives. The human equivalent of chum in the water. The indignity of their pity would never lie upon him again.

Finch glanced at his son, not an arm's length away. With both eyes open, Finch found the sensation of depth intoxicating as he tried to bring Emerson into focus.

The kid's mottled brown hair. Mud-spattered face. His eyes—so tired. Finch had put him through hell today. Put all of them through hell. Forced Emerson to learn a lifetime of lessons in an afternoon. Sacrificed Irene to get to his son. But the cost was nothing next to the prize.

"You understand. You and I, we can redefine this world to our liking. Command whatever we want, Emerson. Will it into existence! Emerson, we are the way!"

"No," Emerson squeaked, his face still slack and unfocused.

Finch must have misheard his son. His melodrama might have been thick, but it was impossible to deny the sensations powering through him like electricity through a wire.

Emerson continued. "You're not the way."

Finch's fresh eyes narrowed.

His son's head pivoted to the shelter steps painted in blood and gore. He sighed, his words carried on the end of the long breath.

"You're just in the way."

Chapter Fifty-Five

I rene pulled the trigger. Finch's head disappeared in a splatter across the wall and ceiling.

And then he turned to her, his face intact.

The pattern was obvious: Emerson was keeping her alive. And Wes. And now his mother. And, to her irritation, Finch. Like in the operating room, when the kid had saved her brother and ended up mending her too.

Finch gaped at her, his umber pupils richer than she had ever seen. His skin was no longer taut on his bones; it swirled now, slackening as the pale patches and flaring red scars mellowed out into a rich sienna. And hair. Finch grew hair. Thick and lush and swelling out of his head like it was being forced. Eyebrows over his eyes. A moustache framing his plump lips.

He beamed. Genuine thrill at seeing her. Without the scars, his joy was obvious. Maybe from the healing. But his stare—the shimmering fixation, the palpable surprise to discover something lost. Irene recognized it, because she had felt it too. The pleasure and turmoil of finding Wes alive at the dispensary.

If she could've breathed, she would have thanked Finch for reuniting her with family.

Instead, she lifted her arm up. Or down. Directions were meaningless at this point.

Finch's face piqued. The gregarious smile stayed, but his eyes soured. Confused.

The shift in her weight pulled on her middle. A part of her was stretching between the steel door under her and the concrete steps above. She was falling apart.

She squeezed. *Crack!* Finch's head snapped, revealing the far side of the metal box for a flash before re-forming. His massive pistol clattered on the ceiling-floor as his arms pinwheeled.

It was pointless. She'd shoot, he'd heal. Repeat. The pattern would break when she was out of bullets. Or when Finch left with Emerson and she died next to her brother.

Resignation cleared her choices. Finch had won, and he'd used her and Wes as fodder for it. Her gaze fell—or lifted. Along Finch's legs. Past them, to the cowering boy. Beyond were the two women. Blair lay bleeding on the floor, and Robin hovered over the children as their wails shook the shelter.

Emerson shook too. Struggling to stand as whatever he was doing racked his tiny form. Tears billowed from his eyes, and his tired face was streaked with grime. It wouldn't take long for him to collapse. And when he did, they would all be dead.

Hawk and his sister remained trapped on the steps, their halos wrecked along with most of their bodies. Mama's aura pulsed on the floor behind him, a bullet lodged deep in her upper arm, letting blood flow out. Their lights teetered on the edge of flitting out, and Emerson knew he was the only thing keeping them alive.

And in the middle of this horror was the monster that was his real father. Laughing as his scars melted back to skin. Smiling even as Hawk's sister shot him in the face.

Emerson's light flailed, threatening to lash out again as he struggled to bend it around the man. To single Finch out of his aura without letting Hawk or Irene or his mother die. The fledgling halo refused any form except the security blanket it always took, drenching everyone nearby with indiscriminate comfort.

A haze covered everything as stretching his power forced him to tears. His gut trembled with fatigue, beyond any tiredness he had experienced.

But it was possible! He had seen his father create tentacles with his black light. Whip them out as if they were fingers. Why couldn't he do it too?

His tears cleared in an involuntary blink when Irene shot Finch in the head once more. The man staggered backwards a few steps, towards the crushed room that entombed Jaime. But he was still well within Emerson's radiating power.

Emerson's tremble bloomed to a rumble. Not fatigue—something closer to desperation. The thought of Finch joining Jaime in that hole stirred Emerson's colors. Jaime had used Emerson. Now Finch was destroying everything Emerson wanted to keep. He saw the truth in his father's writhing black coil of light. Finch would kill all the people he loved. Even worse, he would force Emerson to let them die. Then leave their bodies to rot in this bunker, and take Emerson away from home.

His fingernails scratched his palms as his shaking hands balled into fists. A new color welled out of the places Finch had torn open. An ugliness Emerson detested. One that tasted like the mold in the shelter floor. Passions roiled up that Emerson didn't want to admit he had.

This was anger. And hatred. At Finch for trying to end what he loved. At Mom for hiding the truth from herself. And at Jaime for lying and hurting people and using him to cover it up.

The wound on Finch's head closed. Those charcoal emotions spiraled out of Emerson's core, wrapped through his light. His rage focused on Finch.

Emerson's light formed a chasm.

His father stood in darkness, the healing energy bent away from him. A river of life swirled around a boulder of hate. The aura washed over his mother. Across Hawk and Irene. The fury changing Emerson's power from that cozy blanket to enraged fists that clamped around the things he loved and shunned the things he hated.

Emerson's fiery gaze slipped to the gun in Irene's wobbling hand. Followed it up through her piecemeal emerald halo to her faded stare. Her eyes locked on his, and her face expanded from surrender to surprise.

He held his stance, focused his mind on those negative colors, afraid any motion would shatter the control he had on his light.

He had to protect Irene and the others, but he needed Finch exposed.

And he needed Irene to pull that trigger. One more time.

Through his clenched teeth, a wad of spittle dropping from his lip, he hissed at Hawk's sister. *"Kill... my... father!"*

Irene's hand rattled on her arm. The gunsight scraped over Finch's face as she overcorrected.

Crack!

A small pink bloom puffed from Finch's chest. His boots thumped on the plywood, once... twice...

But he wouldn't fall. Irene's muscles were noodles. No strength. Just tremors and shock. She couldn't hold the gun any longer. It fell up to the hallway floor.

Finch glared, her betrayal etched across his fresh face. The man's supple lips trembled, words failing to form.

So be it. Irene had no way to describe today, either.

Then a gleam of red traced out of the corner of Finch's mouth. The shimmering cherry of oxygenated blood slid into the curve of his full lip. His stare turned to Emerson, the barest of tremors visible in his jaw. After a moment, his gaze fell to the red stain blooming through his gingham shirt. Blood leaving his reborn body, the wound not healing on its own. Finch stiffened, as if afraid to move lest he fall apart.

Vibrations grew as Irene peeled away from the metal clamping her against the steps. She was just a torso. Somehow still living, weightless and unoriented. Her hand slapped against the door as she tried to catch herself.

Then the pressure in her chest released with a sucking pop, the remains of her body falling from the crushing steel. Her breath refused to come—the panic of suffocation set in, her lungs and brain screaming for air, even though she knew Emerson's power wouldn't let her expire.

Through the static eroding her vision, Irene watched Finch crumple to the floor.

Chapter Fifty-Six

Wes leaned into the deck railing, letting the colors of the sun wash through his cigarette smoke. On the underside of the storm's remnants, pinks and oranges exploded, their warmth at odds with the loamy scent of rain, but fitting with the dusty tang of his smoke. Closer to the ground, the canopy of the pecan trees fractured the intense grapefruit shine. The leaves and branches swayed in the last gentle coughs of the storm, giving Wes visions of the painted sky peppered with blinding sun.

He pulled on the cancer stick, the ember sizzling into the filter and sending a sour fiberglass flavor over his tongue. His breath billowed out gray and then ignited as it seeped into the light coming through the orchard. He stubbed the butt under the railing and dropped it into the rusted coffee can Blair kept on her porch.

The screen door creaked on its hinges, and he looked up as Robin crossed the threshold, her boots tapping the wooden porch as she approached. She'd changed clothes since the bunker, and was now wearing deep-blue denim jeans and a crisp V-neck T-shirt over her barreled torso.

"Hey," she offered, her voice strained. Exhaustion had settled over them, but in the ninety minutes since they'd crawled out of the shelter, Robin hadn't sat still. She'd jetted between Emerson, his mother, Irene, and Wes, making sure everyone was okay. She'd even kept that bastard Finch alive and sedated.

Wes smiled. "Hey, Robin. How is she?"

"Which one?" she sighed. "Your sister or Blair?"

He rotated so his ass was on the railing. It was bliss to relax, take just a smidge of pressure off of his body and mind. He positioned himself so Robin fell in his shadow, keeping her from squinting into the fireworks sunset behind him.

"Start with my sister." He chuckled.

Robin nodded. "Still asleep. She's going to be fine, Hawk."

A flinch ran through his shoulders. Hawk was his name now, and something about that didn't sit right now that Irene was back in his life. Whether he wanted it or not, he had earned it.

"Thank you. Anything... weird?" he asked. Both his and his sister's bodies had been destroyed. Emerson had kept their torsos alive until Blair and Robin had pried off the collapsed bunker doors. The experience had been... unreal. Fucking awful. Irene had panicked, to where Robin had to sedate her until her body returned to normal. No Rohypnol; the shitty memories would survive.

Robin shrugged. "There's this kind of ripple of discoloration across her abdomen," she said, her thick finger tracing a line over her own belly. "Can't tell if it's permanent or not."

Wes licked his lips, swallowing the lump of nerves in his throat.

Robin saw it and moved her hand to his face. "Hey," she lilted, "she'll be okay. You and her, y'all will be okay too. I believe that, Hawk."

He nodded again, covering his uncertainty by changing the topic. "What about Blair?"

Her fingers fell, slapping her thigh. Her gaze left his as she sidestepped into the sunset's glow. Her eyes squinted so tight they appeared closed, and she absorbed the spectacle for a few breaths before responding.

"She's pissed. I can tell." Her shoulders shrugged. "I don't think she's going to let us stay here. Now that she knows about the farm. Or remembers, I guess." The ruby sunlight accentuated her worry lines, but her voice carried no hint of the anxiety Hawk saw on her face. They both knew how tentative their presence had always been here. They served at her whim, yet neither had anyplace else to call home.

"I can talk to her," he offered. "With Jaime gone, she'll need us to keep this place running. It makes no sense to cast you out, you know?"

She nodded, her gaze still fixed on the sunset.

"And Emerson loves Layla. You know he does. And despite what she says, she enjoys him too."

Her nods grew emphatic, and her hand rose to wipe away tears. They stood there, Wes facing the house, Robin at his hip, face to the sun, allowing it to glisten in the sweat on her skin.

"I'll talk to her," he repeated, moving an arm across her shoulders and pulling her in for an awkward side hug. She reciprocated, pivoting into him until the embrace was full.

"We don't have anywhere to go, Hawk," she cried. He had never seen Robin lose it. Didn't know she could. But this brief glimpse into her terrors and fears, her vulnerable exposure shaking against him—Wes suddenly realized how Emerson must feel. His closed circle of family and friends in danger. It was no way to live.

He'd had enough of it.

"We won't have to go anywhere, okay?" He took her face in his hands, tilting her head up to capture her gaze. "You and Layla are going to stay here, I promise."

Robin pulled away, smiling—out of gratitude or pity, Wes wasn't sure. "Thanks, Hawk. I need to check on Finch. Make sure he's still knocked out."

Wes nodded. Finch's chest wound would be fatal unless they let Emerson heal him or took Finch to a hospital, but Robin guessed they had a few hours to figure out what to do. A drain in Finch's chest cavity was keeping his lung from collapsing, and now he was sleeping off the heavy sedatives inside of Wes's tiny house.

"Okay. Be safe." He looked past her to the screen door. He could hear movement inside. Blair stirring with nervous energy.

The low whine of the electric engine faded: Robin leaving in the golf cart. Wes pushed himself off the porch railing, his hands trembling at his sides as he paced to the front door. He had just lied to Robin. And to himself. In truth, he wasn't sure any of them had a home at the ranch anymore.

Chapter Fifty-Seven

"**C**an we talk, Blair?"

She sat at her dining room table, stacks of mail segregated into piles in front of her. Her gaze lifted to Wes. Stern as ever. Lips tight with stress. She nodded, then gestured to the seat next to her.

As he sat, she pivoted her compact frame to him, crossing one leg over the other and folding her arms over her chest. Her face was passive and unreadable. Wes wasn't sure if he should expect a flogging or an eviction notice.

She stared at him. He stared back at her. Both waited for the other to start.

Wes made the first effort. "Are you okay, Blair?"

A tremor moved across her lips and cheeks. Whatever she was feeling, she held it in.

"No, I'm not. I'm pretty fucked up, to be honest."

Wes pressed into the chair. It took him a breath to find the right words. "That's okay though, right? No one would be okay after today."

She gave a dismissive shrug. "Hawk," she started, then swallowed the question.

"What is it?" he prompted.

Her tongue moved over her thin lips. "Did you know? About the organ farm?"

He sighed. Ready to lie to her. If only out of habit and exhaustion. But he didn't.

"Yeah," he said. "I had to retrofit the damned space. Keep you and Emerson away from it."

Blair's face cracked. Something was teeming under her skin. Anger, or resentment, or something worse.

"Look," he pleaded, "I wasn't given a choice, okay? Jaime wanted it done, and I had nowhere to go. No one to go to for help."

She nodded, holding up a hand. "I ain't mad, Hawk. I understand how things work here. How they worked, I mean."

He swallowed the flavor of shame and the bitterness of choices he'd unmake if he could.

Blair sucked in a breath, a hollow huff that held the room hostage until she spoke. "Jaime said something in that... that awful room."

A heat rose from his gut into his throat. "What did he say?" he asked, knowing what it was.

Her eyes darted between his face and the table as she spoke. "He said... he said I knew about the organ farm too. That he showed me it. And I wanted him to tear it down, stop the whole thing. But..."

Her hands went to her cheeks. As if she needed to hold her head still to get the words out.

"But that I changed my mind. Jaime said he explained how much money we made by using Emerson for organs. And after that, I was okay with it."

Wes's mind raced for something to say. He didn't get the opportunity.

"Hawk, Jaime said I *chose* to not know about it. That I used one of these needles? With the drug in it that makes you forget?"

"Rohypnol," he said.

Her gaze held his for several breaths before she spoke again.

"Is that true?" she asked, her voice shaking in a way he had never heard from her. He had seen her terrified. Angry, sometimes so full of rage that her skin matched her hair. But this wasn't that. She wasn't angry at anyone; this was shame. "I wouldn't do that, would I?"

He cleared his throat, considering his words.

"Please," she added. "Please don't lie to me, Hawk. I need the truth right now."

He sighed. Truth was the last thing she needed. Her lover was buried under tons of steel and dirt; the sociopathic father of her child was unconscious and tied up in a tiny house on the other side of the hills. The financial future of the ranch remained unknown. The mental welfare of her son was in question after the worst day of his life.

"No," he lied. "No, you didn't know about the shelter until today. Jaime was torturing you. The way he does... did."

Her gaze bounced between his eyes. Searching for a tell. A sign he was protecting her from how awful she could be. His face grew warm from it. From holding his mouth and eyes steady. Not wanting to blink for fear he would give himself away and lose her favor.

Then her studying stare drifted. Off his face. Past him. Eyebrows rising in a signal.

Wes turned in his chair. His gut dropped at the sight of Emerson standing in the doorway of the dining room. Watching him. Skin clean now, hair still wet from the bath, wearing a fresh pair of shorts and his favorite Minecraft T-shirt.

There are no secrets from Emerson Hunt. The words bounced in Wes's skull as his stomach landed in his ass.

The kid's eyes studied him, perceiving more about Wes than Wes could know about himself. Emerson would realize Wes was fibbing. He'd tell his mother, and that would end any future Wes had. Anywhere.

Emerson broke the stare. Looked to his mother.

This was it. The end of the line for Wes.

"He's telling the truth." Emerson's voice was soft. Not a hint of deception or subterfuge in his demeanor. His cheeks soft. Mouth not frowning, but not smiling either. A face beyond tired, where emotions weren't available. "Can I go watch TV now?"

Wes turned to Blair. Her face softened with relief, and his body relaxed. She nodded to her kid. "One hour, okay? Then supper."

Emerson padding away to the living room mimicked the thudding of Wes's pulse. Tentative. Soft. Uncertain. What the hell had just happened?

Blair wasn't giving him time to think it over. She leaned into the table, her posture opening to him.

"Thank you, Hawk," she whispered. "I'm sorry you went through all of that. To hide it for so long."

His mouth flapped, his brain flummoxed and wordless. The television noise carried into the room like vapor. A sitcom. Something generic and benign.

"But it's over now," she said. Her arm stretched over the table to him, her fingers open. He stared at it. The intimacy of holding hands with her was foreign. Unfathomable. Wes was more her property than her friend, but here she was, offering a personal connection.

He took it. Her hand folded around his, a gentle pressure and sway. Like she needed to sense him moving to prove he was real.

His discomfort made him shift in the chair. He changed the topic. "What are we going to do with Finch?"

Her gaze shifted to the table and the tipping stack of opened mail. "I don't know. I want him gone, Hawk. For good, but..." A click ended her sentence as she gulped the rest of her words.

"But Jaime would normally take care of that," he said.

Blair nodded, eyes still down.

"He won't survive that wound. If we do nothing, he dies."

She considered that. Shrugged, as if it was too much. Or not enough.

"I'm not sure, Blair. We could dose him," Wes offered.

She shook her head. "He found us once, like your sister. He'll come back. Those drugs only shred a day or so of memories, right?"

Blair had a point. Whatever machinations Finch built to orchestrate today had taken time and energy. If they dosed him, he'd forget today. But any legwork he'd put in to make it happen would still be in his head.

"I see what you mean," he conceded. He thought for another breath. "He killed Terry. We could call the police."

Her brow knitted. "That's reasonable. What would happen to you if we did that? The cops'll recognize you if they see you, won't they?"

"Probably. Maybe I find someplace to lie low until their investigation is done?"

Her gaze flitted back to his. "Where would that be?" she asked.

He racked his brain for an idea and came up empty. For him, there was nothing beyond the property line of Utopia Farms. "No place," he admitted.

"Hawk, I don't want you leaving. Your blood flows through this place, makes it work."

A knot untied in his chest. "You want me to stay?"

Her face melted with compassion. "Of course I do," she sighed. "Hawk, you're the best thing that's happened to my son in his life. I never could tell you, not with Jaime around, but you are more Daddy to that boy than anyone's ever been."

Her hand squeezed his.

"He loves you, Hawk. I won't take that away from him."

The sentiment knotted his tongue. Compliments from Blair were rare, and Wes had always assumed that was part of her personality. Her gruff and prickly exterior facing the world. Yet here she was, confiding in him the wonderful impact he was having on her child.

He sniffed back his emotions. "Robin thinks you're going to kick her family out. Are you? Considering that?"

Her gentle smile hardened to a line, her gaze sharpening. "I haven't decided yet. I'm not certain I'm comfortable letting her stay after what she's done."

"Emerson also loves Layla."

"Yes," she countered. "He loves her because she's here, Hawk. We can find another friend for him."

Her rapid shift to callousness shocked him, and he released her hand. "Blair, please. Take a couple of days to distance yourself from all the shit that took place before you make that decision."

She nodded, noncommittal, her eyes moving over the mail scattered on the table.

His heart sank. He had promised Robin this would not happen.

"Blair, please, she's paddling the same canoe I am, on the same creek of shit. Her life outside this ranch is gone—she's got nowhere else to go. She can't go work in medicine, not after her drug conviction. And her kid has cerebral palsy."

Her face remained stoic, although her attention skimmed around the room.

"She didn't have a choice, just like me."

Blair crossed her arms, cracking her knuckles before hugging herself tight. "I'll think on it."

"Thank you," Wes said. "That's all I'm asking."

Her aloof demeanor told Wes the conversation was over for now. He pushed the chair from the table, easing to stand. His body remained precarious after the events of the bunker, after Emerson recreated him from near nothing. There was no pain, but a fatigue was building in his bones and muscles. A sleep creeping over him that might last days.

He took a few steps, noting the cylinder on the table, half covered by junk mail. A roofie pen—the one Irene had fetched when they'd armed themselves against Finch in the shelter. His fingers plucked the tube from the lace tablecloth.

"That for your sister?" Blair asked.

Wes glanced at her, finding a curious expression on her face. Not judgmental. But not approving, either.

He shook his head. "It's not for me to use." He dropped the pen into the breast pocket of his denim shirt. "I'm going to stuff that bunker with as much fill dirt as I can find. If you need me, just radio, okay?"

She nodded. He turned, taking another few steps to the door. Blair spoke again. "Hawk?"

He turned to face her. Blair chewed on her lip for a moment. "You never said if you'd stay on the ranch."

He let his thoughts stir for a few breaths. Then his gaze floated. Past the ceiling, to the guest bedroom above them, where Irene was sleeping off the sedative Robin had given her in the bunker to save her from her panic attack.

"I don't think that's up to me," he said. "And call me Wes."

Chapter Fifty-Eight

H is thoughts were mercurial. Propelled by a deep ache in his chest. Confusion at this strange place. It was dark. A small space. Narrow and long. One of the shipping containers? Was he still underground?

No, there were windows, and beyond them was the outdoors. Oranges and reds from the sky pouring through the glass.

The squeak of a door opening. Boots on the floor, stomps leaving an echo trail in his head. Air moving across him now. Cool on his wet skin, then chilling with his soaked clothes. And the smell—marijuana. Not the smoke, but the plant.

The odor pierced him. Found a memory that seemed real. Irene had shot him. Over and over. Emerson should have healed him. But he hadn't. He wouldn't.

Finch had been so sure of himself, confidence spewing like a shaken beer. He had reached his child, torn through his mind. The boy had seen what Finch needed him to see. How he was being used. His gift wasted on his mother's standard of living. Finch had seen the wish Emerson harbored—an edgeless want for it to stop. For his mother's love to be simple and real.

A love that Finch would give to their son. They'd just had to walk out of the shelter together. Run away from Utopia Farms to a better life. No one could have stopped them. Not here. Not outside the ranch.

Through the heavy blanket on his mind, a sticky sensation seeped. His own hollow, expanding without his help, consuming him. Sorrow at his failure. Emerson had been so close to coming with him. He'd sensed it when he was clawing across the boy's fears and wants. Heard it when Emerson stayed close by in the field to listen to this stranger gush about helping him.

A light exploded, like in the field. His soggy mind made it louder than it was. A shadow was here now. Not Irene. She was alive, though. She'd survived today by trying to murder him. Finch might have killed her too. He remembered wanting to raise his gun, the clatter as it hit the wood floor. He wasn't certain he would have pulled the trigger. Even after the violence of the day. Even to get his son. Then again...

The woman's blur squatted by him. She laid something on his belly. The distorted noise of a zipper. His gaze focused enough to see a needle. A vial.

She spoke. I'm going to release your arm. Give you an injection. Some medicine.

"Medicine." Finch was stoned. The drugs fucked with his vision, but he saw through her bullshit.

A snap, then the familiar rattle of a handcuff key. Understanding oozed into his consciousness—the restraints were going to come off him. His eyes scraped in their sockets, looking from the shadow up to the wall. To where the sound was coming from. His hands were there, hanging, cuffed to a metal pipe embedded into the wall. His hands existed. They were asleep. Dead. Not under his control.

The cuffs opened, and his arm floated down to the bed. Something chilled the skin over the elbow, then the pungent punch of alcohol hit his nose. It cleared his thoughts. Let him see the situation as it was.

The pain under his ribs made each breath agonizing. That and his racing heart told Finch he had a collapsed lung. The "medicine" wasn't the only thing making him bleary. He wasn't getting enough oxygen. His body refused to pull it in.

Blair was going to let him die a slow, undignified, lonesome death. And then his son would forget today's lessons. Emerson would remember him the way all children did—as a monster. A walking scar, a sharp memory of something horrific and terrible, and the kid's mind would elaborate and augment him, adding features like horns or fangs or a forked tongue, depending on the stories Blair fed him.

Finch tried to lift his hand. The numbness was abating, replaced with a painful itch crawling down his wrist to his fingertips. Blood returning to his hands.

His precious hands. The means by which he survived in this savage world.

As she worked, filling the syringe, Finch fisted his fingers, then splayed them out, over and over, forcing his heart to deliver his blood faster. Revive the nerves there. Wake up the only weapon he had.

The shadow turned to him. A round face with curly hair catching flakes of the sunset from the window.

And the needle. Crying over him. Wanting his arm.

The itch in his fingers had ignited to a burn. Painful and prickly. The nerves screaming. Less than effective, but it would have to do.

He shot his hand to where the shadow's neck should be. Something coarse burned his waking skin. Hair, maybe? The woman was flinching now. She would jolt up. Leave him to die. Leave his son to flatten under Blair's thumb.

Finch wouldn't allow that to happen. Not after reaching Emerson. He had almost turned the boy. One more chance was all he needed. A little more time with him, alone.

The shadow jerked. A searing spark bit the palm of his hand. The tactile prickle felt odd this time. Intense. Perhaps because of the sleeping limb. But it was exactly what Finch wanted to feel.

The woman's psyche raged open like a tornado. Forces tore through her, ripping at her well-being, the shadows of her wants too many to name, the murky wells of her fear too deep to explore. Images flooded him. Memories of what she had done—bloody things, a countless number; her recognition of it getting easier each time; her guilt dissipating until it was no more. Anxiety, dripping like wet watercolors—this woman, sitting in an idling van at the end of the ranch's driveway, her stomach lurching at the choice to head east or west; no destination safe, no home to go to, no money to spend.

Every thought, every fear, every want: Finch found the epicenter of it all. The focal point. The reason behind those blood-caked memories. The source of every erratic fear.

It sat next to her in the passenger seat of the purring van. Metal arm crutches rested in the crook where the dashboard met the door. Long hair hung over her face to hide her tears from her mother.

The entire cyclone of the woman's psyche spun around her daughter. Her illness. A decent mother's wish to give her child a better life.

Finch understood why. His own inner storm brewed from his son. Frustration over wanting to help Emerson. To straighten every crooked path so he could find his way home.

Finch's drive, his own blooms of desires and fears, they shared the same roots as hers.

He latched onto the thoughts of the daughter. Tore them open. Stretched them out until the winds of the woman's mind found no room to blow and they dissipated.

The shadow woman was crying now, the syringe falling from her hand. Her body paralyzed with indecision, her mind saturated with a single craving to save her daughter. Not give her a future. Not improve her life. Just save her. Right now. At this very moment.

Finch made sure it was the only thing she wanted. Then he dragged her head down, close to him. Her tears fell on his face, and he could feel them. *Drip, drip.* Warm. Tickling. The sensation was immense and unusual, and he wanted more.

His plump and full lips grazed her ear.

"I can help you."

Chapter Fifty-Nine

Wes found the tower leaning, the security lights dark. It must have settled after they'd escaped the shelter beneath it. It was hard to tell, because the field was no longer a consistent height. Farther into the field, the plants crowded together, and they were broader there, taller, crawling up the tower's legs as if to pull it down. The clearing was gone, replaced with an impassible briar of thick stems, tapered leaves, and purple flowering buds the size of Wes's face. The resinous fragrance stung his sinuses, and his eyes watered from the stench.

The excavator was where Finch had left it. Wes's blood, and his sister's blood, had been visible on the bucket's teeth. Wes added Terry's blood to the morbid painting when he used the backhoe to transport the man's corpse across the farm and into the bunker. The blood caked off after the first hauls from the nearby hills.

It took two hours of back and forth in the developing twilight: go to the hill, fill the bucket, move the Caterpillar to the shelter, dump the load in the entrance, and pack it in. Wes lost count of the number of trips. Enough to flatten the growth in a line from the shelter to the hill. Eventually, the dirt filling the bunker entrance offered resistance.

He packed in the last load, creating a solid barrier that would prevent anyone from finding their way into the bunker. For their own safety. To protect whatever future his Farm Family was going to have, whether it was together or apart. What was in that tomb needed to stay entombed, the secret kept close to their collective chest. Never shared, but never forgotten, either. A warning against the allure of the easy path.

Wes drove the excavator around the field rather than over it. The path was longer, but far easier to navigate with the field's overgrowth. As he rounded the western edge, he noticed two flashlights scanning the switchback from the house. He parked and then yanked his radio.

"Wes for Robin. What's the status of our guest?"

Her response echoed without delay. "Sleeping like a baby. Still bleeding, but the chest tube is helping him breathe, at least."

"Secure?" he asked.

The radio hummed with feedback. "Of course, dumbass! I would have led with that!"

Wes chuckled. They hadn't figured out what to do with Finch. Irene might have ideas, and he made a mental note to ask her after she woke.

He killed the engine, then climbed out of the cab. The earth was damp, still giving with each step. Once the downpour had stopped, the ground had slurped down the water. In the end, the quench of rain measured nothing against the thirst of the land.

He turned to the flashlight beams wandering at the base of the hill, and Wes found three figures approaching him out of the blue glow—Blair, Emerson, and their dog, Barfly.

Wes considered closing the distance to them, but didn't need to. As soon as Barfly and Emerson saw him, they broke into a run. The dog bounded ahead, all oozing shapes and flapping ears in the growing dark, and Wes had to sidestep at the last second to avoid getting bulldozed. Emerson was a dozen steps behind the dog, and Wes let the boy crash into him.

Emerson's arms wrapped around his waist, his face turned and pressed into Wes's gut, and he squeezed him like a tube of toothpaste.

"Easy!" Wes laughed. "I just got this body, kid!"

But Emerson didn't let up. Wes embraced him in kind. He owed Emerson so much. His life, but more importantly, the life of his sister. In that moment of gratitude, he wondered what favor could ever repay what Emerson had given him today.

"He was worried. Wanted to see you. Talk to you. Make sure you were okay." Blair's eyebrow cocked, her lips tight in a smirk that restrained the words, *I told you he loves you, didn't I?* Wes knew she was pulling his heartstrings, her way of asking him to do whatever he could to stay on the ranch with them.

Wes shelved the thought—another Mason jar full of something not ready for consumption, stored away to cure in his mental warehouse. He couldn't think about it right now. There would be time later, after he spoke with Irene. In this moment, Wes only wanted to hold Emerson and to be held in turn.

Blair continued, motioning to the field behind Wes with her chin. "And he keeps asking what happened out there. Wants to see it."

Wes patted Emerson's back, retreated a step as Emerson opened his death grip on him. When he had the kid's attention, Wes asked, "You sure? It's dangerous out there. Not like before. The ground is caving in."

Emerson nodded. "I wanna know what I did."

Wes stared at the boy. Was he unsure what had happened around the bunker? It made sense. Emerson hadn't planned it. He'd just acted, and while it had saved Wes's life, the results were devastating.

Wes looked to Blair, his eyebrows raised this time, asking if it was okay with her.

She nodded. "Be careful, both of you."

"You're not coming?" Wes asked.

Blair held up her hands, her flashlight shooting into the heavens. "I'm never going near that place again, H—" She caught herself before using his ranch name. "Wes."

"Fair enough," Wes replied as Emerson pulled him towards the field by his hand. "I'll bring him home after, okay?"

She nodded but didn't turn. Wes watched her watching him as Emerson dragged him another few steps.

"Come *on!*" the kid cried, impatient to witness the destruction he'd wrought.

Wes pivoted to the farm. They entered the main aisle, now extending only two-thirds of the way to the field's center. A mountain of growth consumed the clearing now. Anxiety clutched his nerves. Forced his fingers to grip Emerson's tighter. Wes realized he was alone with this rambunctious kid, walking through a deathtrap that appeared similar to a playground to the boy's young eyes.

"Slow down, Em!" he called, easing on the kid's hand like a brake. "We can't run through here. We need to be careful."

The kid's run petered to a walk, and Wes took point. He held his hand out for the flashlight, and Emerson gave it to him.

Soon, they weren't walking on dirt. They were on a carpet of plants, loose at first, the weave stiffening as they approached the tower.

Wes stopped, and Emerson parked beside him. The pale circle from the flashlight shone up, highlighting the leaf-infested tower against the cooling evening sky. Several enormous flowers reached away from the metal, their size deceptive against the backdrop of silver clouds backed by twilight.

The tower leaned more to the right than earlier. It was sinking, and it would come down at some point.

As if responding to his thoughts, the ground coughed ahead. A sound dusty and wet all at once.

Wes peered down. Emerson's face was awestruck.

"You grew all of this—in about twenty seconds, I think."

The kid was silent for a moment, eyes and mouth agape.

"Why is the tower crooked?" he asked.

Wes followed his stare to the leaning tower. "The dirt under it is opening up." He moved the flashlight's beam down the tower, tracing the nearest leg as it pierced through the tapestry of life until the light found its base. The concrete support on which the leg rested had sunk in the earth, the round, rusted metal of the tower support seeming to poke it, like a finger pushing into soft dough. The flashlight landed on a swath of white, several feet of tangled roots left exposed by the sinking pylon visible through the brush.

"See that?" Wes asked. He wiggled the flashlight.

"That fuzz?"

"Yep. Those are roots for these plants, Em. They probably go as deep as these plants are tall."

The kid took a step forward, and Wes hooked the collar of his shirt to keep him still.

"I just want to see," he said.

Wes wanted to see too, but did not know how stable the area was. "This is close enough. What should be around those roots? What's missing?"

Emerson's gaze drifted to the highlighted spot. His silence told Wes he wasn't seeing it.

"Where do the roots grow?" Wes asked.

Emerson shrugged. "In the ground?"

"Right. So what's missing?"

Emerson's posture straightened. "The ground. The dirt." His voice floated in reverie.

Wes's hand moved to the boy's shoulder. "Yeah, that's right."

"Where did it go?"

It was Wes's turn to shrug. "Down?" he offered. "I think when we came out here every evening, we didn't consider what was happening under us. The plants were strong, which means their roots were strong. But we never see the roots. We don't see what they're doing under the ground."

The kid's face turned up to him, scrunched around a question.

Wes smiled at him. "What happened here didn't start today. I think today pushed it over the edge, but it began when we used you to revive the field. Every day, we asked you to make these plants stronger. Which made their roots thicken. Stretch deeper. The plants were healthy, thanks to you. But the earth wasn't."

Emerson's gaze shifted again. Over the twisting botanical cloth at their feet. "The ground wasn't healthy?" he repeated.

"It was dry," Wes explained. "We planted the field, what... eighteen months ago? Forced its growth during a drought. I think the roots tore up the ground. Softened it. Then today, the rains came, and the loose dirt soaked the water up, eroding it even more."

The rhythmic chirps of crickets rose to greet the coming evening, the insects somehow having survived the torrent of the day.

"The ground gave way," Emerson realized out loud.

Wes nodded. "Yeah. I think this rapid overgrowth forced it to happen, but it was only a matter of time, Emerson. Every time I brought you out here, we made it worse. And one day, I think the Earth would have swallowed this entire field."

The boy's head turned, taking in the expanse. Wes studied it too, a tinge of nerves rushing through him at seeing how far over the unstable area the two of them had ventured.

He wanted to leave, haul their asses off of this uncertain ground before they ended up buried like Jaime. But he had a question burning every neuron in his brain. He needed to ask it now, while it was just him and the kid.

"Emerson?"

"Yep."

"Back at the house... you watched me lie to your mom. I know you could sense my deception. She asked you to tell her if I was being truthful, right? So why did you tell your mother I was being honest when I wasn't?"

Emerson was quiet for a long time, staring into the growth ahead of them. As if sifting through the buried ruins of the bunker with his eyes.

"Because I trust you?" he creaked. His voice was uncertain, but the words walloped Wes in the gut. "I know you lied to Mom, and I don't know why. I didn't want to make things worse by telling her what you were feeling, like I did with Layla and Chris. So I lied to her too. But I did it because you did it. You know the right secrets to keep, Hawk. I don't."

"Jesus," Wes sighed. He couldn't help himself. How could the kid stay so pure? After everything that happened today?

The earth sighed, a groan of settling. The crickets went silent at the deadly portent.

"We should go," Wes said. He patted Emerson's shoulder, turned to the aisle. After a few steps of not hearing Emerson's shoes squishing behind him, Wes glanced back.

The boy stood still. Posture tall. Head drooped. A memory of him on the tower platform came to Wes, along with a spike of panic that the kid might try something.

"Emerson?" he called, his voice warbling with anxiety.

The boy mumbled something. Not to Wes, but to himself.

A few seconds later, Emerson ran to catch up.

"We should go," Hawk said. Not Hawk—Wes. Wes! Wes! Wes! It might take Emerson a long time to relearn his friend's name.

Wes-not-Hawk walked the way they had come, and Emerson returned his attention to the ground. He focused his aura. Probing for the passing glimmer he'd noticed there. Deep. Buried. But unmistakable.

The effort of diving through the purple haze of the plants was immense, especially now that they were so big. So vibrant the air around them left a sourness over his tongue. The dirt teemed with bits of color and life too. But far beneath him, under the pale glow of the field's life force, another color hummed. A darker shade of violet. Dim, but it was there.

Shaping his light again frightened him, especially standing in the aftermath of his earlier attempt. This wasn't something Emerson could do before; he hadn't even known it was possible until today. If he hadn't seen his father do it, he would never have tried.

He stretched it down, his halo spiraling around itself, tightening into a thread. It behaved the way his father's light behaved. Controlled. Purposeful. He wove it between the infinite tight spaces between the roots without disturbing them. Stretching. Thinning. Sensing the life around him without interacting. And then connecting with that putrid, fading indigo halo deep beneath him.

His lips tightened. Trembled with the same heat as in the bunker. That sick and bubbling warmth that balled his fists and barbed his light. The emotions remained new to him, even as their ugliness faded.

"Found you," Emerson whispered.

Chapter Sixty

The fever dream snapped like a twig. Jaime's mind cleared, but the wrongness in his body remained unabated. Pain shook his legs and arms while a pressure squeezed him from the outside.

What the hell had happened to him? Jaime scoured his thoughts. A jumbled mess of hangover snapshots and half-truths. He was in danger, wasn't he? The scenes disconnected in his head, details blurry or sharp, leaving him uncertain which were real and which weren't.

It scared him to move. The pain was beyond anything he had experienced. His arms were pinned out, every inch held in place with something piercing his chilled skin. His legs too. Was he lying down or standing up?

He opened his eyes. He wasn't paralyzed. But there was nothing to see. Just a sting as soon as his lids raised, a burn that hit his corneas and got worse the more he tried to blink it away.

In shock, he sucked in a breath. Something solid shot down his airway. Particulates irritated his lungs.

He coughed and inhaled another wad of the stuff, spewing it into his sinuses.

An odor, fresh and tinted with ammonia and minerals. Recognition snapped in his head, the scent normally pleasant and soothing but now racking him with dread.

Dirt. Jaime had been buried alive. It was the only explanation. An accident on the build site, probably. Something that Terry had done. That seemed right. The memory felt real. It had happened.

He had to have patience. Keep control over his body, prevent it from freaking out and shutting down. Hawk always kept a watchful eye on the construction. If there was an accident, he would call for the bell. Blair would have the radio close. If she wasn't by Emerson, she'd run to the bell on the porch. Slam the iron. Let it ring across the ranch to Emerson's ears.

A tingle caressed his scalp. A bug or worm perhaps.

The prickle grew, seeping into his skin, and Jaime realized it wasn't physical. This was Emerson. He was probing, scanning for Jaime under the ground.

The sensation worked its way through him, a blissful touch that calmed him, let him know everything was okay. His body righted itself, compressed in the ground but free of pain. His chest relaxed, the shit still in there but his body no longer reacting to it. And his eyes, closed now, the underside of the lids full of grime and soot. He reminded himself that this strangeness—knowing his body was broken, that there should be pain where there was none—was temporary.

He would survive. Jaime just needed to calm himself. Control his impulse to cough or blink. To even breathe. Emerson would keep him alive until they dug him out. It shouldn't be long. The deepest holes on the build site were for the shipping containers, only ten or twelve feet deep. Enough to bury the new, larger bunker components. It wouldn't take long for the team to reach him.

Project Money-Maker, he called it. No makeshift operating room this time. Jaime was investing in this effort. Top-of-the-line surgical equipment. Powered freezer for longer storage. Even an autoclave. Not that they needed it with Emerson nearby. Bacterial infections didn't stand a chance against his gift, but Robin had insisted.

Jaime distracted himself by focusing his mind on the money. By his estimates, the ranch would be buy-the-cops rich in a few years. After that, the big business could kick in.

He had ideas—big ones he hadn't shared with anyone yet. Organs were lucrative, sure, but the logistics were costly and difficult to navigate. Plus, that income was a mere step in Jaime's ambition. The perverted desires of the human heart knew no bounds. With Emerson close by, Jaime could charge by the hour. Fixed overhead, practically no operations cost, and with a cornered market, he couldn't be undersold.

His chest spasmed, a silent cough pushing mud up into his mouth. An unexpected reflex from the burn slamming into his ribs as Emerson's warming touch faded. The boy was pulling away. Hawk must be close to digging him out.

The itch returned to his cornea. The dirt scouring his healed eyeballs became jarring and painful again. The waves of suffering in his arms and legs grew fresh, like the bones had shattered anew.

All of it was nothing next to his need to cough. The ache along the inside of his throat and lungs, his diaphragm wanting to heave on its own. To chuck out the mud in his chest only to suck in another lungful.

It was almost over, though. He could hold it. Just a few more minutes, that was all.

Jaime had to hang on for a few more minutes.

Water. Tsunamis of it, pouring down. Pushing her into the ground. Burying everyone she loved in the earth with her. But it smelled wrong. The water had an odor of fire. No, it was smoke. Something burning. How could something be wet and on fire at the same time?

The incongruity forced her conscious. Her eyes opened on a crisp painted space, pale blue glistening with white trim. The bed was a stranger's. Soft and squishy. A Toulouse-style dresser set against the wall, the perfect accent shade of gray. The entire room looked right off a showroom floor.

She pushed herself to sitting on the bed, leaning into the headboard, feeling a pang as the ripples of her spine ran against the firm wood.

Her spine. The sensations of her body. Her whole body. Legs, belly, all of it present and accounted for. A shudder passed through her, her mind replaying when she had only been part of herself. It was a nightmare, recognizing everything broken with her body. But unlike her nightmares, this had happened.

Someone cleared their throat.

Irene looked up. Wes sat on the sill of an open window on the other side of the room. The acrid odor of her dream had come from a lit cigarette he was holding outside. As if the smoke would somehow know to stay out there in the humid night.

She tried to speak but only croaked.

Wes popped the cigarette between his lips and pointed at the nightstand next to her. There, Irene found a glass of water waiting for her. She recognized it then—the thirst through her body. Every cell craving a bath in that water.

She downed the water in a few swallows, relishing the wet, sulfurous tang, and heaved a sigh as she pulled the glass from her lips.

"I thought you said you quit," she huffed.

Wes sucked again, the orange ember growing and fading. He popped the cigarette from his mouth and huffed the smoke out the window.

"Drugs, yes. Booze, yes. Cigarettes? I'm still working on that," he replied, his voice deep and resonant as he exhaled. He moved the butt through the window, where his fingers massaged it against something she couldn't see. As he tucked the stomped dog-end into his shirt pocket, his face grew sheepish. "Please don't tell Blair, though? She doesn't want anyone smoking in her house."

He shifted on the sill, rotating to see her. He looked tired, the same exhaustion that cored out Irene's body. The two of them watched one another, Irene letting the headboard hold her up as the events replayed through her head.

"So, how was your day?" she asked, smirking despite the discomfort between them.

His reply was immediate and surgical. "Not too bad. I only died twice."

Irene laughed. "Three times, dumbass. Chainsawed and left in the morgue, then Jaime stabbed your throat, and then Finch crushed you."

"Well, actually," Wes hummed, "it's only twice *today*. The chainsaw happened earlier this week, remember?"

She rolled her eyes. For a moment, her brother's mansplaining sparked the kindling in her chest. Irene exhaled the embers of anger away. "In that case, you only died one more time than me, so quit your whining."

In the silence that followed, the casual air faded, leaving them floating among everything they weren't saying. Wes's stare fixed on the floor, his posture eroding.

"You know, I used to think our family was fucked up," he finally said.

Another fire bloomed in her throat. The sparkle of a laugh. She let it out, feeling her smile slice through the gap between them. The moment of levity was dark enough to push through the horrific day they had shared. A bookend to the worst day of their lives, last two years of searching and hiding, and the lifetime of conflict between them.

Another pause filled the room, marked by the cadence of rattling insects fading in through the window.

"I don't know how to ask this," Wes said. "I don't even know what words to use."

Irene pulled her legs up to her chest under the bedding. "What do we do now?" she guessed.

Wes nodded. "I don't want to fight with you, Irene. I don't want to run anymore. Searching for me got you killed. Almost more than once. I can't live with... with..."

He broke off, standing up from the windowsill, shaking his head with frustration. His hand went to his rear pocket and pulled out a long silver pen. He held the Rohypnol gently, clearly seeking to make the thing appear harmless between his thumb and fingers.

"What the fuck is that for?" she demanded, cocking an eyebrow as the rush of anxiety scooted her ass to the headboard.

"Look, last time around, you didn't have a choice, Irene." He dropped the roofie pen on the bed, just within her reach. "I dosed you, to protect you. To protect Emerson. And if I'm honest, to save myself. I won't do that again, but I can't ask you to remember today, either. You have a few hours to use this. You can erase your shitty memories of today. But you need to make the choice this time, not me."

"What?!" she asked, dumbfounded. "Are you fucking kidding me, Wes?"

"I'll turn myself over to the police," he huffed, his lips trembling. "You can choose to forget, return to your life at school, and never worry about me fucking things up for—"

"Wes!" she interrupted. "Today wasn't your fault!"

"Wasn't it?" he snapped, eyes pleading. "If I had stayed in the hospital, accepted the consequence of my choices? None of this would have happened!"

Irene considered it. Reviewed the last two years. Her core anger had focused on him, but that resentment was always there. Bubbling on a simmer in her belly. If Wes had gone to prison, where would her rage have wandered next?

"I'm not so sure." Her voice was soft, gentle. Even sisterly. "I want to think that putting you in jail would have satisfied me, but I don't know if that's true. I think I might have ended up here anyway. Maybe searching for Jaime. Trying to find the guy who stole Dad's last moments from me."

Wes wiped away tears. His hands shook. It was a familiar vision of him, but the usual layers of blame and bitterness were missing for Irene.

"I made choices too," she continued. "Told myself I wanted to return to school, but came here instead. Chasing a mystery. And I blamed you, but that was my choice." She closed her eyes, blowing out a deep breath as the yoke of responsibility settled on her shoulders. "I could have justified it lots of ways, but you were the easiest place to lay the blame."

She studied her brother. His lean body remained strange against her expectation of the fat slob she'd grown up with. Those hands were strong now. Calloused and worn. Wes had rebuilt himself these last two years. Spent his borrowed time hardening himself and bettering the lives of those around him, as fucked up as those people were. Irene's gaze fell to her own fingers, the nails snagged and the flesh scratched up, but her sedentary lifestyle plain in her squishy flesh. What had she done in the last two years besides wallow in self-pity and drink herself sick?

"Look, I'm not saying you're off the hook. I'm not okay with what you did, Wes. But I understand why you did it."

She glanced up to find her brother staring at the floor.

"Hey?" she prompted. "Look at me."

His gaze rose to hers, his eyes bloodshot and rheumy.

"How many times did Lady Doctor Frankenstein tear you apart? When was the last time you left the ranch? How many people did Jaime force you to run through that organ farm?"

Wes shrugged, his body rattling.

"And what choice did you have in any of it? You've been paying for that one decision every day since you made it. And you've made the best of it. You're clean now, right?"

"Emerson helped me detox," he demurred.

A familiar wave of anger crashed against her ribs. "No, Wes, don't do that!" she cried. "Don't lay your successes on other people the way you used to blame your failures! You always maintained that staying clean was never a single choice. It's an endless string of small decisions, every moment of every day. And it happens right in the middle of whatever life spills on you." She pointed at the window, into the nothingness of night, where the crickets and frogs chirped back and forth, relishing the moisture. "You live on a massive field of weed, Wes. It's right out there, always available, as much as you want, and despite your fucked-up life on this fucked-up ranch, you don't use it anymore."

Her brother swallowed, tears flowing freely.

"So, is that Emerson, or is that *you*?" she begged.

He took a shuddering breath before responding. "It's me." His smile juxtaposed against his sad stare.

In the wake of Wes's admission, the heat and uncertainty unraveled in Irene's chest. Tight and dense, a knot where threads had worn together after years of neglect and erosion. Her mind raced. Strange thoughts percolated out. Memories of their childhood. Good and bad. Trauma and laughter. Through all of it, Wes had never been the man he had become in this place, under these awful circumstances. Wes had changed himself. He had started over.

It all led Irene to a simple conclusion: she could start over too.

"What benefit would come from sending you to prison, Wes?"

Irene picked up the popper. Held it like a dagger. Her eyes flitted from it to her brother, his gaze pining and sad.

For a moment, the temptation was there. One tiny pinprick and the day from hell would scramble in her brain. Become a fever dream she could dismiss to a night of heavy drinking. But then what? Rediscover Wes was dead? Wonder what ever happened to Finch? Could she even trust what she would do tomorrow, if she didn't have knowledge of today?

She dropped the pen into the empty glass on the nightstand with a crystal *ding*.

"There's been enough forgetting around here. Enough secrets. I don't know how you feel. All I'm sure of at this point is that I've gotten a second chance with you. Another try at being a decent sister. At forgiving you, and hoping to earn your forgiveness in return."

Now her eyes watered. She cleared them with her palms before continuing.

"This time, we keep our memories. Even the shitty ones. Hell, especially those. Treasure them. Share them. Work on letting them in and then letting them back out."

A long moment passed as they shared several breaths of the cooling night air still carrying the mineral flavors of rain.

Wes sniffled, wiped his hand down his face. "I'd love that," he whispered.

She sat cross-legged. The front half of the bed cleared, she leaned over and patted the country quilt, nodding for Wes to join her.

He took the two steps to the bed and sat, one leg on the floor and the other cantilevered off the edge. After the creaks of the box spring settled, Wes opened his hand, and Irene took it in hers. The rough skin on his knuckles and fingertips intrigued her: callouses and scars born from stories she didn't know yet.

"How do we even begin?" he asked.

She didn't have to search for her answer. It was already on her tongue.

"I'd like to start by talking about Dad."

Epilogue

T^{*ap.*}

    Emerson's eyes popped open, the out-of-place sound pulling him from sleep. The room was dark. The only light came from the deep blue glow of night outside.

Barfly lay sprawled beside him, her legs in the air and head hanging off the edge of his bed. She was dreaming, the scratchy pads on her paws twitching and her aura bobbing as she chased something in her dream. Whatever noise had woken him, it hadn't bothered her.

Thunk!

The window. Something bounced against the glass.

Emerson slipped out of the covers. Barfly rotated onto her belly before Emerson's feet were on the floor. Snapping alert, she watched him cross the room, and Emerson put a finger to his lips.

"Shh," he lilted. "Don't wake everyone."

Through the second-story window, spotty clouds dragged between the stars; somewhere, the moon was whole enough to let him see details. The whitewashed silo on the farm next door.

The orchard, calm now, as if sleeping with leaves twitching through their tree dreams.

Movement pulled his gaze to the empty plane of the yard. A figure was there. Features unclear, but Emerson knew who it was. The crutches gave her away.

Layla waved to him, and he waved back with a smile. She beckoned for him to come, and he smiled more. Barfly must have seen it too, the way she thumped to the floor and started nosing his feet—her signal it was time to put shoes on and take her to the yard.

"Okay, girl," he whispered. Emerson padded across the hardwood floor to his door. He cracked it open. Light bounced from downstairs into the hallway outside his room. He heard tinny voices from the television but couldn't tell what show it was.

There was no point in trying to sneak with Barfly. The dog did nothing quietly, but when outside was at stake, she pulled out the stops. She nosed through the cracked door. A moment later, her paws thudded the steps, Emerson unsure if she was running or falling down the stairs. Emerson left his room and found her at the base of the stairs, waiting. Watching him with that excited dog smile on her face and expectant cerulean waves in her halo.

As he descended the steps, he wondered why Layla was out at the house so late instead of asleep in Dr. Travers's little house on wheels. Layla looked fine. Her halo wasn't obvious from the window, but she seemed okay. If something was wrong, she would knock on the door. Maybe she wanted to check on him without bothering everyone else, and that thought made him smile.

Downstairs, Emerson found the lamps on. Hawk lay slumped and snoring on the sofa in the living room with Chris nestled into him. The television showed a movie with a cowboy sitting alone in a motel. Emerson stopped, watching the cowboy notice a shadow move across the thin gap of light at the bottom of a door. The music indicated that something awful was about to occur, so Emerson turned into the entryway.

Barfly pointed out his shoes with her wet nose, so he knew which shoes were his. His feet slid into his Crocs, and the dog spun to the front door. Emerson slid the deadbolt with a scrape, and he opened the door.

Barfly bolted at the first scent, pushing the gap open with her snout and bounding into the darkness with a thick huff. Emerson walked to the porch railing. His dog circled Layla once, twice, and then tore off into the orchard, excited dog squeaks fading in the gloom.

Emerson's shoes squished against the brown grass as he left the porch. The ground was still moist. The air heavy. Almost cool, but it wouldn't last. Tomorrow, the heat and aridity would return.

As he approached his friend, his gut tingled. Something about Layla's posture bothered him. It was difficult to see in the low light. But her halo spoke clearly—bursts of her brick-red anger and sky-blue anxiety fighting with one another.

He jogged the last few steps.

"What is it? What's wrong?" he asked. He was able to read her expression now.

Lines of tears ran from the corners of her eyes, and her mouth twitched and scowled as she worked to speak.

"M... my mom is leaving the ranch," she cried in a whisper, sucking in ragged, panicked breaths. "She says your mom is going to kick us out, or have us arrested, and she wants to leave tonight."

Emerson's heart sank. Spindly legs of panic ran across his skin.

"No, don't go!" he begged. "Mom won't do that, I promise!"

Layla shook her head, her hair wiggling with the motion as she shifted her weight on her crutches.

"Yes, she will, Emerson. She's mad at my mom for something, I don't know what. And we're already packed up; we've got our house hitched to the van and everything!"

"You're leaving... like, right now?" A flitter ran through his veins.

She nodded, wiping her eyes as a mournful wail left her mouth.

A rustle from the orchard captured his attention. Barfly came running out, all flapping ears and slapping paws as she rounded Emerson and his friend, then turned back to the trees. Emerson saw a figure there. An adult. The sickly light of the moon giving her tight curly hair its own glow that seemed to play into the woman's orange aura. Layla's mom emerged from the shadows of the orchard and approached them.

"Hello, Emerson," she said. Her voice was cracking, the way Layla's was. "I guess Layla told you?"

He said nothing. Didn't know what to say. It was happening now. There was no time to fix it. He wrung his mind for a way to keep them here. He'd talk to Mom. Tell her how important these people were to him. She would listen. She had to listen.

He opened his mouth to speak, but Dr. Travers spoke first.

"We have to go, Emerson. We're leaving before your mother does something worse than throw us off the ranch. Layla wanted a chance to talk with you before we go."

Emerson shook his head so hard it rattled. "Mom won't, I promise! I can tell her—"

"We're leaving, Emerson. I'm sorry, but I have to protect my family."

Strange ideas bloomed from his dismay. He'd steal Layla's crutches and run into the house and lock the door and hide in his room, and then they couldn't leave, and he'd only give them back after they promised to never go.

Layla's mom kept talking, but her words bounced off the ringing in his ears. Not a whine, like after a gunshot. This was static. Thoughts trying to get out, not in.

Layla's arms were around him, her body leaning into his, her crutches dangling against his legs as he took her weight. She squeezed him. A wonderful pressure and warmth. Like Mom's hugs, but so much better. And sadder. He loved and hated it. His arms wrapped around her too. Her shirt was wet from the air or her skin, he wasn't sure. And he hugged, and then she clutched him harder, and his nose tickled from her long hair and its fruity scent.

Emerson sucked it in. Wanted to record each sensory detail of this connection. The weight of her face on his shoulder. The heaving movements of her frame as she sobbed against him. He needed to remember every bit. Because this was his last chance to experience it.

"I don't want to say goodbye," he cried. The thoughts pressing against his skull came out as tears. They fell across his nose and wicked into Layla's hair.

Emerson sensed Layla's mom step close, her halo mingling with his. Layla's arms tightened around his waist. The excessive pressure spoiled the bliss of the embrace.

"You don't have to," Layla replied.

Something bit him. A deep pinch on his butt that made his leg jerk. He almost apologized, but then the burn came.

Everything was wrong. His eyes opened to a watery world. Not from rain. He stood on the floor of the ocean, and everything swayed in the tide.

The night darkened. The trees of the orchard blurred, their branches smearing into one another. Something moved among them. Black even in the moonlight, but shiny. And stumbling, walking the way Emerson's mind was moving now.

Layla let go, and Emerson found her mother's face. His body relaxed into her arms as she lifted him off the ground.

The moon hovered before him now. Full and bright, with hazy, luminous clouds drifting around it. A giant eye watching Dr. Travers carry him away.

The eye eased closed, leaving Emerson in a lightless sleep.

"Please be careful," Finch snapped. The sharp twinge in his ribs became a tearing as Robin jerked the van to keep it in the lane.

"Sorry," Robin offered. "Adrenaline is still wearing off."

Finch cursed in his head. She might not be up for this. The passion was there. The woman was desperate. It was useful, but it came with a leaden anxiety that Finch was finding hard to temper.

"It's okay, Robin," he murmured. "We don't want to die before we get there. Emerson can't help Layla if one of 'em's dead, yeah?"

Robin chuckled, a forced sound to cover her nerves. Christ, she was a mess.

"Of course, of course," she replied. "How long until we arrive?"

Finch sighed. "Keep heading south. And stay off the interstate."

"But how long?" she pressed.

Just fucking drive, you cunt! The impulse to scream at her made him bite the inside of the cheek. That, amplified by the sear in his ribs, helped him swallow his impatience. "I don't know for sure. We're taking the back roads. Staying hidden as best we can. Not sure what Blair'll do once she finds him missing."

Finch eased his gaze around the headrest. Emerson remained unconscious, prone on the bench seat, his head on Layla's lap, swaying with the motion of the vehicle. She played with his hair while watching the random lights scattered over the hill country ease past the large window. Once the kid woke up, he'd be in a daze. Have trouble piecing together the events of the day. At least that was what Robin said would happen.

Finch hoped it was soon. The sensations of his new body were exquisite and harsh. His pain was at an intensity difficult to manage. He needed it to stop. Emerson could do that for him.

"You ever use one of them poppers on Emerson before?" he asked her.

She shook her head, the pale green of the dashboard lights giving her a sickly pallor. "No. He reacted the way most folks do, though. Passed right out."

Finch nodded. "And he's breathing normal?"

Robin adjusted the rear-view mirror, presumably to watch Emerson's chest expand and contract. "Yep, he's just sleeping it off."

Over Finch's discomfort flashed a worry that the drugs would dampen Emerson's abilities. He had no reason to think they would. Drugs had never hampered him.

One thing at a time. They'd gotten him in the van. That was the important part: hauling Emerson away from that miserable farm. Now the miles were ticking up between them and Blair. Everything else would work out in time.

A thin, pining whine came from the rear of the vehicle. The dog, demanding to come where the people were.

Robin slid her gaze across to Finch, her round face all tired eyes and twitching cheeks. "How soon will Emerson be able to heal my daughter?"

She'd asked the goddamned question four times since they'd left Tarpley. It wasn't her fault. Robin's fixation wouldn't go away until she got what she wanted. Finch had ripped her emotional wound open to force her to act. Help him get Emerson off the ranch. Out from under the thumb of his bitch mother.

"Not long, don't worry," he repeated. "We have to get where we're going. Let him wake up, you know?"

Finch watched the asphalt congeal out of the night and into their headlights. He sensed Robin's fidgeting eyes on him. Wide and desperate.

"So, where is it? Tell me where we're going!"

Finch sucked in the cool air, taking one last breath of the lush and loamy hill country. He peered back again at rag-doll Emerson sleeping off the drugs. Layla's gentle expression was reflected in the dark window as she dreamed—about new legs, maybe. The dog's tufted snout jutted over the rear row of seats, tongue flapping and searching for a target.

A smile crossed Finch's face. At first, he tried to stop it. But then he remembered his new skin. There was no pain in his smile. He was a monster no more. And he would never need to suffer the pity of others again.

His season of waiting was over.

He ran his tongue over his lips, the rough bumps of its surface overwhelming after years of numbness. The sensation relaxed him into the passenger seat.

"We're going home."

Author's Note

Are you curious how Irene ended up on Utopia Farms in this book's prologue? You can read the story in *This is Goodbye For Now*, a novella you get FREE for subscribing to my newsletter.

Don't miss the next installment of the series! Read the (spoiler-free) teaser for *Cult of Possibility* for FREE by signing up for my newsletter, and get updates when the novel is available!

Please review *Sick as our Secrets*. Leaving a review will help make this book more discoverable by the right readers. The ones like you, with the big brains and fantastic taste in reading material. Having more of those readers motivates and promotes my writing career.

And thank you for reading this book. I hope it was a page-turner that left you thinking. This is my second published novel. I plan to write many more. If you'd like to know when my next book will be available, please subscribe to my mailing list. In exchange, you'll get access to free stories and resources available nowhere else—such as discussion guides for book clubs and chapters that never made it into the final draft.

If you are interested in bringing *Sick as our Secrets* into your book club, a discussion guide is available on my website. I am also happy to make myself available to chat about the book; simply reach out using this contact form.

If you're interested in learning more about me, please visit my author website.

Acknowledgments

Two novels into my career; this one was easier, but it's still a long, difficult process. There are a lot of folks to thank, so let's get started.

Many kudos to Liz Dunbar for working the story with me, reading my earliest drafts, spending hours discussing the characters and the plot. Emma Savant for further developmental and copy editing; you can learn more about her work at http://emeraldinkediting.com. Matthew Revert for the amazing cover design; check out his portfolio at https://www.matthewrevertdesign.com. Geoffrey Hummelke for rapid turnaround on the final proof. And Audrey von Hammonds for fixing my pitch.

Special thanks to all the Jiminions who have subscribed to my newsletter. The ongoing support and excitement you offer is infectious, and I desperately needed that this time around. I love hearing from y'all and appreciate the personal correspondence.

The bottomless love and support of my partner Julie keeps me going, as do my kids and my dog, Gunner. Life got out of whack this past year, fam. Thank you for sticking close, and know that I am proud as hell of each of you.

And finally, I'd like to tell you about my father, Ray Christ opher...

It's difficult at times to tell whether I'm writing about life, or living a story.

I dedicated this book to my father. At 77, his health was decent. He avoided COVID, and he survived a subdermal hematoma several years ago that put him in a coma for days, yet left him with no discernable cognitive impact. He developed a few issues as he aged, like we all do once the warranty on our body expires. About four months into 2021, he started having symptoms we couldn't explain, and after a few rounds of tests, we learned Dad contracted an aggressive form of cancer.

Now, if you haven't read my first novel *Season of Waiting,* allow me to summarize it: the protagonist Caleb Allard is dying of cancer, and his son helps execute a mystical Hail Mary to save his life.

The parallel between my life and my novel was obvious, and I couldn't shake this sickening notion that by writing *Season of Waiting,* I somehow created this reality. I know that kind of causal reasoning is bullshit. I'm a behavioral scientist and understand spurious correlation. And honestly, the story was one I had lived: the character Caleb was dying from the same cancer that took my mother almost seventeen years ago. This was art imitating life, not the other way around.

Wasn't it?

The similarities between my father and Caleb Allard grew as we moved through treatment and into hospice. Dad had trouble differentiating between memories and stories at first. Then the lines between reality and fiction eroded. He saw things that weren't there. Sometimes terrifying ("That's the biggest snake I've ever seen!"), sometimes wonderful ("There are words scribed into the ceiling tiles using all the languages of the world, like a modern Rosetta stone."). At one point, he confused the last book he read—an espionage thriller—with his own life, thinking he was a captured spy and needed to escape. This kind of fabrication isn't uncommon in cancer patients; in fact, from my experience and research, the treatments and pain management cause this as often as the disease.

And, it's another a major plot point in *Season of Waiting*.

If you've ever grieved the living, then you'll recognize that place of idiotic bargaining I reached. I offered exchanges to the gods I don't believe in: *if I really wrote my father into his disease, then give me the chance to write him out of it.*

But there was no barter, and no one to haggle with. Days before I sent *Sick as our Secrets* out for a developmental edit, and a few weeks after his oldest grandkid started their first year of college, Dad passed away.

Sidebar: my wife and I sat by his bed for weeks, advocating for him, holding his hand, keeping him calm, diffusing his hallucinations, telling him jokes, playing music for him. We left the room for a few minutes to get out of the way of medical staff, and that's when the asshole passes on! We're pretty sure he did that on purpose. It was a very Dad thing to do.

Anyway, I wrote this story for Dad, but he never got to read it. I considered reading it to him in hospice, but his inability to discern fiction from reality put the kibosh on that idea. He read *Season of Waiting* last year though, and I wonder if he ever drew comparisons between himself and Caleb Allard. We never talked about it, so I don't know for sure. But Dad was whip-smart and a deep thinker; the similarities must have crossed his mind. I wish I knew how that made him feel. Why I want to know, I can't explain. I suppose it would be a comfort, knowing his thoughts could be as illogical as mine.

He was good about letting me know he loved me, and I was good about letting him know the same. We left nothing unsaid. Our relationship had its discord, especially in my youth. But we transcended father-and-son and moved into close friendship as we aged, thanks to a shared commodity: humor. Our conversations usually turned into competitions, to see which of us could make the other suffocate laughing first.

I usually won, by the way. I'm not as funny as Dad, but his laugh was more energetic. Poor guy would wear himself out over a mediocre "what's in your pants" joke.

I am grateful to him. And I am grateful for him. When I was about twenty, he wrote me a letter—one of the old-fashioned physical ones where pen hits paper. The pages are delicate after so many years, but I still read it when I feel like shit about myself. It's the only letter from him I've saved, because in it, he offered the most endearing compliment I've ever heard, much less received. I won't share it with you, because it belongs to me. I only mention it to say:

I hope I've earned it, Pop.

About the Author

Jim Christopher lives in Decatur, Georgia. His career has been a crooked path, meandering through stagehand, audio engineer, carpenter, cognitive psychologist, behavioral researcher, musician, software developer, learning sciences advisor, to whatever he might be doing today.

He writes speculative fiction, suspense, thrillers, science fiction, and horror. His debut novel *Season of Waiting* was named a finalist in the American Fiction Awards, and the follow-up *Sick as our Secrets* won First Place in the BookFest Awards for Supernatural Thrillers.

To relax, Jim crochets, builds tiny houses, walks his dog, reads, and tries to stay active. His guilty pleasures include laughing, petit fours, end-of-the-world movies, and escape rooms.

More from Jim Christopher

The Utopian Testament

Gradient Descent

Standalone Novels

See Red

Visit https://www.jim-christopher.com for the latest news!